*A Move
in the Game*

KATHLEEN CONLON

A Move in the Game

STEIN AND DAY/*Publishers*/New York

First published in the United States of America in 1979
Copyright © 1979 by Kathleen Conlon
All rights reserved
Printed in the United States of America
Stein and Day/*Publishers*/Scarborough House,
Briarcliff Manor, N.Y. 10510

Library of Congress Cataloging in Publication Data

Conlon, Kathleen, 1943–
   A move in the game.

   I. Title.
PZ4.C7524Aam 1979   [PR6053.0455]   823'.9'14   78-66255
ISBN 0-8128-2603-5

Part One

I

At a quarter to three on the afternoon of the eleventh of September, 1960, Harold Irving, a relief driver employed by a private hire company, suffered a coronary thrombosis. At the moment when the pain crashed into his chest he was negotiating his motor coach, which contained thirteen sixth-form girls and two senior mistresses from the Oxenden High School, around a particularly hazardous bend of a Lakeland pass, known locally as The Drop. He was dead before the wheels of the coach left the tarmacadam surface of the road. His passengers were not so lucky. Out of the strewn wreckage on the riverbank below, police and ambulancemen carried twelve corpses and three bodies so badly injured that their life-expectancy could not be measured in units longer than hours. The survivor, who was assisted through the place where the emergency door had been, unscathed save for a dislocated collar bone and a bruise on her forehead, was referred to by the press as 'The Miracle Girl'.

Joanna McCloud, convalescing from glandular fever, heard the news, faintly and punctuated with static, on the portable radio beside her bed. Beatrice Martin, who had invented a cold in order to avoid the cultural benefits of banging her head on the beams of Dove Cottage, switched on the television and caught the tail-end of the main news headlines. For fifteen minutes they attempted to telephone each other. Eventually Joanna had the sense to put down the receiver and wait. The words 'fate' and 'destiny' figured largely in their conversation. They'd both read accounts of people who'd been prevented from catching trains and aeroplanes which subsequently crashed. Joanna said, 'But lots of people are prevented from catching trains etcetera which subsequently *don't* crash.' 'Miss Mee,' Beatrice said wonderingly, 'and Miss Richardson. And Peggy and Carol.' Miss Mee, a thin classicist; Miss Richardson who was in love with the shade of Robert Browning, Carol and Peggy with their Girton scholarships. Joanna doodled around the outlines of the birds of paradise on the wallpaper beside the phone;

Beatrice flicked through the telephone book which contained unfamiliar names and outdated numbers; each awaited the arrival of an appropriate response, each was aware of the danger of some manifestation of aberrant behaviour: just as you sometimes had an irresistible urge to giggle in the middle of morning prayers.

It took days, and a deserted classroom, and a list of names in smudged black print, and an address from the headmistress, and the sight of twelve embroidered and empty shoebags in the cloakroom, and twenty-odd assorted parents – posh ones that they'd mimicked and shabby, peculiar ones that they'd mocked – weeping and not weeping and trying not to weep at the memorial service presided over by a bishop; it took the combined effect of all these impressions before the full impact registered upon them.

Beatrice's closest friend, Mary Dawson, was among the dead. Also Joanna's closest friend, Hannah Davidson, who had played the violin and had been the only girl in the class to admit to losing her virginity. In English, Miss Richardson read aloud from *Tess of the d'Urbervilles*, read a chapter heading, 'Maiden No More', in her precise, well-modulated voice, and everyone's eyes swivelled in Hannah's direction.

Hannah had carried her secret knowledge to the grave. In the church of St John the Divine, the school choir sang *The Lord is My Shepherd* to the tune of *Brother James's Air* – Mavis Dargue, who sang the soprano solos, was dead, and Moira Bridges, a contralto, who had the biggest bust in the school; they'd reshuffled the ranks, tried to fill in the gaps; the bishop drew upon the Sermon on the Mount, the staff wore their full academic dress, the three remaining members of Form Lower Sixth Remove occupied a pew to themselves. Beatrice pulled a dangling thread from her cardigan, by the end of the service had unravelled two inches of ribbing from its cuff; Joanna experienced the first ominous flashes and sense of blinkered vision that heralded a migraine attack; 'The Miracle Girl', Madeleine Brennan, who was a Roman Catholic, had difficulty in following the order of the proceedings, kept flicking through hymn book and prayer book, was silent during the responses. All three of them were aware of the special position that they occupied, aware of the eyes that were drawn towards them as they rose, knelt, sat, opened their mouths and pretended to sing; some of those eyes expressed curiosity, awe, some betrayed malevolence: what was so special about Joanna McCloud, or Beatrice Martin, that fate,

8

luck, chance, or the architect of the universe should have spared them? Alison Gates had been destined for Lady Margaret Hall, Peggy and Carol for Girton, Jane Porter had played hockey for England. What was so special about Madeleine Brennan?

'Will you hold out until we get home?' Dr McCloud asked his daughter as they hurried towards the car. She nodded. For one terrible moment, during the Lord's Prayer, she had thought she might be sick, then and there, all over her hassock, but the nausea had passed, had been superseded by the pain that bored through her temples, by the optical disturbances that haloed every object that swam into her line of vision.

'It was those damn lilies. Lilies and stained glass, they always trigger it off.'

He put the key into the ignition. He would get her into bed, draw the curtains, give her an ergotamine tablet. He could have shouted for joy. She suffered attacks of migraine, ergo, she was alive.

Helena and Robert Martin comforted the parents of the late Mary Dawson. Their combined charm, tact and graciousness was too much for Beatrice, who moved away and perched herself upon the church wall and unravelled a few more inches of cardigan. The bishop's chauffeur held open the car door for his lordship. His lordship, who had confirmed Beatrice and with whom she had fallen, briefly, in love, hurried past her without recognition. Divested of his costume, his personal glamour was nil: he had two large brown warts on his forehead which were concealed when he wore his mitre. How Mary Dawson would have laughed. They would have filled a vacuum flask with gin and vermouth, taken it up to her bedroom, smoked their way through a packet of Gauloises, practised backcombing their hair and speculated on the endlessly fascinating subject of the men who were destined to love them, men of an altogether different hue from those they encountered in their daily lives. 'Somewhere,' Mary would say, 'there is a man who will fall in love with me and time is drawing us closer together, inexorably. Will he have dark hair, or fair, will he have blue eyes or brown?' 'Or will he have warts?' Beatrice would say, and they'd collapse on to her bed, creased with mirth.

The church wall was damp. Flat gravestones that dated from the eighteenth century were obliterated with outcrops of moss. Mary would laugh no more.

9

'Must you behave with such appalling discourtesy?'

Helena Martin turned in her seat to regard her daughter who sat in the back of the car fidgeting with the edge of her sleeve and chewing the ends of her hair. 'I know that you're upset, but surely you could have managed to say a word to Mary's parents?'

Little beads of moisture glistened on the surface of her sable coat. Beatrice stared insolently at the oval face of her mother, with its discreet and flawless coating of make-up, picked at an incipient spot at the corner of her mouth, made no reply. She wasn't upset. Not exactly *upset*. Disorientated, perhaps. 'Can we go?' her father said, staring straight ahead of him, flicking the ash from his cigarette through the window with nervous little taps.

They'd had a fight the previous night. From her bedroom she'd heard their voices, struggling for ascendancy, heard the stridency of the insults that tripped with such facility from their well-shaped mouths, put a record on the gramophone and turned it to full volume.

Her mother swivelled around, settled herself against the squashy black leather upholstery. 'Of course.'

Madeleine Brennan, in her long school gaberdine which had been bought big enough for her to grow into – unfortunately she hadn't grown – trudged past with her head down towards the centre of the town. 'Poor Madeleine Brennan,' Helena Martin said, irrelevantly and foolishly. Everyone else had said, 'Lucky Madeleine Brennan.'

'Why do you always *say* that?' Beatrice wiped a clear patch on the steamed-up window. Her father switched on the engine, ground the gears. The Jag shot into the mainstream of the traffic. Her mother pursed her mouth, folded the fingers of one hand over those of the other. 'Because I feel sorry for her.'

'Why? She hasn't got a physical disability. She hasn't got a hump back or brain damage or one leg shorter than the other. She's very bright, I've told you, frightfully clever . . .'

'For God's sake, leave your sleeve *alone*.'

Hollywood film stars and Raphael madonnas and Greek heroes depicted in classical statuary apart, Robert and Helena Martin were the two most beautiful, unblemished people that Madeleine Brennan had ever set eyes on. Generations of selective breeding might have resulted in such breathtaking symmetry of feature, such nobility of brow and lustre of eye; it was difficult to believe that a chance and fortuitous collection of dominant genes had combined to produce her perfect oval face, his tender profile, the sweep of her cheekbone, the way his hair curled behind his ear. Beatrice's physical inheritance was evident – or would be, once she got over her spots. The Jaguar, swerving from the kerb, sprayed Madeleine with sludge. She watched it manoeuvre through the traffic, pick up speed, disappear around the corner by the Co-op. Oh lucky, lucky Martins, who were rich and beautiful and self-assured and capable of satisfying their every need and desire, their every whim and fancy.

She walked, in the rain, through the shopping centre. Every plate glass window threw back a cruel reflection: the long macintosh, the unstyled hair, the sensible shoes. The pictures that appeared in the newspapers had been just as unflattering; not one press photographer had managed to capture the attractiveness that lurked, waiting to be discovered, liberated, by decent clothes and a good hairdresser. Joanna McCloud, tall, dashing and famous for straight talking, had paused beside her one day in the cloakroom and had said in a surprised tone, quite out of the blue and apropos of nothing, 'You're really quite pretty, aren't you? You just don't make the best of yourself.'

She turned into Stead and Simpson's where her mother daily fitted the plump feet of howling infants into suitable footwear. It was difficult to make the best of yourself on a limited income, when your clothes had to be purchased to allow for growth, when your shoes had to be selected for stamina rather than style, when a visit to the hairdresser depended upon forgoing something more essential. 'Robbing Peter to pay Paul,' her mother called it, making lists of expenses on the inside of empty cornflake packets. Money was what mattered, the only thing; it meant the difference between a new frock for the school dance and an incompetently-altered hand-me-down, between talking about your summer holiday in Lucerne or Florence and keeping your mouth shut, between exciting envy and being patronized.

'I can't come for lunch,' her mother said. 'Brenda's off with the 'flu and this new girl's clueless. I'll send out for a sandwich. You'll have to open a tin of soup. Or there's some stew left from yesterday. Yes, madam?' A woman held out a pair of strappy silver evening shoes. 'Size five?' Her mother took a brief glance downwards and made for the shelves where the size sixes were situated. Her mother was a small woman with a lined face, an unsuccessful home perm and a figure ruined by years of snatched and starchy meals. On Speech Day the previous year her mother had sat next to Helena Martin who had inclined her head and smiled and engaged in polite trivial conversation. Madeleine, on the platform, waiting to receive the complete works of Tennyson bound in red leatherette, had blushed and cringed and wondered whether her mother was talking about the difficulties of widowhood, the almost insuperable problems involved in bringing up a teenage girl single-handed, and wasn't everything a *price* these days? No one, seeing the two women, would have believed that the elegant, beautiful one was, in fact, three years older than her companion.

The woman pushed her right foot into the silver shoe. Flickers of pain crossed her face. 'How did it go?' her mother asked, massaging the ache in the small of her back with one hand, feeling for her pencil, which rested behind her ear, with the other.

Madeleine shrugged. 'It went on and on. Joanna McCloud had migraine. Hannah Davidson's mother had to be taken out.'

'Nobody else approached you?'

'No.'

The press photographers, the cameras and the microphones had retreated days ago. Certainly it had been a spectacular crash, a heavy death toll, funds had been started, telegrams of consolation sent from high places, a plaque was to be unveiled, but public interest and sympathy was fickle – or was conditioned into being so; a week later there had been an even more spectacular train crash.

'It's for Ladies' Night,' the woman said. 'The Masonic. My dress is gold but I think gold shoes would be a bit much, don't you? Could I try the other one?'

'Yes, dear,' her mother said. Madams quite quickly became dears. 'I should like to have attended. Just to show respect. I expect the Martins and the McClouds were there?'

'Mrs McCloud wasn't.' Mrs McCloud was Dr McCloud as well, an ear, nose and throat specialist at the local hospital.

'She's a working woman too,' her mother said approvingly, as though there could possibly be a connection between pursuing one's vocation in the medical profession and selling shoes to the fat wives of Freemasons.

The woman gazed speculatively at her feet, came to a momentous decision. 'No, dear, I think not. There's something not quite . . .'

'Old bag,' Madeleine said venomously. 'Don't you ever get sick and tired of them ?'

Her mother folded the shoes in tissue paper, replaced them in their box. 'You get used to it.'

'You could *train* for something,' Madeleine said wildly.

'What could I train for?'

Nothing. Absolutely nothing. What were the prospects for an untalented, poorly-educated, unqualified widow of forty? Nil. Absolutely nil.

'Don't be ridiculous. We'll have enough to do with *you* training.'

'I'll get a grant.'

'You'll get those exams passed first before we start worrying about that. What will they do in the way of arranging lessons now? Just the three of you.'

'We're all doing the same subjects. Except that Beatrice is doing Art. She can always be fitted in with another form.'

Her mother sniffed, as much to say: trust Beatrice to be different. 'You'll be very much thrown together, won't you?' she said, casting an eye into the recesses of the shop in case the manager happened to be lurking. 'It's to be hoped that you'll get on.'

Madeleine adjusted her beret to a less unbecoming angle, tightened the belt of her gaberdine, reflected upon the scholastic year that lay ahead of them, herself, confident, bossy Joanna and mocking, unpredictable Beatrice who would smile at you one day, lend you her Parker pen with the gold nib, and ignore you totally the next. It was not a prospect that filled her with joyful anticipation.

For two or three months they were treated with a kind of reverence, approached gingerly, regarded with an awed fascination. Little girls pointed them out to littler girls in the playground, the staff applied the carrot rather than the stick to encouraging their industry, the headmistress invited them into her study, separately and collectively, to discuss any problems that might have arisen. It was both flattering and irritating to inspire such reactions. 'It's like being in the zoo,' Joanna said. Beatrice excused her habitual idleness by reference to 'a sort of recurrent depressiveness' that prevented her from concentrating. Madeleine saw her photograph fade in the window of the local newspaper office. They had thought that they could preserve their former distance but, inevitably, a relationship of sorts was formed: they were the only three people who could treat each other naturally. After the Christmas holiday, when things were beginning to return to normal, when people no longer blushed when they inadvertently mentioned motor coaches or accidents, when Miss Carter was once more referring to Beatrice as 'that conceited lazy child' and Joanna was severely reprimanded for reading *The Tropic of Cancer* under her desk during a history lesson, a solidarity had developed. They were at the age when companionship of any sort is preferable to isolation, and there was, simply, no one else to provide that companionship. The rich man's daughter, who lived in a large white house on the local Millionaires' Row, the scholarship child from the other end of town, and the doctors' daughter with her healthy ego and her troublesome conscience and her inability to dissemble, created common ground between them.

'They're settling down,' the headmistress noted with approval. 'You must invite them round,' Helena Martin told her daughter, looking up from *Vogue* and lighting a mentholated cigarette. 'That Brennan child needs bringing out of herself,' the female Dr McCloud declared, sorting briskly through a sheaf of case notes. 'Why don't you take her with you to the tennis club?' Mrs Brennan wrote: 'butter, eggs, shoe polish, school blouse, subscription for school magazine, ten cigarettes?' on a piece of cardboard torn from the cornflake packet, paused for thought, crossed out 'ten cigarettes?', chewed on the end of her pencil and wondered what further economies could possibly be made in order that Madeleine should not want for the sort of accoutrements that mingling with the Martins and the McClouds might entail.

2

'The history of all hitherto existing society is the history of class struggles,' Joanna said. 'The bourgeoisie cannot exist without constantly revolutionizing the instruments of production.' From Beatrice's bedroom window she delivered these sentiments to the back lawn, accompanied them with suitably histrionic gestures; in her imagination she peopled the deserted garden with hordes of cheering, banner-waving proletarians. She was Lenin, she was

Rosa Luxemburg – the sound of their undying allegiance rang in her eardrums. Beatrice felt around on the floor for the heaviest book that she possessed and threw it at her. 'Hungary,' Beatrice said. Joanna ducked. The book, Bindoff's *Tudor England*, rebounded off the window sill.

'What has Hungary got to do with Marxism?' Joanna said. 'Look – you've split the spine. They'll make you pay for it.'

'We preferred it when you had religious mania.'

At thirteen Joanna had been an atheist, her lips stubbornly pressed together, her eyes determinedly opened wide for the duration of morning prayers. At fifteen she was converted to the Church of Rome, spent hours at the presbytery while Father Kennedy recounted the historical genesis of the Tridentine Mass, explained the distinction between a virgin birth and an immaculate conception, and offered advice on how one recognized a true vocation. Madeleine saw her in church; with the indifference of the true cradle Catholic, wondered what all the fuss was about. It would pass. It did. In the space of a history lesson, when Joanna came to the reluctant conclusion that God's representative on earth, His Holiness Pope Pius XII, had been nothing but an old fascist. And so back to the more mundane ritual of Anglicanism. Until the library shelves yielded up Sartre. And Santayana. Immanuel Kant and Hegel. And hence, by cross reference, Karl Marx.

Beatrice yawned, stretched her legs on the bed, closed her eyes, recited: 'Ramillies, Oudenarde, Malplaquet, the Congress of Vienna, 1815. Aren't you going to do any work?'

'I'm relying on my natural brilliance. Do you know that if I join the Party it will disbar me from a career in the Diplomatic Service?'

'Do you want a career in the Diplomatic Service?'

'No.'

'Well then.'

'It's the principle.' Joanna turned back to the window, saw a small gnarled man emerge from the garden shed with a spade in his hand. 'I say, Beatrice, how much do you pay your gardener?'

'How would I know?'

'You should make it your business to know.' She rested her elbows on the iron bars that were fixed across the window at regular intervals parallel to the sill. 'Did they keep raving lunatics up here, or what?'

Beatrice laid aside *Tudor England* and *The Defeat of the Spanish Armada* and Kennedy's *Shorter Latin Primer*. The print danced before her eyes, the facts refused to embed themselves in her memory store. Could *she* rely upon her natural brilliance? 'It used to be my father's nursery,' she said.

Joanna sneered. 'Mummy and Daddy down there, and up here, Nanny and hot buttered toast. Mummy wore afternoon tea frocks in crêpe-de-chine, and Daddy expropriated the surplus value of the sweat of his workers' brows. They had croquet on the lawn and skivvies who had to run like the wind to put a lump of coal on the fire whenever Mummy rang one of those bells. And they gave the servants one half-day off every fortnight and everybody knew their place and twelve-year-old boys were sent down the mines to lead pit ponies and get their lungs destroyed and it was all pie in the sky bye and bye, Saturday night and Sunday morning, gin palaces and praise the Lord . . .'

'What era are we in now?' Once begun on her such-are-the-evils-of-capitalism tirade, Joanna was liable to continue indefinitely. Beatrice adopted diversionary tactics. 'His parents died when he was a child. He was brought up by this weird old aunt. I once heard Bridget and the char talking about her. Bridget said, "She had syphilis, they smothered her."'

Joanna turned from the window, instantly diverted. 'No! She must have been making it up. They couldn't just go round smothering people. Even in those days. Could they? It's one of Bridget's fictions.' Bridget's fictions included babies born with horns, or tails, or two heads facing each other. They had overheard, they had wanted to believe, but now they were sceptical. 'She had syphilis, they smothered her,' Joanna said. 'It's *beautiful*. Why don't you ask him?'

'I did once. He said, "My *dear* child."' Beatrice imitated the eye-rolling action affected by her father when amused.

They laughed so much that it hurt. After a bit, Joanna said, 'Your father has tremendous chiaroscuro.'

Beatrice raised her face from the pillow. 'Chiaroscuro? That's sort of – light and shade stuff, isn't it? In painting? Caravaggio, etcetera and so forth.'

'I've got the wrong word, haven't I?'

It was a time in their lives when they very often had the wrong word. Or the right word and the wrong pronunciation; for months they said 'epitome' as though it were composed of only three syllables, rhymed clandestine with Appenine, and weren't absolutely certain whether it was Proost or Prowst, Flohbert or Flawbert.

'You mean charisma.'

'Do I?'

'Yes. Hitler had it too.'

'How can anyone who looks so beautiful and intelligent and sensitive as your father allow himself to become a disgusting capitalist?'

'He's as moody as hell, he has a foul temper and the fact that he's a disgusting capitalist won't prevent you from staying to dinner and eating food paid for out of his ill-gotten gains, will it?'

'If I go home,' Joanna said plaintively, 'there won't be anybody in and I'll have to start peeling potatoes. I bet you've never peeled a potato in your life, have you, Beatrice?'

She hadn't. Nor washed an item of clothing. During her brief sojourn in the Girl Guides they'd laughed as she tried to figure out the procedure which resulted in a cup of hot tea.

'You really are most tremendously spoiled and pampered, aren't you?' Spoiled and pampered were the two most damning words in the female Dr McCloud's vocabulary. 'What if you ever have to look after yourself?'

'Then I shall eat in restaurants and send my clothes to the laundry. Where's the problem?' said the idle one, taking up a hand mirror to check on the progress of her skin blemishes. 'When does puberty actually *end*, for Christ's sake?'

'Ages ago. You're retarded.' Joanna put a record on the gramophone, sang along with Lotte Lenya, off key, in an excruciating approximation to the German tongue: '*Surabaya-Johnny, warum bist du so roh? Surabaya-Johnny, mein Gott, und ich liebe dich so,*' picked up a black crayon and defaced one of the eleven photographs of Yehudi Menuhin that were tacked to the walls of Beatrice's bedroom. 'By the way, Chris Adams told Valerie Saunders that Barry Moore fancies you.'

'Barry Moore can fancy away. Barry Moore looks like Neanderthal Man. Imagine Barry Moore's face on the pillow beside you in the morning!'

Joanna began on a second photograph, blacked out two teeth, added a Ramsay MacDonald moustache. She cogitated. 'I bet it turns out to be a terrible let-down. I have this feeling.' When they were thirteen, Hannah Davidson had said, upon seeing her parents in a state of merry inebriation, that if drink was supposed to be so marvellous, then she thought that they ought to give it a try, and to this end she'd filched a bottle of Grand Marnier from the drinks cabinet. They'd shared it between them and then held each other's heads while they were violently sick. 'People enjoy that?' Hannah Davidson had exclaimed wonderingly, afterwards.

Drink had been tried and found wanting. Elucidation of the other great mystery didn't occur for another three years when the first copies of the Penguin Lady Chatterley hit the bookstalls. They'd passed their single copy around the classroom, the corners of the relevant pages turned down. Hannah had mused, turned to Joanna: if sex was supposed to be so marvellous, then . . .

But that experiment had been conducted solo, or rather, with the willing cooperation of a youth who rode a motor-cycle and worked with a travelling fair. Joanna knew of no one suitable. She still didn't know of anyone suitable. Grammar school boys? Those who came back from their first term at university, college scarves flapping ostentatiously, who took you to the pictures and had you in a half-nelson two minutes into the Pathé Pictorial? *Men* were out of reach, deterred, no doubt, by her total lack of aplomb. Who did she know with whom she might possibly want to do that? Apart from Yehudi Menuhin. And Benjamino Gigli. And, anyway, wasn't he *dead*?

Bridget opened the door. 'So there you are. I've been looking hither and thither and yon. Have you been smoking in here again?'

'No we have not. And you could have saved yourself the thither and yon when you knew perfectly well that we'd be here,' Beatrice said, with an attempt at dignity.

'Less old buck from you, my lady. Joanna, your mother rang to say that you're to go into town for the meat.'

Joanna groaned. 'She just doesn't *care* that I have very important exams looming, exams upon which my whole *future* depends. When I'm behind the counter in Woolworth's, she'll be sorry then, she'll wish she hadn't burdened me with the running of the household while she selfishly pursued her career . . .'

'Anyway,' Bridget said, opening the window and admitting a blast of cold air. 'Anyway, I want the pair of you out of here so that this one can give it a going-over.' 'This one' who stood in the doorway, a duster in one hand, a tin of polish in the other, was the latest in the line of cleaners they engaged from a nearby home for subnormal females. 'The half-wits,' Bridget called them and declared that they had blancmange where their brains ought to be.

'I'd like to know what you do up here. It puts me in mind of a Chinese opium den.'

Bridget was an extremely distant relation of Beatrice's mother who had served the household in the capacity of general factotum since before Beatrice's birth. She was an unmarried woman of middle age ('that time of her life,' Helena called it) with short iron-grey hair, legs like pegs, and a note propped up against her dressing-table mirror that said, 'My eyes for the blind.' She, in her unsentimental fashion, had been responsible for a large measure of the spoiling and pampering that might prove to have a deleterious effect upon Beatrice's character.

Beatrice began to slam books into the bookcase. 'I've told you, Bridget, *I'll* do it. After *they've* been in here, I can never find a thing.'

'You said that last week. And the week before. It's a pigsty.'

'All it is,' said Beatrice, 'is a totally unproductive process of moving dust about from one place to the next. Besides which, Freda has quite enough to do already, haven't you, Freda?'

Freda grinned. She had a red potato-shaped face and little slitty Mongol eyes.

'Do they take all their wages?' Joanna asked. 'At the Home?'

'I expect so. Not that they get much. It's supposed to be some kind of occupational therapy for them, keeps them in touch with society.'

'Freda,' Joanna said slowly, fixing Freda with what was meant to be an encouraging smile. Freda looked alarmed, backed away. 'Come *on*,' Beatrice said. 'We'll go and collect your wretched meat. And then perhaps I may be allowed back into my room. I *do* live here. I *do* need to change. And we *are* expecting company.'

The company expected was Joanna and Madeleine. It was the first time that they had been asked for dinner. Previous invitations had been for tea-time sandwiches, or glasses of cider and intriguing things on bits of toast that circulated during the teenage parties that Helena occasionally arranged for her daughter, when the youthful *haut monde* of the district would confront each other glassy-eyed, and Beatrice would retire to the kitchen with a book.

'They *are* seventeen,' Robert Martin had said. Joanna amused him, as engagingly and irrationally Red as only a prosperous middle-class child could be. And, of course, one couldn't exclude the other girl. Under the circumstances.

The other girl was gazing mournfully at the two dresses that were spread out on her bed. Each seemed as unprepossessing as its companion. Even if she'd had the money, she wouldn't have had the taste; taste was something you acquired, gradually, by trial and error, by precept, by means of an expert guidance; she'd never had the opportunity to develop it.

In the kitchen, she assembled soap and towels, spread sheets of newspaper over the lino. She spoke quietly, under her breath: 'Why didn't you let me go to the local grammar? Why won't you, at least, let me take a job in the holidays?' Other girls had done it: worked on the toiletries in Boots or behind the ironmongery counter at Woolworth's. Even Joanna had spent Christmas serving teas to ladies in musquash at The Cheshire Cat. 'Why did my rotten father have to go and get killed in the rotten war?'

The night before, she'd finished reading a book about war criminals in which the author had reached the conclusion that evil astonished one by its banality. Madeleine, soaping herself under the arms, had a similar view of poverty. Only those who had been poor could know the trivial monotonies intrinsic in the situation. Not rags and rickets and tuberculosis, but rather, never being able to make a casual, spur-of-the-moment purchase, never being able to leave a room, for however short a period, without switching off the light, never daring to keep your library books over the due date on account of the fine incurred, always reading your horoscope six months late in the dentist's waiting-room because the money didn't run to brand new copies of women's magazines. There was an old lady down the road who cut matchsticks in two and separated paper tissues, but that was eccentricity: a different thing altogether.

The education man had explained: one could claim free school dinners, a travel pass, vouchers for new school uniform. And her mother had shied as if mortally insulted. It was charity, plain and simple, whatever fancy name they attached to it, and charity she would not accept. They dispensed their charity and they made sure they rubbed your nose in it, ensured that you were made aware of the extent of your obligation: vouchers issued which could only be exchanged in certain shops, meal tickets of a different shade from those given to the paying customers; discrimination of the most invidious kind. Oh no, not *my* daughter.

The gooseflesh rose on Madeleine's thighs and upper arms. She towelled herself vigorously, sprinkled talcum powder between her toes. Joanna, in full spate, her narrow, expensively-shod feet on the desk in front, had spoken scornfully of the indoctrination that resulted in people who didn't pay for their education believing that they owed a debt to the benevolence of the state, whereas, as anyone with an atom of sense ought to realize, the state owed a duty to every individual. The individual *was* the state. And it was the duty of every individual to screw the state for whatever he could get out of it, for his rightful share. *This* crummy state, anyway.

Joanna was brave and tough and expounded her beliefs from a position of security: even if you eradicated the bourgeoisie you'd always need doctors, *particularly* after the revolution. Madeleine put on clean underwear and a fresh pair of stockings that had only one run, up on the thigh where it would never be noticed. She was small-boned with narrow wrists and slender ankles and fingers that looked as though they'd break if you shook her hand; she was built for flight rather than fight.

'Very nice,' her mother said, turning her round, viewing from every angle. And that just about summed it up. The dress had belonged to a cousin who was twenty years older than Madeleine; it was a very nice dress for a thirty-six-year-old matron. Beatrice opened the door, wearing a jumper and skirt so plain and unadorned and well-cut that their exclusiveness was apparent at fifty paces. Bridget, frowning into the hall mirror, stuck pins through her hat and into her hair. Gloves and a missal lay on the hallstand. 'She's one of your lot,' Beatrice said. 'She's going to confess her sins. What is it this week, Bridget? Impure thoughts? Carnal desires?'

'Talk to me when you have some sense in your head. If that day ever comes.'

The hat was finally anchored to her satisfaction. She turned to smile at their guest, a fellow believer in a house full of heathens. The hat was blue with a turned-back brim. In concert with her navy blue macintosh and her stout black laced-up shoes, it made her look like the district nurse about to set off upon a round of bed baths and enemas.

'How do you feel,' said Beatrice, leading Madeleine up the staircase towards her bedroom, 'when your soul is shriven? Uplifted, or comforted, or what? Or ready to start sinning all over again? Not that, I suppose, you've ever done much sinning to begin with. I shouldn't think Bridget has either. Not *sinning*.'

Beatrice was the only one in the class who hadn't passed through a religious phase. For Beatrice, sinning was something that other people did and, essentially, a sexual activity. 'You don't really believe in it, do you?' said Beatrice. 'All that guff?'

It was years since she'd given it any thought. It provided a framework, as school provided a different sort of framework, and a sense of identity. The aesthetics of the ritual: the Agnus Dei at Eastertime, the procession of nervous children in white dresses towards their first communion, the candles at Christmas, flaring into flame one after the other, all these stirred her emotions, but then so did *Land of Hope and Glory* at the end of term. Intellectually, there were certain irreconcilabilities that had to be admitted.

Joanna, never one to countenance ambiguity, had a notice which said, 'Religion is the opiate of the masses,' pasted to the underside of her desk lid, all unaware that the true function of an opiate is to ease pain, rather than to induce oblivion. In Beatrice's bedroom, she riffled through Beatrice's two hundred and thirty albums of the Classics, said, 'How is it that you have all these records and no *music*? Tschaikowsky, yuk, and Johann Strauss, yuk, and *Nights at the Ballet*. How is it that the people who possess masses of records and the very latest and most sophisticated hi-fi equipment never have any taste? Whereas I, who am blessed with bushels of it, can't afford a lousy gramophone needle?' Joanna was lately enamoured of large black blues singers called Sonny Boy this and Little Brother that who made catarrhal wailing noises about life on the levée or the more recondite effects of dope addiction to the accompaniment of steel-bodied guitars. Also acceptable to her exacting standards, for some unexplained reason, was anything written and sung in a foreign language: she kept the record library staff in a constant state of ferment as they endeavoured to secure for her recordings of obscure French chanteuses or pensioned-off performers of German lieder.

'I suppose this isn't quite so foul as the rest.'

The opening chords of Rachmaninov's Second Piano Concerto filled the room, a room which, if it were to be tidied up, would resemble one of those rooms which figured so prominently in the glossy magazines that were stacked on a glass-topped table downstairs: carpet as thick as turf, a wardrobe that occupied the length of an entire wall, blue velvet curtains and a goatskin rug, yards of bookcase that contained shiny art books and the complete works of almost everybody, photographs of Beatrice, at the gymkhana, on the beach at Biarritz, at twelve, soulful and blurred around the edges; propped in the corner was the violin that Beatrice had taken up at the age of eight, the guitar she'd abandoned six months ago, a decorated mandolin from Italy which she'd never even attempted to play.

Some day, in the barely foreseeable future, when her circumstances permitted it, Madeleine would assemble for herself a room just such as this, filled with records and books and a carpet so thick that when you walked across the floor you left your footprints in it. Until then, she could do no other than try to conceal the envy that rose like bile in her throat.

They lolled and lounged, the three of them, in what they fondly imagined was the style of courtesans in boudoirs. Life was so slow, so predictable. Nothing happened. Nothing ever happened. Except for catastrophes. The small, sedate provincial town had nothing to offer them, except the tennis club, the badminton club, the church hall dances, an assortment of gauche youths with raw knuckles and dandruff on their lapels, endless cups of coffee in mock-Italian cafés waiting for the ordained man with mysterious eyes who never showed up. Their only prospect lay in escape. And between that prospect and their present null existence loomed the hurdle of a set of formidable examinations.

Downstairs, Robert Martin poured three glasses of sherry, glanced at the images of his guests reflected in the ormolu mirror above the sideboard, smiled a bit. Seventeen. Barely out of childhood, despite the careful assumption of world-weariness, the concerted refusal to express enthusiasm about anything in case it should betray an unguessed-at naïveté. Three faces: one clear-cut, definite, stamped with its destiny, the other two as yet amorphous, clay to be moulded; you couldn't hazard a guess as to their futures: whatever life did to them, they would become. His daughter's exquisite regularity of feature might harden and set, as her mother's had done, into expressions of discontent; that guarded look that Madeleine presented to the world might be reinforced until every aspect of herself was hidden from view. They'd photographed the eyes of the victims of Jack the Ripper in the belief that the last image one saw remained imprinted on the retina. Looking at Madeleine's eyes gave you that impression, that all you'd see would be yourself, in miniature, sliding from the iris, dissolving into the blue-white aqueous humour. Joanna's eyes were the windows of her soul. He handed her a glass of sherry. Her look said: what a pity it is that you seem so handsome and so charming and so likeable, because we are bound to be implacable, immovable opponents, we two: you, the owner, the boss, and I, who have pledged myself to destroy the balance between the forces and relations of production and thereby the entire class structure.

'And how's my little unemployed revolutionary?' he said, as she raised the glass to her lips. He knew it was unfair, but he couldn't resist it; she rose to the bait so beautifully, every time.

'Quite well, thank you. I'll grow out of it, I know. You told me.'

Beatrice refilled her glass. 'Shut up, please, the pair of you, please, shut up.' The remembrance of previous occasions came into her mind: teenage parties which Joanna had deserted in order to seek out her father and accuse him of nameless atrocities committed in the name of capitalism. In the drawing-room, well-bred adolescents said, 'Thank you *so* much, Mrs Martin,' and then stared at their feet, and in the kitchen, or the dining-room, or the hall, the colour came up into Joanna's cheeks, her arms flailed like windmills and her auburn hair flew round her face while Robert Martin laughed, or hummed the first few bars of the Internationale, or interrupted her harangue to say, 'All class structures are naturally hierarchical,' or 'It's not so much that I object to the ethos of your political position; what I do object to is the incomparable dreariness of those who propound it.'

'All right,' he said, '*pace*. We'll find a nice safe topic with no political overtones whatever and have a civilized discussion, won't we, Joanna?'

Joanna grinned. She was a little bit in love with him. Everybody was a little bit in love with Robert Martin, his romantic profile, his dark velvet voice, his bedroom eyes. It was difficult to believe that he ranted and raved and shouted and stormed and used the kind of language that only Beatrice would not balk at repeating.

'I think that leaves the weather,' she said. 'Or Einstein's Theory of Relativity.'

'We'll talk about that then. The weather, I mean.'

Madeleine placed her sherry glass carefully on a small side table.

Her hand had trembled every time she raised it to her mouth. The strain of mingling with the Martins was almost insupportable. His regard seemed sympathetic but also, she suspected, contained an element of flirtatiousness that she was unequipped to handle. *Her cool smiling glances convinced you that she could see the safety-pin in your underwear, the hole at the top of your stocking.* They seemed so impeccably groomed, so effortlessly suave, so good to look at; in their presence you always felt that some rogue subliminal impulse would manifest itself in the involuntary picking of your nose, scratching of your head.

Joanna ate ravenously, explained that it was a curious fact, but a fact all the same, that food tasted so much better when you didn't have to assist in its preparation. 'It's my dream to spend six months of my life in a four-star hostelry snapping my fingers for plates of Dover sole and profiterôles smothered in chocolate sauce and someone else to do the washing up.'

Madeleine smiled. It was a dream that she shared. Latch-key children, the pair of them, coming home ever since they could remember, to the solitary tin of tomato soup, the sink full of saucepans.

'And before you speak,' Joanna said, scouring her dish for the last remnants of trifle, 'it is just a dream. And I don't have to justify my dreams. Or reconcile them to my beliefs. One gets so sick of returning every day to the same old cold grate and the same old messages scribbled on the telephone pad, just because someone decided to have a baby or their adenoids removed.'

'One does, does one?' Beatrice helped herself to more wine. Unlike Joanna, Beatrice had been introduced to the delights of drink more gradually, could understand exactly why some people held it in such high esteem.

Her father rested his chin on his hands, raised one eyebrow. 'You're not thinking of following in father's footsteps then?'

'No, I am not. I've had it all my life: people coughing and spitting in the next room, phoning up at all hours of the day and night with their kidney stones and their blocked sinuses. I've got a place at the L.S.E., providing . . .' Under the table she crossed the fingers of both hands.

'Are you confident?'

'Yes, I think so. Fairly. It's just a case of the short-term stuffing of your brain with a lot of useless garbage and then regurgitating it in the form they require. God!' She helped herself to a large William pear, began to peel it. 'Half the world is starving and we spend our days learning the uses of the ablative absolute.'

Madeleine and Beatrice – who were not fairly confident, the former because of a terror engendered by the realization that so much depended upon the outcome of those few hours' scribbling, and the latter because constitutional lethargy prevented her from making too much of an effort and because she was famous for going to pieces in examinations – Madeleine and Beatrice gazed at the tablecloth or into their glasses as though seeking omens, in the weft and the warp of the linen, the lees of the wine. 'I had a letter from William,' Beatrice said, in a very obvious attempt to change the direction of the conversation. William, an earnest undergraduate with hair like corn stubble, had been very attached to Beatrice, so attached that he had given her his hardback copy of *Cry, The Beloved Country* with an inscription inside the cover which read: 'To Beatrice – whatever happens – for ever.'

'It said that he was sorry but he felt that our association ought to end because he has met another.'

'It didn't say that.' Joanna made incursions upon the cheese board. 'It didn't say, "I have met another."'

'No.' It had said, actually, 'There's this girl called Linda.' 'What it did say, though, at the bottom, was, "Would you mind awfully returning my *Cry, The Beloved Country*?"'

Joanna thought that William sounded eminently sensible. Beatrice's father choked on his coffee and had to be thumped on the back, thought it the funniest thing he'd heard in ages, said that William reminded him of Dante Gabriel Rossetti: having a good long think and then digging up the remains of Lizzie Siddal in order to salvage his poems.

'Why do I attract such weird specimens?' Beatrice mused. 'Do you remember that one at Rimini who followed us around for a fortnight? And the one we called Daffodil?'

'Yellow hair and khaki shorts and big knees?' Helena smiled. 'Was he in the Boy Scouts?'

'And Paco in San Sebastian, with the gold teeth and the black eye patch. And the awful Barry Moore of the shaggy locks – beware the man whose eyebrows meet, for in his heart there lies deceit.'

'And the Arab who wanted to buy you, in Hammamet.'

Madeleine, who would never have dreamed of discussing her amorous adventures with her mother, even if there had been any to discuss, realized suddenly that not only were there no shared confidences in her house, neither was there any frivolity. When certain kinds of poverty came in at the door, it wasn't love, but light-heartedness, that flew out of the window. Mention a male name to Mrs Brennan and she'd start thinking in terms of wasted time and unwanted pregnancies; the Martins had a way of giving everything exactly the right *weight*, of knowing what mattered and what didn't. Surely the stories of yelling and fighting and allegations of extra-marital doings must be fabrications of Beatrice's perverted imagination?

Joanna, having cleared the table of comestibles, leaned back in her chair, undid the top button of her skirt and said, 'Nobody ever fell in love with me. Not even someone I wouldn't touch with a ten-foot pole.'

Robert Martin looked at her. There was no hint of prettiness, but she had the sort of face that in the due time of womanhood would elicit adjectives such as 'striking' and 'handsome'. 'Does it bother you?' he said.

She yawned. 'Not particularly. It seems to me to be rather a waste of energy that could be put to better uses. Every time *I* ever fell in love, I stopped thinking properly, all of my brain went fuddled, not just that bit reserved for that kind of thing.'

'You're a sensible woman, Joanna,' he said. 'Perhaps you'll be able to identify it for us – that bit reserved for that kind of thing – isolate it, and save us all a tremendous amount of botheration.'

But later, when Madeleine went into the kitchen for a glass of water, she saw him standing with his arms folded around his wife and his mouth on her hair. Their stillness, their rapt attention, had the quality of a tableau. Her face flaming, she closed the door softly behind her and rejoined the others at the Scrabble board. 'What's up?' Beatrice said. 'Are they at it again? They're either throwing things at one another, or else they're at it all over the place. He gets tremendously horny. What on earth can you do with REG if you haven't got IMENT?'

At ten-thirty Joanna pedalled off on her bicycle. Robert Martin, despite her frantic protests that she didn't *need* a lift, she'd *much* prefer to walk, drove Madeleine home. She sat very straight beside him, her hands folded, her knees tight together. Embarrassment paralysed her vocal cords, embarrassment on two counts: the fact that the contrast between the place he'd left and the place to which he was going could not fail to strike him forcibly, and also the fact of his recently-demonstrated maleness, his sexuality.

As he leaned across her to open the car door, his sleeve brushed her arm. The tensing of a hundred tiny muscles was transmitted through the cloth and he recognized her fear. Poor kid, he thought, as he drove home. She's the sort that'll meet some man who'll go at her like a bull at a gate and for ever after she'll have headaches instead of sex.

Helena had never suffered any such inhibition. That night he made love to her. During the twenty years of their marriage they had been unfaithful to each other many times. Not simply because they were continually attracted towards fresh partners, or because there was no relationship to betray, rather, infidelity was just one weapon in the general warfare of their lives together. They fought as they made love, passionately, and with a disregard for the rules of gentlemanly conduct. No one else was strong enough or desirable enough to kindle the same sort of fire as that which flamed between them. 'No one else,' they said, during the peaks of reconciliation, 'no one else would ever do,' and each was speaking the truth. The only sufferers were those others who were sufficiently naïve to believe that the Martins had found in *them* some quality they couldn't find in each other.

He stretched himself, lit a cigarette, flicked the match and missed the ashtray. The match, not properly extinguished, smouldered on the carpet fibres. 'Sod it,' he said, and climbed out of bed to retrieve it. Bridget was always forecasting that one day they'd set each other afire. 'We do that. Quite often,' he'd said. And Bridget had made prune shapes with her mouth. She hated that sort of talk.

'I'd like a new carpet anyway.' Helena moved on to a cool place on the crumpled sheet. 'Oh, and by the way, I rang those landscape gardeners this morning. Emmett simply can't cope any longer. I thought terracing at the bottom and some sort of paved area . . .'

'Those houses,' he said, brushing ash from his chest, 'where I took Madeleine home this evening. Dear God! Back to back terraces with obviously no indoor sanitation. Crumbling walls and rotten roofs and the soot of centuries. I didn't know those sort of places still existed in this day and age.'

'You could have asked Joanna. She would have been able to tell you the precise statistics for. the incidence of shared lavatories throughout the length and breadth of England.'

'Joanna is lovely. They are all three of them lovely. They'll never be so much themselves again, after this. They'll absorb bits and pieces from other people in the process of growing up.' He sighed, leaned his head on his hand. 'Joanna will eventually marry some professional person and become the pillar of every available establishment institution. Madeleine will probably remain the essential scholarship child, stuck for ever in the middle echelons, lacking the confidence to stretch her ability to the full.'

'And Beatrice?'

'Oh, Beatrice. Beatrice might do almost anything and it wouldn't surprise me a bit.'

3

Beatrice decided to fall in love. As the only conceivable means of escaping from a length of grey days composed of bungled Latin unseens and unresearched essays on Henry VIII's foreign policy, the crippling boredom of gazing out at the same landscape – a dog-befouled area of scrubland graced with the name of municipal park – from different windows, while the dry, clipped voices of academe droned interminably on themes that had no relevance whatever.

She wasn't stupid. On her tenth birthday, disturbed by a series of unfavourable progress reports, her parents had taken her to the London clinic of a famous educational psychologist where, after a series of tests, her intelligence quotient had been fixed at a hundred and forty-eight points on the Stanford-Binet scale. Whatever it was that prevented her from achieving her potential, that eminent personage was unable to discover. Questioned about her interests, Beatrice had remained mute. Her interests were playing the violin like Yehudi Menuhin, or dancing like Pavlova, without ever having to undergo the years of strenuous and monotonous application that had made Menuhin into Menuhin, Pavlova into Pavlova.

The psychologist had pulled down her lower eyelids and recommended a physical check-up. But Beatrice's organs proved to be fully functional, her vitamin intake more than adequate, her bloodstream bursting with healthy corpuscles. Her lethargy could be attributed to no physiological abnormality. Why then, asked Helena, her inability to concentrate, to apply herself, except on certain rare occasions when something intrigued her imagination, why did she move so slowly, why did she procrastinate so, find it difficult to make decisions, why would she sleep the clock round if left unattended? 'Some children are like that,' the specialist said, and talked about the mysteries of metabolism. 'She was born idle,' Bridget said. 'Folks like that, they need a stick behind them all their lives.'

So she was marked down as lazy. And accepted the judgement. What hope was there of making anyone understand how it felt to experience daily life as a hurdle race, a series of seemingly insuperable obstacles? Simply waking and getting out of bed demanded an almost superhuman effort of will. The days when there was something planned, something that had to be done – even something as trivial as a dental appointment, or an application form to be filled in – those days loomed like mountains among the flat plateaux of their companion days. Dostoievsky had spoken of the agonies implicit in the creative process, Flaubert had described the way, when confronted with the prospect of work, his brains had turned to porridge, but they were referring to the production of masterpieces, not gazing at their overdue library books, or three weeks' backlog of homework, and trying to summon up the energy to deal with them.

A hundred per cent inspiration and nought per cent perspiration had squeezed her in at the tail-end of all previous tests of ability – she'd received marks for verve, if nothing else, as a result of such efforts as translating strawberries as 'fruits de paille'. But the day of reckoning was at hand. Facts, invaluable facts, facts without which no amount of insight or facility of style could suffice, slid through the interstices of her brain, that organ which existed, it seemed, primarily for the accommodation of daydreams. Once, she had thoughts of becoming a writer: writers, she had heard, spent the greater part of their time in reverie, and certain short essays of hers had been highly praised, but, after five pages on the ruled lines of an exercise book, she'd come to the sad conclusion that, as well as a penchant for preoccupation, writers needed a fair amount of stamina in order to convert their amorphous fantasies into controlled prose. And then there was the dreary business of checking for authenticity: a piece of hers, poignantly lyrical, she had thought, that dealt with swallows hovering lazily on the breast of a sapphire sky, had been returned with the acidulous comment: 'Have you ever seen a swallow?'

She was a reader, not a writer. Novels, she devoured: Dostoievsky, Flaubert, Scott Fitzgerald, Rosamond Lehmann, Graham Greene, Aldous Huxley, any novel that fell into the category of reading for pleasure; let it come within a mile of some syllabus or other, be considered as mind-improving, and her fingers fell away, nerveless, from its outer covers. *Pride and Prejudice*, for instance, the book she was to be examined upon; she simply couldn't read it, however she tried: approached it sideways on, plunged into the heart of it, attacked when it wasn't looking – the block remained, the paragraphs were solid black wedges of incomprehensibility. Instead, she persuaded Joanna and Madeleine to recount the plot, provide a résumé of the characters, select for her certain crucial quotations. Joanna said, 'I think you must have been dropped on your head as a child.'

But the explanation couldn't be that uncomplicated. Bridget simply wasn't the sort to allow anything entrusted to her care to come to harm, least of all the wonder child, removed from the womb two months prematurely by Caesarian section, weighing all of three pounds, maintaining life in an incubator, against all odds.

Perhaps being deprived of those two months had something to do with it, perhaps cutting short one's full term of gestation had a detrimental effect upon one's future development. Though Beatrice found it difficult to convince herself that Helena's womb had been the ultimate in safety and security; to her certain knowledge, Helena had had one abortion before that time and another two afterwards.

She was as she was, whatever the reason, a girl who found boredom intolerable, but even more intolerable did she find the effort needed to alleviate that boredom. Reading, listening to music, daydreaming and falling in love, only then did she feel at one with the world, related to its structures, its possibilities: it didn't occur to her that these were withdrawals from action rather than activities.

Even falling in love. Especially that. She was young, beautiful, physically confident – a number of men would have been only too happy to go through the motions of professing eternal devotion in order to take off her clothes. All she had to do was to choose one and let him; in no time at all he would engender in her those feelings that had been engendered previously by Yehudi Menuhin, by Herbert von Karajan, by My Lord Bishop. Madeleine couldn't dissociate the prospect of sex from visions of a particularly nasty operation, Joanna regarded it as something essentially comical and not to be taken too seriously, Beatrice alone suspected that it might turn out to be as addictive as the French cigarettes and the gin and vermouth in which she and Mary Dawson had so often indulged. The first smoke, the first drink, oh, they weren't pleasurable, you didn't expect them to be. But you persevered. And soon it was difficult to believe that you'd ever shuddered with distaste, ever rushed for the basin.

Not all the men who were attracted to her were weird specimens: a very distinguished teacher of the violin with a tender curved smile and dark blue satyr's eyes had once found all sorts of reasons for correcting her bow action and thus achieving a fair amount of bodily contact, the bronzed tennis professional, who had all the ladies of the club in a lather of longing, had oftentimes pressed himself against her among the privet bushes at the back of the pavilion; there had been an Adonis of a ski-instructor and a strikingly handsome amateur dramatist. It was by a process of elimination that she arrived at David Ross. He was neither as handsome as the violinist or the actor nor as splendidly constructed as the skier and the tennis player, but he did have the advantage of availability; the violinist *et cie* had wives, or other equally restricting relationships.

David Ross's wife was divorced from him, had fled with their child back to her parents' house, which was situated just three doors away from Beatrice's. She was a girl with a face composed mostly of nose and forehead who wheeled out her infant in a coach-built perambulator and informed anyone who cared to listen about her two years of pure and unadulterated purgatory with that man. That man, who drove his scarlet MG with much revving of the engine and slamming of the doors, who was to be seen at all the proper times and in all the right places with a succession of expertly-coiffured and expensively-dressed women on his arm, that man from whose predatory gaze anxious mothers shielded their

32

nubile daughters and sighed for their own lost youth, that man most
definitely fitted Beatrice's bill. The roués of literature had so often
been reformed by the love of a pure young girl.

'Getting yourself talked about,' Bridget said, cracking her knuckles
with vexation, moving agitatedly from foot to foot in the doorway
while Beatrice dolled herself up for her first assignation. Robert
and Helena tended to inhabit some plane far above the level of
gossip and speculation and innuendo; Bridget knew everything,
made it her business to know: who was sleeping with whom, who
was living on borrowed time; pregnancies, Bridget knew about,
before whoever-it-was had missed her first period.

Getting yourself talked about seemed no mean achievement to
Beatrice. She painted black round her eyes, considered, then washed
it off again: pure young girls did not need artifice.

'He's ten years older than you and more.'

'That's what we're doing tonight, we're going to draw his old-
age pension. Oh Bridget, when he smiles – all his teeth fit together
so perfectly in the space, sort of curve to match the shape of his
mouth.' She completed her toilet, spun round from the mirror.
'How do I look?'

'Like a tart.'

'Do I really? I've only ever seen one tart, that one who walks
near the market – Woodbine Mary, or whatever they call her. She's
about sixty-five and she has these repulsive great knotted varicose
veins. I don't look a bit like *her*. As a matter of fact, if she were to
be brushed up a bit and washed and combed, she'd look exactly like
the mayor's wife. Have you noticed? Just like Duchess Thing who
opened the bazaar; she reminded me of the barmaid at The Feathers.
There are probably barmaids who look exactly like duchesses, or
one's idea of duchesses, anyway.'

The palms of her hands were damp and belied her nonchalance.
Suddenly she wished that she could just bicycle round to Joanna's
for a game of Lotto and a mug of Ovaltine.

'You know what I mean.' Bridget buttoned her flowered overall
across her extensive bosom, sat down heavily on Beatrice's bed and
massaged her knees. 'Go around with a character like that and you
start to look like a tart in no time.'

'What's *wrong* with him?'

'What's right?' Bridget ticked off undesirable qualities on the
fingers of her left hand. 'He's a married man with a child, he has

a reputation that stretches from here to next week, he leads a reprobate existence, he got that poor girl down the road into trouble so that she had to marry him . . .'

Beatrice buttoned her coat, turned up the collar, turned it down again. 'He is *not* a married man – except, I suppose, to adherents of your potty religion; getting into trouble, as you call it, is a combined effort rather than a solo performance; and as for leading a reprobate life – you know perfectly well that he has a job, and a good one too.'

Bridget did know perfectly well. David Ross was one of Robert Martin's sales managers. Robert Martin thought very highly of David Ross, had no knowledge of or interest in his extra-mural activities.

'If your father gets to know . . .'

'What do you think he'd do?' Beatrice was genuinely at a loss on the subject of anticipating her father's reaction. 'Why should he do anything? David is free, white and – '

'Well past twenty-one. Oh, Beatrice darling, there are plenty of nice young boys for you.' Demonstrations of affection did not come easily to Bridget. She opened her arms to Beatrice, let them fall to her side. 'Nobody wants to deny you your pleasure. It's just that I'm so afraid . . .'

'I don't know how you could be so disgusting as to even *think* that of me. Parent and children relationships demand *trust*.' The statement sounded irrelevant, but Bridget had been more of a parent than the ones that she had. 'You can say a prayer for my immortal soul.'

Little shivers of apprehension ran up and down her back. Presumably men like David Ross would take great care to ensure that girls like herself did not get pregnant; surely *she* wouldn't be expected to know anything about that sort of stuff?

She looked down on Bridget's grey head, at the dog's hind leg centre parting in her hair. Bridget too must have had a youth, improbable though it seemed. 'Why did you never get married, Bridget?' she asked, for the umpteenth time. And for the umpteenth time, Bridget replied, 'Because.'

'Because nobody ever asked you?'

'I wasn't bad-looking, as a girl,' Bridget said. Nevertheless, Beatrice had hit the nail right on the head; nobody had asked her.

'Nobody will ask you either, not if you continue the way you're going. No decent man wants second-hand goods.'

Beatrice paused in the doorway. 'You won't tell them?' There was a way Helena had of curling her lip that made you feel two inches tall and covered in sores.

'I won't this time. Not if you promise me . . .'

'I promise, I promise.'

It was very odd, Beatrice thought, that after seventeen years' evidence to the contrary, Bridget still had implicit faith in Beatrice's word being her bond. She looked somehow forlorn and faraway, despite her bulk, framed in the doorway, when Beatrice turned at the bottom of the stairs to wave goodbye. Bridget was funny-looking and quaint and her ideas came out of the ark, but whenever Beatrice found occasion to implore the Deity: on the night before examination results were due, or when called to account for some misdemeanour, her prayer always ended with the same supplication: 'Dear God, don't let Bridget die before I do.'

She checked the car park of the Majestic Hotel to make sure that he'd already arrived. Joanna was always bemoaning her lack of aplomb and Beatrice was always insisting that the cloak of self-possession could be donned and discarded at will, but given the same circumstances, Joanna would stifle her qualms and walk boldly inside, whereas Beatrice would pass through fire rather than expose herself, alone, to a battery of curious glances.

He was there. He had a drink waiting for her: a glass of sweet white wine – 'La Flora Plonk' her father called it disdainfully, when obliged to attend official functions and drink such stuff. He stood up. She sank gratefully into a padded sofa, and carried on sinking; by the time she hit the back of it, she could scarcely see over the top of her knees.

'Whoops,' he said and reached out a hand to rescue her. 'Wouldn't you like to take off your coat?'

'Oh. Yes, I suppose so.' He raised a hand and some lackey waited impassively while she disrobed and then bore it away to the nether regions of the ladies' cloakroom. Beatrice, who had never before experienced the slightest twinge of uncertainty over her appearance, suddenly began to get twitchy about such matters as whether or not a sleeveless dress was a very good idea when it displayed the gooseflesh that appeared to be rising like measles on her upper arms, whether she shouldn't have combed her hair backwards instead of forwards, whether she really looked as peculiar as that great ornate mirror on the opposite wall would have her believe.

He clicked his gold lighter, open and shut, open and shut, tapped the cigarette that he intended, eventually, to light, on his thumbnail. 'I never really thought you'd come,' he said.

'Didn't you?' The wine was over-sweet, cloying. She'd have preferred gin.

'Thought that Father might have put down his foot.'

He couldn't really believe that she'd actually sought permission to attend a rendezvous with the acknowledged town rake? Wasn't it obvious to him that this meeting was clandestine? Perhaps he was a bit thick? When he finally bent to light the cigarette, she took a good long look at him. His appearance had a disconcerting tendency to alter totally from one occasion to the next. Or perhaps it was the eye of the beholder that altered totally. The last time, she would have sworn that he was handsome: dark hair that waved back from his brow, big grey eyes, thickly lashed. Tonight she wasn't so sure: a tuft of hair stuck up at the back of his head, there was a smudge on that previously immaculate collar, his nose didn't seem to be such an exquisite shape after all. The lounge was too dimly lighted for her to tell whether or not his eye pupils were dilated. 'The eye pupils become dilated,' Joanna had read, out of some vast tome on psychology – her latest enthusiasm, 'when the subject is excited or aroused.' Perhaps he would take her dancing. Joanna had also acquired the knowledge from somewhere or other that it was an indisputable fact that if a man and a woman found that they danced together well, it was ten to one that they'd be equally well-suited for the other business.

Bored commercial travellers eyed them from behind their newspapers. In the ballroom, across the hall, a twenty-first birthday party was in progress. A slope-shouldered youth in a hired dinner suit aimed a carving knife at the top tier of his birthday cake. Somebody burst a balloon and someone else shrieked. Beatrice scoured her brain for a suitable topic of conversation. With boys one talked about the latest Buddy Holly record and wasn't the Cambridge Entrance a swine and were you going to Angela's party; with the violinist one had discussed musical scores, with the tennis coach, one's backhand drive. He just sat and smoked and watched her.

The last time they'd met, when he'd asked her for a date, in the foyer of the Arts Centre, he'd spent twenty minutes complimenting her on her eyes, her face, her hair, told her how he'd noticed her often, smiled the kind of smiles that made your insides dissolve. Maybe he considered that he'd made his contribution; now it was up to her.

'Do you enjoy your job?' she said at last, and foolishly. 'Are you awfully good at it?'

'You'd better ask your father about that.'

That came as a shock. It had never occurred to her that her position as the boss's daughter might have some bearing on the fact that he found her eyes etcetera so beguiling. Perhaps he hoped to marry her and feather his nest. In that case, she thought, very miffed, I hope my father cuts me off with a shilling.

'I'm not even very sure what it's all about,' she said primly. 'I know you make machines which make machines . . . It always makes me think of big fleas and little fleas.'

'That's about the strength of it.' He hailed the stony-faced waiter and ordered fresh drinks. If only he would smile that smile. Perhaps if I get drunk, she thought.

'David!' A dapper young man in a dinner suit trod carefully across the Turkey carpeting towards them. His hair matched his patent leather shoes. His chin was recently shaved and fiercely blue. When introduced, he held on to her hand for too long. He was, it transpired, the manager of the hotel, and one of David's oldest, dearest and closest friends. He insisted upon providing them with drinks on the house. She thought, if I have to drink one more glass of this muck, I shall probably throw up in the middle of the floor.

In the ballroom, everyone hushed everyone else. The thin voice of the birthday celebrant was heard: 'I would like to thank my mother and father . . .'

David's oldest and dearest friend winked, said, 'And now we wait for Mother to step forward and say, "Your father had nothing at all to do with it, dear."'

She tried to smile, but her jaw felt frozen. In the ballroom, someone proposed a toast. 'Ladies and gentlemen,' said David's friend, 'and those who don't know. Daddy's under the misapprehension that you can stretch seven bottles of Asti Spumante through fifty-six people. They're not even wetting their tongues in there. If I were to tell you some of the things . . . you wouldn't believe me.'

37

The band struck up with *Twenty-One Today*. The birthday boy steered his mother to the centre of the dance floor. This spectacle disproved, once and for all, another of Joanna's indisputable facts: that boys always grow taller than their mothers.

'And how's life with you, David?' asked the manager. 'How's Lord Moneybags and the divine Helena?'

David gestured with his glass. 'Ask Beatrice. She's their daughter.'

The floor didn't open up to swallow him, but providence intervened from another direction. 'I say,' called an elderly gentleman from the other end of the lounge. 'I asked him for a Punt e Mes and look what he's brought me.' He held up a pint of Guinness. 'Can't make him understand.'

Not a flicker of an expression crossed the waiter's impassive features. 'Excuse me,' said the manager.

They looked at one another. She smiled. He smiled. They grinned. 'He's not really your oldest, dearest and closest friend?'

'I've known him six months.'

The smile came naturally this time and had nothing to do with her eyes or her hair. There came a moment early on in every acquaintanceship when you knew whether or not you were going to like someone. That moment had arrived. She was going to like him. There was no way in the world that she was ever going to fall in love with him.

As it turned out, Bridget was expending unnecessary energy wringing her hands and knitting her brow over the condition of Beatrice's maidenhead. She'd been out with him five times before he even attempted anything more than a temperate kiss. The violinist and the tennis coach had gasped and gulped as their passions overcame them; David seemed to want to talk to her, rather than explore her physical geography. And talk they did, after that first strained evening: 'You looked so grand and ladylike and forbidding,' he explained, 'as though you were granting me an audience. I was frightened to death.'

How could they ever have thought that they'd be stumped for conversational topics? They talked until their jaws ached, about life and love and mutual acquaintances, about books and music and painting and films and their peculiar relatives, about food and work and school and their astrological signs, they presented to each other the carefully-edited, potted autobiographies that they'd

38

prepared, but, as the evenings wore on, they forgot what they had intended to disclose and what to conceal: incidents that presented them in a bad light, blunders that they had committed, unpleasant characteristics that they strove to suppress, all surfaced, unbidden, among the more acceptable formalities of their interaction. He told her that at the age of fourteen he had fallen in love with a male schoolfriend and how, although he was told that adolescent homosexuality was but a passing phase, it had worried him for years, long after he'd developed a preference for the female sex. She told him about the time she'd shoplifted a bottle of nail varnish remover from Timothy White's and Taylor's, not because she wanted it or needed it or couldn't afford to pay for it, but simply because always getting what you desired created in you peculiar urges to acquire something totally *undesired*.

She didn't have criminal tendencies. He wasn't queer. They saw one another in a clearer light than they would have done had they fallen in love. She was a spoiled madam and he was an immature man who needed to bolster his ego by escorting a bevy of attractive women around the town; those discoveries couldn't prevent a friendship from developing. He took her dancing and their bodies fell naturally into a complementary rhythm; in his car, in his flat, he kissed her and touched her. 'I would have to be *desperately* in love,' Joanna said. Love or no love, Beatrice was aroused, the albatross of her virginity hung about her neck. Why, she wondered, doesn't he take advantage of me, when I am so ready to be taken advantage of? In literature, arousal led straight into dissolve, fade, and remorse arriving with the morning paper.

Bridget kept her counsel. Her father left for a conference in the Ruhr with an assortment of steel barons. The girl is buckling down at last, making an effort, Helena thought, as Beatrice announced her destination yet again to be the reference library. In his flat, which overlooked the cricket field of a preparatory school, they lay on his bed and kissed and touched and stroked. The sound of leather on willow drifted upwards in the gentle air of the lengthening evenings. 'Played!' the little boys shouted. 'Run, Evans, run! Oh, I say!' He had a sickle-shaped scar above his shoulder-blade, a souvenir, he told her, from his National Service days. All the youths in Beatrice's age-range had escaped National Service by four or five years. 'How old, exactly, are you?' she asked, tracing the shape of the hair that grew cruciform upon his chest. Exactly twenty-

39

seven years, six months and three days. 'Too old for you. Or so they'd say.'

The hair grew darker, progressively, as she traced it downwards. 'They' were not going to get the chance to say anything. 'Do you think,' she said, 'that I have a peculiar navel? It isn't kind of – dished, like other people's. I've noticed at the baths. And it's in a different position, I'm sure, kind of – higher up.'

'It's a perfectly lovely navel.' He followed its contours with his tongue. He said, 'You mustn't do that, you know. Not unless . . .'

'Unless what?'

'Unless you really want me to.'

She really did want him to. 'How amazing,' she said. *Lady Chatterley's Lover, Tropic Of Cancer,* Gray's *Anatomy*: all the theory in the world couldn't throw more than the faintest glimmer of light upon the practical. 'Isn't it funny?' she said. 'Oh, I'm not being personal. Everybody's is, I suppose.'

Too funny by half. Or not half funny enough.

At nine o'clock she rose, dressed herself, collected her books together. 'The reference library closes at seven-thirty. I'm at Joanna's now. It's a bit silly, isn't it? I mean, there's no need for all this hole and corner stuff, is there? No need whatsoever.'

He inhaled deeply on his cigarette, bit the side of his lip. 'You're very young, Beatrice.'

'Mm. I know. Perhaps after I'm weaned . . .'

'It can happen, you know. Sometimes, you want to *too* much.'

'Is that why your wife left you?' She juggled with Kennedy's *Shorter Latin Primer,* tucked her hair behind her ears. Everything had been going so marvellously, a logical progression, when, suddenly: a power failure, the Angel of the Lord passing overhead. Beatrice, at that moment, had had a sharp and vivid mental picture of Bridget on her knees, telling her rosary beads, imploring the Sacred Heart.

'No.' He pushed the ashtray with his forefinger around the bedside table. Eventually it fell off.

'Maybe it's me.'

He collected cigarette ends from the carpet, ground ash under his bare foot.

'Maybe you just don't fancy me enough.'

'Maybe I fancy you too much.'

'Well then, if it's something that happens sometimes, there's

40

no need to make a song and dance about it, is there?' She crossed over to him, crouched beside him on the floor, put her arms around him. Male pride, she knew, was such a delicate article. 'You haven't gone off me?'

'The question is – have you gone off me?'

'Not a bit. So that's all right then.'

She walked home through the park. Intacta. That kind of situation never figured prominently in literature. In fact, she'd never known it to figure at all. In literature, the period of time between the removal of clothes and the achievement of climax, on average, occupied the space of a dozen lines. She wasn't sure whether or not she should feel humiliation, or pity, or nothing at all. It had been – kind of sweet. In a way. And she certainly didn't like him any the less because of it. They were friends, and friends could forgive each other things that might cause irretrievable breakdown between lovers.

Helena was on the phone to someone. 'Yes,' she said, 'goodbye,' as soon as Beatrice came in. She glanced at her watch. 'I fully appreciate the importance of these examinations,' she said, 'but, really, you go from the sublime to the ridiculous. Or vice-versa. You look shattered. You need a *bit* of relaxation, a *bit* of fun.'

4

Bridget brought bread and milk upstairs, fed her with it, a mouthful at a time, brushed back the damp hair from her forehead. 'You need your strength,' Bridget said, wiping dribbles from the bedclothes. And, for fifteen minutes or so, she relaxed into the rôle of invalid, allowed her pillows to be plumped, the corners of her sheets to be mitred, her face bathed with a warm flannel.

Bridget trod quietly, spoke softly, as you would do in a sick room. She opened the curtains. The garden shimmered in the August heat-haze. At the bottom of it, two men and a machine transformed a paradise of rampant growth into a landscape of regular terracing.

'It's not the end of the world.'

One of the men whistled the Harry Lime theme as he stacked

paving stones one on top of the other. A melancholy tune. She let the curtain fall back into place, excluded the sunlight, sat down on the edge of the bed, took off her pink plastic National Health glasses and polished their lenses with the corner of the sheet. The glasses left dark red indentations in the flesh at the sides of her nose; her eyes, bequeathed to the blind, were pale grey, protuberant and encircled with white rings at the edge of the iris.

'You can't stay up here any longer,' she said. 'You must put it behind you, start again. It was a setback, that's all. Do you think you're the only one in the world who ever experienced a setback?'

The girl turned her face into the pillow as the trite phrases – a forlorn attempt at comfort – tripped off Bridget's tongue.

'That Joanna has phoned three times. Why won't you talk to her?'

Beatrice opened her puffy eyelids, bit her bitten lips, gazed beseechingly at Yehudi Menuhin with his blacked out teeth and his moustache. 'Joanna got a State Schol.'

'Ah, well. She was never backward at coming forward, that one.'

'It's got nothing to do . . .' Beatrice closed her mouth. Bridget's grasp of the ramifications of the British educational system was feeble in the extreme.

'Tomorrow,' Bridget said coaxingly, 'you'll get up tomorrow?' She was at a loss. Years ago, disappointments could be soothed with boiled sweets or Fenning's Little Healers. At eighteen, you could no longer kiss it better.

Beatrice made no response. The space between four walls and a closed door represented the only kind of sanctuary available.

Bridget sighed, picked up the tray with one hand, stroked the girl's forehead with the other. 'Sleep, then.' She didn't even convince herself. Sleep, they said, proposing it as a remedy for all ills. But you had to wake up again, to the same reality.

The landscape gardener switched to a rendition of *Sweet Georgia Brown*. A vibrating blow-fly swooped in ever-decreasing circles around Beatrice's bed. Behind her closed eyelids the examination room reconstructed itself in every monstrous detail: the varnished dais, the bars of sunlight that penetrated the gaps in the Venetian blinds, the rows and rows of backs and legs and scuffed shoes, the scratch of nibs, the nervous coughing and the sighing.

The War of the Spanish Succession? Total blank. Henry VIII and the Dissolution of the Monasteries? '*L'état, c'est moi*' – Discuss?

She filled in her name and the date, cudgelled her brain for the catchword, the key that would unlock her memory, permit the outflow of information. It remained elusive. The black hands of the clock whirled around its white dial. The mnemonics, the allusions, the clues assembled to assist the process of recall, all deserted her, as ever. There was only Madeleine's inky second finger and Joanna, crossing and uncrossing her ankles: her down-at-heel shoes that had once been all the rage, 'Logrollers' they were called, a type of moccasin – and the calm voice of the invigilator saying, 'Half an hour more.'

Different days, but the disjunction persisted. The Uses of Simile and Metaphor in *Sohrab and Rustum*. Sohrab and Rustum? 'On either side the river lie long fields of barley and of rye.' No, no. 'As in the country, on a morn in June, when the dew glistens on the pearled ears, A shiver runs through the deep corn for joy . . .' *That* was it. A rent in the veil, a flash of lucidity, and it was gone. Jane Austen? A woman in the cinema queue, behind Beatrice, waiting to see the film – Greer Garson and Laurence Olivier – had referred to it as *Pride and Prejustice*. There was somebody called Mr Darcy and somebody else called Elizabeth. Or something. 'Far and few, far and few are the lands where the Jumblies live. Their heads are green and their hands are blue . . .' And somebody called Mrs Bennet.

Some foul fiend, some *espèce du con*, had transcribed a passage from the *Aeneid* into Serbo-Croat: '*Infandum, regina, iubes renovare dolorem.*' That was never Latin. Was it? She was falling, she was flying, her heart thumped. 'Ten minutes more,' said the voice. 'Willie, Willie, Harry, Ste, Harry, Dick, John, Harry Three. Most gracious Queen we thee implore, to go away and sin no more. I'm His Highness's dog at Kew. Pray tell me, sir, whose dog are you?' Joanna fetched up a sigh that fairly rocked the room. 'Put your pens down – now!' 'She left the web, she left the loom, she made three paces through the room . . .' From the municipal park came the drone of an electrical saw.

She handed in her papers, a few pages of meandering inaccuracies, and with them her hopes: of matriculation, of freshers' balls and rag weeks, of letters home, of escape, of a future.

'Nonsense.'

Her self-imposed exile was curtailed, abruptly. A summons was issued. She washed her face and combed her hair, came down from her bedroom and presented herself at school. Helena, arranging delphiniums in the hall, looked away. The bone of her nose showed white and prominent. Respectable failure was one thing. But this! A retarded chimpanzee could have put up a better show. Even Art. *Nobody* failed Art. The reference library!

The headmistress, who had cut short a month's holiday in Bournemouth with her friend Gwen, twisted the cornelian ring round and round her little finger. A white piece of paper, *the* piece of paper, lay in front of her on the desk. It said, five per cent, ten per cent, ten per cent, and blank.

'I have written to the Matriculation Board and explained the circumstances,' the headmistress said.

They looked at one another. They both knew that she'd written to the Matriculation Board and explained the circumstances long before the event and that her letter wouldn't make any difference at all to those black figures on that white paper.

'The doctor prescribed you a tranquillizer before the examination?'

Beatrice nodded. When all else failed, they called it nerves. She'd been tranquillized from birth.

The headmistress caressed the barrel of her fountain pen between forefinger and thumb, leaned forward. 'There was nothing else – bothering you, was there, Beatrice? Your – home life, perhaps?' She'd read more psychology than Joanna, prided herself on the rapport that she established with her senior girls, had, inevitably, heard reports of some marital discord between the Martins.

Beatrice recited in her head: 'They sailed away for a year and a day. To the hills of the Chankly Bore. My heart aches and a drowsy numbness pains my sense. They say the lion and the lizard keep the courts where Jamshyd gloried and drank deep. Will you, won't you, will you, won't you, will you join the dance? Will you, won't you, will you, won't you, won't you join the dance?'

Some girls – the *odd* girl – cropped up, with whom there was no possibility of rapport.

'You will, of course, resit these examinations in November. In the meantime we will have to discuss a revision of your plans.' The sunlight glinted on the carriage clock, the crystal paperweight, the pewter vase. Perhaps Gwen would be able to manage a week-end. Her mother wasn't as helpless as she tried to make out. She'd ring that evening.

Beatrice walked home. The longest way. Into the centre of the town. In Stead and Simpson's Madeleine's mother laced up green suède brogues on to a pair of matronly feet. The Kodak Girl smiled flawlessly from the doorway of Boots the Chemist. She crossed over by the railway station and walked straight into Joanna, bicycling home with her Cash's name tapes and her luggage labels.

Joanna swerved into the kerb and dismounted. The bicycle was of the sit-up-and-beg variety, with a wicker basket affixed to its handlebars and her name writ large on the back mudguard.

'You saw Her Ladyship?'

Beatrice nodded. Joanna waited expectantly. Ladies with shopping bags passed to and fro in the space between them.

'She thinks I'm going to take those exams again.'

'Aren't you?' Joanna devoted her entire attention to testing the air pressure in her front tyre. It was a bit like visiting the terminally ill; one didn't know quite what to say or the precise tone in which to say it.

'What would be the point? I'm just not cut out for it. I don't think I'm cut out for anything.' The horizon closed in, upon the narrow main street, the little cramped shops, the blackened railway station from which, since Dr Beeching and his axe, trains ran to two destinations only. She wasn't going to Bristol. She wasn't going to Edinburgh. She wasn't even going to the University College of Aberystwyth.

The distance between them seemed symbolic. Conversational topics were limited. Joanna flicked her finger at the nickel-plated dome of her bicycle bell, sought for words that would express her apologies for gaining a State Scholarship on the strength of her natural brilliance. Beatrice said wanly, 'How does it feel to be covered in glory?'

'There are plenty of careers and so forth that don't involve passing examinations.'

'Oh yeah?' Perhaps Joanna would tell her that examinations were merely another capitalist con trick. 'I'll get out there among the workers, shall I, start raising the consciousness of the proletariat? Isn't that what you should be doing, rather than accepting state patronage?'

Joanna grasped her handlebars. 'You have to fight it from the inside, from a position of strength. You take from them and then use it against them. The bourgeoisie sows the seeds of its own destruction.'

She fell silent. Somehow, she couldn't think of a single thing that Marx had ever said which might be applicable to Beatrice's sorry situation.

'Where are you off to now? Can I join you? It isn't exactly the Palace of Varieties at home. Bridget lights candles for me and prays to St Jude, my mother has this bad-smell-under-the-nose expression on her face all day long, my father looks continually puzzled, as though he's wondering how on earth he managed to produce a cretin.'

'I'm going back for lunch. Actually. Ma's off this afternoon. We're supposed to be sorting through my various shabby garments to see what'll be suitable for . . . October,' Joanna said awkwardly. 'You're perfectly welcome to come . . .'

Beatrice shook her head. There was no place for her any longer in the scheme of things that included buying name tapes and assembling an appropriate undergraduate wardrobe, looking up the times of trains and hauling cabin trunks down from the attic. In fact, there was only one place for her, as far as she could tell: with the man who had also failed a test.

She went round to his flat that evening, unannounced. Perhaps there would be some glamorous female installed there, some lacquered and perfumed creature more adept at arousing and maintaining his potency than she.

'The reference library?' Helena had said snidely, *en passant*, as she was leaving. The girl probably needed sympathy, but Helena's capacity for sympathy, never very strongly developed, was severely limited of late. 'Oh, don't bother to lie. It's your own life you're ruining, nobody else's.'

He answered the door in his shirt-sleeves. In the corner, the television set flickered. There were three empty Worthington bottles on the floor. The room was grey with smoke. His jacket hung on the back of one chair, his tie over another.

'What a gay and glamorous existence you do lead.'

She picked up the silver-framed photograph of his child from the mantelpiece; a male child of four years who bore no resemblance to his father. 'You've heard, I suppose?'

'Heard what?' He moved around the room, emptying ashtrays, straightening cushions. He was nicely proportioned: the breadth of his shoulders balanced by the length of his legs; his hair, recently washed, flopped across his forehead.

46

'I thought my father might have pinned it up on notice boards: "My daughter has just been nominated as moron of the year." How does it feel to be a parent and have it brought home to you that your offspring is not going to gladden your heart and fill your spirit with parental pride? Is *your* son bright?'

'It's a bit early to tell.' He looked at her blankly. 'I wondered why you didn't ring me.'

'I saw you and him last Sunday. You'd just collected him from the Bellamys. From my bedroom window, I saw you,' she explained.

He buttoned up his shirt. Which was a pity. He had a broad brown chest covered with curly dark hair; he spent his Sundays at the open-air swimming pool with his son. 'What's all this moron business?' he said.

She took a mouthful of beer from his glass. The glass was slightly dusty and smeared. 'I failed all my exams,' she said. 'Spectacularly. If the Northern Universities Joint Matriculation Board went in for wooden spoons, they'd have presented me with one. Ceremonially.' Beer always looked better than it tasted.

'Oh,' he said. His brow cleared. 'And?'

'*And* it is a terrible disaster. For my mother and my father and all my teachers, it is equivalent to the death of a thousand cuts. If there was any justice, I'd be walking round with my head shaved, carrying a leper bell.'

He fetched a clean glass and another bottle from the kitchen, performed a neat bit of wrist work with the opener. 'Didn't you work hard enough, or what?'

His face hadn't altered. Obviously, he didn't realize the implications. 'It means I shan't be going to university.'

Beige froth flowed from the neck of the bottle and over his hand. He licked it off, handed her the glass. 'Well, I'm glad about that,' he said. 'Come and sit down,' he said. 'I've missed you, you know. I thought perhaps you wouldn't want to see me again. I wouldn't have blamed you.'

They sat together on the sofa and he stroked the hair back from her face. 'You'll have to think of something else to do, I expect?' he said, running his forefinger gently down her cheek to the point of her jaw. He didn't think that it was a sin she'd committed, a crime. Failing exams was something that happened. Her determined flippancy had fooled him into thinking that she didn't care, that she could cope. She allowed two tears to drop on to his

47

checked shirt. He held her away from him, tilted her chin. So it was comfort that she needed. Poor kid. She tightened her arms around his waist. To comfort her, he laid her back against the cushions and made love to her. And this time it wasn't funny at all.

'You'll forget about me,' Beatrice said lugubriously over the phone. 'We'll drift apart. It's inevitable.'

After all, it was only the crash, the deaths, that had drawn them together in the first place. Beatrice had always regarded Joanna as being insufferably affected; for Joanna, Beatrice had been a shining example of the results of hereditary social privileges. Both of them had considered Madeleine to be too wet for words.

'I give you my solemn promise,' Joanna said, holding the receiver in place between her ear and her shoulder, struggling to unloose knotted string with her fingernails and her teeth – there was so much still to *do*, so much to be sorted and packed and organized, 'my solemn promise that I shall keep in touch.'

'What?'

The string fell apart. She unwrapped the two shining new books: Max Weber's *The Protestant Ethic and the Spirit of Capitalism*, Hobbes's *Leviathan*, repeated what she'd said.

'You say that *now*. Just wait till you've been there a term or two. You'll be as superior and touch-me-not as the rest of them. It seems to have that sort of effect on people. And Brennan – she'll be ten times worse. I believe there are banners strung across her street: "Madeleine is going to the University, Madeleine is a very clever little girl."'

The reaction in Madeleine's neighbourhood was rather different. Most of the neighbours were of the opinion that Madeleine should have been out working, helping to support her mother at the earliest opportunity. Education was all well and good for those who were suitably placed in life to receive it. She'd leave home, meet a boy and marry him and make nought of all those sacrifices made by poor Mrs Brennan.

'I hope you'll always bear in mind what your mother has done for you, Madeleine,' said Mrs Snow, their next-door neighbour, a vixen-faced woman with hairs growing out of her mole.

Madeleine gritted her teeth and dug her fingernails into the palms of her hands. In Joanna's circle all was congratulation and plaudits.

Still, she could be in Beatrice's position. Although Beatrice's position seemed, on certain occasions when the terrors came – first thing in the morning and last thing at night – not entirely undesirable. The idea of London frightened her, the idea of finding a place for herself inside that vast institution made her blood congeal; she had only to picture platform four and the eight o'clock train and her heart palpitated, her stomach lurched. Did other people suffer such fears?

Mrs Brennan moved about the house, uncovering small caches of money that she had hidden from herself. The grant, of course, was a godsend; without the grant, there would have been no possibility of Madeleine going to university, but these little hoards, representing all those packets of ten cigarettes that had been crossed off the bottom of shopping lists, all those ladders in her stockings stopped with nail varnish so that they'd last that little bit longer, all those tea leaves dried out and re-used, these little hoards would purchase the extras not covered by grants: the college scarf, the leather briefcase, the wristwatch engraved with her name.

'All I ask,' said Mrs Brennan, counting notes and stacking silver, 'all I ask is that she works hard and makes something of herself.' Given that, every scraped penny, every laddered stocking, would have been worthwhile. She demanded nothing more. Madeleine would move out of her orbit; she knew that, she accepted it.

'Is it true about the Martin girl?' Mrs Snow said, sitting forward, her hands on her knees, avid for information. Having been brought to the forefront of public attention as a result of the events of September 11, there the three of them had remained. If it hadn't been for the crash, no one would have batted an eyelid over the Martin girl.

'Beatrice could never cope with exams.' Madeleine bent her head, wrote 'M. Brennan' in marking ink on endless lengths of tape.

'Thinks she's the bees' knees, I believe,' said Mrs Snow, who wouldn't have known Beatrice if she'd fallen over her in the street. 'I dare say this will bring her down to earth with a bump. Though, of course, her father can always set her up in something, can't he?'

'In a flat with a maid,' Beatrice said, 'and I'll put cards in newsagents' windows: "Miss Martin – Correction and French Lessons, £5." I'd probably be no good at that either. I wouldn't hit 'em hard enough. Or I'd get a dose of the pox within the first fortnight.'

'They'd smother you,' Joanna said. But it didn't raise even the ghost of a smile.

It was their farewell meeting: coffee and cakes in The Cheshire Cat. Beatrice, who had refused point blank to return to school, stubbed out one cigarette and immediately lit another. Joanna, after greeting the waitresses she knew and asking them if they'd done anything yet about the exploitative conditions of their employment, ate three chocolate éclairs and a vast meringue.

'Have you got a tapeworm?'

Joanna licked her forefinger, mopped up crumbs from her plate. 'I might as well make the most of it; I dare say I shall be on fairly short rations from now on. There's no way I shall be able to do all I want to do and eat as well. Beatrice, you can send us food parcels!'

Beatrice just wasn't going to be amused. She drew patterns in the ashtray with a match, looked across at Madeleine. 'Are you all ready, all prepared? Has Mother packed up all your nice warm vests?'

Madeleine kept her eyes fixed on her coffee cup. In moods such as this, Beatrice invariably struck out at the easiest target.

'I don't know what *you're* looking so damn doleful about. Don't you want to go? Is little Madeleine afraid of stepping out into the big naughty world? Does she want to stay safe at home with Mother?'

In a word, Madeleine thought, in a word, yes.

'Shut your face,' Joanna said. 'It isn't our fault that you blew a fuse. We're not to blame for your examination phobia. Try counting your not inconsiderable number of silver linings. If she or I had failed, it would have been a sentence for life in the library or the rates office or the Department of Health Insurance. *You*, on the other hand, can sit on your backside and smoke yourself to death while you wait for inspiration to strike. Don't you want that piece of cake?'

Beatrice tipped the remains of a brioche on to Joanna's plate, bit at the ragged cuticle on her index finger, said quietly, after a pause, 'I'm ten days late.'

'Ten days late for what?' Joanna signalled the waitress – Doris, or was it Elsie? she couldn't remember – the one with the bandy legs, for more coffee.

Beatrice groaned, bent her head until her brow touched the

tablecloth, began to laugh in a slightly hysterical way. Doris, or Elsie, watched her anxiously. Madeleine looked at Joanna, looked long and hard until light eventually dawned.

'Some more coffee, please, Elsie,' Joanna said. She couldn't take her eyes off Beatrice's long dark hair, her shaking shoulders. At the civilized hour of four p.m., all among the ladies in musquash sipping Russian tea, the deep pile carpet, the blue Delft plates and the silver cake knives, sat Beatrice with her head on the tablecloth, Beatrice to whom the worst thing that could possibly happen had happened.

'David Whatsit?' Joanna said.

Beatrice moved her head up and down. Doris/Elsie, returning with fresh coffee, said, 'Is there something the matter?'

'You could say that.' She raised her face, regarded the waitress gravely. 'When sorrows come, they come not single spies, but in battalions. How's that for recall? And they have me marked down as a total dead loss.'

'Thanks, Doris,' Joanna said quickly. 'It's all right. She's not going off her rocker. She's just quoting.'

The waitress, whose name was Ethel, banged down the coffee pot, cast a cold eye upon Beatrice. Well-educated girls like that – acting like lunatics. They were all off their rockers, if you asked her, including that McCloud girl who'd pestered them to death all over Christmas, telling them they were overworked and underpaid and then had had to be shielded from the wrath of the management because she couldn't carry an empty plate without dropping it.

Suddenly Joanna didn't have the stomach for the remains of the half-chewed brioche. She pushed away her plate, ran her fingers through her hair in the same manner as she did on the occasions when Beatrice's father teased her about her politics. 'Shock can do it, you know. Or a cold. Once I went for three months. All kinds of things can do it. Nerves. Or an emotional upset.'

'Or going to bed with someone,' Beatrice said. 'You've got icing sugar in your hair.' She stubbed out her fifth cigarette. Her face was impassive but her hand was trembling. '*You're* very quiet. Are you shocked to the core? Of course, good little Catholic girls don't do such things, do they? Good little Catholic girls save it for their husbands. Oh Christ, Bridget will go mad and tear paper.' Down went her head again towards the table top.

'*Stop* that,' Joanna said. 'Everyone's looking. Didn't you take any precautions?'

'Not the first time. Not properly. It was all sort of impromptu.' She began to shred cigarette ends into their component parts of tobacco and paper. 'Only, what do you call it – that Latin thing – *ceteris paribue – dulce et decorum* – ask *her*; she'll know.'

Madeleine was gazing at Beatrice as rabbits are reputed to gaze at snakes, as an arachnophobe would contemplate an advancing tarantula. A chasm had opened up between them: on the one side, she and Joanna who hadn't, on the other, Beatrice who had, not once but several times, Beatrice with her lovely face and her expensive suède jacket, set apart, untouchable, one of that army of women who *knew*.

Joanna, who had once overheard her father remarking to her mother that those who wished to make babies would be well advised to practise *coitus interruptus* – a prematurely middle-aged woman in a shabby coat with tears on her cheeks and a tribe of young children at her heels had just left the surgery – Joanna said briskly, 'The chances of conception are a million to one. You've been very worried these past few weeks. I expect that's the reason.'

'It's not just that. I feel peculiar.'

'Ill?'

'No. Sort of sleepy.'

'You're always sleepy.'

'Sleepi*er*, then,' Beatrice said. 'How soon can you have that frogs and rabbits thing?'

'Not so soon, I don't think.' Joanna racked her brains for snippets of conversation, dislocated facts, that had, over the years, penetrated the green baize door that separated the surgery from the house proper. 'There is a test, I believe. You have to pay for it. They don't do it on the National Health.' There had been tense young women, she remembered, sitting on the very edge of their seats, white round the mouth with apprehension, at the tail-end of surgery time.

'Have you told him?'

'Who? Oh, him. No. Not yet. Perhaps you're right, perhaps it's just that my hormones have got themselves into a twist. The difference between a hormone and a vitamin is that you can't make a vitamin,' Beatrice said mechanically. Nobody smiled. They'd fallen out of their cradles laughing at that one.

'Do you want me to make an appointment for you?' Joanna

said. 'Then you won't have to go through the rigmarole with Dorothy.' Dorothy was her father's receptionist who was wont to enquire somewhat over-zealously into the reasons for one's appointment requests. Beatrice, afflicted once with a sore throat, had replied to Dorothy's query as to the nature of her complaint: 'Tertiary syphilis,' just for the pleasure of hearing Dorothy's rapid intake of breath.

'Not unless he's decided to forswear the Hippocratic oath.'

She crumpled the empty packet of Gauloises. Quinine, there was, and ergot, and slippery elm and tansy, and regiments of old women armed with crochet hooks. How did one locate them? Look in the phone book under A for Abortionists? At home, there were bottles of gin and gallons of running hot water; only the willpower was lacking. That, and the inclination. For ethics and morality, she didn't give a sod, but there was something pretty awe-inspiring about the thought that life could be created so very easily, without any undue concentration or effort. I've succeeded at something, she thought. Madeleine and Joanna, as well as being horrorstruck, couldn't conceal from their faces glimmers of a sort of respect. At one stroke, the failed exams and the ruined career had been cancelled out; there was a certain cachet in having achieved her probable condition, even if it had occurred no mean distance outside wedlock.

5

She had never known her father to use physical violence. Over the years, the house had reverberated to the sound of his periodic fury; he had cursed every part of Helena's anatomy most comprehensively, using, abusively, the words that he'd use in a different context later, after it was all over, when he was in bed with her. Bridget, after the early years of unwise intervention, would put on her hat and leave for a meeting of the League of Catholic Women, or a walk around the park; Beatrice would turn up Gigli to full volume in order to drown out what Bridget called their barrack-room language. Sometimes there was a genuine reason for the quarrel, but more often than not they would create one out of nothing. He'd had a bad day, so had she. He'd come into the house with a face like thunder and she'd goad him until he reacted. It had become a ritual, an essential ingredient, it seemed, of their marriage. Beatrice might sit on the stairs with her hands over her ears to blot out the litany of bitches and bastards, but never once had she suspected that the nastiness might develop from the verbal to the physical.

Consequently when, on that autumn afternoon, he raised his arm and fetched her a blow that sent her reeling from one side of the room to the other, her first reaction was one of astonishment.

She picked herself off the floor, raised her hand to her ear which was bleeding as a result of her impact with the door-handle. He was panting, as though an enormous expenditure of effort had been needed to knock one small slight female off balance. The noise of her fall had brought Bridget to the door. Bridget placed herself between him and his daughter. 'The strong arm stuff now?' she said. Whatever the justification of the circumstances, there were some situations when women must band together against the traditional enemy: man. 'Makes you feel big, does it?' she said. 'Hitting a child?' The number of times that Bridget had asserted that Beatrice would have benefited from a swift clip round the ear would have filled the pages of the *Encyclopaedia Britannica*.

He stood with his back to them, looking out at the new arrangement of rockeries and patios and terracing. Emmett swept copper leaves into a heap. Smoke from his bonfire rose perpendicular towards the still dun sky.

'I never thought,' he said, 'never in my life, that I would want to do that.' He was trembling and what could be seen of his face was colourless.

'It's time you learned to control that temper of yours,' Bridget said. And a few other things as well, she thought. It's no wonder the child has no sense of moral decency when, for years, she's had evidence of your barnyard antics shoved under her nose. There was a time and a place for everything, Bridget thought, remembering how, during the early years of their marriage, she'd had to knock on every single door – even the kitchen – before she dared to enter, in case they were doing something that should have been reserved for the bedroom and until after dark. A child brought up in such a household was bound to be lacking in a sense of what was proper; it stood to reason.

'Come along, Beatrice, let's get that ear seen to.' Little drops of Beatrice's crimson blood splashed on to the white collar of her blouse. The imprint of his hand faded slowly from the right side of her face. She kept her eyes fixed on his motionless back, moved slowly towards him, touched him on the shoulder and, when he turned towards her, slipped wordlessly into his embrace. 'Oh, Beatrice,' he said, 'are all your stars in opposition?'

In the bathroom, Bridget attended to the ear ungently. It looked worse than it was. She shook iodine on to a piece of cotton wool, applied it without warning or preamble. Beatrice howled. 'Howl away. It isn't half what you deserve,' Bridget said grimly, dabbing at the wound. 'I suppose him clouting you and then loving you, that makes it all right? I suppose the next thing will be the arrangements made?'

Four times the arrangements had been made since she'd come to live in this house, four times Helena had greeted the smiling morn with her head over the lavatory bowl, the signal for the phone call, and the journey to London from which she would return frail and pale and have to be helped up the stairs to bed. Four innocent souls had been extinguished; Beatrice, had she but known it, owed her existence to a wily trick of nature: the fact that Helena had continued to bleed into the fourth month of her pregnancy; by the time she realized the truth, a termination would have been too risky – and she balked at the idea of an actual operation; that was as bad if not worse than having a child.

'Don't let them do it,' Bridget said, discarding the cotton wool and the iodine, taking the girl's face between two gentle hands. 'Don't be a party to murder.'

Beatrice sat down on the edge of the bath. You couldn't call it murder, not the process that Helena had described for her: the nursing home, the merciful injection, the anaesthetic and the surgeon with the genial smile who, for the sum of two hundred pounds, helped distressed women out of their difficulties. A formless lump of jelly, that was all it was, Helena had said; there was absolutely no need to get emotional. Her distant attitude implied that this intimate knowledge of the procedure was part of any sophisticated woman's repertoire, rather than the result of personal experience.

Beatrice closed her eyes while a green wave of nausea passed from her. 'How can it mean so much to you?' she asked, when she could trust herself to speak.

'You've created life,' Bridget said. Behind her glasses, her pale eyes were teary, her forehead ridged with earnestness. 'It may have happened against your will, but it's happened all the same.' She gesticulated towards Beatrice's taut midriff. 'That's another *person*. What gives you the right to destroy it?'

A mortal sin, Madeleine had called it, for which you were condemned to fry eternally, world without end.

'You'd rather I married him and risked unhappiness?'

'Marry him or not, it doesn't matter. It's the child that matters.'

'One out of every four brides walks pregnant up the aisle,' Beatrice said. It used to be one of their favourite pastimes, hers and Joanna's, checking the matched and hatched columns of the local paper for news of their acquaintances and noting the discrepancies. Mrs Pritchard, who sewed occasionally for Helena, confided that she had been called upon time without number to insert extra front panels into wedding dresses. 'This god-damned supposed pregnancy hasn't even been *confirmed* yet,' Beatrice said, swallowing hard on the sickness that rose to disprove her words. 'I may not even *be*. People have had *phantom* pregnancies. They've swelled up to an enormous size, had cravings, everything . . . Oh God!' The nausea could no longer be contained. She lunged for the lavatory and retched till her guts ached. 'I shall die,' she moaned, as Bridget held a damp flannel to her forehead. 'There won't be any need for arrangements because I shall be dead.'

'Nothing is ever as bad as you think it's going to be.'

But Beatrice believed that if there was one infallible law of life it was that everything, invariably, turns out worse than you thought it was going to be.

Tomorrow, she had thought, each night as she got into bed, tomorrow I will tell David. But the days had passed and he remained in blissful ignorance. It wasn't that she continued to hope for a miracle – she knew now, test or no test, that she wasn't going to wake up one morning with that old familiar dragging pain in her belly and blood between her thighs; her reluctance to act was simply part of the same process that meant nursing a toothache for days because it was too much trouble to pick up the telephone receiver and ring the dentist. The evil fairy excluded from Beatrice's christening had probably flown in and written Mañana above her cradle in letters of fire.

The disturbing news was imparted to him, at last, visually rather than verbally, when, one evening, at the critical moment of their activity, she had to leap out of bed to be sick in the washbasin.

She rested her head on the blessedly cool porcelain of the sink, asked if he'd make her a cup of tea. 'How can you have morning sickness at eight o'clock in the evening?' she said.

'Amy had it all day long for six months solid. The day it stopped was the day she said that if it didn't stop she was going to put her head in the gas oven. You can't be,' he said.

She watched him, watched the startlingly rapid detumescent effect that her words had had upon him. 'I expect you said that to Amy too. You do seem to make rather a habit of it. Perhaps you're just tremendously fertile. Or perhaps I am. One of those females who need only a pair of men's pants hanging over the bedrail in order to get pregnant.'

In silence he got out of bed and dressed, went into the kitchen and filled the kettle with water. She followed him. 'It was exactly the wrong date,' she said, 'that first time. And you must have stayed too long.' Before her departure, Joanna had searched her father's bookshelves for the relevant volume, quoted it in the same precise, dispassionate way that she used to quote Latin poetry: stuff about ovulation and the life-cycle of the average spermatozöon.

He struck a match and lit the gas. He grinned. 'You put it so delicately. You make me sound like an unwelcome guest, the sort that doesn't get the message until you change into your pyjamas and put out the cat.'

Swamped with relief, she hugged him. 'I thought you'd say something horrible.'

'Such as?'

'Oh, I don't know. I thought perhaps you'd deny it, insinuate . . ., say, "tough luck, go away and get on with it," I thought you'd be furious.'

They held each other peaceably while they waited for the kettle to boil. She felt safe, protected. Between solitary worry and mutual worry there was no comparison. 'Have you been to the doctor? Have you told your parents?' he asked, as he guided the cup of weak fragrant tea towards her mouth.

'I haven't done anything yet. Do you *have* to smoke? It fair turns me up, as they say in the classics.'

He extinguished the cigarette. 'What do you want to do?'

'They'll want me to get rid of it.'

'And you don't want that?'

It was one of his days for looking beautiful. There was a trust-worthiness, a certain *gravitas* about him that comforted her. 'I don't know. I don't think so.'

'There's nothing to prevent us from getting married,' he said, 'provided that your father gives his consent.'

'Did you love Amy?' Amy! What a name. Sounded like someone who played the harmonium and organized sewing bees.

'I think so.'

But you don't love me. And I don't love you. Not *love* you. That is to say, my heart doesn't spring from its moorings and float free whenever I see you, my days and nights aren't filled with the thoughts of you, my appetite isn't diminished (well, it is, but not for that reason), I don't sit a yard away from the telephone willing it to ring, I don't ask God to keep you from having an accident when you're out of my sight. If *that's* being in love, then I'm not in love with you. 'So why did she leave you, Amy?'

'I don't think she liked me very much.'

'*I* like you.'

'I like you too.' He got out a packet of plain biscuits, fed her with little pieces in an attempt to settle her stomach and, later, when her stomach rebelled and disgorged its contents quite unexpectedly over his carpet, he mopped it up without either demur or the tiniest flicker of disgust.

In the public library, Amy Ross, née Bellamy, selected two Daphne du Mauriers. She wasn't sure whether or not she'd read one of them before and it bothered her. She'd never knowingly re-read a book in her life. Beatrice followed her from BAG – BOW to MAC – MUL. Frail elderly ladies elbowed her out of the way, snatched arthritically at volumes stamped with an R: *Passionate Friends*, *The Captive Heart*. Amy read the back of the jacket, the blurb and the first page. 'I just can't remember,' Amy said. 'Can we talk somewhere?' Beatrice said. There was a copy of *Middlemarch* that hadn't been issued since September, 1959, and a whole shelf of Henry James in a uniform edition that had gathered dust ever since Beatrice could remember. In the reading-room, grizzled old men stripped the sticky tape, furtively, off the racing results and the mad lady who had no home except for the reading-room and a bus shelter beside the War Memorial, rearranged the newspaper parcels that contained her belongings around herself.

'Was it *Jamaica Inn* or *Frenchman's Creek*?' Amy said. 'Or was it *My Cousin Rachel*? The one about smuggling?'

'That's right,' Beatrice said. 'It was that one.' An old gentleman browsing through PAL – POT turned and hushed them severely. A library official evicted the mad lady from the reading-room. This happened with monotonous regularity, every time there was a general consensus of opinion that her smell was too pungent to be endured. She always returned.

Next door, in the Café El Morocco, Amy gazed suspiciously at a plastic cup containing a beige liquid surmounted with three inches of froth that was described as coffee, took off her gloves and enquired of Beatrice her business. 'I have to collect Matthew at half past three,' she said, consulting her elegant gold watch, a present from Daddy. There had been a lot of presents from Daddy; they'd helped to assuage the pangs during that terrible period of solicitors and decrees this and that.

Dear God, do not let me be sick, Beatrice prayed, concentrating fiercely on the yellow sunburst that was set into the centre of the tiled table. 'It's about David,' she said.

'David who?' Amy said, in the tone of one whose life has been overrun by a variety of Davids.

'The one you were married to.'

'Oh yes?'

Beatrice filled her lungs with breath. 'What would you say if I were to tell you that I was thinking of marrying him?'

Amy paused with her morning coffee biscuit half way to her mouth. Her mouth hung open. Slackly. There was a lot of expensive bridgework and fillings in there. 'Cradle-snatching now, is he?' she said at length. Amy was twenty-four. At school, the recalcitrant eleven-year-old Beatrice had often been reprimanded by Amy Bellamy, a big girl with a prefect's badge and an air of exquisite condescension.

Amy's teeth crunched into her biscuit. 'I'd say you wanted your head examining,' she said. She'd taken a vow, after the divorce, that that man's name would never pass her lips again, but curiosity wasn't stifled so easily.

'Mm,' Beatrice said, 'this is strictly *entre nous*, you understand?' Amy stared. She might have had a prefect's badge but she'd always been thick as a plank. 'Between ourselves. I just wanted to know why you left him.'

Amy ate Beatrice's biscuits. 'Because he was a self-centred, insensitive pig,' Amy said, 'who ruined my life.'

Amy's parents were wealthy. She had a flat of her own in their house, a dark blue Daimler coupé and an allowance to be spent on whatever took her fancy. Granted she was thick and had the sort of face that made you think of sanatoria, but she was young still, her holidays were spent in Jamaica and Nassau, her father, a stockbroker, had lined up for her a positive retinue of eligible escorts: the sons of merchant bankers, mostly, with good prospects and conspicuous Adam's apples. Was that a ruined life?

'Yes, but, apart from that, what was wrong with him?' said Beatrice.

'I expect you're pregnant,' Amy said equably. 'Otherwise you wouldn't be asking me. It's the only thing he's good at, making people pregnant. If you want my advice, you'll find yourself a sympathetic gynaecologist, as I should have done five years ago.'

'But you're glad you had him?' Beatrice said anxiously. 'Matthew? You're glad you didn't find a gynaecologist?'

'Why should I be glad? What's so marvellous about motherhood? You spend nine months throwing up your guts and the rest of your life encumbered.'

Encumbered. It was a good word. Not a word, Beatrice would have suspected, that featured in Amy's vocabulary. Encumbered? Children grew up, didn't they, flew the nest? Beatrice's parents had never given the impression of harbouring an encumbrance.

'Who wants to take on another man's child?' Amy said bitterly and drained her coffee cup. Only those for whom Daddy might make it worth their while. 'You're too young to realize. Will your parents *let* you marry him? I shouldn't think they will. Not if they've any sense.'

Entering a long-term relationship with David would mean, of course, Beatrice realized, entering a relationship with Amy. And Matthew. Eighteen was fearfully young to be somebody's stepmother.

'You still haven't said why you left him.'

Amy took out a suède make-up bag, began to repaint her face. 'I've told you. Because we didn't get on.'

'But what does it mean: not getting on?' If it meant rows, then

60

her parents didn't get on, but they hadn't left one another.

'It means,' Amy said, outlining her mouth with Romantic Russet – for all her airs and graces, she had the social manners of a shop girl, 'it means that when you've spent hours getting yourself ready to go out, he sits and sulks because he wants to go somewhere different; it means that when you're feeling affectionate, he turns over and goes to sleep; it means that he yells at you when you scorch his damn shirt or lose his damn car keys; it means that he denigrates you in front of his awful friends and makes jokes about you that aren't funny and calls it your child when it keeps you up all night. It means he has secrets from you and never, never once gives in to you. It means he stops opening car doors for you and hangs up the telephone receiver when you come into the room. It means that he's snide about your family and your friends and the whole of your life before you met him. It means that he sits with his eyes closed and says, "I'm not asleep," when you complain. It means that he prefers to be with somebody else, anybody else, than with you, that everything you do gets on his nerves, even breathing, that everything you ask him is interpreted as a *demand*, that he doesn't laugh at your jokes and you don't laugh at his . . .'

The list was obviously inexhaustible but she had run out of breath. When presented with the same question, David had said, 'She was such a *whiner*.'

'But he didn't hit you? Or get drunk every night? Or commit adultery?'

'Only for the divorce. Adultery, I mean. That we could *prove*,' Amy said. 'He was too null and void,' Amy said, 'for any of those other things. He was *boring*,' Amy said, as if she'd only just realized it.

Her father said, 'It never occurred to you, I suppose, that he might have done it on purpose? Pretty damn coincidental, isn't it, first Bellamy's girl and then you? He shows a fine sense of discrimination in where he chooses to plant his seed. And don't turn away your face and blush,' he said, as Beatrice did just that, 'if you're old enough to do it, you're old enough to talk about it. She was a catch,' her father said, 'and so are you. Open any door along this road and wherever you discover an unmarried daughter of the house, you can bet your life that she's a catch. He doesn't impregnate factory girls or the daughters of unskilled labourers. Or does he?'

It had never occurred to her. Pregnancy was such a ghastly state of affairs that it had never entered her head that anybody might do it deliberately.

They were awaiting his arrival. The heating in the house was going full blast but apprehension froze the blood in Beatrice's veins. Helena sat in the far corner of the sitting-room, symbolically removed from them, with the air of a spectator rather than a participant. Helena had evinced little surprise upon learning of her daughter's shameful condition. Bridget had said – when the evidence of her own eyes could no longer be ignored – 'Either that girl's expecting, or I'm the Emperor of Japan,' and Helena had raised one curved eyebrow. She knew Beatrice. She hadn't really expected that fate would be so kind as to spare her the bearing of *that* particular cross.

Now, in the waning light of the October afternoon, she sat at a distance from them, flipping a pack of Tarot cards. They were very beautiful, old and valuable, brought back for her from Marseille by a fanciful ex-lover. She shuffled and re-shuffled them. She kept getting The Hanged Man.

How vulnerable he looked, his entrance preceded by no revving of engine, no slamming of door. He walked up the drive as though he were negotiating the Matterhorn on roller skates. His manipulation of the doorbell was so diffident that if they hadn't witnessed his approach he'd have been standing on the doorstep until the current half-wit finished her chores and let herself out. It was a repeat performance of the interview that he must have undergone five years earlier, but practice hadn't made him perfect. A glass of whisky clasped to his chest, he kept flicking little glances from under his eyebrows at Beatrice – sole ally, or was she? – while her father shot him full of holes with hostile questions and her mother surveyed him silently from every angle: the length and the breadth of him, the height and the weight, the set of his shoulders and the cut of his coat, the hollow at the base of his skull, the plane of his cheek, the line of his jaw and the shape of his fingernails.

Beatrice felt as though she ought to be circulating with dishes of nuts and plates of canapés; there seemed to be no real rôle for her in this charade. She was simply the object of their conversation: one who could not be blamed, whose youth and impressionability had been taken advantage of, whose future must be settled between the rest of them. Whatever they decided, they would expect her to abide by it. Such was the sense of unreality generated by the proceedings that it wasn't until her father looked towards her and said, 'You're quite sure that you want to marry him?' and she had an instantaneous impression of the two of them side by side – her father was taller and broader and handsomer and richer and more powerful, and the comparison was so unfavourable: made David seem somebody whom nobody could *want* to marry – that she became aware of any positive feeling whatever. 'Yes,' she said. 'I do.' Because in that instant she had realized that there was a stronger bond between herself and this man than that forged throughout eighteen years of filial duty. She had detected in him that lack, of grit, inner compulsion, of a centre of energy, that she recognized in herself. Beethoven wrote music when he was as deaf as a post and Dostoievsky struggled with epilepsy and madness and Sarah Bernhardt hopped around the stage on her wooden leg and paralysed persons in iron lungs learned to type with one toe. And then there were the other sort: those who had the full use of their faculties, who had been granted ability and perception and good looks and a secure social position and, for the life of them, couldn't organize all these attributes so that they amounted to anything.

'I take it that that's what you want too?'

Delivered in the same tone that he used to secretaries: 'Get me Frankfurt. Pronto,' or the half-wits when they left their cleaning materials as obstacles in his path.

'You can always sack him without references,' Beatrice said, 'if he won't.'

They turned to look at her briefly, resumed their one to one confrontation. She was too young to know any better. 'I want to marry her,' David said, 'on one condition: that I marry her and not you as well. That she's my wife first and your daughter second. That I keep her, on my income and the sort of style it affords. Not yours.' Oh, shades of the Bellamys and allegations of mixed motives: 'If it hadn't been for the money, you wouldn't have seen him for dust.'

'I will not be parcelled about from person to person,' Beatrice said. (There must be a verb which described the transfer of parcels, but she couldn't think of it.) 'Like a foundling on a doorstep.'

Helena snapped the cards together, her patience at an end. Her cool, low-toned voice cut to the core of the matter: 'She's pregnant and she'd prefer marriage to an abortion. It's hardly an ideal situation but perhaps she likes the idea of the simple life. There is absolutely no need for melodrama, and it seems to me that the sooner they get themselves legalized, the better it will be for all concerned.' She touched the tender skin below her eyelids. When she was accompanied by Beatrice, people said, 'You're not old enough to have a daughter of that age! I can't believe it!' That was flattering. The idea of a man who found her desirable discovering that she had a grandchild was a thought of an altogether different and disconcerting nature.

Robert glared at her. 'I want her to be happy,' he said. He did. He wanted all those years of casual neglect, all those times he'd said, 'Go away and don't bother me, I'm busy,' all the occasions the bedroom door had been locked against her, all the information she'd imparted that he'd received with half an ear, the skimped comfort, all of it to be cancelled out. He'd discovered too late that a man and a woman who are obsessed with one another do not make the best kind of parents.

They were married quietly and bewilderingly quickly in the register office. David's parents were dead. He had a brother, she discovered – an RAF pilot stationed in Germany – when that brother flew over to bear witness to their nuptials. Throughout the brief ceremony the registrar's clerk kept her eyes fixed on the area that lay between Beatrice's waist and the top of her thighs. Beatrice intoned her responses in the correct sequence and wondered whether this was intentional: whether perhaps they laid bets in registrars' offices as to who was and who wasn't, or whether registrars' clerks didn't want to remember your face in case you were one of the ones they were destined to meet again in the same circumstances.

Helena wore a grey suède Garbo-ish cloche hat and Bridget had put curlers in the ends of her hair the night before. A cleaner swept the corridor outside the wedding room and the mayor emerged, resplendent, from his parlour on his way to some official function. Nobody cried. Nobody smiled much either. Joanna sent a postcard which said, 'Wot no tulle and confetti?' and Madeleine sent a sedate card of congratulation embellished with inaccurately-drawn violets.

6

'I go into the shop and I ask for a piece of topside – about so – or a leg of lamb, or rump steak. If we haven't got much money, I ask for brisket, or three-quarters of a pound of shin beef, or mince. Topside and legs and shoulders, I roast – that's fat; shin beef or best neck, I stew – that's water with stuff in it – *stock*. Chickens and ducklings are economical. First of all I put my hand inside and there'll be a little bag full of things which I don't throw away – I make gravy with them. I turn on the oven and while I'm waiting for it to heat up, I rub the chicken all over with butter and put stuffing where that little bag of things – giblets – used to be. It takes about twenty minutes for each pound, so I must remember to weigh it. Potatoes also take about twenty minutes and I have to put salt in. I chop up cabbage into bits and cook it in a very *little* water. Carrots take ages. Chops I fry or grill. Also steak. When I ask for liver, I must make sure that it's *lamb's* liver. Oh, Bridget, don't go so fast! Batter has to stand and sausages have to be pricked and cheese sweats and there are two sorts of flour – oh Christ, I'll never remember it all. Does anybody remember it all? Why can't we just eat sandwiches? And drink milk? Did Amy manage to remember all that?'

'I seem to recall that we tended to work on one principle, rely on one golden rule: when it's brown it's done, when it's black, it's buggered.'

Of course, Amy too had been the only sprig of rich parents, brought up in the same unreal world of leaving your clothes where they fell on the bedroom floor and not being able to connect the raw ingredients of a meal with the end product.

'Did she learn?' During those two short (or long!) years that she spent with you.

'Oh yes. You will too.'

But it wasn't just the cooking; it was everything else as well: ironing the fiddly bits of shirts, and did one wait until one could actually *see* dust before one dusted? Turning mattresses (how often?)

and making sure one didn't run out of something absolutely vital on a Sunday afternoon, and how long did clothes take to dry and how could one be sure that they *were*? The prospect of coping with a baby on top of everything else was unthinkable. She refused to contemplate it. Bridget would have to join the household, that was all. However strenuously he objected. By then they would have a house and a spare bedroom. It was only the lack of this facility that prevented Bridget from joining them now. As it was, she spent a great deal of time with Beatrice despite Helena's advice, which was to keep her nose out and let Beatrice get on with it. 'Otherwise she'll never learn,' said Helena, who had had servants to call upon all her life, whose domestic activity was confined to cooking (a natural talent and a Cordon Bleu course) and the arranging of flowers.

'The child will never learn if she isn't tutored,' Bridget had replied. To Bridget, Beatrice would for ever be the child. And so, in the mornings and the afternoons, while David was at work, Bridget coached her in the correct commission of her household duties and, because it is so much easier to demonstrate than to explain, Bridget usually ended up baking the pies or polishing the furniture or making the bed while Beatrice sank gratefully on to the sofa and sipped at a glass of soda water to settle her digestion. Bridget would pause, a duster in her hand or an armful of bedding, en route to bedroom or kitchen, and ask, over and over again, whether Beatrice was happy. And Beatrice would reply, 'Yes,' and 'Yes, of course I am. If only I could stop being sick.'

Sickness apart, she was happy. Or as near to happiness, she suspected, as she would ever be. With Bridget's assistance, the housework was soon finished, leaving the rest of the day free for her own pursuits: leisurely walks around the town, library books gulped down at one sitting, afternoon sessions of her favourite despised music, or, best of all, doing nothing whatsoever except recline and nibble at Matsos. (Amy's craving, David reported, had been Morello cherries; Matsos was both cheaper and more easily available.) And indulge in a dream of perfect motherhood. This fantasy, sanitized and expurgated, consisted mainly of mental pictures of herself as painted by Raphael, wearing a lace bedjacket, pale and brave upon satin pillows, surrounded by bunches of bloomy black grapes and sprays of deep red roses.

So far, there was only one aspect of marriage that compared

66

unfavourably with not being married. And that was the financial arrangement. On the morning after their wedding night, instead of turning to her, awed and stirred by the sight of her, ready to worship again at the shrine of her sacred feminine sexuality, he'd supported his weight on one elbow, coughed till his lungs were clear and said, 'Let's get one thing straight at the earliest opportunity: we are not, repeat not, accepting hand-outs from your father. Or your mother. Or your father and mother via Bridget. Understood?'

Moral principles were something of which Beatrice had no understanding, with which she could feel no affinity. Those who suffered for their beliefs aroused in her only irritation and incomprehension. What did it matter if they were subsidized by her father? He could well afford it. What was so noble about refusing offers of help from those who were only too eager to distribute their largesse? What greater satisfaction could there be than taking from those who wished to give? However, the first day of one's marriage, she thought, was hardly the time to bring up such deep philosophical differences. She nodded. Understood.

And, after all, her wants were hardly wildly extravagant. Just books and records and, eventually, if and when she returned to her original shape, a few decent clothes. It was only when they'd been married a couple of months and she couldn't resist buying a pair of lizard-skin shoes and a brand new copy of *Franny and Zooey* and a record of Stefan Askenase playing the Chopin Polonaises that it came to her that she wouldn't have enough money left to last till the end of the month. A lifetime's habit of spontaneous buying is hard to break – if you like something, you buy it – and, although he earned a good salary, by the time he'd paid out child maintenance and the bills and the regular amount that went into the building society towards the deposit for a house, there wasn't a great deal left over for impetuous purchases. Beatrice borrowed three quid off Bridget and paid her back, religiously, at the rate of ten shillings a week.

For the time being the desire to acquire remained dormant mostly. It was as if all her actions and reactions had been muted. Women during pregnancy became lethargic, she knew, it was a form of self and child protection, but, she had thought, as lassitude was her normal state, perhaps being with child might have the opposite effect on her: liberate unsuspected sources of vigour. It wasn't so.

She became slower and more dreamy (more sow-like, Joanna said, during a flying half-term visit) as the months went by, and the luxury of fantasy became one that she indulged more and more and for longer periods. Bridget shelled peas or wrapped puddings in cloths to steam and Beatrice shifted her bulk from side to side upon the sofa and saw the child at two years old, naked and brown on a beach; at six, copying sums with its tongue between its teeth and mastering its shoe-laces; at eight, fighting off sleep on Christmas Eve; at thirteen, locking away its diary from prying eyes. The child was as neutral as an angel and its face was a composite of the best features of its parents' faces. It did not cry, neither did it scream, nor sulk, nor defecate nor throw tantrums. In this respect it was utterly unlike its sibling, her step-child.

Matthew was and was going to be a problem. His weekly visit inspired in her a peculiar sort of fear. There was a song sung by Billie Holiday that Joanna had played until its grooves wore out: 'Sunday is gloomy, my hours are slumberless, dearest, the shadows I live with are numberless.' Beatrice's Sundays were not so much gloomy as fraught. The gloom was engendered by the fact that they seemed to recur with such frequency: no sooner had you breathed a sigh of relief on Monday morning than it was Saturday evening again. She knew that she must be calm and tolerant and kind. After all, he was the product of a broken home and children from broken homes were destined for the psychiatrist's couch, the juvenile court and the remand home, unless they were treated with kid gloves. Or at least that was what Joanna's psychology book had said. Beatrice inclined sneakingly to the view that children come into the world fully fashioned in the department of the psyche, and whether they are brought up well or badly, in the end they will be themselves.

It was an unfashionable opinion. Folk singers sang, 'There but for fortune go you and I' and social workers and quality journalists drew a picture of the infant as an empty slate to be written upon, with environment as the dominant factor. Beatrice remembered her schooldays in the company of little swine who had understanding parents and every advantage. Matthew was not a little swine; he was just a disconcerting child who would treat you with grave courtesy one week and kick you the next. 'You're a big boy,' David said, when he turned his face from her, pleaded to be carried, to be taken home. She found it rather touching: his stumbling attempt to communicate with his son. He was as ill at ease as she; he had never acquired the knack, he was, by turns, too soft or too harsh, and his lack of confidence transmitted itself with every gesture, every fumbled embrace. She hoped that he would be better with his next offspring, more assured. Meanwhile, Matthew sometimes hid behind the sofa and sulked, sometimes clasped his hands around his body and rocked himself to and fro, or rampaged around the flat, kicking the furniture and knocking things off shelves, or shrieked himself hoarse and refused every conceivable cajolement. Or, sometimes, he regarded her with those adult grey eyes and stroked her hand, allowed her to read to him, presented for her inspection the cobbled calendars and the wobbly drawings he'd made at school.

'Children need to respect,' Joanna said. 'Like animals, you've got to let them know who's boss right from the start.'

'You pass this on to me from the depths of your profound experience? Or did Engels say it? Or Kropotkin? Or that other one – I forget his name – who had the nasty accident with the ice pick?'

Joanna looked at her in disbelief. 'Trotsky. Don't pretend to be more stupid than you are. Nobody said it. It's simple common sense.'

Beatrice had a sudden vision of the future Joanna: a don's wife in a flowered cotton smock who baked her own bread from stone-ground flour, gave shelter to unmarried mothers, reformed alcoholics and social misfits, and who brooked no nonsense from her children who would be called Abel and Dorcas and Tabitha, and brush their teeth unbidden.

'Are you expecting a baby?' Joanna said. 'Or a detached residence? Should you be so huge quite so soon?'

She crossed and uncrossed her lean thighs. At school, Joanna had been known to carry with her four rounds of toast and a packet of biscuits to satisfy the voracious demands of her appetite that might occur between breakfast and lunch. Life was so unfair: not simply in terms of hereditary social privileges and inequality of opportunity, but basically, biologically; men acquired handsomeness with their wrinkles, women's wrinkles signified nothing more than hormonal activity reaching the end of its tether; girls like Joanna could consume calories by the bushel without ill effect and girls like Beatrice gained flesh and spots situated in eye-catching positions.

'Your father says that I am coming along very nicely indeed.'

Joanna smiled, recognizing the vocabulary that her father reserved for children, mothers-to-be and geriatrics. 'Is he still using that culinary metaphor?' A great deal of fondness, simple and uncomplicated, existed between Joanna and her father.

'Incidentally, *can* you cook yet and so forth?' she said. 'How is it generally?'

Unashamed curiosity all over her face. She meant, how is it, specifically. How is it to lie beside a man every night and have a sexual life? How is it to have something alive inside you that will soon burst forth like a pea from a pod?

'It's all right. It's fine.'

A matinée jacket, originally snow-white, had by now, after various unpickings and re-knittings, assumed the colour and texture of a dishrag. Nevertheless, Beatrice persevered patiently. Occasionally she shifted her position in the chair. Occasionally Joanna saw a faint ripple of movement beneath the taut surface of her smock. The pleasant aroma of a casserole cooking wafted in from the kitchen. The room they sat in was clean and neat and polished and tastefully, if sparsely, furnished. New bookshelves had been built to accommodate Beatrice's library; cupboards had been cleared of junk to house Beatrice's record collection. A painting of Beatrice's, after Stanley Spencer, hung above the fireplace. A wedding photograph, taken by Bridget with her Box Brownie after the ceremony, in the garden of Beatrice's home, occupied pride of place on the mantelpiece. Both bride and groom looked out at the world with an expression of mingled apprehension and determination. We are unsure and afraid and there may be a snowball's chance in hell of success, but we are going to have a damn good try, the expression said.

Poor Beatrice, they had said, the kind people, in much the same tone as Helena Martin used to say, 'Poor Madeleine Brennan.' The unkind people said that she'd had it coming. 'Would you have married him?' Joanna asked, point-blank, spitting pips from a Christmas tangerine in the general direction of the fireplace. 'If it hadn't been forced upon you?' Tact and Joanna made uneasy bedfellows: if you wanted information, you asked.

'If I'd stayed here, probably yes. If not, probably no.' Beatrice held out her knitting at arm's length. 'Is there any way of dealing with a dropped stitch other than pulling out the whole shooting match? I have this feeling,' Beatrice said, 'that all that business about making momentous decisions throughout our lives is a lot of nonsense. I think what we are programmes us to do what we do.'

'Here I stand, I can do no other? People like you always rely upon that argument. It's an excuse for no action, the easy way out.'

The phone rang. Beatrice rose unhurriedly to her feet. It would be David, calling to ask if she wanted anything bringing in on his way home. Joanna heard a 'darling', a joke exchanged, the truncated sentences and half-uttered phrases of relaxed familiarity. 'Oh – and some celery,' Beatrice said. She explained that her craving for Matsos had given way to a craving for celery. 'With my mother, it was coal,' Joanna said. 'She had to be very furtive about it because of funny looks.' She began to gather together her belongings in order to make her getaway before Beatrice's husband returned, bearing celery. He was polite and friendly, but all the same one felt *de trop*.

'Oh don't go. Tell me some more about academic life. Make me jealous.'

Well: there was the fear and the newness and the strange faces that gradually metamorphosed into the faces of friends and the inevitable bores who made first contact and had to be shaken off and the cold bathroom shared with six other people and the early assumption that everybody else, but everybody else, was more talented, more knowledgeable, more poised than oneself. There was the slow and painful novitiate of learning the correct clothes to wear and the right words to use and which artists and writers and musicians were to be held in high esteem. There were subtitled foreign films and glamorous lecturers doomed to be the target of unrequited love and accustoming oneself to switching one's allegiance from food to drink. There was the spluttering gas fire for which you never had enough shillings and the Swede across the landing who did exercises and the Nigerian above your head who couldn't keep warm, and there was doing up your face for dances and, once there, the strategies of moving around the ballroom until someone half-way presentable asked you to dance, or spending an hour in the cloakroom because nobody did, and there were the parties which you attended, clutching your entrance fee of a bottle of brown ale, realizing as the evening wore on that all the best men were already spoken for, drinking anything within reach because it enabled you to sparkle, put a fine cutting edge on your wit and, finally, one of those men did notice you and danced with you and you floated in his arms for a few brief moments, but it was only for a few brief moments because, in a sudden lucid flash, you knew that you were going to be sick, and oh, the shame, you didn't quite make the lavatory, and, after it was over, he gallantly supported you home to your digs and your voice wouldn't stop talking, it boomed and slurred in your ears and your tongue was too large for your mouth and there was no way that you could get your key to fit the keyhole, so he did it for you and steered you gently towards your bed and left you, and you never saw him again except at a distance.

Would that make Beatrice jealous, Beatrice who had a husband to whom she belonged, returning at the appointed hour with sticks of celery and eyes full of tender loving concern? Beatrice knitted on, making her nest, cocooned. On the other hand, Beatrice had closed the door, for ever, to that which made all the sad dances, the unproductive parties, the cheap booze, the hangovers and the foolishness worth enduring: the opportunity: of the unexpected occurrence, the appearance of a face, a form, at once strange and familiar, the soul mate, the other half of one's whole.

'Is Brennan behaving herself?' Beatrice said. 'Girls like Brennan usually go berserk at the first sniff of freedom, start sleeping with Italian waiters and Puerto Rican drug pushers.'

'No. Girls like Brennan fall madly in love and *give* themselves as though they were priceless objects. They invariably get pregnant first time.' Beatrice raised her head, unstartled. 'Whereas girls like you,' Joanna said, 'usually pass themselves around generously, absolutely never get caught, and end up marrying the sons of earls or the chairmen of boards.'

'Which is she doing then? Seeing that you seem to have reversed our rôles.'

'Neither. She's still tagging along, worrying that she hasn't got a name tape sewn in her vest or clean knickers in case of an accident, and she still wears these too-large garments and she hands all her essays in on time and she has a note-book in which she records the dates of her tutorials and the times of the buses, and she regards every male who speaks to her as a potential rapist and nearly gets killed every time she crosses the road because she's so cautious. I try to shake her off. Gently. But she won't be shaken. Besides, I was glad of her during the first few weeks,' Joanna said honestly.

'You mustn't give up with her,' Beatrice said. Unexpected waves of compassion towards the timid Madeleine arose in her. Perhaps it was her condition.

'I shall persevere but, really, she's far happier beavering away and writing letters to her mum and washing her stockings. Don't be sorry for *Madeleine*,' Joanna said. 'She'll get a First and a job where she'll make herself so indispensable that she'll end controlling the whole set-up. Be sorry for me. I'm skint, I'm always hungry, everybody expects me to play a blinder because of that *verdammte* State Schol, and if I wore striped pyjamas I'd look like the last survivor out of Belsen. Men like women to have flesh, don't they? When I was sixteen, that cow, Muriel Benson, you remember?' – Muriel Benson had not died in the coach crash and subsequently been canonized; Muriel Benson had moved to High Wycombe and could, therefore, still be called a cow – 'She said the only way I'd get a fellow would be by standing outside St Dunstan's and then I'd have to wait for someone who'd had his arms amputated as well. I used to stick pins into Muriel Benson, in the school photograph. I wonder if it worked?'

But Joanna's were trivial complaints: her looks satisfied certain aesthetic standards, she would learn to stop scaring people away with her rather aggressive displays of learning or political fervour, and once she had found a path through the social jungle she would stick to it and apply herself seriously to justifying the faith that the state had placed in her. Whereas Madeleine's problems, Beatrice thought, were fundamental. Madeleine would have heartily endorsed Sartre's view about hell being other people. Madeleine looked for hostility and found it, expected disaster and conjured it into being, had eighteen years' absorption of guilt engendered by her mother's self-sacrifice behind her.

It was only a token gesture, but the next afternoon Beatrice invited Madeleine for tea. Joanna's report had been accurate: Madeleine's clothes were still on the large side, a lifetime's conditioning. She and Beatrice were practically the same size, or had been, five months ago. Beatrice opened her wardrobe door, said casually, 'If there's anything you particularly fancy, speak now, because they are all destined for the jumble sale. I intend to re-deck myself from top to toe when I'm normal again. If I ever am. I asked Joanna yesterday, but of course she's quite the wrong size and shape . . .'

Madeleine's hand moved involuntarily towards velvet and cashmere and tailored grey flannel. By a great effort of will, the hand was stayed. 'No thank you,' Madeleine said, 'I couldn't. Not possibly.'

'Of course you could.' Beatrice pulled garments from their hangers, filled Madeleine's arms. 'Look – that's quite nice. And that. I don't think I ever *wore* that.' Benevolence rushed to her head like wine. 'And that jacket. And those dance frocks. I shan't be going to any dances for quite a while, I shouldn't think. Joanna said food parcels. Well, I can't manage food parcels, but . . .'

The clothes were mostly French, cut narrow, with over-stitched seams, silk linings, labels embroidered with famous names. You knew, before you even tried them on, that they would transform you: the lizard-skin jacket, the velvet trousers, the silk-chiffon evening dress. 'We don't accept charity,' Mrs Brennan said, trying to make the figures on the cardboard add up to what she had in her purse. But Beatrice's marvellous wardrobe could not be construed as charity, rather, as a gift from heaven.

Beatrice moved in a rosy glow for days afterwards and then forgot about it completely. Madeleine covered the clothes in cotton sheeting and hung them in her wardrobe. She couldn't wear them. There was a sore place inside her chest, like the time she had pleurisy. She told herself that she was a fool, that throughout history gifted people had received the patronage of those who possessed nothing but money – perhaps not in terms of old clothes, but it amounted to the same thing. Still it rankled. Offered them to Joanna? A likely story. One day, please God, their positions would be reversed and Beatrice, kind cruel Beatrice, would need help, help that only Madeleine could provide.

74

7

'"Beatrice gave birth to a baby boy at three-thirty yesterday morning. Six and a half pounds. Your father delivered her. They are both well."'

'Does she mean Beatrice and the baby, or Beatrice and my father?' Joanna read aloud from her mother's letter at the breakfast table. Joanna had found herself a bedsitter (a procedure that was strictly against the rules during one's first year) and was therefore no longer entitled to eat in the hall of residence. That fact didn't deter her. Every morning she entered by the back door and joined the queue in the dining-room where the catering staff, unaware of her defection, served her with food. One day she'd run the gauntlet once too often. In the meantime, she spread her toast thickly with marmalade and imparted the news to Madeleine and a couple of uninterested female social psychologists.

'Why can't my mother write normally? "Your father delivered her." Sounds frantically biblical somehow: "and she was delivered of a man child". Six and a half pounds. That's not very big, is it? She must have been carrying *gallons* of water. Heavens – Beatrice, a mother. It's astonishing. I can't see Madame Martin adapting gracefully to the rôle of Grandma, can you? I mean, it involves acknowledging the fact that her daughter has actually reached puberty.'

The second page of the letter drifted into somebody's abandoned bowl of cornflakes. Joanna rescued it, mopped it with the edge of the tablecloth, continued to quote from it: '"No doubt Beatrice will write to you herself in due course..."' No doubt Beatrice will. What's the betting we get a blow by blow account, right from the midnight alarums to the disposal of the afterbirth? "... I tried to phone you on Friday evening. The person who answered said you weren't in. This is the sixth time I've tried. Really, Joanna ..."'

Joanna folded the letter, replaced it in its envelope. 'The rest is just the usual screed of belated parental concern. Do you suppose that Beatrice *suffered*?' She contorted her features into a series of grimaces. The two social psychologists departed, looking faintly disapproving.

Coincidentally, they formed the audience for the recital of the expected letter which arrived a week later. 'Graphic,' Joanna said, 'graphic, is the word,' and proceeded to read it, uncensored. 'Over breakfast,' the first one said, the one with the teeth and frizzy hair. 'Must you?' 'I didn't think you lived here any more,' the other one said, the bloodless one with the pointed nose. They picked up their shiny briefcases and excused themselves from the table. 'D'you think they're Lesbians?' Joanna said, picking absently at the pieces of bacon left on their abandoned plates. Joanna detected sexual perversion in the most unlikely places: the widowed Domestic Bursar, their moral tutor who was married with five children.

'Can I read it? Now that you've successfully put them off their breakfasts.'

The letter had obviously been written direct from a hospital bed: the writing was shaky and sloped all over the place, indicative of the resting of a writing-pad on one's knees rather than extreme weakness. On the subject of accouchement it was a model of discretion. 'What do you mean: graphic? All she says is that she went into labour at six o'clock on Thursday evening and the baby was born early next morning. Where's all the blood and guts stuff you were spouting?'

'Oh, that was just for *their* benefit.' Joanna stretched herself luxuriously, her arms above her head. Madeleine trembled for her lest this exhibition should attract the attention of someone in authority who would effect instant eviction. 'Do you know,' Joanna said, 'that at the age of nine or so I asked my mother about reproduction, and she told me. *Your* mother would have talked about the Holy Ghost or the gooseberry bush; mine had to speak the truth, the *entire* truth, embellished with every gruesome detail. It sounded so absolutely foul and incredible. I refused to believe it for years. It wasn't until I got hold of the medical books and saw it there in incontrovertible black and white that I was reluctantly convinced. What *did* your mother tell you, incidentally?'

'She didn't. I think she hopes I'll never need to find out.'

They lingered among the spilt marmalade and the crumbs, thinking of Beatrice and the fact of her motherhood. It was a sort of personal two minutes' silence: if sex had caused a gulf between them, maternity created an unbridgeable chasm. 'Next week,'

Joanna said, 'I expect we'll have to go along and drool.' Next week was half term. 'I loathe babies,' Joanna said. 'I don't intend to have any. Ever.'

'Neither did Beatrice.'

'Then why didn't she make sure that she didn't? Beatrice was always too slow to catch cold. Nobody needs to get pregnant.'

Madeleine rose to her feet. There was every possibility that Joanna would embark on a lecture concerning contraception for her benefit and the benefit of every other remaining inhabitant of the dining-room.

'Can I have a shufti at your Hume essay before you hand it in?'

'You can, but I don't see the point.'

'The point is that I haven't done it yet, that I have a tutorial at eleven and it'll be a start if I can rabbit on about something vaguely relevant because I shan't be able to do it tonight on account of that Brecht thing.'

'What's your excuse this time? Another migraine?' Joanna hadn't suffered a single attack since coming to London.

She nodded, put her hands to her temples, contorted her face. 'Wicked, it is. Get them something cruel, I do. A martyr to it, I am. I read this article the other day which said that migraine sufferers are invariably high achievers of above average intelligence.'

'Written by a migraine sufferer?'

'But of course.' Joanna licked her forefinger and mopped crumbs from the surface of the tablecloth. 'You are coming tonight, aren't you? Yes you are. You've no more work left to do and you've written to your mum and darned all your stockings and there's a great big world out there where things are happening to people and it's time that you conquered it.'

Easy to say. Upstairs, in her room, Madeleine unpacked the usual Friday morning parcel that had 'From: Margaret Brennan' written on the back in indelible pencil. It contained three stamped envelopes, a pot of jam, a tin of French Fern talcum powder, a pair of fleecy-lined pyjamas and two stiff new face flannels. The postage alone was astronomical. 'Please don't,' Madeleine wrote over and over again. 'I know that you can't afford it and I don't need these things, really I don't.' To no avail. The parcels continued to arrive, punctually. Self-denial was a habit of the most addictive sort. Each small lovingly-pondered gift represented a luxury forgone: one bar of the electric fire switched on instead of two, an egg once again for lunch. Sometimes Madeleine wrote 'Leave me alone' in thick black capitals, underscored, at the top of her letters, before tearing off the page in a sickness of shame and throwing it into the waste basket.

Her feelings were ambivalent. There was safety: home and parcels and letters full of worry and concern and exhortation, the retreat of her hostel room where she wrote those letters and washed out those face flannels and prepared her essays and went to bed at ten-thirty with a mug of hot chocolate and *Religion and the Rise of Capitalism* and listened to the footsteps of others who creaked past her door on their way out into that other life.

Some of those others were so bright, so knowing, so hard-edged. It was difficult to believe that they were the same age and intellectually, at least, no better endowed. Many of them were Londoners, assumed an automatic superiority. Joanna's response had been to adopt a broad clogs and shawl accent and profess ignorance of which fork to use. If it hadn't been for Joanna, she'd have turned back at Euston. 'Don't be so wet,' Joanna said. 'We're every bit as good as they are. Better, in fact. Nesh Southerners with no nous!' Never afraid of making a fool of herself, Joanna never did.

And Madeleine moved in the wake of her swift-striding shadow, always afraid of being left behind, stranded, unarmed in a hostile environment. Within the first fortnight Joanna had mastered the routes to the Students Union, the registrar's office, the lecture theatres, located the best and cheapest places to eat, garnered every scrap of relevant information about the teaching staff, formed a wide and fluid circle of acquaintance. Everything Joanna did was performed *con brio*, from standing during class to contest a point to tearing a strip off the Nigerian upstairs for continually missing his aim when visiting the lavatory. 'We came here so that things might happen to us,' Joanna said. 'They sure as hell won't happen if we sit in reading *The Wealth of Nations* every night of the week.' Clubs there were to be joined: the Young Socialists, the Theosophical Society, Nuclear Disarmament, War on Want, trips out to CP meetings in Camden Town, dances where, as the central faceted globe revolved slowly, violet, turquoise, sea-green, illuminating the faces of the assembly, you knew with a sinking certainty that he, yes, he of the buck teeth or the greased quiff or the outcrop of spots, he was the one coming to claim you. Though the dances were preferable to the parties. At the dances you could say, 'Not

78

this one, thank you,' or, 'I'm waiting for my friend,' and then escape to the cloakroom. The parties offered no refuge at all, other than striking out alone into the night that seethed with menace. And Joanna's parties were the worst because it was safer to stay where she was for the night and as Joanna's territory consisted of one room, that meant sitting it out, a glass of poisonous red biddy in her hand, until the last inebriate had staggered off homewards.

'Enjoy yourself!' Joanna would say, stepping over a couple who were almost having sexual intercourse on the stairs, to put the kettle on, uncorking another bottle of poison, raising her voice to make herself heard above Bessie Smith singing 'Gimme a pigfoot', Big Bill Broonzy, Sonny Terry and Brownie McGhee, 'Nutrocker' by B Bumble and The Stingers. 'You look as though you've lost a shilling and found sixpence,' Joanna said. 'What ails you?'

Difficult to explain. Lack of self-esteem. Fear of wanting too much and being disappointed. Dread at the thought of opening her mouth and uttering some comment of stunning banality at any one of those gilded party-goers: the Greek profile philosophy don, the liquid-eyed girl who smoked the silver-tipped cigarettes. A vision of her mother, alone, listening to *Friday Night is Music Night* and counting the pennies. Guilt. A feeling of waste as she came out of the library into one of those long soft twilights that mark the passage of spring into summer and saw couples strolling by, their arms wound around one another. Pangs. And vague longings: herself and X in a boat on a river, floating through a Renoir landscape. The horrid suspicion that it was not bound to happen.

Impossible to explain to Joanna. In Joanna's opinion there was always something that could be done to alleviate discontent. In the same way, her mother advised the bored, the desolate, the melancholic, to consider others worse off than themselves, to join the League of Hospital Friends, the purveyors of Meals on Wheels. 'Fill every minute of your day with activity and you won't have *time* to feel depressed,' she'd tell whoever it was: the unmarried mother, the deserted wife, the menopausal matron. Dr McCloud was a wizard at diagnosing turbulent tonsils but suffered from a curious kind of emotional blindness, a failure of the imagination. It was a quality that her daughter had inherited. In their clear gaze life seemed so straightforward, the possibilities of order and harmony so limitless, that they simply could not comprehend the squint angles, the distorting lenses through which the afflicted viewed their surroundings.

'Meet Hugh,' Joanna would say. 'Meet Brian. Desmond.' And Desmond (or Hugh or Brian) would draw her into the middle of the room, lean himself against her to remain upright and move his arms and his shoulders and his hips in time to the music and close his eyes and silently mouth the words of the song and occasionally reach for the nearest glass and drink from it. Someone would put the needle back on to 'Peggy Sue' so many times that it finally crackled to a premature demise and he (Brian or Desmond or Hugh) would steer her into a corner and proceed to clutch at various parts of her anatomy. Vacant-faced, blank-eyed, his mouth would search out her mouth and fasten upon it. While she endured this assault, images would float into her mind, of sea-anemones and tentacles and cattle markets. Flesh was all that she was required to be, passive, dough to be kneaded. Sometimes she tried to will a response to his mouth and his hands, tried to catch the current of his desire as though it were a contagious disease. It was impossible. No matter how fervent his tongue, how accomplished his hands, she couldn't banish from her mind the certainty that, sober and in daylight, he would fail to recognize her.

And experiences like that were the result of her forays into the life out there, the place that contained all she needed but was reluctant to yield up its secrets. There was more to it than just music and drink and grappling, she felt sure. But perhaps the music and the drink and the grappling were a kind of obligatory ante-chamber to that place of something more. Joanna, at the breakfast table, stretched her arms and said, 'Great night.' All that Joanna seemed to require from life was a healthy intellect against which, or in concert with which, she could exercise her own. Joanna would never mope through an April twilight, smell hyacinths across a garden, waste her time on what might be or mightn't be when what *could* be was present in such abundance.

The Rise and Fall of the City of Mahagonny. An amateur production. And although Brecht and Weill had themselves specified actors rather than singers to form the cast, surely some musical ability was desirable? They were all much too young anyway, couldn't begin to assume the masks of depravity so essential for the suspension of disbelief. Nevertheless, not even the most inept performance could detract from the insistence of the tunes; they came out into the night singing, 'Oh *moon* of Alabama', and 'Show us the way to the next whisky bar', Joanna, enthusiastic, but completely tone-deaf, Madeleine performing a quiet descant, Desmond, whom they'd encountered in the rush to the exit, contributing snatches from a song that he insisted belonged to the same opus but had been mysteriously excised from the evening's entertainment. 'It's *The Threepenny Opera*,' Joanna insisted. 'How could it be? I've never seen or heard *The Threepenny Opera* in my entire life.' 'At some subliminal level . . .' 'Balls. Mutter Goddam's Puff in Mandalay,' Desmond sang, *basso profundo*. 'It's from *Happy End*,' Madeleine said. She remembered the information catching her eye at the tail-end of a page of the *Radio Times* or some such publication.

'*Yes*. That's right. *Happy End*.' He stopped dead in the middle of the pavement, beamed at her. It was the first time that she had met him when he wasn't fairly drunk or about to be fairly drunk. She was convinced that he believed that this was their first encounter. 'You remember Madeleine, don't you?' Joanna had said, and he'd made the kind of gesture that could be interpreted as either positive or negative.

'Well, now you've settled that particular controversy – as if it mattered' (though, of course, it *did* matter; Joanna herself had been known to rise from her bed at two a.m. to consult a reference book in order to confirm or disprove, once and for all, some irritating uncertainty), 'shall we find the way to the next whisky bar? Or the next pretty boy? You're not a pretty boy, Desmond.'

'I should hope not. Though I think the Brechtian interpretation had more virile connotations than yours.'

Madeleine, a step or two behind them, surveyed him sideways on. Perhaps, during the parties, she had been as guilty as he, seeing him only in terms of mouth and hands whereas, in actuality, he was undoubtedly a real solid person: smallish, slim, with dark curly hair that grew low on the back of his neck and poked, alarmingly, from above his collar and beneath his cuffs. In his rôle as predator, his eyes seemed always to have been closed; now she saw that they were alert and light grey and sparkling. Dressed in corduroy trousers and a blue donkey jacket, there was a thoroughly unintellectual look about him, as though he would be more at home on a building site or the deck of a trawler. He was, in fact, in his final year, specializing in economic history; quite bright,

Joanna said, when he chose to be. Which wasn't often.

'I haven't got any loot for whisky bars,' he said. 'Have you?'

They hadn't. Joanna because she had held too many parties and bought too many records of Lotte Lenya singing decadent German songs, and Madeleine because she received her grant in a kind of dole system: postal orders at monthly intervals; her mother thought that it would be better that way, that temptation could be resisted more easily.

'We could rove over to my place and see if Pedro has anything.'

The pavement was crowded and they were obliged to perform a sort of square dance, permutations of two abreast. He stepped into the gutter in order to be in line with them, turned his head to receive Madeleine's reply to his invitation. Or so it seemed to her.

'It's late. I ought to get back.' She had a horror of being stranded somewhere, miles from a point of reference, unable to reach the haven of her austere hostel room, even though Joanna told her continually that this was London and there was always *something* running and they put up little coloured maps in Underground stations specifically for morons like Madeleine.

'It's only eleven o'clock. Do come. I'll let you listen to my Ragas.'

Whatever they might be. She'd never catch up with the latest trend, it was hopeless to try. No sooner had you been converted to Woody Guthrie than he became terribly *vieux-jeu* and everyone else had moved on to Traditional jazz or Indian music.

It was a room similar to dozens of other rooms of that era: the walls covered with bullfight posters, table lamps adapted from Chianti bottles, a record-player in the middle of the floor, its cord plugged, unwisely, into the overhead light socket, a threadbare curtain that half-concealed a stone sink and a decaying Belling cooker, a wardrobe with a spotted mirror, a couple of shelves containing textbooks and the obligatory paperbacks of the period: *The Catcher in the Rye, Catch 22, The Alexandria Quartet* minus one (somebody always borrowed one and never returned it), *Cry, The Beloved Country.*

He followed the direction of her gaze. 'It's no use your trying to figure me out by referring to my literature. That was left behind by the chap who had the room before me. He flitted. The only things that belong to me are the textbooks and the clothes and the empty bottles.' He went to the doorway, shouted, 'Pedro,' at the top of his lungs, received no reply, so followed the reverberations of his shout up the stairs to the next floor.

Joanna lit a cigarette, looked at her index finger with an expression of disgust. 'There must be some way of smoking a fag so that you *don't* get covered in nicotine. I shall equip myself with a cigarette-holder.'

'And ostrich feathers for your hair and a sequined thing to go round your forehead.'

'God, yes. And blood-red fingernails. And silk stockings that make a noise when your thighs brush together. Like those tarts in *Mahagonny*.'

'Not tarts. Good-time girls.'

'Rainy-day women.'

'Ladies of the roadside.'

Better than a semi-detached, with a rectangle of lawn. A shrine to materialism. 'We'll never come to that, will we?' Joanna said, 'stainless steel sink units and matching sets of pans and watching the potter's wheel on the telly? Will we?'

As Beatrice had come to it, Beatrice in her new house, surrounded by her curtains and her cushions and her carpets, going into raptures over her glass-topped coffee table.

'Spanish prick,' Desmond said, entering with two glasses and a bottle of red wine. 'They come over here, taking our jobs, pinching our women . . .'

'What *are* you on about? And why only two glasses?'

'He owes me, the Dago,' Desmond said darkly. 'I'm off it for the time being. Too many roses, flung roses, riotously, whatever it is. I'll stick to coffee. If we only had an opener, you two could have a drink of this.'

'Have you got a Boy Scout knife?'

'I'm never without one. Have I buggery.'

He had a potato peeler and a key that was meant to open tins of sardines. It took twenty minutes and a ripped thumb which Desmond insisted was next door to being a mortal wound before they succeeded in making a hole in the cork sizeable enough to allow a flow of wine through it.

He wound Madeleine's handkerchief around his thumb, blew into the glasses, poured them each a drink. Little bits of cork floated on the surface. 'I once worked in a restaurant,' he said. 'Silly sods were always sending the wine back, screaming about it being corked.'

83

'That's not what it means,' Joanna said automatically, 'corked wine.'

'Just giving you the chance to betray your nice middle-class origins, Joanna dear.' He treated her to a smile of unmixed nastiness. 'We didn't go in for it much in my particular milieu.'

'Pardon *me*.' Joanna drank the nasty-tasting stuff enthusiastically, held out her glass for more. 'You do go on about it a bit, don't you? I bet it's all a load of crap. I bet you're the issue of a high court judge or a brigadier-general. If there are such persons. Brigadier-generals.'

'That's right. I'm a changeling. The gypsies swopped me.' He stirred his coffee, flung the spoon into the sink, sat down on the floor beside Madeleine's chair and rested the back of his head against her legs. His hair was coarse and black and curly. She was overcome with a sudden and almost irresistible urge to run her hand through those curls just for the sensual delight of doing so. She sat on her hands, sipped at her wine. The monotonous Ragas followed one another around the record. His taste in music stank, but as for Desmond himself – a reappraisal seemed to be in order. It was as if she was seeing him clearly for the first time, as though that person who had groped at her in the corners of Joanna's room had been a different character altogether. Her ideal of masculine beauty had always been dictated by Robert Martin: tall, fair, pale-skinned and patrician, but there were other kinds of attractiveness, she realized, which encompassed bodies constructed for action rather than elegant languor. One couldn't, for instance, imagine Robert Martin doing anything *physical*. Not even *that*. Though Beatrice maintained that he did, constantly. Whereas you looked at Desmond and you thought immediately of muscle and tendon and tissue all functioning at the peak of their form.

'You're always aggressive when you're sober,' Joanna said reflectively, hooking out bits of cork from her wine with her little finger.

'Isn't that the whole point of drinking, to induce a feeling of euphoria, contentment with one's lot?'

'No. Some people drink to give themselves confidence.'

'Ah well. Those are your potential alcoholics, the ones who need a glass in order to face the day, and then two glasses, and so on.'

Perhaps he was talking through his hat. Nevertheless Madeleine put down her glass on the floor. That was precisely the reason why she forced down various unpleasant-tasting liquids, so that she could look people in the eye and contribute to conversations without blushing and stammering and trembling at the knees.

'Why have you packed it in, then?' asked Joanna, from the bed. 'When you admit that it has such a beneficial effect upon you. Your thesis?'

'Because I am skint. I owe rent, I owe the bookshop, I owe just about every second person I meet. I don't owe you by any chance, do I?' He turned his head to look up at Madeleine. His cheek was warm against her knee. She shook her head. 'My thesis is written,' he said. 'I finished it over Easter. I shut myself in this room and never budged. Pedro brought in food. God, I got so sick of warmed-up paella and sherry trifle. It got so that I put it out for the birds after a bit, but even the birds turned up their noses – their beaks, I suppose – at it.'

'Why always paella and sherry trifle?'

'Left-overs. From the Wop restaurant where he works. I'm not surprised they were the left-overs.'

Joanna frowned, finding these references to Dagos and Wops most distasteful. Desmond, whose political views were almost in complete accordance with her own, should know better. 'Haven't you got any music other than that mournful Asiatic dirge?' she said. 'It sounds like the kind of background to which widows committed suttee.'

He rose to his feet and stopped the record in mid-mourn. 'You can have this. Or you can have Ravel's *Bolero*. That's all he left behind him.'

'The flitter? Don't you possess *anything* of your own?'

'Not if I can help it.' He changed the record. 'The sexiest music ever written, this. Listen out for the post-coital heartbeats.'

They refrained from enlightening him about their total ignorance as to the form and nature of post-coital heartbeats. Joanna said instead that it was too obvious, that the sexiest music was that which hinted at rather than blasted you with its implications. Examples of sexy music were: the voice of Billie Holiday echoing the clarinet on 'Yesterdays', certain parts of *Der Rosenkavalier*, the Procurer's Ballad from *The Threepenny Opera*.

He poured the remainder of his coffee down the sink, scratched his head, said that she had depraved tastes. 'Women amaze me,' he said. 'They expect absolute devotion from men in their own personal relationships, yet the characters they secretly admire are pimps and cads and rotters. There seems to be this ineradicable streak of sentimentality in even the most sensible of women. You want us to worship at your feet and yet if we do, we're boring. Beat you and cheat you and discard you and you'll love us for ever. You just don't know what you do want.'

'Do you?'

'Pedro does. He wants a woman – so.' He spread his hands apart to indicate girth. 'A big strong woman who'll work like a navvy and drop kids with the minimum of drama. Then they'll open a restaurant in Tossa de Mar and she'll cook uncomplainingly from sunrise to sunset and provide him with heirs to look after him in his old age. It's a refreshingly pre-industrial view of the mating game, I must say. Much more sensible than simply wanting the usual rich nympho living over a pub.'

'Capitalism has made the concept of the extended family redundant,' Joanna said mechanically. There were two topics that Joanna found endlessly fascinating: capitalism and sex. The chance to expound upon the two of them, in concert, was irresistible. It was capitalism, Joanna said, that was responsible for the myth of romantic love. In socialist societies, men and women retained the dignity of their sex, toiling in their respective rôles towards the common good. Whereas capitalism had spawned the idea of social mobility, the Prince Charming syndrome whereby one way of moving from a disadvantaged position was to pick yourself a mate from the higher echelons. All those shop-girls and factory workers, Joanna said, reading cheap magazines and dreaming of the sons of earls. Instead of elevating their own men to the status of dignified human beings. Capitalism had provided people with the fantasy of romance in order to consolidate the status quo. Cleaned-up sex, Joanna said, draped sex, orgasm tastefully depicted as the hand grasping and slowly releasing its grasp on the bed-rail of a fourposter spread with silk sheets. What could be more perverted than a camera focused on every other part of the anatomy except the relevant parts? Gin, religion, and the unreality of romance, the three soporifics by means of which capitalism maintained its hold upon society, Joanna said.

She drank from her glass. Desmond stroked Madeleine's leg, slowly, from knee to ankle and back again, said, 'Are you a virgin, Joanna?'

86

'Yes. What does that have to do with anything?'

'A great deal. You wouldn't speak with such certainty and passion on the subject of nuclear physics, or molecular biology, would you?'

'I don't know the first thing about them,' Joanna said innocently.

'You don't know the first thing about a real working-class environment, either, or factory conditions, or the reasons why tarts decide to become tarts, but that doesn't stop you exercising your jaw, does it?'

His touch was so gentle that it was barely discernible. 'I don't like you when you're stone cold sober,' Joanna said. 'After all, not everyone can speak from experience about everything. Remember about bystanders seeing more of the game.'

'That enables them to draw logical conclusions rather than express wildly partisan views.'

Joanna uncrossed her legs from the Lotus position, pulled on her coat. 'We will renew our acquaintance when you've ceased to be so deliberately contrary.'

'Don't you want me to escort you home? You might get attacked and molested.'

'Please don't trouble yourself. If I do, I'll be able to speak from experience then, shan't I? See *her* home. She needs looking after.' And off she stumped, down the stairs, out of the front door. 'You will take care of Madeleine, won't you?' Mrs Brennan had besought her on the station platform that previous October, as though she, Joanna, were older, tougher and altogether more sensible. She had felt, then, for Madeleine, standing apart from them, tearing at the edge of her ticket, wishing for the ground to open. Well, there were limits. She hadn't come to university to spend her time acting as unpaid protector and moral guide. Anyway, Madeleine hadn't the gumption to get up to anything she shouldn't.

Imprisoned in her chair behind his back, Madeleine contemplated the homeward journey. One turned the first corner, walked a hundred yards down a dimly lit road bristling with black gateways and alleys, took the second left and came to a Tube station no doubt seething, at this time of night, with rapists and drug addicts and slave traffickers. And then there was the train itself, the frantic scanning of the carriages as they slid past, seeking for one that contained at least a single respectable middle-aged woman. And then there was the walk at the other end: the street of overhanging shrubbery that would provide the perfect concealment, the trees planted at intervals along the pavement that, in the dark, assumed the shape of loiterers with evil intent . . .

'Don't look so anxious,' he said. He had resumed his leg-stroking activities, though she hadn't noticed. 'I shan't leap on you, if that's what you're worried about. I almost never do. Not on first acquaintance.'

In view of the terror that lay ahead of her, she wasn't at all sure that she wouldn't prefer to stay where she was and take that risk.

'Not unless you want me to?'

She gazed, over his shoulder, at the opposite wall. He smiled, touched her cheek, got to his feet and handed her her coat. 'Come on, I'll take you back.'

Oh, thank the Lord for men. Judo classes were no substitute; after all, what use would Judo be when you were paralysed with fear? You'd be robbed and violated and murdered before you could raise a finger in your own defence.

It was a warm, moonlit night that presented a completely different prospect when you were protected. She didn't see a single soul who looked capable, or even desirous, of nefarious doings. They talked, inconsequentially, of this and that: a film they'd both seen, the mounting pressure of his work, the drawbacks to hostel living – at least, he thought so: she was quite happy with the comforting routine, the cushioning effect of hostel life.

'I once had a big thing going with a girl who lived here.' They stood in the shadow of the portico. In the lighted foyer the night porter watered his geraniums, coughed into his handkerchief, inspected the results. 'Room 65,' he said.

'That's my room.'

'Is it now? Have they mended the bed leg yet?'

The bed seemed to be perfectly stable. Not that she'd subjected it to any rigorous test. The idea that he should, once, have been familiar with the room in which she now dressed and brushed her teeth and picked the sleep out of her eyes gave her a curious fluttering feeling in the pit of the stomach. The spilled ink on the rug – could that have been him? The discoloured patch on the wall? The message written, in pencil, over the doorway: *Lasciate ogni speranza voi ch'entrate!*? 'What happened? Where is she now?'

'I'm not sure. She left, I think, went home.'

She determined to find out all that she could about the girl, her predecessor, *his* girl. The night porter took a folded *Evening Standard* from his pocket; a few yards away a couple entwined themselves into an even closer embrace, muffled noises arose from them. He was about to depart from her and it seemed all wrong, all wrong that she would not be seeing him again except perhaps as a lecherous stranger at one of Joanna's parties.

'Well, *buenos noches,* as Pedro absolutely never says.' He squeezed the upper part of her arm, rocked a little on his heels, turned from her. 'Who exactly is Pedro?' she said in desperation.

'I told you. A very lovely Spanish man who occasionally provides me with food in return for introducing him to members of the female sex. So if you know of any big girls . . .'

He was half way to the gate before he turned again, walked slowly to within a couple of yards of where she still stood, pretending to search for something in her handbag for which she had a sudden and vital need. 'What do you do with yourself?' he said. 'In the evenings.'

Sometimes, she thought, I go to parties and you are there and you make drunken advances towards me.

'What are you doing on Tuesday?' he said. 'No, not Tuesday. Wednesday?'

The neighbouring couple uncoupled themselves, dusted themselves down. They were both singularly unattractive. The fantasy of the boat on the river floated into her mind, she in Beatrice's dress; X was no longer X, he was Desmond. It wasn't until she was in bed that she remembered that Wednesday was the third day of half term, and by then she would be at home.

8

'Go round and tell him that you can't, on account of a miscalculation, but that you'd be delighted to agree to a rendezvous on any other date. Christ, *I'll* go round and tell him. What's the drama? It's only Desmond.'

In Joanna's opinion, this was an incestuous kind of relationship. Or might develop into one. Desmond was a member of the crowd, the Film Society crowd, the party crowd, who went home afterwards with whoever was nearest to hand and/or obliging. If one wanted love and so on, one sought for it outside the family circle.

'You'll have to go home,' Joanna said. 'Your mother will be up here on the first train otherwise. It's only a week, for heaven's sake. He's not going to disappear off the face of the earth.'

But she had a feeling that if she didn't keep this appointment, no such similar concrete arrangement would obtain again. And it was as she supposed: when she finally plucked up the courage to intercept him on his way into a lecture, he said, 'Of course, I forgot. I suppose you have a home to go to. I'll give you a ring when you get back.' He had been deep in conversation with a red-haired woman – you couldn't have called her a girl, she was much too composed and self-assured to be a girl – who hovered while they spoke. 'I'm sorry,' he'd said, 'I have to rush. I'm not in your fortunate position: two years to go before you need to start working. For me, the evil day is at hand. See you,' he'd said, and resumed his absorbing conversation with the red-headed creature. *When* will you phone me? she'd wanted to say. How do you know I'll be there? Are you quite sure you can remember where I live? She didn't, of course, say any of those things.

'Clean sheets!' Joanna said on the train. 'Food! Warmth!' She said it over and over, at Rugby, and at Stafford, and again at Crewe. They were the only occupants of their carriage which was littered with discarded magazines and newspapers. Madeleine collected them and read the horoscopes. All of them were depressing, warned of untrustworthy companions, unwise partnerships, advised retrenchment.

'She won't be there, will she, waiting to meet you?' Joanna craned her head out of the window. There was a notice above the window warning against this practice; you could be decapitated by a train travelling in the opposite direction.

'Please God, no.'

But she was. Clutching her platform ticket, scanning with anxious eyes the railway tracks which stretched ever onward, to meet in infinity. Her face was the face of a stranger: older, wearier, more lined than Madeleine remembered.

'I think it's rather sweet,' Joanna said. 'It wouldn't occur to anyone to come to meet me. I go home and if there's anyone in they glance up from whatever they're doing and they say, "Good grief, is it May already?"' But preferable, infinitely preferable, to being smothered in maternal affection, she thought as she parted from them, lugged her case to the bus stop and composed herself for half an hour's wait.

Maternal affection seemed to be the theme of the vacation. The two of them, bearing hastily selected baby gifts, wended a fairly reluctant way to Beatrice's new address: a small detached residence, newly-built, on a housing estate that backed on to the golf links. The ghetto, Joanna called it. Crescents of houses ran one into the other, doubled back on themselves. Every so often a crescent petered out into a wasteland of empty plot or a ragged area of foundations and sewer pipes where men in yellow helmets drank tea and whistled at them as they passed. Of the houses that had been completed, some had french windows that stretched the length of the frontage, some had small bow windows complete with mullions, some had integral garages and some were clad with weatherboarding; none of these individual differences relieved the general impression of uniformity, of three small bedrooms and one large downstairs room, of identical herbaceous borders and square tiled patios, of perambulators and children of nursery school age, of vinyl floor coverings and white paint and Elizabeth David cookery books and mass produced teak-veneered furniture. 'If you roll home drunk, how on earth do you figure out which one's yours?' Joanna asked, peering into picture windows and bow windows, seeing a series of three-piece suites and Axminster rugs and long low sideboards adorned with ceramic table lamps.

'You look at the number on the gate. Besides, you don't have far to roll. All your entertaining takes place in one another's houses so that you can keep nipping home to see if the children are OK.'

'Community living? Your actual *Gemeinschaft*? But they don't have any shops or cinemas or cafés. And what's the point of sitting on your own Scandinavian-style sofa all day long looking at your coal-effect electric fire and then going somewhere else to sit on someone else's Scandinavian-style sofa etcetera?'

'This is a residential area. Why would they need shops? They all have cars. At least, they all have garages.'

'That's the only way that you can distinguish this *arrondissement* from the council estate. That, and the fact that the council houses have flying ducks or Whatshisname's Chinese Lady on their walls and here they have – ' Joanna peered, ever more rudely – 'Van

91

Gogh's Sunflowers, or Paul Klee or – hang on – oh yes, of course, Breughel, those scenes that they use for the fronts of Christmas cards.'

'Don't be such a snob.' In Madeleine's opinion, the houses were highly desirable: warm, weatherproof, clean and neat and possessing every modern labour-saving device. What more could any reasonable person expect from a habitation than efficient plumbing and indoor sanitation and machines that washed your clothes and sucked up your dust? There were infinitely worse places to live than in identical little boxes made out of ticky-tacky.

'No, he won't be in,' Beatrice had said on the phone. 'He's going back to work today. What about it? You make him sound like Bluebeard. I am allowed the occasional visitor, you know.'

It was simply an impression that each of them had received, separately. He smiled at them, plied them with drinks, placed ashtrays at their elbows and offered to drive them home, but they were always aware, somehow, that Beatrice's husband regarded them as little girls with whom there could be very few points of contact. Joanna said to Madeleine, 'He looks at us with a kind of amused and condescending smile, an exact replica of Beatrice's father's attitude; somehow, coming from Beatrice's father, it doesn't matter, coming from him, it does. I suppose he's very charming and pleasant and all that, but every time I see him I get this overwhelming urge to kick him in the crutch.'

Since most people had this effect upon Madeleine, made her feel childish and gauche and lacking in the social graces, her feelings on the subject were not nearly so vehement. Beatrice's husband was an experienced man of twenty-nine summers who had accumulated a wife, an ex-wife, two children and a detached house, and who, most probably, had every right and reason to think them immature. Perhaps Beatrice too would now think them immature.

But oh three cheers and hooray for our side. Because Beatrice isn't a grown-up person after all. She is reclining on her Scandinavian-style sofa in her usual Beulah-peel-me-a-grape attitude and her face shows no trace of the torment that she may or may not have suffered and her belly is once again flat as a board (well, not really – Beatrice always tended to a pleasant rotundity in that area) and if there is torn flesh, or stretch marks, or a slight drooping of those formerly firm young breasts, all of that is concealed. And she jumps to her feet and greets them with cries of delight and tucks her thick straight heavy dark hair behind her ears just as she did of yore. And she says, 'How you've changed, both of you,' which surprises them because *she* certainly hasn't changed, to outward view at any rate, and they weren't aware that they had either. When pressed to describe the exact nature of these changes she retreats into vagueness: Joanna looks – wilder, Madeleine less wary. That has to suffice; after all, this afternoon, they are merely background figures, attendant lords; centre stage must perforce be relinquished to the newest addition to their circle.

Joanna shifted uneasily in her chair (pine and sludge-green tweed, to match the sofa), said, 'Where is it?' and looked around her fearfully as though awaiting the entrance of a member of some unfamiliar species.

'It? It is he. Bridget is changing him. Samuel,' Beatrice said. 'It's a compromise. I really wanted Valentine. *Would* it have been too much?'

'Depends on how he looks.' Beatrice sounded as though she might have been naming a doll.

On cue, Bridget entered, the child pressed against her shoulder. She walked to the centre of the room, waited until all eyes were upon her and then proceeded to draw back the edge of the shawl. An unveiling ceremony, every bit as solemn as the one when they'd uncovered the plaque commemorating fifteen dead.

He had a little screwed-up waxy face and tiny hands with flaking fingernails that pawed blindly and ineffectually at the flowered surface of Bridget's overall. He was quite bald and there was a frightful pulsing area of eggshell fragility on the top of his head. Joanna suppressed shudders, thought of the nest of new-born mice they'd once uncovered in a corner of the garden: tiny squirming pieces of red flesh, veiled still. Madeleine suppressed the desire to reach out and touch: that tender quivering fontanelle, those white miniature waving fingers, those two faint arched lines where eyebrows would appear.

'Bridget,' Beatrice said, 'be an angel and make us some coffee. I'll take him.'

She held him carefully, his wobbling head supported in the crook of her arm. Contrasted with Bridget's professionalism, her lack of confidence was evident. Tentatively she held out a finger and the child's fingers closed around it. 'What do you think?' she said in the same way that she'd once produced an essay or a painting for their

93

critical opinion, saying, 'What do you think?' 'Aren't I clever?' she said. 'Does he really look like me, or is that just a figment of Bridget's imagination?'

'He looks like a baby,' Joanna said judiciously. 'And babies all look alike.'

Beatrice, more knowledgeable than that now, smiled, remained silent, foresaw either a rapid and sudden change in Joanna's attitudes or else a long hard road towards inevitable parenthood.

'It hasn't sunk in yet. I keep telling myself: I am a mother, I have a son. But it hasn't sunk in.'

Bridget re-entered with the coffee, deposited it, cast an anxious glance in the baby's direction – 'Don't be too long now. I want to put him down for his rest' – and retired.

'He's resting now, isn't he?' Joanna poured coffee from a thick, misshapen, unglazed jug into cups of similar crude design; the trend among the newly-married managerial set was obviously towards the ethnic: hand-thrown pottery, hand-woven curtains, natural knotted-pine tables. In Beatrice's case, it probably made a refreshing change from the Persian rugs and the tapestries and the translucent Spode banded in gold among which she had spent her formative years.

'Not resting properly. Bridget says that he must be free to kick and squirm and exercise his limbs.'

'Bridget's in residence then, is she? Wouldn't it be better for you to learn to cope alone from the word go?' Joanna thought that Bridget was the world's prize fool, despaired of trying to reform a society which contained such characters who took to slavery as though they'd been programmed to it from birth.

'Don't smoke, Joanna, if you don't mind. It won't kill you to do without one for ten minutes. And when *you've* had a baby, then I'll be perfectly willing to accept your advice. It's a shattering experience, having a baby.'

The child's eyes were tightly shut. Occasionally he pursed his lips and made faint sucking noises. Madeleine sat forward. 'What *is* it like?' she asked. There was no one else of whom she would ever dare to enquire. And although she had practically resigned herself to lifelong virginity, one had to prepare for the unlikeliest eventuality.

'Actually having it?' Beatrice, in her enthusiasm to impart information, reverted to a neuter description of her offspring. 'Oh there's nothing to *that*. It was a piece of cake. I was floating a yard in the air on Pethidine. Nevertheless, I think I'm very good at having babies. I think I've discovered my métier. Everyone else shrieked the place down.'

Madeleine spread her fingers wide and studied them. Undoubtedly she would turn out to be one of life's shriekers.

'It's *afterwards*,' Beatrice said. 'You feel as though you've climbed Everest or trekked across the Gobi. Your legs kind of buckle under you, and your stitches hurt like hell and you daren't even *contemplate* going to the loo.'

'Thank you,' Joanna said, 'thank you and goodnight.' Joanna held to the opinion that prior information was usually unreliable; far better to take things as they came, to face up to every fresh occurrence innocent of the half-digested snippets of other people's experiences. 'Why can't I smoke? Your father smokes like a chimney. Did it have some awful effect upon you?'

'Probably. He doesn't smoke when he comes here. Or, at least, he goes out into the garden to do it.'

They were silent, relishing the picture of Robert Martin, that most masterful of men, trooping obediently outside to light a cigarette.

'Not that he comes here very often. *She's* terribly unamused at the idea of being a grandparent. *Most* unbecoming and style-cramping. Her friends, I believe, bring up the subject at every possible opportunity. Oh, I do hope he cares for me more than I care for my mother,' Beatrice said, anxiously rocking. 'I mean, how on earth do you strike a happy medium between encouraging total dependency and neglecting them?'

It was beginning to sink in: the years and years that lay ahead that were destined to be filled with mistakes, over-concern, too little concern, perplexity, guilt, ambiguity, fear. She looked from one to the other of her guests: one who had become totally dependent, the other, offspring of two career-minded parents, who had inevitably suffered a certain amount of neglect.

Madeleine said, 'I think you just have to more or less play it by ear and hope for the best.'

Joanna said, 'Well, obviously you have to have some sort of *modus vivendi*, certain standards to which you intend to adhere, certain guidelines. After all, it's how you behave towards him that will determine how he turns out.'

Joanna had lately decided to throw in her lot wholeheartedly with the environmentalists. For ten minutes she bored Madeleine rigid and worried Beatrice sick with explanations of operant conditioning, behaviourism and Pavlov's dogs.

'My child does not salivate and I shall not be ringing any bells and I wish you'd shut up.'

'Don't be so dim . . .'

But Beatrice misunderstood wilfully, refused to believe, to accept such an enormous responsibility. Her child was formed temperamentally, just as he was formed physically; whatever happened would be due to him as much as to her.

They drank their coffee and mused. He *does* look like me, Beatrice thought, and not at all like David. Just as Matthew is the image of Amy. Yet isn't it a fact that each parent contributes fifty per cent of the total number of genes? I must ask Joanna.

I am worrying unnecessarily, Madeleine thought. Of course he will remember the number of the hostel, and my room number too, in view of that girl for whom he once had a big thing. Though it might have been as long as three years ago and they might have changed the number since then. She tried to ignore the voice that repeated insistently: if he wants to get in touch with you, he will get in touch with you, somehow or other.

Joanna waited, on tenterhooks, for the terrible moment when Beatrice would unbutton her blouse and proceed to feed the wretched thing. Joanna had always favoured unashamed nudity, had wandered, naked and unconcerned, in and out of the shower after games at school, much to the chagrin of the games mistress who interpreted this behaviour as exhibitionism, pure and simple. She knew that this reluctance to view Beatrice suckling her child must be a symptom of inhibition and it worried her because she thought she'd succeeded in sweeping away all inhibitions donkeys' years ago.

To her immense relief, Bridget came in with a bottle, tested the temperature of the milk on the back of her hand and swept the child – so confident a gesture – on to her lap. His eyes were closed still but his mouth opened instinctively at the approach of the teat, the muscles of his cheeks moved in and out rhythmically.

'Why aren't you doing it yourself?' Joanna was all in favour of the natural method, theoretically, and when she wasn't obliged to spectate.

'I can't,' Beatrice said happily. She would nurse him and change him and watch his development most dutifully, but the idea of such intimate contact was a little disturbing; her failure to lactate effectively had been an enormous relief. Nature had stepped in to prevent the development of a trauma arising from the dissonant facts of loving him and yet not wanting to enter, with him, into the closest bond of all.

Because she did love him. Unless there was some other word to describe the emotion, some technical term that occurred in the description of post-partum behaviour. I'm not maternal, she'd thought, as the pains came closer and closer together and she was subjected to examinations of an increasingly undignified nature, I'm not a bit maternal. But the minute, the very minute, they placed him in her arms, she knew that if he were to be taken away from her she would be bereft.

Bridget tipped the baby over her shoulder. A dribble of milk ran down her back. 'You see – just wind him occasionally,' she said to Beatrice. 'And never mind all those books and the clinic, feed him when he's hungry. It's what I did with you and you've not turned out so badly, have you?' Bridget's days were numbered and so she tried to instil into Beatrice hints and methods of procedure at every available opportunity. She understood and sympathized with Beatrice's lack of confidence; she'd felt the same way herself eighteen years ago, presented with a tiny baby whose mother demonstrated no instinct whatever and precious little enthusiasm. When you had to do it, you did it. It was as simple as that. Besides, she, Bridget, would be round every day, as before, just as soon as she'd finished her own chores. For Helena wouldn't let her go, wouldn't agree to a permanent change of residence, had stood in the middle of Bridget's bedroom and raised the roof. Was Bridget quite mad? This household depended upon Bridget, always had done. Beatrice was young, strong and healthy, with a husband who was quite prepared to shoulder his share of the burden of domestic life. Unlike Helena herself whose husband would never relax his exacting standards, who expected the house to function as efficiently as one of his factories.

'You know very well that we can't manage without you.' She twisted the aquamarine ring round and round her finger. Bridget read her face. The message was plain: Robert is critical and no less demanding than he was twenty years ago. There are girls, young girls everywhere, only too eager to accommodate him. The ominous black cloud of the menopause hovers on the horizon and every moment must be devoted to maintaining my attractiveness. What time does that leave me for sorting the laundry and organizing the half-wits? And Bridget felt pity for this spoiled wilful woman who was battling with every weapon at her disposal against the inevitable waning of her sexual magnetism.

So she had replaced her clothes in the wardrobe, her cards of grey hairpins on the dressing-table, her shoes beneath the bed. To be needed was perhaps the best that you could expect from life. It would be hard work, but she'd never been known to balk at hard work.

'You'll probably become addicted to it,' Joanna said sadly, 'having kids. One of those women who buy a pram when they're twenty and don't relinquish it until they're forty.' They were the surgery women; you looked at the face of the child in its mother's lap and you thought, Good God, it must be older than that by now, and then you realized it was a different child, a newer child. Joanna pressed her forehead against the cool glass of the picture window. This house induced feelings of claustrophobia, something she had never experienced in her small cramped Islington room, even when it contained a dozen and a half carousing individuals. She felt stifled, uneasy and sad. When you came home, everything seemed smaller, and Beatrice's situation assumed a symbolic quality. Perhaps those days, those long golden afternoons spent waiting for the future, perhaps they had been the days of wine and roses after all: the days when time dragged, lame-footed, and they sat in Beatrice's bedroom under the eaves, fantasizing, quoting chunks from 'The Waste Land' and 'A Subaltern's Love Song' and 'The Ballad of Reading Gaol', irrespective of their relevance, and Emmett swept leaves and the smoke from his bonfire shrouded the setting sun and Beatrice said that the most beautiful and evocative line in the whole canon of English poetry was: 'Do you remember an inn, Miranda?' and their three pairs of eyes went misty, contemplating a time in their lives when a line such as that *would* have some relevance.

'Roll on next week,' Joanna said, as they waited at the bus stop. The bus service was infrequent owing to all those garages. Specks of mica in the pavement glittered in the late afternoon sun, a child pedalled a red toy tractor to the end of a driveway and back again. One young woman unpegged sheets from a clothesline, pressed them against her cheek to check whether they were thoroughly dry. Another dug couch grass out of her lawn with a trowel. Yet another mounted a pair of step-ladders to clean her front window. The garages were all vacant and there wasn't a masculine figure to be seen. How could people bear to lead such lives, how could they reconcile themselves to a lifetime of washing and window-cleaning, of shopping lists and the numbing chatter of small children, of three regular meals a day and sex 2.8 times a week, and the only thing changing, the calendar on the wall? Next week there would be people of assorted varieties, and noise, and conversation and lectures and cheap wine and music and the feeling once again that anything was possible.

Roll on four o'clock, we used to say, Madeleine thought; now it's roll on next week, next month, next year. I suppose the realization of age comes when you prefer to look back because the future no longer holds out any hope.

Her mother stirred soup with one hand, pressed the other to a place just below her ribs. It was a gesture, a seemingly unconscious gesture that Madeleine had noticed several times since her return. She carried plates and cutlery to the table. 'Do you have a pain?' She was almost too afraid to ask, to ask invited a response that could result in a term's worry.

'It's indigestion,' her mother said, pouring tomato soup into bowls. 'Dr McCloud has given me some tablets.'

Madeleine's face cleared. She spooned her soup with relish. Beatrice, losing her lunch every day, her head over a bowl, had referred to Joanna's father as an old sadist who enjoyed the idea of female suffering, but Madeleine, the delicate child, with a history of respiratory infections, steam kettles, M and B tablets and visits to the doctor, had great faith in him. She ate three slices of bread. Roll on next week. She would be sitting at her desk and she'd hear feet along the passage and a knock at the door and a voice would say, 'Madeleine Brennan! You're wanted on the phone.'

Mrs Brennan forced down two spoonfuls of soup and then had to abandon it. Dr McCloud's actual words had been, 'Try these and if they don't make any difference, come back again and we'll send you for a barium meal, get it sorted out.' He was a forthright man, a kind man, vastly overworked, whose practice included most of the inhabitants of the poorer part of the town. 'Try these,' he said, fifty times a day: white tablets and blue tablets and yellow capsules, poor substitutes for a psychoanalyst's couch or a complete new lifestyle.

Mrs Brennan's tablets were large and white and tasted of chalk and so far they hadn't made any difference at all.

9

'I'm afraid it's only instant.'

Joanna emptied the remains of the Nescafé tin into two mugs. 'I bet that's what they say on Beatrice's estate when they're playing that musical chairs dinner-party business, moving to and from their identical houses. I bet they undress underneath their dressing-gowns and talk about the toilet and go into screaming hysterics if they find their kids playing with themselves.' Ridicule seemed the best form of defence against a way of life that threatened to entrap the most unconventional of characters, the free-est of spirits.

Strains of Greek music arose from the basement where a young Cypriot resided. Joanna sat on the landing beside the gas stove, waiting for the kettle to boil, Kant's *Critique of Pure Reason* on her knees. 'I understood this once,' she said. 'I must have softening of the brain. I can no longer work up any enthusiasm on the subject of whether clocks continue to tick when I leave the room. Is it too late to switch to Anglo-Saxon studies? Is it too late for a complete change of direction? Please, sir, I should like to become a Zeppelin-maker. Or a shepherd.'

Madeleine gazed out of the window, counted chimney pots and wondered whether there was the slightest chance that a phone might be ringing for her back at the hostel.

'Why don't you go round,' Joanna said, 'and say, "Hello, I'm back. How about the big night out?" Desmond,' Joanna said, 'has always treated women in a very cavalier fashion. He's well known for it. Oh please!' Joanna said, 'will somebody teach that bloody Greek another *tune*. Or I shall take his bazouki and *insert* it. Kant, and bazoukis, and it's sweltering! He'll be working, of course,' Joanna said. '*That's* why he hasn't rung or shown up. Finals in a fortnight. You'll have to give him till then. I never *thought*.'

Of course. Of *course*. Oh. Now she could settle down to her own revision in that happy three-week hiatus, travelling hopefully once more. If one could only live eternally in happy anticipation.

'Damn Kant,' Joanna said. 'Damn all philosophers. Let's go for a swim.'

They stepped outside into glaring sunlight, rolled towels under their arms. The Cypriot's curtains were drawn. 'He lives like a mole,' Joanna said, 'strumming and weeping alternately. And going to sign on on a Friday morning.'

'He's homesick. And lonely.' He had a gentle face and eyes that were prone to brim if someone so much as looked in his direction.

'There's no need for him to be lonely. Or homesick. I tried to introduce him to some of his compatriots at that party. They didn't seem to want to have anything to do with him. I can't say I blame them. Face like a wet weekend. And he smells as well. I just wish he'd find fresh lodgings.'

Madeleine said, 'You cry over starving children and you rage about political prisoners and injustice and inequality and class divisions, and yet there is a poor, confused, unhappy man living beneath your feet and you're totally unsympathetic and scornful of his very natural apprehensions.'

'He's the author of most of his misfortunes.'

'Perhaps some of the starving millions are too. And the political dissidents and the social misfits. You're great on humanity, Joanna, but you're hopeless when it comes to human beings.'

'The schools aren't on holiday, are they?' Joanna said. 'Else the pool will be full of little kids not bothering to leave the water when they want to pee. Do your individual vertebrae stick out like door-knobs when you wear a swimming costume? No? I'm starting on Complan tomorrow. Complan and Mars bars. And sit on my bum a lot. Develop an anal orientation. Cheer up,' Joanna said. 'I won't let you drown. Not until after the next three weeks at any rate.'

The examinations came and they went. Madeleine came second of her year and was awarded a prize, 'the second-best prize', Joanna called it. Joanna scraped through by the skin of her teeth, was felled by an excruciating attack of migraine, and gave up smoking because she had discovered great boulder-like lumps of tartar forming on the back of her teeth and, besides, smoking kept you thin. Mrs Brennan chewed another white tablet – a compound of magnesium trisilicate and sodium bicarbonate – and wrote Madeleine a letter of congratulation inside which she folded two five-pound notes with the instruction to 'spend it on some little luxury for a change, treat yourself'. Madeleine bought a dress which was almost, but not quite, a replica of Beatrice's Snow Queen frock; when she got it home she discovered that the discrepancy between the two of them was greater than she'd thought. Still, she would need more than one frock like that for the time after the telephone rang.

The results of the Finals were pinned up on the main notice board. She scrambled her way to the front through the ranks of those whose names appeared there and the attendant gloaters and gawpers. He hadn't got a First. That didn't surprise her. Neither had he got a 2.1. 'A 2.2,' someone said, behind her, 'a stinking Plodder's. It's almost worse than those Indian gentlemen who carry around cards saying, "B.A. – Failed". What price the doctorate and the fellowship and the life of indolent scholarship now? Ah well. So it goes.' Desmond hadn't even gained a respectable Plodder's. Desmond's name occupied a position down at the bottom of the list. Desmond had a degree. Just. She, in the afterglow of receiving the second-best prize, could envisage nothing more galling. She would pluck up her courage and visit him, offer tactful condolences, comfort him, cherish him and reconcile him to the fact of his now non-existent brilliant academic future. No wonder he had chosen to lie low. Obviously he'd been aware of the dog's breakfast he'd made of it.

Desmond had been aware of the course that his life was taking ever since around about half way through his second year. Either you worked or you didn't. And if you didn't work you got a lousy degree. The news, delivered *en passant* by a fellow student who lived on the top floor, came as no surprise. It came as no surprise, but there were slight twinges of disappointment all the same. 'The bastards,' he said once or twice, before returning his attention to the problem that was, quite literally, at hand.

Desmond was not suffering from a terrible illness. That was not the reason for his failure to telephone Madeleine. He had forgotten all about his promise to telephone Madeleine. Nevertheless he did have an illness. And that illness was the reason for his forgetting.

He'd ignored it for as long as he could, refused to acknowledge it, immersed himself in the impenetrable prose of David Ricardo, blotted it out with bottle upon bottle of Pedro's knock-off red wine that tasted like shoe polish. But it hadn't gone away. And after the exams were over and there was no longer anything to take his mind off it, he realized that something was going to have to be done about it.

A dozen times a day he dropped his trousers, arranged shaving mirrors at strategic angles and contemplated it. Some days it seemed worse than others. He borrowed money from Pedro and bought a dozen pairs of underpants; every night he threw away the pair he'd worn that day. Heat rash? a little optimistic voice kept saying. In a pig's eye. Pedro couldn't enlighten him either. 'Is bad,' was all Pedro could say, gazing from a safe distance, 'is bad,' and, 'Doctor. Go to doctor.' He didn't have a doctor and, he suspected, even if he had he wouldn't have gone to him. He tried Dettol. And calamine lotion. And once, in desperation and diluted in water, some sort of disinfectant stuff that the landlady kept for the drains. None of these made any difference to the condition. Except for the disinfectant stuff. Which stung and burned to such a degree that he was tempted to reach for the bread knife and end the torment once and for all.

In bed at night he tossed and turned and besought sleep. Sleep did not come. Instead, voices came, voices which insinuated the dread litany that he banished from his mind during the daylight hours: Syphilis, they said, the pox, sores and ulcerated flesh and blindness. Locomotor ataxia, they said. And general paralysis of the insane. Every night he looked inside his socks to see whether his toes had dropped off.

Eventually he betook himself to one of the Underground's less salubrious urinals and there, on the wall, defaced but still legible, was a notice giving him the information that he required.

'You have got a dose,' Pedro said gleefully. Smug bloody Spaniard. Of course, Spanish girls didn't. And Spanish tarts were probably inspected. Or did that happen only in the hygiene-conscious Protestant Northern European countries? The *sensible* Northern European countries. 'I hope you find a very big woman,' he said, 'and she smothers you.'

The poster had said complete confidentiality, but he hadn't so much as unzipped himself before they started asking about contacts. Contacts? He couldn't for the life of him remember. Names and faces floated through his memory as he sweated, trying to recall a specific name, a specific face and tie it in with the period prior to his infection. Of one thing he was certain, he would never again sleep with anyone he'd previously slept with. And that fact produced a corollary: he would simply not sleep with anyone again. Period.

The nurse did all sorts of unpleasant things with a variety of cold steel instruments. And took pleasure in it. You could tell. She was middle-aged and Scottish and she didn't care that what she was doing probably defied some universal law of physics about exits and entrances. She gave him a lecture on personal hygiene and a bottle of lotion and told him to come back in three days. And in three days he came back and it was a doctor. And his bowels turned to water. The doctor opened his mouth to speak. His lips formed the shape of a word. Syphilis. Oh God, please God, I'll never touch another woman again. I swear. I'll put it under the cold tap first. Dear God. 'You can breathe again,' the doctor said. 'A secondary infection. Very mild.'

He waltzed along the pavement, his pocket full of pills and unction. Report again in a fortnight's time. Observe certain rules. Get in touch with suspected partner and send her along. There wasn't much chance of that. He'd remembered. A dark girl with hairy legs. Mavis Something. A nurse down on a visit from Tyneside. Well, she was probably spreading it half across Newcastle by now. Let the Geordies look to their own *moutons*. Abstain from sexual activity blah, blah, blah. *That* wouldn't be any hardship. Venereal disease. Probably everybody had had it. One time or another. A mark of the experienced man. Like a duelling scar. Baudelaire had died of it, and Schubert, and the entire population of Restoration England was bedevilled with it. Just take the pills and praise the Lord for Alexander Fleming.

It was then that he remembered Madeleine. A virgin if ever there was one. A pure young virgin, host to no foul spirochete, no seething bacteria. He'd give her a ring. Just as soon as they pronounced him fit to return to the company of those decent, clean members of the community who practised sexual restraint.

Throughout the dying days of June, when everyone else was celebrating success or, at least, the end of unsuccessful effort, and the sun scorched the grass in the gardens and the balmy evenings gave back the soft echo of the voices of young girls on their way to encounters, Madeleine sat in her small square room waiting. Desmond travelled to and from the clinic and Madeleine counted the number of books in her bookcase, the number of circles in the pattern on the rug and the number of times the conducting wire was convoluted around the element of the electric fire. People tapped on her door, stuck their heads around the jamb, said, 'You're not staying in again? On a night like *this*?' and disappeared in a flurry of cotton frocks and starched petticoats. She took up smoking. It was something to do. Reading demanded a degree of concentration that she couldn't bring to it. For her courage had failed her. She could no more make the journey to his house, ascend the stairs and knock at the door than fly. She dared not lay herself open to probable rejection. If he'd wanted her, he'd have found her.

Wholesome again at last, Desmond celebrated by means of a ritual cleansing: a bonfire in the area at the back of the house. Grey sheets sprinkled with paraffin, a dozen pairs of underpants, the pillowcase upon which she had laid her dark head – all exploded in a burst of orange flame, belched forth black smoke, subsided into a heap of grey ash. The landlady pounded on her window. He ignored her, thought instead of Room 65 at the hostel and the girl he'd known there. Pretty and pliant she was, and amazingly sexy. With her he ran what must surely be the gamut of sexual inventiveness and between them they broke the bed leg. Once, he hit her. Hard. He'd never imagined that he'd want to do that. Her eyes were surprised, but she'd liked it, he thought. He was besotted with her. For twenty-eight weeks. On the first morning of the twenty-ninth week he woke up and it was gone, that feeling. A magnificent obsession had run its course.

And now the new girl. With light brown hair and green-blue eyes and a skin the colour of pale biscuits. Timid and wary like a young animal. Once he'd wanted to become a vet. At school he'd volunteered to look after the mice and the guinea pigs and the tropical fish, had superintended various confinements, watched the progress of the newborn with an intense absorption. But the big fish ate the little fish and the male mice attacked their young and the guinea pigs grew and acquired an independence, demonstrated a distinct lack of affection or gratitude, and gradually his interest waned and the floors of the cages became carpeted and befouled with droppings, the surface of the fish tank grew green with algae and stank and the biology master said that if he, Desmond, couldn't be bothered, then Hopkinson of the Lower Fifth might as well take over the job.

The last of the orange flames burned blue and died in the sun. He scattered the ashes with his heel. Pakistani faces were pressed to the basement window; they probably thought it was a display of yet another curious English custom: a midsummer version of Guy Fawkes Night.

In the hall, he put twopence into the call-box, waited for a reply and pressed button A. 'I'd like to speak to Madeleine please,' he said. 'Madeleine who?' the voice said.

'I don't know. Room 65.'

'Oh hell. That's right at the top. Hang on and I'll see if she's in. You can dial direct to the top floor now, you know,' the voice said.

He hadn't known. That facility had not been in existence during the days of the broken bed leg.

Stephanie Carr, the girl who had taken the call, was famous for her absent-mindedness. Dizzy Stephanie Carr who'd once come down to breakfast wearing odd shoes and who couldn't remember her home telephone number without looking it up. On the first landing she bumped into Joyce Fawcett whom she hadn't seen since Saturday night when they'd made up a foursome with two Earth Scientists. There was a lot to tell, a lot of ground to be covered. 'No!' Stephanie Carr said. 'You didn't! Mine flaked out. It was like being buried alive. Thirteen stones of him. I nearly suffocated.' Madeleine stubbed out another cigarette in the brimming ashtray. She had sixty-three books on her shelves, of which twenty-one were published by Penguin, eleven by the OUP, five by Secker and Warburg, seven by Macmillan, eight by Longman & Co – or was it nine? She got up to check the colophon. 'Hello?' Desmond said. 'Hello?' And the reverberation of his voice echoed around the empty kiosk. 'Oh God,' Stephanie Carr said, 'that phone call! Madeleine Thingamajig. That brainy one. *What* room is it?'

'Sixty-five,' said Joyce, who wouldn't have had a clue except that she lived next door.

As Madeleine reached out a trembling hand towards the receiver, Desmond, having despatched a series of oaths into the ether, hung up. She continued to listen, long after it was obvious that the line was dead. It was probably only Joanna anyway. In a rush. Unable to hang on for long. Tearing off towards some other pressing engagement.

I'll send a message via Joanna, Desmond thought. Much more sensible than relying upon one of those dozy mares at the hostel.

He'd had a gutful of *them* three years ago.

Joanna's door was closed. It was locked. Which was odd. And although there wasn't a sound to be heard, he had the distinct impression of somebody or something inside there. But whoever, whatever it was didn't answer. The landlady was out and the thick Cypriot merely shrugged his shoulders and ceased to be bilingual. Some days were like that, of course. You rose, full of good intentions, determined upon action, and some malignant providence saw to it that your every attempt was frustrated. Still, he was bound to run into her sooner or later. You couldn't attend the same educational establishment and not run into one another, however infrequently. And now he thought about it, he had a stack of things to do, arrangements to be made, a further year to be signed up for – he'd do a Dip.Ed. if they'd have him and if they'd renew his grant; he had no desire to teach, no intention of teaching, but at least it gave you a year's breathing space and anything was better than working. And then there was the question of a job for the summer vacation; he still had so many unpaid debts and Pedro was getting distinctly stroppy about the underpants money, had ceased to return with parcels of stringy chicken legs and bowls of melted pimento ice cream. And he'd look for another room while he was about it; he could have sworn that it was a giant cockroach that had darted through a hole in the skirting-board last night. Though he had had a bit to drink and perhaps they were breeding beetles bigger these days.

'Were you expecting anybody?' Fred said, releasing his pent-up breath in a long sigh.

'No.' Joanna pulled up the sheet over them because she didn't want Fred's gaze to dwell for too long upon her knobbly vertebrae and her razor-sharp hip-bones. He'd felt them, certainly, but tactile impressions were perhaps less vivid. The Complan and the Mars bars hadn't increased her weight by an ounce.

'They can always come again if it was anything important.'

'That's what I want to do,' Fred said and took hold of her face between his two hands and kissed her on the lips because he'd found that the only way of stilling Joanna's insistent tongue was to cover her mouth with his own for long periods of time.

She'd met Fred in Camden Town. The appearance of most of the Communists would have confirmed Robert Martin's assertion about the ineffable dreariness of the protagonists of the workers' revolution: earnestness and obsessive attention paid to the minutiae of protocol. Fred was facetious, disruptive and clearly an embarrassment to the rest of the group. He leaned across the table and winked at Joanna. 'Do you want to come to a party?' he said. 'Comrade?' right in the middle of somebody's boring dissertation on the concept of on-going revolution.

He was a graduate of Trinity College, Oxford, and earned his living as a stevedore. He wore a loud check shirt and had mad eyes and a tattoo on his forearm that said '*Merde*' and he took her to this party where, towards morning, somebody passed around a thin mangled-looking cigarette that smelled peculiar. Marjorie-Anna, Fred said and showed her how one coped with it. She had the same squeamish feeling that she used to experience when taking communion wine: the idea of all those previous mouths – ugh! Nevertheless she took it and drew the smoke down into her belly and waited for the roses on the wallpaper to expand and blossom, the carpet to increase its dimensions to desert-like proportions. The background music assumed a more insistent beat and all that happened was that she felt a trifle giddy and recognized within herself a slight and uncharacteristic tendency to giggle.

'Cheap crap,' Fred said afterwards. 'I've had more of a high from a Craven A,' and described the enlightening experiences he'd achieved from the use of the good stuff. Fred had experimented with a fair amount of chemical substances. He was interested in the theory that the successful functioning of one's mind and body might depend upon the maintenance of an exact and complementary chemical balance. Joanna had implicit faith in the capacity of her mind and her body to function successfully without the aid of any synthetic agent. Still, she didn't doubt his sincerity. There weren't that many socialists prepared to hump crates day after day in the interests of participant observation for a real understanding of the trials and tribulations of the manual worker.

He took her home and stayed and they discussed William Burroughs and Aldous Huxley and the possible fallibility of Hegel's theory of dialectic social change and the year he'd spent on the kibbutz and Wilhelm Reich and Jungian dream interpretation and how infiltration was the only political course left to them and how it was important that Joanna should achieve a bloody good degree and then she too could become a stevedore (or whatever a stevedore's female equivalent was) rather than wasting away her life in the back row of the bourgeoisie.

And then it was much too late for him to leave because he lived somewhere incredible, unheard-of, south of the river and tomorrow was Sunday anyhow. Today was Sunday, actually. She spread an eiderdown for him on the floor but even as she was doing it she was telling herself that it had to happen some time and now was as good a time as any.

He grinned and unbuttoned the tartan shirt. The memory of the Palestinian sunshine lingered on his skin. 'You're a great girl, Joanna,' he said. 'Fancy finding you among that bunch of old farts. I only go there for a laugh.'

She reached out her hand and touched his chest. It was warm and brown and so was the hand that came to encircle her own. The eiderdown lay spread between them. 'Ah, sod the eiderdown,' he said.

And it wasn't some ghastly competitive-type activity after all with rules and procedure as rigid as a sixteenth-century courtly dance or the Annual General Meeting of the CP in Camden Town: you do this and then I do that. It was simply the mutual desire to give pleasure of a progressive nature. And desire itself, after all, was nothing but a chemical reaction. 'Oh, good heavens,' she said, sitting up straight in the bed, 'what about contraception?' She'd been so absorbed by the reactions – chemical and otherwise – that he was arousing in her, that the necessity for sensible precautions had momentarily slipped her mind. Where, at three o'clock on a Sunday morning in Islington, did you find an open chemist's shop or a branch of the Marie Stopes Memorial Clinic?

And he pushed her back against the pillow and said not to be so silly, that he always travelled prepared for such eventualities, that casual conception was the most immoral act on God's earth. He knew, he was a bastard himself, an abandoned bastard at that, who'd had eighteen years of Doctor Barnardo's and foster homes. And she was so busy feeling sympathetic towards the poignant tale of his youth that she hardly noticed it happening.

Desmond was accepted for a course leading to the acquisition of a teaching diploma, found himself another room, in a West Indian household, and a job in a timber yard, and felt so knackered every evening when he got home that he couldn't even contemplate the *idea* of women, generally or in particular.

Fred said, one Sunday morning in July when they were in bed and all the church bells in creation were competing with one another, 'How do you fancy a trip to France? I've amassed a fair pile of loot this year and it's time I had a change. We'll have to hitch, of course, but I've got a couple of mates in Avignon. Good types. I'll show you Marseille. Marseille is somewhere everyone should see. You hadn't anything fixed, had you?' Joanna rang her parents and said, 'I'm going to France with a very nice man. Don't start screaming. I've been to the clinic and the bottom's fallen out of the white slavery market. He's a docker called Fred,' Joanna said, waited for the expected reaction and then said, 'With an Oxford degree. First Class Honours. Travel broadens the mind.' She then rang the branch of Woolworth's in her home town to cancel the job she'd intended to take during the summer vacation.

Madeleine went to Mass, came back and packed her trunk. She took the record of the songs from *Mahagonny* that she'd bought in remembrance of that evening and she broke it into two equal pieces and threw them both in the waste-paper basket. The end of her hoping. She would never see him again. There was no possibility. The sun shone and shone and everything within her field of vision was grey.

10

'He doesn't look remotely like David, does he?' Amy said, peering into the pram in a manner which suggested that Samuel might be suffering from smallpox.

'Neither does Matthew. Perhaps we both had virgin births. Well – not exactly virgin births – asexual reproductions, spontaneous conceptions.'

Beatrice yawned widely, felt dizzy and had to reach for the fence to steady herself. 'Would you like some tea?' she said.

How civilized we are being, she thought, as she filled the kettle, I and my husband's ex-wife, sitting down to tea together, passing each other the sugar. I really ought to be desperately jealous of

Amy and she of me and if David knew he'd throw a fit; he'd have visions of us chewing over the intimate details of our marriages, analysing his character, his habits and his performance. He'd be quite wrong. Amy simply isn't sufficiently interested and the idea of *that* sort of heart to heart makes me feel queasy. As if I didn't feel queasy to start with.

David didn't know, and this was Amy's second visit. They'd met by chance, both gazing into the same shop window, a jeweller's: Amy because she was trying to decide which ring Daddy was going to buy her for her birthday, and Beatrice because she'd walked all the way into town with the pram and her feet were aching. 'I adore opals,' Amy had said, 'but aren't they supposed to be unlucky? That diamond cluster is nice but perhaps a bit ostentatious, don't you think?' It was then that Beatrice, who considered an obsessive interest in jewellery to be symbolic of a hopeless sinking into middle age, had said, 'Why don't you come round to see me some after-noon?' and Amy had done a double-take and then replied, 'Yes. All right. As long as *he* won't be there.'

It wasn't that she had any particular liking for Amy or her com-pany; the fact was that the days dragged so, seemed so identical, one after the other, that any new experience was welcome. House-work, she knew, should have kept her occupied, but Bridget did most of that, despite her half-hearted protests. 'I can have it done while you're looking at it,' Bridget would say, arriving every day promptly at eleven and rolling up her sleeves. 'Besides, you've just had a baby. You ought to take it easy. You've never been strong.' This last was a myth that Bridget had created for herself, just like the one about her father's aunt and syphilis and smotheration. Her father's aunt had gone potty all right but it wasn't syphilis, it was progressive senile dementia. And apart from the early weeks when they'd kept her alive with cotton wool and incubators, Beatrice had always been as fit as a flea.

At one o'clock they ate lunch, she and Bridget: boiled eggs or salads or bowls of soup, and at three o'clock, after she'd rinsed the dusters through and hung up the tea-cloths and mopped the kitchen floor, Bridget would depart to catch the three-fifteen bus and resume her duties on the other side of town. And for three hours the clock would tick and the baby would cry and the sun would change its position on the carpet and Beatrice, who had once relished the idea

III

of an uninterrupted interlude of idle hours, drooped with boredom and yearned for the sound of his tyres on the drive, his key in the lock.

Beatrice tried, really tried, to make contact with the Carols and the Barbaras and the Susans who dropped by with their assorted children to eat ginger nuts and discuss their figures and their mortgages and the length of time they'd been in labour. Beatrice joined the Pram Club and the Young Wives' Association, she bought women's magazines and followed instructions in cookery books produced for cretins and she invented gory tales about her time in the maternity home. Sometimes she persuaded Bridget to cook a fancy dinner and entertained one or two of the couples. Inevitably, she got on better with the husbands than she did with their wives. The Peters, the Richards and the Tonys at least brought a breath of the real world into the sage-green close-carpeted lounges where one juggled with a small whisky and a cigarette and contemplated the hi-fi unit in one corner and the nest of G Plan coffee tables in the other. Some of the husbands treated her with an exaggerated, if impotent, gallantry; she was much younger than most of them and extremely attractive. Sometimes, when discussing the economy with them, or the iniquities of personal taxation or disgraces and corruption in local politics, she would daydream a bit and try to decide which of them would eventually run off with his secretary, take to drink, remain a true and devoted husband and father. This was mere speculation, for none of them had been married long enough to realize the hideous inevitability of it all, their wives had not yet grown cold, or too demanding, their children were charming toddlers not turbulent adolescents, their jobs seemed still to offer unlimited prospects. When one or other of them held on too long to her hand when refilling her glass, she'd stare straight through him until her total lack of response had transmitted itself. Even if she'd been looking for an extra-marital flirtation – which she wasn't – she would never have chosen any one of them; how could you fall for a man who carried a shopping basket around the Home and Colonial and looked furtive whenever his wife cast a cold eye in his direction?

They all of them were too organized, too content with the narrow limits of their existence, too concerned with climbing aboard the latest trend and making it respectable for Beatrice's taste. Beatrice liked odd, eccentric people who refused to fit into any preconceived category, who'd buy a book in preference to a loaf of bread, who'd stay up all night and sleep all day if it suited them, who'd live on scraps for a year so that they could visit the Greek Islands. And persons of such unconventionality had not taken up residence on the estate.

Which was why she welcomed Amy. Amy's conversation didn't exactly extend the intellect but at least Amy's life was a rag-bag of colour and incident compared with those of Carol and Barbara and Susan. That afternoon Amy was debating the decision whether or not to marry a man called George who was in the hotel business in Bermuda. He was a widower of forty-five with a grown-up son, but he was loaded and his parental experience could only be to the good as far as Matthew was concerned.

'You'd take Matthew to Bermuda?' Beatrice stirred her tea, very slowly.

'Well, naturally.'

'Don't you think David might object?'

'I don't see why. I think he might be quite relieved. He's got that one now.' Amy gestured through the window in Samuel's direction. 'Why should he need another?'

'They're not *parcels*.'

'David never struck me as being particularly attached to Matthew.'

'You talk about him,' Beatrice said, 'as though he was a slight acquaintance that you'd once known for a brief period, as though you'd never been married to him, had his child.'

'I'm just glad that it *was* a brief period. When I think of my life then and my life now, I just give thanks that I saw the light when I did. Your baby seems to be crying. Oughtn't you to bring him in? It's getting quite chilly out there.'

If my husband's second wife had a kid, Beatrice thought, I'd want to kill it, I'd want it to die of exposure in a January snowstorm. 'Don't you hate me?' she asked curiously.

'Why should I hate you? I feel sorry for you.'

There was no malice detectable in her voice or her expression. Beatrice remembered the Amy of not two years ago, bewailing her ruined life. Now she flew off to Nassau by the minute, gold bracelets rattled at her wrist and a very rich man was willing to put his life and his money at her disposal. Was that sufficient reason to feel sorry for someone who didn't *want* any of those things, who simply wanted a normal, straightforward, steadfast man to love her, to give her a home and a family and an identity? It was most galling to be the object of Amy Bellamy's pity. 'I have what I want,' Beatrice said. She said it so vehemently that she was certain that she believed it.

She reached for Sam's bottle which was soaking in a solution of Milton. The blood rushed from her head, her knees buckled. She held on to the edge of the sink until the giddiness had passed. Her reflection in the window confronted her sternly. You can fool yourself for only so long, it said. You can't have forgotten already, it said, not in the brief space of fifteen months – the giddiness, the nausea, the languor?

'Are you all right, Beatrice?' Amy said from a great distance, the sound of her jewellery ringing in Beatrice's ears like the entire percussion section of an orchestra. 'You're as white as chalk.' And Beatrice ran the cold tap and bathed her face and determined to look up parthenogenesis in the uniform edition of the encyclopaedia that they kept on the top shelf of the bookcase.

Dr McCloud washed his hands very thoroughly. His hands were freckled and raw-looking around the knuckle area. A few strands of his remaining sandy-coloured hair lay across the top of his head at regular intervals; whether by accident or design, she couldn't tell. He looked at her through the top part of his bi-focals; this produced the effect that he wasn't actually looking at her but at a spot some distance above her head. 'There's precious little point in me doing this,' he said, 'at this stage. But if it'll make you any happier . . .'

She never failed to feel embarrassed at the idea of this man – who'd known her from childhood, who'd played the piano for musical chairs at Joanna's birthday parties and taken her upon his knee for comfort when she sulked because she never won any of the prizes – probing the innermost intimate recesses of her body. She breathed deeply and rhythmically through her mouth while he prodded and poked at her. She wondered if doctors ever got aroused in such situations and, if so, how they concealed it. Or did familiarity breed contempt and did it mean no more to them than a line of carcasses hanging in a cold store would mean to a butcher? Perhaps it all depended upon the quality and regularity of their own sex lives. She tried to imagine Joanna's mother out of her starched coat and in the throes of passion. It was impossible. Anyway, her own sex life was regular and satisfying, but that didn't prevent her from entertaining the odd erotic thought about some other man: the curve of a jowl, the cut of a pair of trousers. Mysterious, it was.

He straightened up with a creaking sound, peeled the glove from his hand and threw it into the bin. He shook his head. 'At this stage,' he said, 'we might just as well consult a crystal ball. If you're *that* anxious to know, you'd better bring in a specimen.'

She rearranged her clothing, swung her legs off the couch. She felt wet and sore and uncomfortable. He rolled down his shirtsleeves. 'You're quick off the mark,' he said. 'What happened? Did you forget to use it?'

'No, I did not.' The tone he used towards her was the same tone he'd used when she was eleven and he'd told her to stop picking at her chicken-pox vesicles.

And she hadn't. Regularly, religiously, even when it was cold and she was tired, she had attended to the ritual.

'I believe you,' he said, fending off her indignant glare. Though he didn't. Beatrice was the sort who'd burst into flame before she could summon up the energy to move back from the fire. 'Perhaps you didn't position it properly,' he said, as though that was some sort of comfort. 'There is a failure rate, you know. Nothing is a hundred per cent effective.'

She did know, something like five pregnancies per hundred woman-years. And she had to be one of the five.

'Well,' he said, unscrewing a small bottle and taking a large white pill from it, 'if you're going to have a family, you might as well get it over with at one fell swoop.' He slipped the tablet into his mouth and chewed at it; it was a tablet of the same sort prescribed for Mrs Brennan. 'Your fertility is obviously high,' he said. 'I had a woman in this morning who'd change places with you like a shot. She's been trying for five years.'

That piece of information solaced her no end. I should have been around during the time of dynastic marriages, she thought, and empires that depended upon the production of heirs. One of those times when you were judged on the fecundity of your womb rather than the evidence of your intellect.

In the encyclopaedia she read every single entry that appertained to the subject. Parthenogenesis occurred only among aphids, or so it seemed; there was screeds of information concerning aphids. Pygmies achieved population control by means of abortifacients and the misguided assumption that the most propitious time for conception was during the period of the menses. A woman in Ohio was pregnant for thirteen months. King Richard III came into the world with teeth and Macduff, like Beatrice, was from his mother's womb untimely ripp'd. Fascinating stuff. She was so absorbed that Pamela Glover, the pink and white wife of pink and white Derek Glover next door, eventually had to knock at the window to ask if Samuel really ought to be left *yelling* like that and shouldn't someone just check to see if he was *OK*? 'He's merely exercising his lungs,' Beatrice said in a very chilly tone. Pamela Glover always waited for her husband to speak first and had to ask his permission before she drank a glass of sherry or visited the cinema or painted her fingernails a different shade of pink.

'It's come back positive,' Dr McCloud said, over the phone. 'And next time you can just wait, as all the rest of my patients have to do. Of course, it's not gospel,' he said, 'not at this stage.' If he said that just once more she'd run lunatic. However, he went on to explain, whereas negative results quite often turned out to be erroneous so early on, the chances of a positive result being sub-sequently reversed were almost nil. 'By the way,' he said, 'have you had any communication with Joanna recently? If so, the next time you write, would you mind reminding her of her home address?'

'The last time I heard from her she'd just got back from France. With that docker,' Beatrice said sweetly, wishing to cause Dr McCloud – with his hearty assumption that women ought to accept the effects of their fertility and get on with the business of having babies without undue fuss – a moment's pain and humiliation.

'No, not a docker any more,' he said gloomily. 'He works as a street trader now. If you need a bedspread handwoven by Mexican peasants or a set of Ceylonese table mats, I'm sure he'll be able to fix you up.' He rang off, chewed another tablet, thought nostalgi-cally of the days of National Service and that generation of clever working-class children who regarded education as a stepping-stone to an improved social position rather than an end in itself.

Beatrice mashed rusks for Samuel, brought him into the lounge, propped him in a corner of the sofa with cushions and proceeded to feed him. As he grinned at her and nuzzled greedily and gummily at the spoon, she heard the sound of a car door slamming and looked up. Helena's Renault Floride stood outside the gate and Helena herself, in her new lambskin coat, was walking up the path.

She surrounded Samuel with cushions and went to open the door.

Helena had just had a sauna and a massage and a facial. She smelled of Joy and fur and cleanliness and her clear skin glowed. But the little lines were forming, there in their infancy at the corner of her eyes and her mouth. She took off her coat and handed it to Beatrice. Underneath it she was wearing a suède suit and a silk blouse and a number of gold chains that hung in the valley between her uplifted breasts. Beatrice, in down-at-heel slippers and a big shapeless cardigan and a pair of David's cast-off corduroy trousers cut down to fit, hung the coat in the hall and marvelled at the discipline of the woman: that régime of moisturizing and plucking and shaving and combing and colouring and diet that she followed so conscientiously every single day of her life in order to present herself as a work of art. *Il faut souffrir pour être belle* might have been engraved above her bedroom door.

Bridget was unwell. Just a cold. But she didn't want to spread her infection to the baby. Therefore Helena had come in her place. To offer her assistance.

'Oh good,' Beatrice said, 'I've got a week's washing and all the windows need cleaning and after that you can do out the bedrooms. Have you ever "done out" a bedroom, Mother dear? I'll bet you haven't. Don't look so disconcerted. There's no need to disturb a hair of your carefully-lacquered head.'

'Do you *know* what you look like?' Helena said, following her daughter into the lounge, stepping gingerly around an assortment of nappies and baby powder and teething rings and rattles.

'There's not much point poncing myself up when I spend half the day covered in baby food and sick and gripe water.'

'You do change, I take it, before David gets home?'

'Oh yeah.' Beatrice guided a spoonful of mush towards Samuel's mouth. He spat joyously. 'Into black stockings and a lacy suspender belt and I put flowers in my hair and he chases me round the sofa.'

Helena said that men wanted to come home to order and tranquillity and wives smelling of scent. Helena said that there was nothing more certain to drive a man to seek distraction than returning nightly to a slut. Helena said.

Beatrice scraped the spoon round the dish, tucked what she'd gathered inside Samuel's left cheek. He opened his eyes wide. The irises were a jewel-like green-blue colour and the whites were tinged with the same shade. 'Isn't he lovely! Say hello to your grandma.' Helena winced. 'Don't you want to hold him and cuddle him? You're a most unnatural woman.'

'Perhaps if you wiped his chin. Is he dry?'

Helena placed her hands under his armpits and lifted him carefully on to the point of her knee. Once he'd peed all over the skirt of a Chanel suit simply because stupid Beatrice hadn't thought to put on his plastic pants. 'How long do they stay bald?' she said, touching his few feathery fronds of hair with her forefinger. 'I can't remember.'

'You don't remember much, do you? I used to ask you about my childhood and you used to say, "Ask Bridget." I used to ask you what I looked like when I was born and whether I cried much and what my first words were. And you couldn't remember.'

Samuel reached out a hand towards the gold chains. Helena moved him back on her knee, out of harm's way. He retaliated by turning his attention to the ring with the aquamarine stone that she wore on her right hand. 'I never even *saw* you for the first three weeks of your life,' Helena said. 'I had to rely upon your father for accurate reports as to your appearance, whether you had the requisite number of fingers and toes, etcetera. You were in an incubator and I was recovering from the operation.' There was a faint reminder of the incision still, across her belly. How she'd hated that scar, those primitive wartime conditions, the surly gynaecologist who'd refused to give her a general anaesthetic.

'Is my father back yet?' He was attending a conference of industrialists in Torquay.

'Tonight.' Samuel tried to inch his way along her knee towards those gold chains, swinging and glinting with every rise and fall of her bosom. She handed him back to his mother, brushed her skirt, gazed pensively at the backs of her white hands. *Still* they fell for him: silly young girls, scheming middle-aged women, dazzled by his slow smile, and his sleepy eyes that always seemed to contain a sexual invitation, assuming him to be lovely all the way through, like a perfect diamond or a slice of sponge cake. The particular game they'd played for so long was turning into a one-sided contest. What possible comparison could there be between a young man after her money and a young girl after his body? There was so much that she could tell Beatrice and so much that Beatrice simply didn't want to know: how men possessed a minimum degree of resistance to the female come-hither, how monogamy was simply not in their natures, how, compared with women, they were mere straws in the wind. Beatrice said, 'So you think I ought to get myself up like a dog's dinner every night of the week just to make sure that my husband's fancy doesn't stray? How degrading! We aren't like that any more, Ma. We've given over being sexual objects relying upon artifice and hypocrisy to keep our marriages intact. We accept each other these days as fellow human beings, warts and all.'

This was Joanna speaking, Joanna echoing the thoughts of her Fred. And it wasn't true. At least it wasn't true in Beatrice's immediate vicinity: the majority of the Carols and Barbaras and Susans still put their children to bed, tidied their houses, laid their tables and were waiting, in kaftans, with their hair pinned up, for their husbands' return.

'Don't say I didn't warn you.' Though perhaps David was one of those men who needed to bolster a weak ego and who'd run a mile if some woman took him at face value. Helena knew *those* sort.

'You've warned me. I'll embroider it on a sampler, frame it and hang it on the wall: "My mother warned me." Now, what would you like for lunch?'

'I've brought it.'

Helena unpacked a basket. There were slices of what Bridget – who'd made it – called bacon and egg pie and Helena called quiche Lorraine, some asparagus, crisp French bread and a piece of Emmenthal, a punnet of raspberries – raspberries in November! – and a jar of cream. Beatrice salivated, set out this feast on the Formica top of her kitchen table, gorged herself and was promptly sick in the sink.

Helena averted her eyes from her daughter's heaving, found they had come to rest upon Samuel who was pinioned in his high chair with the remains of a Heinz baby dinner spread half across his face, and averted them again. 'Well, it can't be the food,' she said, 'it's completely fresh. You've not suddenly become allergic to something, have you? The raspberries?' She stirred at the remaining raspberries with her spoon, wrinkled her nose above the cheese crumbs, and behind her smooth brow an idea was forming, taking shape. 'Oh no,' she said. 'Oh *no*.'

'Oh yes.' Beatrice shivered, pulled the edges of her cardigan together, hitched up David's trousers, attempted a wan smile. 'It reminds me of those Roman vomiting posts – they stuffed themselves with food and then made themselves sick so that they could start all over again.'

'For heaven's *sake*,' Helena said and flung the spoon across the table. Samuel looked up, alerted to the movement of any bright shiny object. 'What's the *matter* with you? Haven't you any sense at all? You're hardly over *this* one yet. I thought you'd been to the Family *Planning* Clinic.' She shuddered. The idea of pregnancy, even someone else's, horrified her.

'I'm like you,' Beatrice said. 'We don't have to work at it, do we? It's easier for us than blinking.'

Helena levelled at her a long cool stare. Eventually she said, 'I don't know what you're talking about. And I don't think that you do either.'

'Oh come *on*. I have ears and eyes. I must say it took some time before it registered. I used to think that you were ill. That last time, I suppose I must have been about thirteen – you didn't go away that time, did you? – I saw the sheets that Bridget put to wash and they were soaked with blood and I was terrified. I thought you must be dying. Tell me,' Beatrice said conversationally, 'what did he think about it? Didn't he mind? Bridget used to pray for you. And for herself. Making her an accomplice to your criminal acts. Her immortal soul is probably doomed. It hasn't happened recently, has it? Is that indicative of a general decline in fertility, or did you finally get yourself sterilized?'

She returned Helena's gaze steadily. They read messages from each other's eyes. I wanted him, Helena's said, not his babies. I'd seen other women grow gross and flabby with childbearing, devote more and more of their attention to their babies and less to their husbands, lose interest in the sexual side of life. He wouldn't have wanted a woman like that. I don't think he'd have wanted a woman like that. It was my beauty and my strength that attracted him. Where would I have been without them? So I aborted my pregnancies and, yes, eventually, I did get myself sterilized and after it was done I cried for a week. I don't know why. I thought it was relief. But perhaps it was something else as well.

Beatrice's said, I am a woman now. In my own right. And I will have children and I will love them as you never loved me, leaving me at home with Bridget and the chicken-pox, or the measles, or the time I broke my arm, while you accompanied him on a business trip or a holiday. You were jealous of the attention he paid to me so you started having affairs with horrible men so that he had to devote himself entirely to you. You locked the bedroom door and you said, 'Go away,' when I had a sore throat or a nightmare, while you entrapped him there with your rotten sexuality. I put my arms around your neck and you drew away, you said, 'Bridget, this child's face is dirty.' You slept with a man one afternoon on the Reina del Mar when he and I were playing deck quoits and you made sure that he knew about it. He sleeps with women because he's highly sexed and he can't resist an attractive face, a pliant body; you slept with men (because it's the past tense now, isn't it, Mother: straighten your shoulders and confront the menopause); you slept with them for subtler, darker reasons than that. I don't hate you. You are as you are and life has a way of dishing out its own penalties. But my child, my children, they will have me and I won't give a sod if they smudge my make-up or demand to be taken into my bed when they wake with night terrors. Because I know that the way children are treated is the most important thing on earth. Not from reading Joanna's joke psychology books, but because I didn't just have your example, I had another one: Bridget's; a woman who acquired grey hair and lines over my upbringing, who sat up all night and filled my hot-water bottles, who comforted me when I first got the curse and I thought something terrible was happening, even though she was desperately embarrassed and stuck for words, who let me cry in her arms when I failed an exam or somebody gave me the brush-off, a woman who even now would defend me with her life. You, what have you got, apart from your expensive possessions and your youthful face and your slim figure and a handsome man to walk beside you and the memory of all those brief spasms of pleasure?

Samuel blew out his red cheeks and stuffed his fingers into his mouth. He had two tiny white teeth dependent from his gum and a red sore place where another one was due to appear. He had tugged at the ends of her hair and made noises that might be interpreted as Ma and he had howled and bunched his fists and drawn up his legs in a frenzy of anguish when she left him alone in his pram. She was young and strong and she would overcome her congenital lassitude and if her children managed to get themselves conceived despite caps and barriers and spermicidal creams, then she would be a mother. And a damn good one at that.

121

I I

Somebody had written that if you sat in the Charing Cross Hotel for long enough everyone you'd ever known would pass through its portals. Madeleine didn't really know what her personal equivalent of the Charing Cross Hotel might be; the Students Union, perhaps? It wasn't a particular haunt of hers. In fact she did her best to avoid it, its common room filled with girls waiting for excuses to cease the half-hearted concentration that they were applying to their work, its bars brimming with drunks. Nevertheless it was the focus of undergraduate life and even though he had probably left and was certainly no longer an undergraduate, she spent many afternoons gazing unseeingly at textbooks and breaking off small squares of Cadbury's Fruit and Nut for sustenance. Occasionally she even ventured into a bar and sat for a long time behind a glass of beer, watching the entrance, while idiots stood on tables and poured drink over one another.

'You'll never have a better time in your life,' they said. They said to relish this golden period, of freedom from responsibility and opportunity to benefit from the interaction of like minds, of instant community and membership of an intellectual élite. So she attended folk evenings and voluntary lectures on the subject of Marx as a power theorist and gatherings where one danced to Traditional jazz, she waited for late-night buses and found her voice in tutorials and sat in bedsitters watching the dawn break and yawning and discussing profiteering landlords and Dizzy Gillespie and Kerouac and Zen, nervous breakdowns and the theory of natural selection. And none of it was enough. There were fine minds and beautiful faces and exotic personalities, but he refused to be dislodged from the niche that he occupied in her mind and though she knew, she knew for a fact, that you couldn't fall in love on the basis of a short journey through a night in May and the hazy memory of a face and a regret for what it might have amounted to, she could find no other explanation for her heartsickness.

'I have a feeling that he's still about,' Joanna said. 'Don't ask me why. Perhaps he's giving off energy waves close enough for me to pick them up.' She and Fred had lately extended their interests to include the paranormal, spent evenings testing one another with pieces of card upon which were transcribed rudimentary symbols: circles, squares and the like. Some evenings their success rate was high, statistically significant. Fred said that those occasions coincided with the evenings when he smoked, but the distribution curve that she plotted refuted this assumption. Joanna herself never smoked now. She had been afraid, one evening in the yellow stone house in Avignon when everything had slipped out of control and fear was there, it was pushing at the door and all the stars were needle-sharp and pointed and there was so much air that it could choke you. None of the others could understand it, having experienced only euphoria. One of them described a similar encounter with terror, but that had been an acid trip and, perception be buggered, he'd never try that again.

Next morning she had awoken to the joys of a day-long migraine attack. Fred closed the shutters, bathed her temples and administered her pills and it was then that she decided that never again would she delve into the prohibited list: the benny for the exam, the barb to counteract the benny, the slow weekend joint smoked to a background of joss sticks and Dylan. Her migraine acted as a kind of personal litmus paper; beware of stained glass and lilies, it told her, nicotine and horsehair, and now, a particular variety of cannabis resin. She had faith in her attacks of migraine, they were a mechanism which warned, in no uncertain terms, of substances and situations to be avoided.

Nothing seemed to affect Fred's constitution, neither wind nor weather, nor downers nor uppers. Perhaps institution life toughened you up. In Oxford Street he touted his wares in the grey sleet of a November afternoon, his shirt unbuttoned to the waist. He'd eat anything. Anything. Or not eat at all. Wine made him a little more sentimental, speed more energetic, tranquillizers a little more relaxed. In December he forswore all of them and bought a mandala and spent entire evenings meditating in Joanna's room. Joanna was bored silly. She tried very hard to concentrate, to fill her whole mind with the word and thus alter her consciousness. Fred said that she tried too hard. Eventually she left him to it and sought out Madeleine to whom she delivered her visionary message of cheer.

It was a mistake, obviously, because it rekindled in Madeleine a spark of the hope that she'd abandoned in July, or so she thought. She began once again to pester Joanna about contacting friends of friends for information. Joanna explained that Desmond had no friends, not in the strict sense of the word. 'i.e.,' Joanna said, 'there is no one who shares Desmond's hopes and fears or knowledge of his new address. That I know of. Everybody knows him and nobody knows him, if you understand me. Can't you make a big effort and expunge him? It's been nine months now and it's getting to be an obsession. I'll find you a very nice man,' Joanna said. 'Much nicer than Desmond.' Which wouldn't be difficult. Desmond had been all right, occasionally, infrequently, and in small doses, before it became painfully clear that he was unreliable, emotionally perverse, sexually indiscriminate, intellectually disorganized, and that Desmond's entire thinking tended to revolve around Desmond and related concerns.

Madeleine was with one of Joanna's very nice men when the stars in their courses or the hand of fate or the long arm of coincidence engineered it so that their paths, so diverse for so long, crossed once again.

The very nice young man whose name was Jeremy had taken her to see a French film called *Les Amants*. This film, which displayed a lot of surging flesh in soft focus, aroused in the audience two different types of reaction, either a heavy-breathing sexual excitement, or a tendency to collapse with mirth, whistle and catcall. Madeleine very much feared that Jeremy's response belonged to the first category. His arm was around her shoulders, his hand squeezed rhythmically at the flesh of her upper arm, every so often he raised his other hand from where it lay inert half way up her thigh, twisted her face towards his and thrust his tongue inside her mouth. She thought wearily, during intermissions in this grappling, of films that she'd never seen from start to finish – good films, some of them, *A Taste of Honey*, *Guys and Dolls* – because the Jeremy of the time had decided to use the cinema as other, more fortunate individuals used the front room or the backs of their cars.

Afterwards he took her for a coffee. He was calm again, unaffectionate. In cinemas one behaved in a certain way, in coffee bars in another. She blew foam across her cup and listened while he recounted to her the plot of *La Règle du Jeu* from start to finish. After that, he explained *Last Year at Marienbad* and *Les Quatre Cent Coups*. There was no possibility of discussion; on the subject of the

European cinema she was relatively ignorant because of people like Jeremy who never allowed her to concentrate.

Eventually, after hours it seemed – though a glance at her watch informed her, to her astonishment, that it was only eleven-fifteen, he began to button his jacket, adjust his scarf and talk about the times of the buses. The dead weight of boredom lifted from her head.

The pavements were bright with frost. It was bitterly cold. She hoped to heaven that she would not be expected to participate in another wrestling session outside the hostel, her arm going into cramp, her feet numb. They turned a corner into Tottenham Court Road and walked straight into Desmond.

There was one dreadful moment when she thought that he wasn't going to recognize her, then he said, 'Well, hello. Where have you been hiding yourself?'

She almost said, 'It's rather more a case of where *you've* been hiding *yourself*,' but stopped herself in time. As if she knew or cared!

'We never had that night out, did we?'

He looked so much the same that she couldn't believe it, so identical to the picture in her mind that she'd carried for all these months: his curly mouth, his swarthy complexion, his compact, tightly-muscled body; so entirely beautiful. His eyes moved from her to Jeremy and back again. He might assume that she and the ghastly Jeremy formed some kind of couple, some relationship. She closed her eyes in an agony of humiliation, prayed that he would just disappear, vanish, enter a different dimension. But the ghastly Jeremy remained, moving from foot to foot and banging his gloved hands together.

'Are you still in the same place?' Desmond said. And when she nodded, said, 'I thought everyone escaped from there at the earliest opportunity. How's Mad Joanna? Still trying to rally the proles?'

'She's taken up with a street trader called Fred.'

'Well, naturally. Girls of Joanna's ilk always do. Before they marry solicitors or accountants or stockbrokers.'

She tried, unsuccessfully, to imagine Joanna inhabiting the gin and Jag belt. The pause between them assumed gigantic proportions, punctuated only by the heel-clicking and the slap of leather upon leather that was Jeremy trying to keep warm. She supposed that she ought to be performing introductions but hoped that, by omitting to do so, Desmond would perhaps assume that he was some casual acquaintance with whom she'd had a chance encounter. So much was implicit, so much was self-defined. It would be so simple to say, 'It's lovely to see you. This is Jeremy, a friend of Joanna's.' But she couldn't. She said, 'Well –' and began to make that agonizing turn from him and back towards her companion.

'You don't have a pen, by any chance, do you?' he said. 'Because if you did, I could note down that number that goes through to you direct, couldn't I?'

Of course she had a pen, being a thoroughly organized creature. She also had a piece of card inscribed with her name, address and her blood group, a spare key, a clean handkerchief and a map of the Underground. She handed the pen to him, and he took a pound note from his pocket, balanced it on his knee and wrote the number down the side of it as she recited it to him.

'You'll spend it,' she said, 'on a packet of cigarettes or a pint of beer and then I shall receive phone calls from barmen and tobacconists.'

He gazed at her. 'It *is* a bit unnecessary, isn't it?' he said. 'I'm sorry – it's all this bloody child psychology and teaching practice, it's turning my brain. We could actually arrange a date, couldn't we?'

They could. They did. And he winked at her, turned up his coat collar and continued on his way. He still had her pen. 'I'm frozen stiff,' Jeremy said petulantly. He had condensation on his glasses and his nose had turned blue. When it came to the social graces, women were right down the field. Standing there, talking to that oik Russell, whom he knew of, from a distance – as many people knew of Desmond – and disliked. And now he was expected to trail all the way back to her rotten hostel with her. And all for the sake of a frozen-fingered fumble at the end of it. If he was lucky. And the odds against that were about a hundred to one, if her response in the cinema was anything to go by.

'It's not as cold as all that,' Madeleine said. 'I'm quite warm. Feel me.' But he was too far gone in wounded pride and annoyance to even attempt to misinterpret that remark.

'It's horrible,' Desmond said. 'I cannot convey to you the full horribleness – horribleness? – horror of it. They know that I hate it and I hate them and I don't give a sod whether or not they learn anything or don't learn anything just so long as they sit still and shut up. In my day,' Desmond said gloomily, sipping his beer, 'fourteen-year-old boys did not read *Playboy* quite openly in class, and fourteen-year-old girls did not flaunt their revolting over-developed chests under one's very nose. It's the lousy welfare state, all that free milk and orange juice, it's turning them all into sodding giants. I wish I was back in the days when the working class was a race of runts. There is a certain psychological advantage in being able to look over somebody's head rather than at the second button of his shirt.'

He was talking of the school in which he did his teaching practice, an ex-Victorian slum workhouse staffed by incompetents and housing Amazonian girls and Grade A psychopathic youths. For the first half-hour in the pub he poured out his woes to her while she drank a glass of shandy very slowly indeed because she knew that she quickly became inebriated and, once inebriated, if he suggested anything improper, she might agree to it.

'If you're so antipathetic towards teaching, why on earth did you go in for it in the first place?' she said. She was wearing Beatrice's velvet suit, Lady Muck in the sawdust and spittoon pub to which he'd brought her.

'What else?' He spread his hands in a gesture of helplessness. 'Just tell me – what else?'

'Wasn't the Appointments Board any help?'

'Oh, them! Fantasy land. They sit there with their barmy pieces of paper about the Forestry Commission and community leadership in some Devil's Island New Town and how about becoming a rep for Shellmex or do you fancy teaching maladjusted kids in Nether Wapping or adult illiterates in Sierra Leone? It's a joke. Three years of my life and I'm no nearer knowing what I want to do, let alone getting there, than I was at the beginning.'

'What does your father do?' There was nothing about his appearance, or the cast of his features, or his accent to give you a clue. His father might be a refuse collector or a belted earl.

'Pushes up the daisies. Next door to my mum.'

The colour of her face matched that of Beatrice's suit – a crushed damson shade. She made her apologies. He waved them away. 'He's better off,' he said. 'So's she. He spent thirty years wrecking his lungs in an asbestos factory while she cleaned the houses of his bosses. Almost a feudal arrangement. Heart-rending, isn't it? How about yours?'

'My father's dead. My mother works in a shoe-shop.'

He took a little machine from his pocket and a packet of papers and proceeded to fashion a cigarette. His movements were deft, precise. She could imagine his father, with his ruined lungs, doing the same thing, equally adept. 'I would have put you down as middle-class,' he said, 'like your friend Joanna. I expect, like me, you almost had it educated out of you.'

'Had what educated out of me?'

'Your accent, your dialect, your nasty dirty working-class habits – you know, sleeping in your vest, bathing once a week, your guts.' He tapped the cigarette on the table, applied a match to it. It lit in a shower of sparks. 'Grammar school?'

'Direct grant.'

'Me too. Bleeding neighbourhood prodigy, I was. *Wunderkind.* Till it came to the Oxford Entrance. Did they turn you down too?'

'I never applied.'

'Just as well. They send for you for an interview. You know perfectly well that you've passed their rotten exam, otherwise they wouldn't be interviewing you, and then they ask you about your father's occupation and you tell them and they look at one another. And from then on you know the situation.' He brushed at his jacket. 'Why can everyone but me smoke without covering themselves in ash?'

Her hand had stopped trembling. She raised her glass. 'Don't you think,' she said, 'that your view is a bit jaundiced? Joanna's Fred got in and he spent half his life in Dr Barnardo's. He doesn't even know who his father was.'

'Oh, they have a quota. Token niggers. To counterbalance the cretinous heirs to defunct European dynasties and the retardate issue of Middle-Eastern potentates. It was probably laid down in the 1944 Education Act: so many places for the offspring of the horny-handed sons of toil.'

'This conversation is developing in the same way that all conversations with Joanna tend to develop. You make her a cup of tea and she starts telling you about the iniquitous working conditions of Ceylonese tea pluckers, or whatever they are. If you don't jump in pretty fast with something else you're on to Marx and the falling rate of profit in no time at all.'

'Oh, Joanna,' he said. 'Girls like Joanna give me a pain. All that half-digested polemic and *aux armes, citoyens*. It's the same spirit that led to the Nuremberg rallies. Joanna has a soft heart and so she embraces Communism; Priscilla, or whoever, has a heart of stone and turns into a right little Junior Fascist. Granted that Joanna's vision is moral, she is still a little middle-class girl thumbing her nose at Mummy and Daddy.'

'She wants social justice. Just as you do.'

'You can stuff your social justice. I want revenge. The CP's bursting with paranoiacs. Didn't you know?'

They all knew and cared so very much more than she did. Just staying alive and functioning in a fairly average fashion demanded all her energy. His grey eyes were distant, lost in contemplation of the apocalyptic day when justice would be seen to be done and the souls of all his exploited ancestors, vindicated at last, would rest easy. It must be wonderful to be capable, as Desmond was, of projecting your personal inadequacies upon the system. But perhaps he didn't have any personal inadequacies. Perhaps he was right.

'So you've nobody to bail you out if you make a cock-up of it?' he said, taking little short nervous puffs at his cigarette. You had to do that of course. Otherwise they went out. No saltpetre. You saved on fags but you spent a fortune on matches. 'In thrall to the local authority? Don't let it get you down. From my own bitter experience, I'd advise you to work, though. Otherwise you'll have to go back. And I wouldn't like that at all.'

Oh, wouldn't you? Wouldn't you really? Why? She kept her eyes fixed on her glass. 'I have to work,' she said. 'I'm not Joanna. She seems able to put it down and pick it up at will and still she understands it and remembers it.'

'The road to intellectual sloth,' he said. And told her how he had never acquired the habit of effort simply because, from his earliest childhood, everything had come too easily. 'I had a retentive memory and a fairly quick perception. I never had to exert myself. By the time I got here, the habit of indolence was fixed. Talking of indolence,' he said, passing a hand around the back of his collar, 'do you think I need a haircut? Is it really getting a bit too rabbinical? My landlord called me Shirley Temple this morning. I don't suppose you'd care to have a go at it? Women are supposed to have more of a talent for that sort of thing.'

In his room she wielded an open razor. The skirt of Beatrice's suit was covered with glossy black locks and tendrils. She had to support one hand with the other because it trembled so and she was terrified that she might sever the odd ear. Joanna cut her hair with a Stanley knife. Regularly. Joanna obviously had more of a talent for that sort of thing. 'Oh dear,' she kept saying, 'oh dear, I can't seem to get it level. I don't think you're going to be pleased.'

'Just so long as it's above my collar and I don't lose my strength, I couldn't give a monkey's.'

A grave-faced Delilah, she sawed at every recalcitrant curl until neck was to be seen once more. 'There,' she said dubiously, 'there. I daren't attempt the front. That curls back anyway, so it doesn't matter.' The texture of his hair and the skin beneath it affected her hand like electricity.

'It's marvellous,' he said, taking her word for it. 'Most people, I couldn't trust not to cut my throat.' He pulled his jersey over his head, began to unbutton his shirt. 'You don't mind? You won't faint away with shock? Only I've got offcuts all down my back and they'll itch like hell if I leave 'em.'

She wondered how on earth he could tell. For he was black, from the pit of his throat to the waistband of his trousers, covered, coated, furred with thick black luxuriant hair. Over his chest, under his arms, across his shoulder-blades. Like some sort of shaggy forest creature. Pan. A sign of virility, it was, she had read. The bed in the corner which she couldn't help noticing out of the corner of her eye seemed to increase in size until it dominated the room.

He brushed his hair and his chest, shook his shirt. At this moment, to her horror, the door opened and a face came round the edge of it, a large coal-black shiny face that split open into a grin. 'Sorry, man,' the face said. 'Some other time, eh?'

'What is it, Percy?' Desmond said. 'There's no need to be so coy. I'm getting rid of hairs, you daft bugger, not stripping for action.'

The black face continued to grin. A hand appeared around the door, a hand that clutched a wad of folded pound notes. 'Will you pay the man for me, friend?'

'But of course.' Desmond pocketed the money. And the face disappeared, leaving in its wake the echo of a laugh that made you think of ripe fruit and strong liquor.

'It says something for racial solidarity when Percy prefers to entrust his rent money to me rather than one of his black brethren. What's up?' Desmond said. 'Have I compromised your honour with Percy? He's got a one-track mind. People take their clothes off for one reason only in Percy's experience. I think he sleeps in his.'

He spun out the process of shirt-shaking and jersey-plucking, observing her reaction. He'd put clean sheets on the bed just in case she surprised him as that other hostel girl had done, avid for it, when she'd seemed as prim as you like. There should be a way of telling, a sign that appeared on their foreheads saying 'Go ahead', or 'If you touch me, I'll scream'.

He dressed himself. Her brow cleared. He poured out two glasses of the beer that he'd brought from the pub. 'There's that chair and the bed,' he said, 'for sitting down upon. It's what my landlord laughingly describes as a furnished room.'

She chose the chair. As he had suspected she would. 'It's nicer than your last place,' she said.

'The cockroaches aren't so big. There aren't as many pieces of cheese going mouldy under the floorboards.'

'The proportions of the house are more attractive. I expect that these were once the desirable residences of prosperous businessmen.'

'The skivvies would have been up here, Annie and Fanny and Rose. In their combs. Waiting for Sunday afternoon when they could walk out with their young men. That'd have been us, fifty years ago. You'd have been Fanny, carting in the coal and black-leading the grate and starching your – well, whatever it was they had to starch.'

'And you'd have been my young man.'

'Waiting beside the area steps with a box of chocolates.'

'We'd have gone to the park to listen to the band. And then to a tea-shop.'

And how lovely it would have been, to listen to the German band and eat maids of honour and not have to bother your head about the decent interval of time that ought to elapse before you surrendered your virtue; too soon and he'd think you a tramp, not soon enough and you must be frigid. Lucky Fanny, your combs firmly buttoned, your maidenhead intact until you reached the marriage bed, or at least until you were within hailing distance of it.

'Would I have kissed you?' he said, from the bed.

'No. Not until we'd got to know each other quite well. If you were honourable.'

'What if I was a cad?'

'I wouldn't be walking out with you if you were a cad.'

'You'd know?'

'I think so.' Unless, of course, I fell in love with you almost on first acquaintance. She remembered Joanna's parties and the taste of his skin, the feeling of his hand on her shoulder, her waist, the rhythm of his heartbeat. What was it that had occurred to change a feeling of disquiet into one of longing? It was the same Desmond then who'd pawed her as the one who now sat across the room stroking her with his eyes. Then, she had been so unmemorable as to be part of the furniture. Or he had been so drunk that he couldn't distinguish one face from the next.

He'd been off drink, that kind of drinking, for quite some time and he hadn't had a woman since that bit of trouble. She sat there demurely in her fancy gear, soft pale hair falling around her face. It was a face that incorporated a steady gaze, high colour that came and went and a mouth that could be shaped to your own, and he didn't half fancy her. 'It's a bit unfriendly, isn't it,' he said, 'me over here and you miles over there? We ought to be communicating in semaphore. I won't bite. Honest.'

It was the longest journey that she'd ever taken in her life. But he didn't bite. He just took off her jacket because he said it was too nice to get crumpled and put his arms around her and his mouth over hers and began to kiss her. And she stopped giving a damn whether he might think she was cheap, even when he unbuttoned her blouse and put his hand there, and gave herself up wholly to sensation. The only worry she had, as his hands moved around her, unzipping and opening, was the fact of that door, unlocked as it obviously was. How many more black faces could be expected to appear, grin, and disappear? She wanted to remind him of this omission, but was afraid that he'd interpret it as an invitation to further intimacies. And, as time went on, there were really only a very few further intimacies left for them. Logically. That she knew of.

All masculine bodies were alien and formidable. Except for his. His seemed so familiar, so unfrightening, so – unfamiliar word – so desirable. And all the cringings and the squirmings and the ideas she'd had of knives and operations vanished from her mind as his hands found places in her that she'd never known about and their tongues entwined and she stroked his hair and his chest and the tender nape of his neck.

He had never, in his entire sexual experience, refused any compliant woman, never drawn back, before it was too late, to consider. He had always continued doggedly, even with the ones that weren't so compliant, until the please no's turned into yeses. He'd felt affection, fondness and various degrees of desire towards a number of girls. He'd not made any of them pregnant nor led them to believe that there was a chance of him falling in love with them. At school, some of his friends had mooned over girls, written poetry, waited for hours on street corners for the sake of a glimpse of the beloved. It was an emotion quite alien to him; he took nice girls to the pictures in the hope of a bit of intelligent conversation afterwards, and for relief of sexual tension he sought out the town bike. Love was that which you felt for your parents who had made sacrifices for your sake, and that love included hostility, resentment and bitterness. It was far too complex an emotion to be applied to some seventeen-year-old nymphet without an inkling of the ways of the world.

She came, rapidly and tumultuously, in response to his practised hand, her head buried in his shoulder. He stroked her hair, moved her gently away from him, tried to compose himself. Never before had he felt – kind of responsible. He couldn't make it out at all. With the blood beating in his temples and no resistance offered, he'd begun to think that she wouldn't know what a painful business it could be – well, she might know, but only theoretically – and what right had he to take his own pleasure from her discomfort, and how trusting she was and how, in a peculiar way, he wanted their closeness to continue rather than be chopped off short by the expiry of his lust. He drew down her skirt and fastened up her blouse. 'Come on,' he said, 'let's get you back before it's too late.' Christ, he thought, what's this now? She wants to and I want to, and instead of making us both happy, I'm going out in a hell of a state into a bitterly cold night to travel miles across London. And then I suppose I'll kiss her and ask if I can see her again. I must be raving mad. As if I don't have enough to contend with: poverty and uncongenial work and bone idleness, without being lumbered with *concern*.

12

And then, for Madeleine: the days transformed. Contracted. Until they contained only him and his face in her dreams as it was in reality; no condensation, sublimation or symbolic distortion – his image was too powerful, too persuasive to bow to any psychic alteration; it blotted out entirely the pale landscape of the rest of her life. Her virginity surrendered with the merest gasp, her letters unwritten, her textbooks open around her as she closed her eyes to recall the texture and scent of his skin. And lectures that passed in a blur as she strove to reconstruct their meetings, every unit of time, every touch, every inflection of tone and gradation of gesture. He was what life had had in store for her, the reason why she hadn't died with the others.

'Love's young dream,' Joanna said. 'Ah, sweet mystery of life at last I've found you. That first fine careless rapture – You make me want to throw up.'

'You're jealous.'

'I am not jealous. Just nauseated. Look, Madeleine – he's an affectionless loner. Women are for penetrating and borrowing from. He'll use you, he'll tire of you and he'll drop you. That's what he does. He wouldn't recognize an ongoing caring relationship if it introduced itself to him. And then there's his drinking.'

'His drinking?' Joanna was a fine one to talk.

'There's drinking and drinking. Oh, I know, we've all said, "Never again" through endless mornings-after, but it's more than that with him. I've seen him pissed out of his mind for days on end. He's half way to alcoholism if you ask me.'

'I'm not asking you. He doesn't drink much any more.'

'All right, Madeleine – he's quite intelligent, he can be amusing, I'd invite him to any party. But I wouldn't even *contemplate* a relationship with him. And neither should you. You're just not in his league.'

'You're jealous. When is Fred leaving?'

'In a month.'

Overland to India. The Golden Road to Samarkand. He would send her postcards en route and in the summer he would send her enough money for her to join him, wherever he might be by that time. He was determined upon it. 'You could chuck it all and join me,' he'd said, 'but I wouldn't if I were you.'

'Why can't you wait? It's only a year and a bit. It'll still be there.'

'I might not be. There are times for doing things. And the time for this is now. What are you getting into such a sweat about? You've not started to want me to give you a roof over your head and a couple of kids, have you?'

'Of course not.' The very idea made her go cold.

'Well, then. Don't try to put fetters on me.'

'Surely it's a pretty natural reaction, me not wanting you to go?'

'Nothing natural about it. Conditioning, that's all it is. There's no divine law I know of that states that a man and a woman must be manacled to one another.'

'I'll miss you.' She nestled close to him, uncovered. She no longer cared about her knobbly vertebrae.

'I'll miss you. But we'll get over it.'

'I'll suffer from sexual deprivation.'

'Well, you know what to do about that.'

Coaxing, rational appeal, emotional blackmail, none of them had any effect. His mind was made up. She saw him, fornicating cheerfully across Europe. Perhaps children brought up in institutions were incapable, in later life, of devoting themselves to a single emotional relationship. In her room the mandala and the ESP cards had given way to maps. She knew the terrain he would traverse almost by heart: the green fertile plateaux, the beige-coloured mountain ranges, the red areas of dense population and the white uninhabited spaces. He expected her to share his enthusiasm, said, 'What I first fancied about you, Joanna, was your sensible attitude. No female shit. You wouldn't try to turn me into something I could never be.'

She derived little consolation from that thought. And Madeleine besotted, Madeleine smitten, Madeleine climbing in over the hostel wall at three a.m. just like everyone else, was salt in the wound. Besides, she felt responsible; it was she who had drawn the two of them together in the first place. But that had been when she lacked information.

'Why?' Madeleine said, on the way to Joanna's room to borrow a book. It was Madeleine now who requested 'a quick shufti at your essay, a glance at your notes; I should have done it last night but I didn't.' 'What *is* it? You used to get on together.'

'I just happen to think that he's a bit of a bastard. Obviously he doesn't agree.'

'But what is this opinion based on? *Why* do you think that?'

'Where the hell did I put my key?' Joanna searched her pockets, produced half a packet of biscuits, her cheque-book, several CND leaflets, a ticket admitting one person to the public baths – and, eventually, the key. She had almost decided to keep quiet about her discovery. But perhaps half the trouble in the world was caused by people keeping quiet when they ought to speak up. 'You remember him telling you that he'd once known a girl who'd occupied your room?' Madeleine nodded. She'd made discreet enquiries about that girl but even the longest-standing residents knew only that she'd left half way through her second year, dropped out, they supposed. Joanna said, 'She's dead. She committed suicide.'

Raindrops slid down the landing window. What little light there was filtered through that window which was set with squares of coloured glass, ugly colours: chartreuse yellow, vomit green. 'How do you know this?' Madeleine said.

Joanna wasn't sure whether or not she regretted her impulse. Perhaps half the world's trouble was caused by people opening their big mouths when they ought to have bitten their tongues. 'Fred and I went to this lecture about Oriental religions. You remember? Just before he got into Zen? We stayed afterwards to talk. There was a chap there who reminded me of Desmond. I said to Fred, "Isn't he the spitting image of Desmond?" and this girl who was sitting next to me said, "Do you mean Desmond Russell?" and I said yes, that Desmond Russell was going out with a friend of mine, and she said, "Oh, I know Desmond Russell – "'

'Oh, get to the point.'

Joanna, who had been pursuing the most circuitous route available to the point, said, 'She was a friend of that girl. Polly. It seems that Desmond dropped Polly like a hot brick after having had his wicked way with her for some months, and Polly went home and did herself in.'

It was perfectly quiet. The friendless and mournful Cypriot, after an unsuccessful attempt at hanging himself from the central light fitment, had been carted away. Joanna, remorseful, had visited him once, carrying an armful of back numbers of *Punch* that she'd purloined from the library. He was too polite to tell her that he couldn't read English.

Madeleine moistened her lips, said, 'Does he know about it?'

'Don't think so. This girl only knew because she happened to come from the same place as Polly. It was kept as quiet as possible. Accidental death and so forth.'

Two minutes ago, Madeleine thought, I didn't know about this. 'How?' she said.

'Drowned herself in a river. Or fell into a river. They put it about that she'd returned home because of ill health, gone for a walk and lost her footing. But this girl said that she was in a terrible state.'

'And he never knew?'

'Why should he have known? He'd severed all connections with her. And they don't exactly stick it on notice boards when one of our number cracks up, do they?'

'But it would have been in the papers. Surely?'

'The local papers. Probably. She was Scottish. Do you often take the *Glasgow Herald* or the *Highland Gazette* or whatever?' Joanna said, 'To be fair, I ought to point out that this Polly was known to be emotionally unstable long before Desmond chanced upon the scene, that as far as her work was concerned she was up the creek without a paddle and she was always prone to Ophelia-like poses. I'm not saying that Desmond was responsible for her suicide –'

'What are you saying? Exactly?'

'I'm saying that, according to this girl, for the period of their affair, Polly and Desmond were inseparable, wildly in love, gave off a bleedin' mutual glow – however you care to describe it – and then suddenly, and for no apparent reason, he packed her in. Without apology or explanation or kiss my arse. I am saying that it seems to me that we are watching a re-run, that the Desmond who pines for your presence is, in the not-too-distant future, just as likely to say ta-ta, change his address and abandon you for ever. And,' Joanna said, 'I don't much care for people who behave like that.'

She unlocked the door. Her room was furnished with the usual amenities and two hideous plaster statuettes that occupied pride of place at either end of the mantelpiece: epicene figures, swathed in drapery, their vacant eye sockets staring heavenwards; Prometheus and Epimetheus, Joanna had christened them, and added moustaches. She was a long time growing out of that habit.

'I just thought that you ought to be forewarned,' she said, fiddling with the appropriate figure, 'in case he dumps you as he's dumped your predecessors. That Polly – she thought they were going to be married.'

Human beings, of course, alter according to their experiences; she'd argued that point of view through many a rosy-fingered dawn. But deep inside her, beneath her carefully-constructed convictions, was a lurking belief about leopards and the intransigent arrangement of their spots.

'You've not had much experience,' she said. 'Box clever. Don't jump in there with both feet until you're entirely convinced.'

From the look on Madeleine's face, she knew that this advice had been delivered far too long after the event.

Fred wasn't another Desmond. He might be quixotic and opinionated and much too self-sufficient, but he kept his word. Postcards arrived. At irregular intervals. From France, from Spain, from Italy, Greece and Turkey. They were rarely inscribed with more than single-sentence greetings, but from them she was able to deduce that he wasn't keeping to his proposed route. He'd reach a certain place, meet up with a gang of people and be sidetracked: a stamp from Florence postdated one from Ankara. Occasionally he sent a photograph. Always he was in a group surrounded by bearded men and braided girls. He looked darker and shaggier and more remote on each succeeding photograph.

At first she'd watched for the postman. She'd pondered over the terse messages: heat stroke here, dysentery there, 'me, Mabel (an American girl), Tad and Jonathon in the soukh.' He would get it out of his system. Perhaps he would come home, put on a collar and tie and take out a mortgage. But postman-watching was a fruitless activity when his progress was so erratic, his correspondence so irregular. Sometimes there was nothing for three weeks and then two postcards would fall on to the mat at once. From Europe into Africa and back into Europe. She saved the stamps for Beatrice's Matthew.

By the time the money arrived and the address – he hadn't made it as far as India after all, he was back in Greece – she could no longer assemble his face in her memory. The money had arrived after a letter of authorization to his bank in England. Naïvely she'd imagined him sending over bundles of drachmas or whatever the hell they used over there. There was sufficient for her to travel by boat and train in comparative comfort along the route he'd organized for her. There would be people looking out for her at various stations along the way – he'd organized that too; Mabel, she supposed, and Tad and Jonathon, welcoming smiles pasted across their brown faces, full of tales to recount while she changed platforms or traversed cities.

She doubted whether she'd ever meet anyone whom she'd admire so much. Her fondness for Fred, or its memory, would remain with her all her life. But Fred was fleeing. He thought he was travelling *to* somewhere, but what he was doing actually was fleeing *away* from somewhere else, from a place where there was work to be done, responsibility to be accepted. The collective good was greater than the individual search for fulfilment. What if everyone swanned off to the mysterious East in their sandals?

She returned the cheque to Barclay's Bank and she wrote a letter to Fred. She said that she hoped that they would never lose touch, that she would ever be grateful for the function he'd performed in opening her eyes to areas of knowledge that she might not have sought to explore otherwise. And that summer in France had been idyllic. But. Her nature was not contemplative. She couldn't just sit around waiting for enlightenment. She wasn't all that bothered about the sound made by one hand clapping or how you got a goose out of a bottle without breaking the bottle or harming the goose. Not when there were racketeer landlords and asset-strippers and a deliberately divisive educational policy and female laundry workers earning four pounds ten a week.

She wrote at such length that she had to pay excess postage. That night, after her soup-serving stint at a hostel for the homeless, she went on to a party and there she met a young registrar with symmetrical creases down the front of his trousers and a way of raising his eyebrows that had her spluttering and gibbering with indignation while he took apart each of the concepts upon which she'd based her ideology and exposed them to the light with the same sort of precision as he no doubt wielded his scalpel.

'Joanna's staying in London. She has a new chap and a holiday job and in the evenings she rehabilitates meths drinkers.'

'But I'll be seeing you?'

'Yes, I'm coming home. For a while, at any rate.'

The kiosk was stuffy and blue with the previous occupant's cigarette smoke. Madeleine opened the door a fraction but was immediately assaulted by the post-prandial clamour issuing from the common room so had to close it again. Seats should be provided in telephone boxes. Beatrice was ringing from her parents' home and could therefore be expected to talk for hours.

'He looks like my father,' Beatrice said. 'You'll say how can a new-born baby look like a middle-aged man but, really, he does. He's blond and he already has that "Be warned, I'm in a lousy mood" expression off to a T. Sam can't make him out at all. He hides his face whenever he sees him. Do you think that's a sign of incipient sibling rivalry?'

'Don't you read Dr Spock?'

'Absolutely not. I'm all in favour of recipe books for cakes, but not for babies. I have Bridget's old wives' tales instead – spaces between the teeth being lucky, and witches' marks, and not sleeping in the full moon's glare – they might not be testable hypotheses but they're a lot more fun. I thought Joanna was following the opium trail this summer. What happened?'

'She had doubts about Fred's social conscience, I think. I don't see her all that often and when I do we spend the entire time doing tests to discover our verbal, spatial and numerical abilities.'

'How do you come out of them?'

'*I* come out of them very well. Joanna's results would seem to suggest that she's severely sub-normal, if not a downright imbecile.'

'Perhaps we could use them as a basis for appeal to the examination board. Perhaps they'll give me the State Scholarship and tell Joanna that she might just as well get married and populate the earth.'

It's still with her, Madeleine thought. She still minds about it. And as the years go by she'll probably mind about it more. She said, 'Should you be up and about so soon?'

'I might as well recline downstairs as recline upstairs or, better still, I might as well recline here. I don't *do* anything. Just read my way through *Vogues* and *Tatlers* and watch Ma filing her nails and consulting with interior decorators and berating the half-wit. *You* like Felix, don't you? Say you do. David moans on about it sounding poofy. This interior decorator's a poof. He has *the* most gorgeous hairstyle and those lovely long-fingered sensitive hands. Ma's trying to dazzle him; I don't think the penny's dropped yet. You'd think, wouldn't you, with all her experience she'd be a pretty good judge of degrees of masculinity? Well, *do* you like it? *He* says that when he gets older – Felix, that is – he won't thank me for it. I think the least you can do is to give someone a nice name.'

'I think it's a lovely name. I hope it's significant.'

'Oh, so do I. Imagine starting life saddled with Dolores. Or Perdita.'

Desmond tapped on the glass, made gestures of impatience. Madeleine halted Beatrice in full spate: Felix's birth weight, regularity of feature, Samuel's extensive vocabulary – 'I have to go. I'll see you next week.'

'Oh. Why? We could have chatted for ages. And all for free. She's too involved in making big decisions about sanded floors and lowered ceilings and silk wallpaper to notice. David's put a box beside ours. He says he's going to fix up one of those devices which mean that you have to pay before you can use it, if I don't exert a measure of self-control. I can see David developing into one of those old persons whose lives are ruled by the making of economies.'

Desmond pointed to the clock, mouthed exhortations for her to hurry up. 'I'm sorry, I really have to go,' said Madeleine.

'Oh, all right. Misery. One day *you'll* be becalmed in domesticity and you'll long for somebody to have a long conversation with . . .'

'Christ,' Desmond said, 'she does go on, doesn't she? Is she like that in the flesh? If so, you're not getting me round there. Can't abide women who can't give their jaws a rest. I thought Joanna held the world record for that: the ability to rabbit for hours without saying anything.'

If only one could so arrange it that one's friends found each other congenial. 'How did you get on?' she said. He'd just returned from a job interview.

He dug a dog-end out of his pocket, struck a match on his shoe. 'I didn't. It never happened. One look at the place was enough. It reminded me of a penal institution. The smashing of empty milk bottles seemed to be the major recreational activity.'

'But perhaps if you'd actually gone in – '

He squeezed her elbow. 'Don't nag, there's a love. If it's to be my career, then I can at least make sure I start off in some place that looks vaguely as though it might have been established for the pursuit of learning rather than the correction of offenders. I'm a bit particular about the type of swine I cast my pearls before. There's bound to be something better. There couldn't be anything worse. We'll have another gander through the TES later on. OK?'

OK. He'd had three interviews already and all of them had been disastrous. Either the headmaster was the original authoritarian personality, or the chief education officer was fifty years behind the times, or he was expected to teach some subject that bore no relation to his specialization. One of the advertisements he'd answered was for the post of an assistant master in a (very) minor public school: 'The proprietor, headmaster, whatever he called himself, had jam roly-poly on his lapel,' Desmond said, 'and asked me if I thought I'd fit in. I said probably not in view of the notoriously low academic standards of the establishment.' She pointed out to him that such responses were hardly likely to endear him to those upon whom his future prospects depended. He knew it; there was just no way he could hold his tongue when he felt that he was being patronized.

'Don't worry. Something more suitable will turn up. It's bound to do. I'll leave those other places for Joanna and her crusading zeal.'

'Joanna won't teach. She hasn't the patience. Rabble-rousing, yes; the inculcation of knowledge, no.'

He ground the cigarette end out on the immaculate parquet floor. 'What's the point of it, anyway? What benefit have you derived from your education? Were you ever taught to think, to relate your work to reality, to draw your bits of knowledge together into a whole? No, of course you weren't. You were taught to supply correct answers and work the system. Any thinking you might have done was due to your own private personality and determination. And I'm expected to go into one of those places and bang facts into kids' heads as though they were empty pitchers and hope to Christ that they've memories sufficiently retentive so they can spew them all out again in something like the right order at exam time. Because good exam results will reflect favourably upon *me*, enhance my career. Education! It's a contradiction in terms.'

Girls, on their way to the library or the television room, paused and turned their heads to look at him. 'Let's get out of here,' he said. 'Lots of women together – they smell, haven't you noticed?'

She bought some eggs at the corner shop because once they got inside his room they'd go to bed and they wouldn't leave it until the pangs of hunger drove them out again. She'd make omelettes on his gas ring – that would save the bother of getting dressed. If anyone had told her this time last year that twelve months hence she would be sexually in thrall to him, she'd have laughed in their faces (well, no, she wouldn't have done that; she'd have blushed and changed the subject). Emotionally in thrall, yes, certainly, she'd known that was on the cards. But she'd never suspected that you could fall in love with someone's body, that physical proximity could make you ache with desire and that you'd spend the greater part of your time hurrying bedwards. The extent of her sexual dependency was awe-inspiring, frightening even. Beatrice had compared it with learning to swim and Joanna had mentioned pain and discomfort; neither of them had said that it could take over your life to the point of obsession. Perhaps it hadn't. For them.

Hand in hand they walked the dry dusty streets to the oasis of his room. The eggs had been placed carefully in a carrier bag, above the shirts she'd laundered for him. 'Concubine *and* washerwoman?' Joanna had said, her lip curled upwards. But she derived great pleasure from washing his clothes. She'd press them to her face, inhaling the odour of him, feeling against the smooth plane of her cheek the little rough curly hairs that he shed continually and which adhered to his shirts and his sheets and his pillowcases. She would have performed any service for him, however distasteful, quite gladly.

'What would you really like to do, Desmond? If you had a completely free choice of career.' The sole of his shoe was parting from its upper; she must remember to take it to the mender's.

He thought for a bit and then he said, 'Playboy.'

'Yes, but seriously.'

'I am serious. I can't think of anything I'm desperately interested in. And most jobs are monotonous some of the time, aren't they? Apart from perhaps parachute-jumping or being a front-line war correspondent. And I'd be too scared for that.'

'What did you most enjoy doing as a child?'

'What is this? Vocational guidance? Let me think: I used to enjoy winning prizes, so long as it didn't involve much effort –

and it never did. I used to enjoy – imagining how famous and celebrated I was destined to become – a famous and celebrated *what*, I couldn't have told you. I enjoy making love to you, and sleeping, and getting pleasantly tight. I *used* to enjoy shutting the door and being on my own.'

'You *must* meet Beatrice. Those are exactly the kind of things that she used to enjoy. Before she discovered her true vocation.'

They fed each other with pieces of omelette, mopping up the odd spillages from the sheets. The sheets were always clean now; she took them to the launderette every Friday evening. He said, 'We won't be able to do this next week, will we?'

Oh no. Most definitely not. Her mother would send for the priest. Her mother would send for the Pope, if she thought that her daughter was having carnal knowledge of a man.

'In that case,' he said, 'we won't stay very long. And when we get back, you'll go to that clinic place Joanna told you of, won't you? Because this is costing me a fortune. God won't strike you dead. You never go to Confession any more, anyway. And *don't* start on about safe times. That's just a wicked rumour put about by the church in order to swell the Catholic population. From what I can gather, we could make love without holding our breath for about five minutes every month – always providing we keep our fingers crossed and don't spill any salt. I'm not playing Vatican roulette. Not even for you.'

She put the empty plate on the floor and curled herself into the curves of his body. His shoulder was warm and tasted salty. She would screw up her courage and do as he asked. She was not nearly so shy and self-conscious these days anyway. The only area in which her confidence was as lacking as ever it had been was the home area. She wondered how her mother would react to him. Her mother didn't know he was coming. Her mother didn't know of his existence. She relied upon the element of surprise to prevent any active hostility, any explicit statement of displeasure.

He put out his cigarette and began to devote himself in earnest to what he'd been doing lazily and absent-mindedly during their conversation. She closed her eyes while her body flowed beneath his hands and his questing tongue. Oh, this was better than getting a term of straight A's, better than receiving the complete works of Tennyson and the second-best prize. Her exam results had been disappointing. She didn't care at all. Every moment out of bed was a moment wasted. He raised his head. He said, 'Will she like me, do you think?'

She looked down at his beautiful face, his unique, irreplaceable face. How could she fail to like him? How could anybody?

She was altogether too disconcerted to know whether she liked him or not. She went into the kitchen and she collected together another knife and fork, another cup and saucer and buttered herself a slice of bread because there were only two chops.

It had been foolish of her to imagine that there wouldn't be somebody, sooner or later. She'd fallen in love herself and married. The war had intervened, demanded his life, before she really needed to face the realization that she'd made an unwise choice. He'd died a hero; if he'd lived he'd have been a failure. She'd hoped that Madeleine would have the sense to postpone any emotional entanglements until such time as she had her future certain. For Madeleine, after she'd gained a good degree and a good job, she'd had a dream of a certain sort of man: a man of means and position, an older man perhaps who would treat her as he treated one of his precious possessions. This young man didn't give you the impression that he possessed anything, let alone anything precious.

She lit the gas under the kettle, held her breath until the pain had gone away. She chewed the tablets now instead of eating. She had lost weight, from her arms and her legs, her face and her hips, everywhere, in fact, apart from her stomach which seemed permanently distended. She'd had to let out the waistbands on all her skirts. 'Come back,' Dr McCloud had said, 'if there's no sign of improvement and we'll send you for an investigation.' She hadn't been back, except for repeat prescriptions of the tablets. She knew what an investigation meant, it meant the knife. And it was almost as if the knife conjured the disease into being, or if not that, encouraged a dormant malignancy to activate itself and multiply. The discomfort was bearable, even the pain was bearable. Every night she prayed to St Anthony, asking him to keep her alive until Madeleine had someone else to look after her.

'How long will you stay?' she asked, not wanting to hear the answer, not wanting to betray to them how her whole life was geared to these three breaks in the academic year.

'About a fortnight,' Madeleine said, studied the tablecloth. In London, guilt could be suppressed; here, it was inescapable. Her mother, under those odd loose garments she was wearing, seemed unusually thin. 'We both need jobs,' she said. 'And there's not much prospect round here.'

'They were advertising for pea-pickers in the paper on Saturday. Thoroughgood's have vacancies for temporary staff. And they need a car park attendant and a lifeguard for the swimming pool. And leaflet-deliverers. They're crying out for leaflet-deliverers.' She looked from one to the other of them. They were silent. They wanted the anonymity of a single room in a big city. They were lovers. They hadn't touched one another, they'd hardly looked at one another, but she knew. You couldn't devote yourself obsessively to a daughter for twenty years and not know. She wouldn't say anything. She daren't say anything. But if this Desmond were to cause Madeleine a moment's pain, she'd seek him out and set fire to him.

She made him a bed up on the sofa. She wouldn't sleep tonight. She'd strain her ears and if she heard the slightest hint of nocturnal wanderings she'd be out of bed in a flash. He might be taking her in London but he certainly wasn't going to take her here. Even as she was fitting a cushion into a pillowcase she knew that such precautions were redundant. They were out, an evening stroll around the town they'd said. They'd find themselves a quiet place – a hedgerow, a shelter in the park – and they'd do it there. She tried to arrange her feelings into some semblance of order. Children might find the idea of sexual activity between their parents disturbing; it was nothing to the way parents felt when their children demonstrated the fact that they were no longer ignorant in that sphere. Somehow one always felt (hoped?) that one's children would have more sense than to enter voluntarily that gate that led to so much pain and regret and wasted hours. Mrs McCloud, encountered briefly one Saturday afternoon in the supermarket – she was in a tearing rush, as usual, picking foodstuffs seemingly at random from the shelves and throwing them into her trolley – had said, in connection with Joanna's absence from home, 'They're grown women now with lives of their own – sexual and emotional. We mustn't interfere. Just hope to God they remember to take precautions. Goodbye,' Joanna's mother had said and left Mrs Brennan standing open-mouthed beside the cooked meats. Of course Joanna's mother had no religion.

And neither had Desmond. At that moment she was very glad.

Heathens were less likely to rely on the goodwill of God in the matter of preventing conception. She knew from her own experience that one minute devoted to precautionary measures was worth two dozen prayers to St Anthony.

13

'I must be getting old,' Bridget said. She hung the tea-towel on its hook behind the kitchen door, bent and rubbed her knees. 'My legs never used to ache like this. I got these elastic stockings but they don't make any difference. I suppose elastic stockings can't turn the clock back.'

'Oh Bridget, don't *moan*. Nobody asks you to slave your guts out the way you do.' But you don't actually prevent her from slaving, do you? said the voice of Beatrice's conscience. She lifted Samuel into his high chair. He protested vigorously. He hated to be confined. When she put him in his playpen in the garden he'd manoeuvre it by dint of pushing with his hands and shoving with his bottom until he was near enough to shout at her through the kitchen door. 'Perhaps it's your age,' Beatrice said. 'Doesn't the change of life have those sort of weird effects?'

'The change of life! I waved that goodbye long since.'

'Did you? How long since?'

'So long since that I can't remember,' Bridget said and formed her lips into a straight line. There were topics that Bridget refused to discuss. Except with persons of her own age and sensible attitude and even then only in veiled allusions and hints that seethed with unspoken meaning. She unfastened her apron. 'Well, everything's ready for your guests. I'd defy anybody to find a speck of dirt in this house.'

'They're hardly likely to be looking for dirt. From Joanna's account, it seems that they're too besotted with one another to notice anything. Can you imagine? Madeleine!' Samuel sucked greedily at the spout of his milk mug, interspersed his sucking with a tuneless crooning about ducks and water.

Bridget jammed her hat on to her head. 'Why ever not Madeleine?

She's as much right to fall in love as the next.'

'It's just that she was always so prim and restrained. I simply can't visualize her all rumpled with passion.'

'I said fall in love. We don't all have to go to those lengths.' Bridget buttoned up her macintosh, checked to see that the baby's feeds were all made up until tomorrow. 'Right then. I'll love you and leave you.'

Beatrice dropped blobs of strawberry jam into Samuel's semolina pudding. He stirred it furiously. 'Not eat?' he said hopefully. It was too pretty to eat. 'Yes, eat.' She guided the spoon to his mouth, waited until he decided to open it. 'Bridget,' she said, 'you will look after yourself? You'll take it easy when you're feeling tired?'

Anxiety was not an expression that Bridget was accustomed to seeing on Beatrice's face. She collected her shopping bag and spectacles with brisk gestures. 'Oh, I need a good moan from time to time just like everyone else. I'll not give in to it, old age and weariness, you needn't fret about that.'

She didn't slow her pace until she was out of sight of the house. Sometimes her ankles swelled and her legs gave her gyp. It was funny how, if you'd always been fit and active, you couldn't accept a decline in your body's efficiency, a diminution of your strength. Slow down, your body was saying, via those aching legs and swollen ankles. Well, she simply couldn't do that. She'd taken her usual two weeks in Scarborough with Cousin Molly and they'd done nothing more energetic than stroll slowly along the promenade of an evening and sit in deckchairs, and at the end of the first week she'd been bored stiff, would have welcomed a few floors to scrub. Work was her métier and although work was perhaps now a little too demanding, what with two babies at one end of town and Helena at the other – prone these days to successive nervous headaches, prone also to spur-of-the-moment dinner-parties for which she would create complicated and exotic dishes and for which Bridget would have to start peeling and blanching and dicing and puréeing and washing up while Madame performed all the fancy stuff – still it was preferable to twiddling her thumbs in a boarding-house or joining the rest of the lone people, the spare people, on a bench in the park or a table in the tea-rooms.

Alderman Pitcher had provided a seat for the bus stop. God bless Alderman Pitcher. Her eyelids dropped like shutters and she allowed herself to doze. The noise of the bus, grinding gears up the

148

hill, would wake her. 'Not a pretty sight,' Desmond said to Madeleine as they passed by on the opposite side of the road. 'My mum used to tell me to close my mouth and stop catching flies.'

Madeleine shaded her eyes. 'It's Beatrice's Bridget. She used to say that too. Or else, "Your face is enough to stop a clock."'

'Who on earth is Beatrice's Bridget?'

Madeleine considered. 'I suppose you'd say that she was once her nanny, or a kind of housekeeper. She more or less brought Beatrice up.'

'Oh Christ, old retainers yet. Who is this posh cow you're dragging me to meet? Will we have finger bowls and port passed from the left? I shall embarrass you by asking for the toilet and saying, "Pardon my glove."'

Consequently, until he was introduced, he assumed that the very beautiful girl in the food-stained smock and the dilapidated sandals who opened the door to them was the au pair or someone. He'd never seen such a beautiful girl except on the covers of magazines or still photographs from Hollywood films. Never in the flesh. When he was six years old in school and they asked him to draw a princess, Beatrice's face was the one he tried to draw and never succeeded because his artistic talent was nil. Not pink cheeks and bright blue eyes and long flowing golden tresses; he tried to create a woman in his own image: a dark woman with thick dark silky hair and a perfectly oval face and a straight nose and just the right amount of chin and lips that complemented one another in shape and curvature and eyebrows that arched without resort to artifice and great big wide-apart eyes thickly fringed. Miss Macdonald would look over his shoulder at his daub and say, 'Very nice, Desmond, but we don't really have mud-coloured faces, do we?' and afterwards he'd tear it up because the shade he'd been aiming at – somewhere between pink and white and mud – obviously didn't occur in the Reeves Number One paint-box.

Beatrice's skin was that long-ago-sought-after-and-never-achieved colour: a kind of opaque beige with maybe just a hint of carmine above the cheekbone. Or was it rose madder? Or even Indian red? He couldn't remember. He knew only that she approximated exactly to that childhood vision. He'd always believed that the fantasies one created were precisely that: fantastic, over and above anything that might occur in reality. To come face to face with one of them was a disconcerting experience.

149

'You'll permit me to boast and drool a *bit*?' Beatrice said. 'And then I'll shut up and you can discuss with me whatever it is intelligent people these days who are *au courant* do discuss.' She led them into a room where one male child was throwing plastic bricks over the top bar of a kind of wooden cage set in the middle of the floor and another slept in a carry-cot on the sofa, one fist tucked beneath his cheek. 'Dr McCloud called this morning and I said, "Isn't Felix the most beautiful baby you ever saw?" and he said, "My dear girl, if you'd hauled out as many as I have over the years, you'd understand that each one looks the same as the next and the one that went before." But really, it isn't just blind prejudice, is it? He is rather remarkable?' She lifted the larger child out of his wooden prison. 'Come on, Sam, you can have your liberty now that I can keep an eye on you,' she said and set him down on the carpet. He staggered, bandy-legged, his thighs separated one from the other by a great swathe of napkin, until he reached Madeleine's feet whereupon he fell on to his bottom and proceeded to tug at the buckle of her shoe. She slipped her foot out of it and relinquished it to him. Beatrice said, 'Don't do that, he'll chew it. We buy him all these fantastic toys that are meant to stimulate his creativity and he prefers old shoes and tin lids and empty detergent packets. I'm not worried about the effect of your shoe on him, I'm worried about the effect of him on your shoe. Here, Sam!' She coaxed his attention with a rubber duck that made an appalling noise when squeezed. He looked from one to the other and then made a grab for both of them. 'No, Sam. One thing at a time. That way you get the maximum of enjoyment. Don't you?'

Desmond, who had experienced some of his most pleasurable moments when having his cake and eating it, didn't agree with that particular precept, but he couldn't take his eyes off her. Admiring Sam's precocity and Felix's pulchritude, his gaze would slide Beatrice-wards, as if magnetically attracted. It was no love at first sight that he was experiencing, no *coup de foudre* – she was an ideal figure and you didn't entertain emotions of that nature in connection with ideal figures; it was more akin to goddess worship. For the first time since his voice broke he felt tongue-tied in the presence of a woman. His feeble conversational contributions went unnoticed, however, in the flow of her unceasing chatter. She went on just as she had gone on on the telephone. Either she was naturally loquacious or else she had been starved of congenial company for too long.

They made obeisance at the carry-cot. Madeleine was struck by the resemblance between the child and his grandfather and remembered, with a kind of fond and vague amusement, how her ideal of manhood had once been Robert Martin. Desmond's babies would be dark, they would wriggle and squirm and howl till they were purple in the face. She observed his reaction to Beatrice's children, was pleased to note that there was none of the drawing back, the fear, that had been so painfully evident in Joanna. At one point he lifted Sam on to his shoulders and carried him around the room. Sam squawked with delight and Beatrice fell silent and thought, David never does anything like that, not spontaneously like that. Of course, David is older, David has a responsible job and is tired when he gets home in the evenings, for David, it's the third time around and, naturally, enthusiasm is bound to wane somewhat.

'You will stay to dinner, won't you?'

They looked at one another. While the weather was fine, they had planned on taking a bus to the outskirts of the town and finding themselves an abandoned barn or a dry ditch, any place away from puritanical parents. 'Oh please!' Beatrice said. 'It's not often that I see you, and there's a very fancy thing in the oven that Bridget has sweated over for hours, and David's looking forward to it, and I want to hear absolutely everything, all about Joanna's progress through the philosophies – from your point of view, not hers. Joanna's all right but she won't *gossip*, she just wants to convert me, and I can't restrict my diet to organic food or become a Zen-adept and meditate for three hours every day. It's just not practical. Not with two kids.'

She was so insistent that they felt they couldn't refuse. For them it meant a delay, a postponement in the satisfying of their desire; they needed no one else. But Beatrice did. For Beatrice their presence was a treat, an exciting occurrence in a series of days that varied only in minor detail: the milkman calling on Friday, Susan and Richard coming for drinks on Wednesday, library books being exchanged on Thursday.

While Desmond built structures out of plastic bricks for Samuel to demolish, Beatrice took Madeleine on a guided tour of the house, through the sparkling surfaces of the kitchen and up to the rigid neatnesses of the bedrooms. 'Bridget has been polishing and vacuuming like crazy so that you wouldn't be shocked and alarmed by my slovenliness. I told her you couldn't care less. Do you like the colour scheme? We're furnishing. Slowly. I don't want cheap and cheerful stuff. I'd rather save until we can afford decent things. There's a lovely leather Chesterfield in Simpson's. It makes my mouth water every time I see it. I gaze through that window so often I'll probably be picked up for loitering . . .' Beatrice sank down on to the candle-wick bed-cover, suddenly became aware that she sounded exactly like Carol or Susan or Barbara when they went into ecstasies over dishwashers or split-level cookers or Swedish glass. Why did she feel the need to justify her lifestyle to Madeleine, to convey the idea: this is my home and setting up a home is a very satisfying activity? Because Madeleine had Desmond and was obviously very much in love with Desmond, and all that mattered to Madeleine was the ownership of a bed and a door that could be locked against intrusion. But life was procreation, the furbishing of a nest, the contract with a partner for the safeguard of one's young and thus the continuance of the species; marriage, home and babies: *that* was life and everything else was simply the trimmings – youth, yearning and philosophical debates, tenuous connections and the reading of Proust. It was only when Beatrice was presented with the evidence of all this unimportant extraneity that she thought about the period of her life that had been forfeited, the period you were allowed before you had to buckle down to the basic essentials. And that was the reason for her ostentatious display of status, just a way of saying, 'I have something too, something much more real and worthwhile.'

'That's a lovely dress,' she said. 'I thought that you lot all wore big jumpers and white lipstick and despised female frippery.'

Madeleine looked very hard at Beatrice's upturned face. But Beatrice's face was quite devoid of dissimulation. She genuinely hadn't realized that she was looking at one of her own cast-offs. It tied in with the way she used to be for ever leaving her Parker pens in someone else's form room, her eighteen-jewelled wrist-watches on the sink, her monogrammed school cases on the number nine bus.

'I don't have any truck with clothes any more,' Beatrice said. 'I just go into Mothercare every now and then to replace my smock.

But of course, in a year or so it'll be different, when we've finally waved goodbye to the extremely messy stage. I shall go out then and spend all the housekeeping on glad rags.'

'You're not having any more?'

'Not if I can possibly avoid it. I mean, I *like* having babies and I quite like looking after them, and I like not having to go through all that business of hairdos and hems that don't dip and ladderless stockings that's involved in presenting yourself publicly. At least at home I have a *certain* freedom from routine. It doesn't really matter which day I wash the sheets or precisely when I dust the shelves.' She rubbed at an encrustation of dried milk that adhered to her sleeve. 'Of course, I don't suppose I'd manage at all without Bridget. Everyone round here makes snide comments, they call me Lady Ross. They don't realize how much I'd like to be like them. To possess their energy and organizational ability, I mean – I wouldn't want to be like them in any other way. Joanna says they're all arrested at the anal-retentive stage. What does that *mean*?'

'It means they're afraid of mess and disorder.'

'That's them all right,' Beatrice said gloomily, lifting the edge of the curtain and seeing the neat rows of Pamela Glover's white washing, Susan Burton's gleaming window-panes.

'That's most of us, probably.'

'You don't look very inhibited and afraid of things any more.'

Beatrice wasn't sure whether or not she was happy about this transformation. Madeleine was shy, timid and repressed, not confident, calm and wearing dresses that showed off a fair amount of flesh. You got used to people being one thing: it broke down your structure of certainties when they turned out to be another.

If David had been so looking forward to the pleasure of their company, then, for the first few moments after entering the house, he managed to conceal it quite effectively. 'Beatrice!' he called, as he hung up his jacket in the hall, 'I asked you to remind me to take that beige folder this morning. I've spent a fruitless afternoon trying to hold my end of the argument without having a clue as to the relevant figures. I distinctly remember *asking* you. Good God . . . Oh hello,' he said, as he came into the room and saw their visitors who were politely assuming total deafness in deference to Beatrice's anxious expression. 'Well, hell,' he said, 'I can't remember every damn thing.'

'You could have rung,' Beatrice said.

'What would have been the point of that? Could you have raced over with it?'

'Stop complaining and greet your son.' Samuel was tugging at his trouser leg. He bent and patted his head in a perfunctory way. He looked tired and very much older than the man who'd whizzed around the town in a scarlet MG and been a talking point among stoutly-corseted matrons over morning coffee at The Cheshire Cat.

'He should be in bed.'

'He's going. He likes to see you.' 'Dad,' Samuel said helpfully. 'You see?'

'He calls your father Dad, he calls Derek next door Dad.'

He called me Dad, Desmond thought, but refrained from volunteering this information. Beatrice lifted Samuel into her arms. 'Perhaps you would like to offer our guests a drink?' she said as she left the room, in a tone strongly reminiscent of her mother in high dudgeon.

He made an obvious effort at sociability. He poured them drinks and introduced himself properly to Desmond. 'Women!' he said, and, 'Bad day. You know how it is,' as though the simple fact of their shared masculinity made some bond between them. Desmond drank his whisky and thought, Fancy a girl like that being married to a clod like him. If I was a girl, I'd have taken my love-child and begged on the streets before I'd have married him. Madeleine remembered how in awe of him she'd once been: David Ross, the embodiment of world-weary sophistication. Perhaps being in love cleared your gaze. She saw now that he was simply a very ordinary, conventionally handsome man who looked as though he rarely enthused about anything or found anything more than faintly amusing and who hadn't the good grace to disguise his bad humour in front of his wife's friends. She wished Joanna was present. Joanna would have said, 'What on earth do you mean: women!?' and given him a lecture on the subject of sexual stereotypy.

They talked of Joanna over dinner. David said that Joanna was an adopter of attitudes, that Joanna read too many books and couldn't make the mental link between the theoretical and the practical. Joanna was simply a tilter at windmills, David said. It was very difficult to believe in the sincerity of someone who moved with such astonishing rapidity between beliefs in Marxism and Zen, parapsychology and Existentialism. Every statement that Joanna made, David said, contradicted an earlier statement.

'She is quite sincere,' Desmond said. 'How can she know what she believes until she discovers what there is to believe ?' Madeleine's fork was halted half way to her mouth. Privately, Desmond always maintained that Joanna's half-baked theories gave him a pain. Beatrice wondered if her apple fritters would match up to the excellence of Bridget's goulash. Sometimes they turned out and sometimes they didn't.

'I'd place bets that ten years from now Joanna will be voting Tory and screaming for the return of capital punishment,' David said. He was mellowing with every bite of food, every sip of wine. He even smiled at Beatrice and patted her bottom when she passed him, her arms full of plates.

'That shows how little you know of Joanna,' Desmond said. 'She may be floundering a bit, but she accepts certain basic principles, like not growing fat off the sweat of someone else's brow. You won't find Joanna in the thick of the managerial revolution. She'll be doing something that can be defined as useful, not one of those jobs that somehow escape definition but exist, as far as I can tell, to shield the owners against the rapacity of the working man.'

Even if he hadn't been a clod, Desmond would have felt the need to attack him, simply on the basis of his having married Beatrice. A girl like Beatrice ought not to be married and serving up apple fritters. It diminished her. He suspected that she also blew her nose, went to the lavatory and dislodged morsels of food from her back molars and, equally, such knowledge was dissonant with the image he preferred to entertain.

Madeleine said, 'Your baby really is beautiful, isn't he ? Those eyes!'

David said, 'If Labour gets in, there won't be any owners left and we might as well all fold up our tents and leave. If state control is so desirable, how is it that as soon as an industry's nationalized it starts to lose money ?'

'Do you know the percentage of this country's wealth that is concentrated in the hands of a very small proportion of this country's population ?' Desmond said. He hoped that he wouldn't be called upon to elaborate because he couldn't recall the exact figures himself. 'And the only difference a Labour government will make is in such vital areas as whether or not we have to pay for our bottles of cough mixture, or whether we allow our poor to move up from starvation level to subsistence level. I'm talking about socialism, not self-seekers wearing different hats and playing musical chairs at Westminster.'

'Starve?' David said. 'Who starves these days?'

'Only those who won't work. Or so they'd have us believe.'

Beatrice ladled cream on to the fritters. 'The logical course of this conversation is how everything's the fault of the evil trades unions, and then how difficult it is for private enterprise because of the depredations of the tax man, and then how the Nuclear Disarmers need locking away and do they *really* want us to become a Russian satellite? At least that's the way it usually goes at the dinnerparties we attend,' Beatrice said. 'Except there everybody's more or less in agreement. So if we have to have it, can we get it over quickly, and then we can talk to each other like people?'

'Your apple fritters are lovely,' Desmond said. David said, 'We'll agree to differ.'

Oh I know you, Desmond thought, shooting off your mouth from a position of entrenched ignorance, going off every day to your work, touring your factories. You call your foremen Fred or Bill and they call you Sir and you sign your expense account and you drive home and you think politics is something apart from all that, just a subject for discussion, like power-boat racing or tomato growing.

So you're one of the reasons why I pay my rates and my taxes, David thought, so that you can piss about for three or four years airing your Commie views, biting the hand that feeds you, the system that took you out of your hovel and put you into a grammar school blazer. State-subsidized screwing, that's what you represent. And boozing. And scratching your backside, and curling your lip at anyone who works hard to provide himself with a reasonable standard of living.

While Beatrice and Madeleine washed up in the kitchen, they sought vainly for uncontroversial topics of conversation. Desmond knew nothing and cared less about cricket, about gardening, about cars, National Service or foreign travel, the joys of parenthood, do-it-yourself home joinery or the mortgage rate. And David supposed that a discussion of Desmond's interests could lead only to further argument. Eventually he switched on the radio and they drank whisky to a background of the Palm Court Orchestra and tried to will the hands of the clock around its face.

'You're crazy about him, aren't you?' said Beatrice as she wiped the sink. 'Oh to hell with the pans. I'll leave them to soak. And it seems as though he's crazy about you. Aren't you both lucky. Will it last, do you think?' The tone of her voice betrayed her assumption that such an intensity of emotion was, necessarily, bound to burn itself out. Whether it burned itself out to a state of affection or eventual hostility, who could tell? Beatrice thought of her parents who were also crazy about one another – and that involved hating each other as well – and ceased to be envious of Madeleine. Who would deliberately choose a relationship of that nature unless he or she had a streak of masochism? 'You must be bored to death,' her mother would say, arriving on quiet Sunday afternoons to find Beatrice knitting baby clothes and David mowing the lawn. They behaved towards one another, in Helena's estimation, like a couple who might be approaching their thirty-fifth wedding anniversary, their interaction had that dreadful taken-for-granted quality about it. Beatrice would knit to the end of the row and then say, 'You really do have a threepenny novelette conception of a man-woman relationship, don't you? After eighteen years of storms and tempests, a quiet life suits me very well.' So maybe she was bored. Occasionally. To be bored, occasionally, was a small price to pay for the companionship of an equable temperament and the feeling that you were proceeding in harness, a partnership, rather than rushing at one another head on.

Madeleine and Desmond wended their way slowly and reluctantly homewards. 'Patronizing twat,' Desmond said. 'I feel very sorry for her. She's wasted on him. She seems to have a tremendous amount of potential and he'll smother it.'

Madeleine was not unaware of the effect that Beatrice had had on Desmond. And of course she misinterpreted it. She was accustomed to men being bowled over by Beatrice's looks – even tatty hair and unflattering clothes couldn't really disguise Beatrice's beauty. Beatrice was safely married, thank the Lord. But, all the same, she'd get him back to London at the earliest possible opportunity.

14

On the first day of November 1963 Joanna woke up beside Neville the registrar and pondered on their conversation of the previous night. Stupid, he had called her, criminally stupid, to forfeit the sort of chances that other, less privileged, people might sell their grandmothers for. 'All this flag-waving,' he'd said, 'and then you prove to the world that you can't write two coherent sentences about the very subjects you expound upon. Not altogether convincing, is it?' Neville was solemn, slightly taciturn and extremely career-minded. Every time he rang her for a date she accepted and then wondered why. For he seemed to epitomize everything that she scorned: he was precise, orderly, rule-bound, conventional and determined upon forcing her into a confrontation with every illogicality that was contained within her private manifesto. 'What price the thoughts of someone who can't even organize her own academic career?' he'd said. Unwillingly, she reassessed her progress. There were seven months left before her final examinations. She decided to devote those seven months to intensive intellectual effort. She was capable of gaining a good degree; perhaps it would be foolish, as Neville said, to lose out on account of mere idleness.

On the first day of November 1963 Beatrice was fitted with an inter-uterine device. Three weeks later Beatrice became pregnant.

On that same morning, Desmond, who had spent September and October turning down or being turned down for teaching posts all over London, boarded a train at Euston station which would take him to Crewe where he would change for North Wales and thence proceed to attend an interview for a job in the history department of a rural grammar school.

The school, which served a small nearby town and a number of outlying villages, was built of mellow grey stone and set in a valley. As the train crossed a viaduct on his homeward journey, he caught sight of it, framed by a plantation of fir trees, neat cultivated fields stretching away on either side of it, a red sun sinking behind its chimneys. Everything about the landscape seemed grey, green and gold, a respite for eyes clogged with city soot. The quiet, which at first had alarmed him, was a quiet compounded of birdsong and the wind through grasses. The lilt of soft voices was balm to ears dulled by the clangour of red buses and black taxis and cosmopolitan voices raised in strenuous disagreement. He closed his eyes and the scene – the house in the valley with its rapid river and its dark trees and its mullioned windows ablaze in the sunset – remained imprinted behind his eyelids. It wasn't a bad job either. He would have a measure of autonomy and the academic standard was high and his immediate superior had a year to go before retirement and there was an empty cottage to rent, vacated by his predecessor. 'Our staff are mainly local,' the headmaster had said. 'It's not ideal for anyone who needs a rather more stimulating environment.' Desmond thought of the rather more stimulating environments – the grimier reaches administered by the Greater London Council – in which he'd previously sought employment. A group of boys, en route to the playing fields, passed outside the window. They looked serious and sensible and he compared them with the towering youths who had hurled milk bottles and kicked stones aimlessly across concrete playgrounds in Southwark and East Ham.

Madeleine met him at the station. He took her into the buffet and imparted his enthusiasm over a couple of lagers, told her how there was absolutely no comparison between this place and those that had gone before, how he'd felt, somehow, at home in that valley; it seemed a place to which you could belong. How could anyone belong in Brent or Haringey? How could anyone belong to a preparatory school in Esher? Who'd want to?

She let him run on, describing the stone cottages and the shrouded hills, the peace of it all, the way total strangers had smiled at him, the green fertile valley protected on all sides from assault, the hedgerows full of whatever the hell hedgerows were full of in November. She let him transmit his vision and she said nothing, not until they were out in the Euston Road where the wind blew litter into spirals and vagrants on benches wrapped newspapers around their legs. Then she said, 'When would you have to go?'

'Spring term. January. They're making do with a supply until then. Did I tell you about the cottage? The rent is less than I pay for my *room*. It's empty at the moment. The supply drives in from Denbigh. It's just down the road from the school. I went and had a look. You'd love it.'

'What makes you think I'd love it?'

'Well, you don't like this, do you?' He gestured around him. 'Pavements and glass and concrete and sooty trees and shrivelled shrubs. I don't like it. I'm not a city person. I escaped to London for the sake of broadening my mind. Well, it's broadened now and I want to get back to where real people lead real lives.'

Somehow, she had accepted their relationship as being something that would continue. Perhaps that had been an unwise assumption. They had never made their plans explicit, Madeleine because she hadn't sufficient confidence in her own worth to feel that she had the right to enquire of him his intentions, Desmond simply because, for Desmond, life was very much a day to day business and attempts to shape the future were tantamount to tempting a malevolent providence to hit you with both barrels.

'I can't work in a timber yard for the rest of my days.'

Seven months, that was all. Until she would be free to follow him to the ends of the earth. 'Surely there must be *something* around here . . . ?'

'There isn't. You know it as well as I do. Nothing that doesn't involve me living in one stinking room and running the daily risk of grievous bodily harm from some kid that's on probation and just waiting for his Borstal common entrance. Or else moving out to the suburbs and subscribing to an educational ethos that revolts me.'

'I shall miss you.' That was the most that it was permissible to say out loud. I won't be able to bear it, don't leave me, seven months is an eternity and you can't love me as much as I love you, you can't, or you wouldn't leave me: all of this had to be said inside yourself, in that cold place where all your hopes were laid to rest.

They sat side by side on the bus. She rested her head on his shoulder, inhaled the scent of rough wool and tweed and skin that was Desmond and Desmond alone. So many other shoulders and no other shoulder would do. If there was only some way to tie him to her. The only way she could do that was in bed. But she couldn't keep him in a state of sexual excitement indefinitely. Not until the post was filled.

And it wasn't until they had picked up two portions of King Prawn, eaten it and got into bed together that he traced a line down the middle of her face with his forefinger and said, 'I don't want to leave *you*.'

'What about all those buxom Welsh maidens?' She blinked her eyes and bit the inside of her lips to stop the tears from coming. She'd let him go, she'd lose him, simply because she wasn't able to admit her need of him.

'Why don't you come too?'

He began to do things of a very intimate nature. For all the response he was getting he might just as well have saved his energy. 'In what capacity?' she said at length, in a little voice.

He guided her hand downward. 'I was thinking,' he said, 'on the train. We've known each other a year, haven't we? And I'm still mad for you. And we get on very well, don't we? And you're a good influence on me – that's a fact. I used to drink and smoke and go out with loose women before I met you. I was thinking,' he said, 'if it mightn't be a good idea for us to get married. At least we wouldn't need to keep pissing about, pushing you over that hostel wall every morning and pretending to your mum that we haven't got round to holding hands yet.' It was an image that had superseded that image of the valley behind his eyelids as he dozed on the homeward journey, an image that involved himself, Madeleine and a cottage, a succession of tranquil days and unlimited opportunities to go to bed together. Until that time the idea of marriage had never entered his head except as a bloody silly activity that other people apparently wished to indulge in. 'Mm,' he said, 'that's nice. Well, do you have any thoughts on the subject?'

'Hundreds of them. Oh Desmond, don't. How can I think?'

'Don't think. Just feel.'

'I can't concentrate while you're doing that.'

'Instinctive reactions are the best. Hey, how about my instinctive reaction!'

'Will you be serious!'

'Only on one condition. That you don't stop what you're doing.'

'Well, in that case, we might as well get it over with and talk afterwards.'

'Get it over with! I take great exception to that remark. There have been women, you know, who've begged me, begged me, when I did this, and this. And particularly this. I'll stop though, if you like, and we'll get out the Book of Common Prayer and go through the marriage service . . .'

'Oh no,' she said. 'Don't stop now.'

Of course it was totally impracticable. She wasn't yet twenty-one, her mother would never give her consent, they'd stop her grant and he'd be expected to keep her. To be married in a Roman Catholic church it would be necessary for them to obtain a dispensation, for them to be married properly, he would need to take instruction and that could be a lengthy process.

'What is your religion?' she asked, quite well aware of what the answer would be: 'Nothing. That makes me C of E, I suppose.'

'You'd turn?'

'I'd *turn*? What a peculiar expression. I'd go along with the externals. If it'd make you happy. Till we were married. And then I'd devote myself to ridding you of your superstitious notions. You'll not get me paying to keep the Pope on his Chrysanthemum Throne.'

'That's the Emperor of Japan.'

'Him as well. I'll keep you in bed all day Sunday and every Holy Day of Obligation and whenever it is you're supposed to confess your sins. I'm warning you.'

When we are married. The more they talked about it, the more the idea appealed to him. He'd look around him at the cracked linoleum and the brown-beige wallpaper and the piece of cardboard that replaced a broken pane of glass in the window and he'd see instead a cottage parlour bright with chintz and a garden blooming with hollyhocks and bees and night-scented stock. This vision assembled itself autonomously; he never saw himself actually painting walls or hoeing the earth.

But reality was something different. Reality was Madeleine needing to stay in London to finish her course and waiting for her twenty-first birthday, reality was Madeleine's dependence being shifted from her mother to himself, and obdurate education authorities. They must needs wait. She didn't mind at all: seven months with the prospect of marriage to him at the end of it was a different state of affairs compared with seven months and no prospect. They must wait and keep it to themselves. They would write every single day. He would prepare the cottage for her coming and she would wall herself up and work. And the time would pass in the blinking of an eye. She said, 'I want to tell the world. Can't I tell just one person? Can't I tell Joanna? She'll keep her mouth shut. Otherwise I'll burst.'

'Joanna will try to dissuade you. She thinks I'm an evil influence. I can't quite figure out why.'

It was while she was seeking out Joanna that she thought, for the first time in months, of the girl Polly. The mental shutter that she'd bolted across that unwelcome piece of knowledge swung open to reveal a series of images, second-hand and unconvincing most of them, culled from the cinema version of *Hamlet* when the audience had hooted at the spectacle of Ophelia's amazing buoyancy. Real people – Polly – they sank, didn't they? Sank with their hopes of marriage. She had never confronted him with her information. The girl had been known to be unstable – Joanna had said so. Unstable people were liable to read too much into casual relationships and then over-react when forced to acknowledge their misinterpretation. To tell him, to burden him with the responsibility, was unthinkable. A girl had died. It didn't make any difference. It wasn't going to be allowed to make any difference. She pulled the shutter across just as she had done over the memory of the crash. They'd watched her for ages then, watching for signs of psychological disturbance, unaware that she'd pushed it away to where it couldn't affect her.

She tracked Joanna down in the library. Joanna was sighing and making copious notes and trying to eat an apple quietly. 'I aim to astonish them with my erudition,' she said. 'The trick is to acquaint oneself with vaguely relevant works that *aren't* on the syllabus. You know: "as Friedrich von Schweinerei so succinctly sums it up." What's the betting they'll be too damned idle to check? They'll just think, "This girl's read widely round her subject," and give me a lovely mark. At least I hope so.'

'I hope it pays off. We're going to be married,' Madeleine said. 'In July.'

Joanna crunched loudly. The sound reverberated around the stacks. The librarian raised her head. There were several large notices pinned up forbidding the consumption of food on the premises. 'What else can you consume except food?' Joanna said.

'Energy,' Madeleine replied. 'Did you hear what I said?'

'Clever arse. Yes, I heard you.'

'And?'

Joanna tipped the apple core into her briefcase. 'Am I supposed to register surprise?' she said. 'If so, I'll postpone that reaction if I may, until you've actually got a ring on your finger and a bit of paper testifying to the fact. He has a habit of changing what passes for his mind, does our friend Desmond.'

'Thank you very much.'

Joanna, who had not ceased her scribbling throughout this conversation, scribbled on. 'You certainly don't want my opinion. You know it already, anyway. If I had the choice between the Boston Strangler and Desmond, I'd probably choose the Boston Strangler. Still, *chacun à son goût*. I hope you'll be very happy. Now, are you going to push off so that I can get *on*?'

Jealousy took various forms. She looked across the quadrangle. The sky was the colour of milk and very soon the dusk would push gently at the windows and she would prepare a meal for Desmond coming home weary with blisters on his hands and wood shavings in his hair. And then they would lie in one another's arms, quietly contemplating future bliss.

Joanna sighed again, rubbed a hand across her eyes. She'd never admit to jealousy, not in a thousand years, thought Madeleine. Neville looked as though he was composed out of cardboard.

On December 4 Joanna wrote a letter to her mother saying that she might as well come home for Christmas in view of the fact that all the libraries would be closed. 'Just don't expect me to start cooking Xmas dinners, etc. Not unless you want me to plough these exams and ruin my entire life.' Desmond went to Burton's during his lunch hour and bought himself two suits: a grey worsted and one that was described as a charcoal pinstripe. He didn't recognize the reflection in the full-length mirror as being that of himself; it was a weird feeling. One of the suits was for getting married in. He had already been to see the priest at Our Lady of Lourdes, a sexless old creature with watery eyes who smelled of rubbing liniment and who told him that faith was a big responsibility and offered him a cup of weak tea and a Marie biscuit.

On December 4 Madeleine, too late for breakfast as usual, grabbed two letters from her pigeon-hole as she scurried out of the building on her way to her first lecture. During the lecture, she opened them and read them and the voice of the speaker receded and the planes of the room buckled inwards and a hand that was made out of ice clawed at her solar plexus and the girl next to her was prompted to ask if there was anything the matter.

The first letter, which was from Mrs Snow, informed her that, in Mrs Snow's opinion, there was something very wrong with Madeleine's mother. 'The least you could do,' Mrs Snow wrote, 'would be to come home and see for yourself. She's like a walking skeleton. I thought you might have noticed it during the summer. Though perhaps you weren't home long enough to notice anything.'

Written with equal parts of ink and vitriol. Mrs Snow and her ilk, they regarded Madeleine as a traitor to her class: 'getting big ideas', 'too good for us now'; she marvelled irrelevantly at the enormity of Joanna's task, Joanna seemed to regard class barriers as being reinforced constantly from above rather than below.

Perhaps Mrs Snow's letter could be disregarded, perhaps it was merely an excuse, woven about a tiny germ of truth, to get everything off her chest. The second letter could not be disregarded. It was from Joanna's mother, written in Joanna's mother's fast-flowing, free-form script and its contents ran thus:

My dear Madeleine,
The task of writing this letter is an unwelcome one. I have tried to persuade your mother to get in touch with you but she refuses on the grounds that you must not be worried at this stage in your career. I sympathize with this view and I have no wish to cause you unnecessary alarm, but the facts of the matter are these: your mother who, it seems, has been suffering from various unpleasant symptoms for quite some time, has finally agreed to a specialist's examination. Further examinations have proved to be necessary and therefore she is being admitted to hospital tomorrow morning. I am not qualified to go into the medical details – and neither would it be ethical for me to do so – but my husband wishes me to tell you that her illness may possibly be of a serious nature.

As I said before, I don't wish to frighten you – no definite diagnosis has been made as yet – and I quite realize the pressure that you are under. But in view of her intractability in the matter of communicating with you, I felt it my duty to write. I think you should come home, Madeleine, if only for a short time. I'm sure the college authorities will be sympathetic when apprised of the facts, and despite her insistence to the contrary, I'm sure your mother needs you at this time.
Yours sincerely,
Dora McCloud

PS. We would be very pleased to have you to stay with us for however long it may be necessary. I tried to telephone you several times yesterday, but neither you nor Joanna ever seems to be in. Anyway, just ring me as soon as you decide – Joanna has all the relevant numbers – and someone will meet you at the station.

Joanna sat at the back of the lecture theatre surreptitiously eating toast. She had kept on her coat – ready for instant flight. The voice of the lecturer, mellifluous and pleasantly pitched, boomed in her ears. And instant reactions – those that Desmond had said were to be trusted – battered at Madeleine's consciousness.

Her life was finished, of course. That was the first reaction. She must go home and nurse her invalid mother. She must abandon all hope of a degree and a decent job and marriage and Desmond, for Desmond could not be expected to share the burden of bedpans and sheet-changing and getting up in the middle of the night to see that all was well. How reluctantly she had left home more than two years ago and now how her soul rebelled at the prospect of being forced to return. She might have known that fate had something of this nature in store. Everything had been running too smoothly for too long. She re-read Mrs McCloud's letter; Joanna was right, her mother wrote as though she was speaking, addressing the board: 'the facts of the matter are these.' On the whole, she thought she preferred the spiteful hinting fashion employed by Mrs Snow.

Time crawled. She should have stood up and excused herself, she knew. But she sat on, fantasizing vividly and at length about the way her life would be ordered from now on. They would have to live on whatever pittance the National Assistance Board cared to hand out. There wouldn't even be the occasional luxury to relieve the horror of it all: the imprisonment between four garishly-papered walls, the ghastly routine. She would grow old, prematurely, without intellectual stimulation, without a man, without a hope. The nature of her mother's illness was vague in her mind: something incapacitating, she thought, something that involved constant nagging pain and the inability to control one's own physical functions. Margaret Brennan was only forty-four but, already in Madeleine's imagination, she had assumed the appearance of one of those old women she'd seen in a television documentary about hospitals: one of those *things* – shrunken skulls and sunken eyes and gibbering mouths – that had been propped up against pillows and caged in with bedrails in a ward for geriatrics.

When at last the lecture ended, she didn't make straight for Joanna and the nearest telephone, she made for the woodyard and Desmond. All the way there on the bus she was thinking, there must be a solution, something I haven't thought of, a compromise;

life surely doesn't offer only clear-cut alternatives.

He was helping to load joists on to a lorry. It was raining and his jacket was drenched and his hands red-raw. 'Sorry,' he said, when he saw her, 'no chance. We're not taking on this week and you're not well enough qualified anyway. You need a degree before you can appreciate the satisfaction intrinsic in getting splinters in your hands and soaking wet through all at the same time. Isn't that right, Cyril?'

Cyril, who wore a woollen hat pulled down over his ears and drew on a cigarette that was positioned dead centre of his mouth, adjusted the tail-board of the lorry and said, 'By Christ, mate, if I had one you wouldn't see me for dust. I wouldn't be so choosy. Anywhere'd suit me, anywhere in the warm where I could attach my bum to a seat and keep it there. Why don't you tell him, love? He reckons to be clever but I think, myself personally, that he's only ten pence in the shilling.'

'Can you spare a minute?'

'Can I spare a minute, Cyril?'

'Spare as long as you like, lad. You'll only get the sack. And that doesn't matter to you. Anyway it's time for a brew.'

She showed him the letters. He read Mrs Snow's unaided but she had to translate the other one for him. 'Clarity of handwriting degenerates in direct ratio to intellectual ability,' he said. 'Oh hell, Mad. What a swine of a thing to happen. Hey, Cyril, bring out another mug, will you?' He re-read the first letter. 'This one's an old cow, isn't she? Look, love, it probably isn't nearly as bad as they're trying to make out. And even if it is serious, well, people recover from serious illnesses, don't they? Hell, there are people climbing mountains on crutches and walking about with batteries in their hearts and only one kidney or half a stomach. The human body has fantastic powers of regeneration.'

Cyril carried three mugs across the yard, breathing hard through his nose with the effort of trying not to spill. 'For Madam,' he said. 'Sorry about the tin mug. Only all the Crown Derby's dirty at the present moment. What's up? You look as though you've had bad news. Oh bloody hell, you've not slipped up, have you, Desmond?'

'Her mother's ill,' Desmond said.

'Oh,' said Cyril, 'I'm sorry, love. Just my joke. It's tough luck that. What's the matter with her?'

'They don't know yet. She's going into hospital.'

She warmed her hands around the mug. The tea was strong and sugary. The thought that her mother might die had never entered her head. When she was a little girl, she'd prayed every afternoon in school that her mother wouldn't have died during their separation. When she was a bigger girl too.

'You'll have to go,' Desmond said. 'Have you been on to your tutor and the registrar's office? They'll make arrangements, you know – excusal of work and allowances in the exam, even hold your place open if necessary. Not that it'll come to that,' he said quickly.

She'd never thought of her mother dying. Not for the last year, at any rate. Not since Desmond. It wasn't a thought that she was capable of sustaining, alone.

'Will you come with me?' she said.

Well. There was a month to go before he started his job and he was skint. Buying those suits had cleaned him out. Perhaps they'd take them back and return his money. He had a feeling that they wouldn't. Illness gave him the creeps, illness and shows of emotion. He looked at her face. It was closed up, expressionless, the way your face went when you were afraid of everything behind it collapsing into chaos.

' 'Course he'll go with you,' Cyril said. 'It's not a thing to face alone, isn't that.'

'Of course I'll come with you,' he said.

15

She rang Mrs McCloud from the station when she reached home. She said thank you so much for your kind offer but my fiancé is with me, so we'll stay at my house. It was the first time she'd thought of him as her fiancé; it seemed an incongruous word to be applied to Desmond.

Joanna's mother wasn't at all shocked at the idea of two unmarried persons of different sexes sleeping, unchaperoned, under the same roof, but the neighbours were. They reckoned that if

Margaret Brennan got to hear about it her chances of recovery would be set right back. London behaviour. They knew all about London behaviour: black stockings and fornication and putting out your washing on a Sunday. What they didn't know was that there was little hope of recovery. Little, very little, none. The doctor at the hospital did not say, 'These are the facts.' He broke the news as gently as he knew how.

'When such a disease reaches this stage . . .' he said. 'The liver is a vital organ. Irreplaceable.' He'd played this scene many many times. There were those who broke down at the first mention of the word, those who sobbed and wailed and had to be sedated; they were the most difficult to deal with in the short run. And there were those who listened to what he had to say and gave no sign of caring, and they were often the ones who caused far more trouble long term, the ones who could function only when heavily tranquillized, the ones who gobbled down their barbiturates or slashed their wrists, the ones who were admitted eventually to in-patient care. Or so his colleagues in psychiatry informed him. And some cases were worse than others. Among them cases which involved twenty-year-old girls who looked as though they'd break if the wind blew on them and who had no near relations to turn to for solace.

'Does she know?' Madeleine asked. If I can just get out of here without making a fool of myself, she thought, and wondered at the same time why the maintaining of what she thought of as her dignity should be so important to her.

He shook his head. 'She hasn't asked any direct questions. Most patients, when they are as ill as your mother, are determined to know the odds.' It was an unfortunate phrase; he was aware of that as soon as he'd uttered it. 'I mean, it's a difficult decision: we have to make them aware of the seriousness of the situation without condemning them to absolute hopelessness.'

'You mean there is some hope?'

She stared past his shoulder and through the window to a flower-bed where a solitary rose bloomed. It was almost as if her whole future depended upon the precise words that this gentle, pale-faced man with his silver hair brushed back so attractively, might speak, as though the decision whether her mother would live or die rested with him instead of God, or the growth that was taking over her liver and destroying its functions.

He chickened out, as he had always chickened out at this juncture.

He spread his hands and he said, 'There's *always* hope.'

'Can I see her?'

'Not until the morning. She hasn't come round yet.'

'From the operation?'

He nodded. The operation. They'd opened her and they'd looked and he'd said to Pryce-Davies, 'Do you know, I once had an inflamed thumb, a spot of sepsis, and I was rolling about in agony all night – my wife threatened to send for an ambulance if I didn't pull myself together. And yet this woman has walked around for God knows how long, has, presumably, worked and talked and functioned fairly normally, with this inside her.'

'It's a beauty, isn't it?' Pryce-Davies had said. And then they'd closed her up again.

She didn't cry, not that evening, nor through the night when Desmond lay on his back and smoked and held her close, which was the only form of comfort he could dispense. He couldn't mouth platitudes as those idiot neighbours had done earlier, stuff about it always being darkest before the dawn and stories about persons who'd returned from the brink of the grave. Neither could he encourage her to accept the truth softened with the triteness of it being a happy release. We are no use, he thought, one to another, not when it gets down to basics.

She didn't cry until the next day, after she'd seen her mother. Margaret Brennan had awakened from the anaesthetic and the first thing she'd noticed was the absence of pain. She moved, very cautiously, she turned her head from side to side. There was soreness. And her throat was terribly dry. But there was no pain. And she knew then that her prayers had been answered. For a time, when the pain had driven her back to Dr McCloud and he'd seemed unwilling to commit himself, she'd been very much afraid that she was really ill. She'd got out her insurance policies and her Trustee Savings book, she'd written frantically, to distant cousins and remote in-laws, requesting assurances about Madeleine's welfare. Two or three of them had written back, told her that she mustn't be morbid, that they would like to help but they had families and responsibilities of their own and wasn't Madeleine practically a grown woman by now? The day before yesterday, packing her case, she'd been at her wits' end, unsure whether it would have been better to contact Madeleine at the risk of worrying her, just in case something went wrong. And then Mrs McCloud had breezed in, had said that Madeleine knew and Madeleine was coming and that, should anything happen, Madeleine would always have a home with the McClouds. After all, they *were* linked, weren't they, the Brennans, the Martins and the McClouds? Had been ever since the day of the disaster.

Mrs McCloud was waiting outside the ward. In her white coat. She forestalled Madeleine, extended a cheek towards her. She smelled of hospital. 'She thinks that she has had a successful operation,' Mrs McCloud said. Desmond counted the tiles which were affixed to the lower half of the walls around the corridor, the upper part was covered with mustard-coloured lincrusta.

'You'll need to be very brave,' Mrs McCloud said. 'Don't disillusion her. If you can possibly manage it.' She glanced at her watch. She had a queue of adenoids awaiting her. The girl showed no emotion whatever, apart from a faint air of resentment. The young man looked as though he very much wanted to be elsewhere. 'If there is anything. Anything at all . . .' She *had* to dash. Those kids would be lining the corridors by now, howling themselves hoarse.

And yes, Mrs Snow had not exaggerated. Her mother looked dreadful. She'd probably looked dreadful in the summer. Madeleine hadn't looked at her all that closely. But she smiled and she said, 'I *told* them not to bother you. I feel so well. I expect it was an ulcer. I expect they've taken it away. They haven't told me. And you don't like to ask, do you? Not when they're so busy. I don't care. It's such bliss to feel well again. Well, I wouldn't exactly say that I'm up to doing cartwheels. But it's gone, that pain I had.'

And she asked Madeleine about her grades and how she'd managed to take time off, and told her that she looked tired and was she getting enough sleep? And Madeleine gazed at the wall and Desmond gazed out of the window and they both answered her questions briefly, monosyllabically. They didn't mention their decision to get married and when she leaned back on her pillow and said, 'At any rate I can rest easy knowing you're with Mrs McCloud,' they didn't disabuse her of this mistaken assumption.

'When I get out of here,' she said, 'and when you get your next holiday, we'll go away somewhere. There's an endowment due very soon. We've never really had a holiday, have we? Except for that time when we stayed with your Aunt Myra before she died.'

It was then that Madeleine cried. Took hold of her mother's

hand and pressed her face against her mother's face and soaked the pillows with her tears and had to be drawn away gently by Desmond who said, 'It's just reaction. She's been dreadfully upset. I'll bring her back when she's recovered,' Desmond who gabbled the first thing that came into his head while he got her out of the room and steered her towards a nurse who led her into another room and got a cup of tea and a yellow pill down her.

She called him back from the doorway. Her eyes were closing. Her periods of lucid wakefulness would become fewer and fewer. 'You tell her I'm going to be all right,' she said. 'She'll believe you. Talk to that doctor. That one with the grey hair. He knows.'

'I'll tell her,' he said. He wanted to smash the world to bits, to kill whoever it was, whatever it was, that had decreed that we must be born and we must die.

Madeleine cried all the way home in the taxi and continued to cry until half past eight that evening when Dr McCloud called and gave her an injection. She thought of the joyless years of her mother's life and how she'd never had a new coat, only a second-hand one that someone had advertised in a shop window, how she'd never had a proper holiday except for the time in Whitby which Aunt Myra had offered in exchange for a fortnight's house-work, how she'd liked the occasional cigarette but had denied herself in order to send those weekly parcels. And she thought of the way that she, Madeleine, had accepted, always accepted, this self-sacrifice without thinking it in any way odd, how she'd abandoned her mother just as she'd abandoned her religion. But God was not mocked. The wicked might flourish like the green bay tree, but not for very long. She was being punished for her lack of caring, for the way she'd averted her eyes from her mother's suffering, for all the Sunday mornings celebrated in Desmond's bed rather than at the altar rail. Mumbo-jumbo, Desmond had called it, superstitious nonsense: 'It will be my life's mission,' Desmond had said, 'to rid you of it.' Well then, she'd allow him to do so. If her mother died. And she cursed and blasphemed and beat her fists against the wall and fell on to her knees and vowed that she would discard what little faith she had left, if they let her mother die: God and all his angels. She clung to Desmond, so that he had to prise her away in order to answer the door. And she made him promise that he would never, ever leave her, even though she was rotten and deserved to be punished. And she cried until no tears came and her chest hurt and she couldn't focus her eyes any more. And Desmond held her and stroked her and kissed her bruised knuckles and wished to Christ that the doctor would arrive with his syringe full of oblivion.

After that there were days of calm, when the fact of death receded. Mrs Brennan was allowed unrestricted visiting. They'd sit, one each side of the bed, while she talked of feeling stronger all the time. She didn't seem to realize that she was awake for shorter and shorter intervals each successive day. Her eyes would close, quite suddenly, in mid-sentence. And then they'd tiptoe out of the room and go along to the cafeteria and drink cups of coffee they didn't want and mash cigarette ends into ashtrays. And Madeleine would experience alternating feelings of remorse and resentment: I could have helped her more than I did, comforted her, sympathized with her; she was a lousy mother, tying me back on to her, making me afraid, it was always no, don't, be careful, you'll hurt yourself. Never: go ahead, try it, take the risk.

There were fourteen of those days, ominously calm. On the fifteenth day Margaret Brennan didn't seem to recognize anybody, lapsed constantly into sleep or unconsciousness. On the sixteenth day her bed, in the private ward, was slung about with contraptions and every so often Madeleine and Desmond were shunted out into the corridor while the nursing staff performed mysterious rituals. On the seventeenth day she opened her eyes and cried, 'No!' and called and called for Madeleine and when she came rambled to her about dead days, about the father she'd never known and the garden of the house in which she'd spent her childhood. After that all was flurry and hurried footsteps and screens rattling and Father Kennedy arriving to administer Extreme Unction. Afterwards he spoke to Madeleine, put his hand stiffly on her stiff shoulder. 'The four last things,' Madeleine recited to herself, as he talked of the resurrection of the body and the life everlasting, 'the four last things are Death, Judgement, Hell and Heaven.' For all that it meant to her she might have been reciting the nine times table.

She died two days before Christmas, while a ward maid pinned tinsel above the doorway and a staff nurse with a piece of mistletoe kept a look out for lovely Dr Bridge from Gynae, while Desmond boiled a pan full of potatoes and boiled the bottom out of the pan and Madeleine alighted from a number seven bus at the hospital gates. She'd hung on for forty-eight hours longer than they'd

173

expected, forty-eight hours after Father Kennedy had shriven her soul and administered the sacrament. She did not expire peacefully, a prayer on her lips. She struggled against the morphine, she clasped at the bedrail, she cursed and she said that she could not go. She died wrestling with death.

Other people did what was necessary. All that she was required to do was to put on a dark coat and climb into a black limousine and follow the coffin to its place in the cemetery. The cemetery was of the traditional kind, its perimeter enclosed by yew trees: something to do with yew being poisonous and therefore deterring wild animals from desecrating the graves, she remembered. She was full of Librium and every time she put one foot in front of the other she was afraid that the ground wouldn't be there to meet it. Coffins always looked smaller than the persons they had been constructed to enclose. Helena Martin wore a black fur coat and her hair was bright beneath her hat. Helena Martin had devoted her life to keeping her man and Margaret Brennan, widowed at the age of twenty-four, had lived celibate for twenty years. From choice, surely? She had been a pretty woman, a woman happy to subject herself to catering to someone else's wants. 'I never met a man who I could be certain would love you enough.' Those words, spoken once, years ago in a rare moment of honesty between them, her mother's reflection in the dressing-table mirror, naked and, for that brief moment, full of regret. Did it matter, in the long run, how many you'd loved, how deeply you'd loved, who'd loved you?

The agony began at the graveside. A mean north-easter blew through the gaps in the enclosing trees, fluttered the ribbons on the wreaths and billowed the priest's cassock behind him. She pressed her hand to the right side of her face and waited for the paroxysm to pass. Which it did. And then returned, again and again, ever more violently. Throughout the remainder of the service and the subsequent buffet meal hosted by the McClouds and the condolences she was obliged to receive from people she barely recognized. Between the spasms, she tried to remember the worst pain that she had ever experienced and the nature of that pain. There had been an abscessed tooth once and, once, an attack of gastro-intestinal colic. But neither of those pains, as she recalled, approximated in any way to this pain which attacked, at intervals, like an army with banners, travelling the length of her trigeminal nerve from the top of her cheekbone to the point of her jaw. It began slowly, mildly, insidiously, the pain – ignore it, you thought, refuse to acknowledge its existence – and then it gathered momentum, blotted out everything outside itself, occupied your entire consciousness, until you were a body attached to a searing agony that felt like a huge cold blunt instrument being forced through a resistance of bone and gristle from your ear to your jaw. Each period of remission encouraged you to believe that it was over, and just when, with a kind of faint mad optimism, you dared to think that it had run its course, back it came, tenfold.

She was in a doctor's house. Her neuralgia could have been diagnosed and dealt with in a matter of moments. She would have received sympathy and expert attention. But instead she clenched her fists inside her pockets and when it was at its worst, when she thought that she might be going to faint, she sat down and put her head in her hands, which action was, naturally, interpreted as a sign of uncontrollable grief.

For she recognized the pain for what it was, its twofold significance: as a tormentor and a friend. She had sinned and therefore must be punished. On the other hand, if it hadn't been for the pain, there was no doubt in her mind that she would, on this terrible afternoon, have taken leave of her senses. She would have screamed and yelled and torn out her hair and attempted to follow her mother into the grave. But the pain out-countenanced everything, it was total, complete in itself, allowing no quarter to sorrow or remorse or even mental collapse.

She couldn't keep it from Desmond. At home she writhed on the bed and stuffed the sheet into her mouth and at last had to admit it to him. He put on his jacket and said that he would ring Dr McCloud. She forbade it. She held on to the tail of his coat and swore that she would kill herself if he left her. She screamed at him and eventually he called her a silly hysterical bitch because the violence he saw in her eyes was something more than the natural pain of bereavement. But he acceded to her will and he warmed cloths in the oven and held them to her cheek while she clutched at him and moaned and told him nothing mattered to her any more except him, except Desmond.

'She was everything to me and I was everything to her. I neglected her, and I paid for it. How will I manage on my own? I've never learned.'

'There'll be no need for you to manage on your own.' He replaced the cooling cloth with a warm one, held her head in the angle of his shoulder. He would marry her, of course, as quickly as possible. Was it not marvellous how, left to itself, life made the decisions for you? The idea of total dependence unnerved him a bit. He had never been everything to anyone before. Not as far as he knew.

He bought a special licence. Out of Mrs Brennan's insurance money. There were all sorts of formalities and objections to be sorted out on account of Madeleine not being twenty-one. There was a visit to the education office where the powers-that-be had some idea that they might require repayment in full of the money she'd received from them for two and a half years. He told them that she was pregnant. He told them that at the register office too. Their objections seemed to melt away at the word. Bereaved and pregnant. An awesome combination when it came to battling with bureaucracy. He didn't know how he'd managed to dream it up, this masterstroke; he was suffering from lack of sleep and he'd soaked up enough tears to float the *Titanic* and he felt as though he was moving, muddle-headed, through a maze. Occasionally, when sitting in someone's outer office, or waiting at a bus stop in the driving sleet, he thought of his valley. If they could only make it to the valley they would be all right. They would begin anew, with the spring.

Robert Martin, recognizing him from the funeral, rescued him from one particular bus stop, held open the door of the Jaguar and gave him a lift into town. Desmond leaned back gingerly in the seat, aware that his clothes were wet through and that he was spoiling the upholstery. Still, that wouldn't matter much, would it? Not to a fellow like Martin. He could always buy another.

'I was coming round to see Madeleine, to see if she needed any financial assistance.'

'What concern is it of yours? Or do you practise casual phil-anthropy?' He didn't feel hostile, but he couldn't check an automatic reaction any more than Joanna could have checked it, sitting next to this man in his vicuna coat and his silk shirt, with the faint odour of expensive cologne in your nostrils, purring along the highway while the plebs queued at the bus stops.

Robert Martin didn't take offence. He just offered Desmond a cigarette and said that he felt a kind of responsibility for all three of them, the survivors. And that financial assistance was all that he could provide.

Desmond ignited his cigarette on the dashboard lighter. He said, 'We don't need money.'

'We?'

'I'm marrying her.'

Robert Martin drew up at the traffic lights, turned to look at him. 'Why?' he said. 'Out of pity?'

'No.'

'Good.' He tapped his fingers on the steering-wheel, exhaled smoke elegantly through his nostrils. 'It's not the best basis for marriage.'

'What is?'

'I don't know. Equal stamina perhaps. Do you want to be married?'

Desmond clasped his hands between the sodden corduroy knees of his trousers. 'Doesn't everybody, sooner or later? Did you want to be married?'

He looked a bit startled, postponed his answer until he'd changed gear and turned a corner. 'In my day,' he said, 'you got married for regular sex.'

'Oh come on. There was more to it than that. Even then.'

He removed a shred of tobacco from his lip. He was bloody good-looking, for his age. Even Desmond, who wasn't used to assessing masculine attractiveness, could tell that. Correction: he was just bloody good-looking. He'd probably had to fight them off, battalions of women, beseeching him to marry them.

He didn't answer Desmond's question. He said instead, 'She's not pregnant?' And then, 'What's so funny?'

'Nothing. No, she's not pregnant. I'm marrying her because she needs me and I need her to be with me. Can you think of any better reason?'

The car slid gently to a halt. Robert Martin treated him to one of those famous tender remote smiles usually reserved for his womenfolk. 'No,' he said. 'I can't. As long as that need is reciprocal to the same degree.'

And the chances of that, he thought as he drove away, are extremely remote.

It was left to Joanna to kick up the fuss. Which she did, so successfully that eventually he had to tell her to piss off and keep her nose out.

Madeleine was answering letters of sympathy. She wrote the same words on each piece of paper. There was a comforting property generated in performing routine tasks. She didn't speak, she didn't even raise her head very often while Joanna ranted on, emphasizing her points by pounding on the rickety sideboard. During one of her more vehement stresses, a handle fell off. 'How can you *do* this to her?' Joanna said. 'How can you take advantage of the state she's in?'

'It's not a punishment. She's marrying me of her own free will. Ask her.'

At first he was determined to regard Joanna with an amused tolerance. Her outburst was, after all, to be expected. But his patience was on a shorter rein than he had realized. Anyone would think, from the way she was going on, that he was abandoning Madeleine to some ghastly fate, rather than marrying her, standing by her.

Joanna said, 'Oh, marry her if you must. Who's stopping you? But don't, for God's sake, screw up her life. Let her finish the year and get qualified at least. Otherwise it's such a bloody stupid waste. And once she's chucked it in they'll never let her back. You know that. Half a year, that's all. And she'll have *something*.' They'd been quite right, those old female schoolteachers, when they said first get your qualifications and then indulge your emotions; she saw that now. It wasn't some high-flown philosophy of liberation; it was just practical. Where will you be, they'd meant, when your husband dies, deserts you, leaves you with mouths to feed, if you haven't got some kind of a piece of paper to intermediate between yourself and the world? – that's what they'd meant though they hadn't said it.

'She doesn't *want* to go back. Do you?'

Madeleine shook her head, continued to write: 'I very much appreciate your letter . . .'

'She doesn't know what she does want. Not at this moment.'

'And you do, I suppose? You know what everyone wants? You're typical of your kind, Joanna. You preach about democracy and everybody having a share in decision-making, but what you mean is – as long as it concurs with your feelings on the matter. Why should you imagine that you know what's for the best?'

'Bloody common sense, that's why. She'll regret it for the rest of her days. What's she going to do – follow in Beatrice's footsteps, turn into a baby machine?'

'If that's what she wants. She's not a child.'

That was not true. He recognized the fact that she was a child, a child who had never been given the confidence to stand on her own two feet and tackle the world.

'You're very good at buggering up people's lives, aren't you, Desmond? And using as your excuse the fact that they did what they did of their own free will. The concept of free will is an extremely controversial one anyway. Everybody's influenced by something or other, someone . . .'

'What are you influenced by? Sour grapes? What she needs is help and support. Not pressure.'

'And you're the one to supply help and support? Your track record doesn't exactly bear that out.'

'Oh piss off, Joanna, and keep your nose out of what doesn't concern you.'

She surveyed them both: Desmond, hostile, Madeleine seemingly indifferent. 'Right,' she said, and made the gesture of twitching her mantle blue, except that what she twitched was a very old corduroy jacket worn almost naked of its nap. 'Right,' she said, 'go to hell your own way,' and stalked out of the house.

Then Madeleine spoke. She said, 'We have to make a success of it now, if it's only to spite Joanna.'

They were married: Desmond in his corduroy trousers and his donkey jacket, because his suits were still in London, Madeleine in her funeral coat. They assembled their belongings and, hand in hand, they boarded the train for Wales. And all through the journey he talked to her of their destination and how important it was that she should feel the same way about it as he did. By the time they arrived she had been conditioned into seeing it through his eyes, even though the rain streamed and the wind howled and there were three slates off the roof of the cottage and several ominous-looking damp patches on the ceiling.

He shielded her gaze from evidence of mouse and woodworm of long-standing residence. He said, 'With a bit of work put into it, it could be a palace.'

And how they worked, painting and papering, mending and

refurbishing, hoeing and sewing. The valley became green and bursting with blossom and the milkman sang on his delivery round, while Madeleine hemmed up the edges of curtains and Desmond hammered shelves into position and put down little heaps of Warfarin in strategic positions and ordered ten pounds of seed potatoes as the first step towards self-sufficiency. That was the time when everything was good, when every bulb they'd bought to edge the garden proved to be fertile, every seed they sowed germinated into a healthy plant, when the mice obligingly died and hole-boring insects took off for fresh woods and the boys were alert and attentive and eager to learn, the staff most congenial, and their pleasures were cheap and easy to come by and mostly to be found in the bedroom.

Beatrice sent off little cards depicting a stork with a bundle to announce the birth of her third child, another boy: Toby. Once Beatrice would have scorned such twee examples of lower middle-class mores. Robert Martin gave his son-in-law a rise – strictly on the grounds of nepotism – and told him to invest it in a stock of contraceptives. Dr McCloud wrote Beatrice a prescription for the Pill. 'If it hasn't harmed God-knows-how-many Puerto-Rican women,' he said, 'I don't suppose it can harm you.' The Pill had a 99.3% success rate; Beatrice swallowed it resignedly, quite prepared to discover that she was among the unlucky .7%.

And Joanna pulled all the rabbits out of the hat and got a First.

16

Dear Madeleine,

This is probably the first letter you've had from me for a long time that isn't to say I'm pregnant. Well, I'm not. Isn't science wonderful? Three children is just about right, isn't it? Though David would have liked a girl. Apparently he only makes boys.

Actually we've been a family of six rather than a family of five for the past few weeks. Mrs Bellamy's been in hospital and Amy's been having husband trouble so Matthew's been in residence here. I do wish I knew how to approach him and help him. They haven't actually expelled him from the latest school, just asked him to leave. It seems he smashed up the art room. He was bored, he said, when asked for an explanation. The psychologist says he has difficulty in relating. Bridget says he's a good lad ruined. She can handle him better than anybody. Why is it that childless people seem to get on best with children? There just isn't time to give him loads of attention. Not with three others clamouring all at once. Sometimes I feel like booking in at a Retreat for a year or so. Even though they are lovely, really they are. Sam's going to be the practical, steady one and Felix is going to be the brilliant one and I'm not sure about Toby – Toby has all the signs of not giving a monkey's. David says that Bridget spoils them rotten. I don't see anything wrong with a bit of spoiling, as long as it's love spoiling and not the other sort – spoiling with possessions to make up for parental neglect, the sort Matthew had. As I write this, he's just broken Sam's train and Sam is howling with fury. What is it that makes people want to destroy things? I expect Joanna would know. Amy's sending him to a new school next term, one of those progressive places where the kids are allowed to do exactly as they please on the assumption that what kids really want to do are socially acceptable things – the idea is, I think, that Matthew will at first burn down a few garden sheds and wreck a few classrooms and then discover that he'd prefer to be learning Latin grammar and building a rabbit hutch.

My mother has gone into partnership with that poof who redesigned their house for them. They're opening a shop. My father is furious. He says that he refuses to fill his house with shrieking homosexuals. Though Archie isn't really the shrieking sort at all. And you'd think that my father would be comforted, knowing that she's at last turned to relationships that can only be platonic. They say that male hostility towards queers is because it makes men aware of the precariousness of their own sexual proclivities (what a good word! See, I'm not really a cretin, despite evidence to the contrary). I would have supposed that my father, of all people, was pretty sure of his masculinity. Aren't men funny? The idea of lesbians doesn't bother me in the slightest. Does it you?

What about you? I expect you're madly happy and self-absorbed and that's why we haven't heard from you. We'd love to come and visit you. So why don't you invite us? I don't go anywhere much. Whenever we make a plan, somebody gets chicken-pox or a bilious attack or something, or David's too tired, or else we're saving up for a new carpet or whatever. (A word of advice: if you do decide to have kids, do not, repeat, not, fill your house with anything half-way decent until they're about twelve years old. You wouldn't believe the damage they do. All the springs are poking out of the sofa and the paintwork's kicked to bits and Sam's just discovered swear words so we have 'Sod' written at intervals on the wallpaper all the way up the stairs, in red Biro.) I must say you're showing remarkable restraint in that direction. I thought

Catholics were supposed to go forth and multiply. Or have you packed it up entirely? Mother Church, I mean? I can't really imagine Desmond among the incense. Bridget has just looked over my shoulder and told me that it's a sign of ignorance to talk about a person's religion in a facetious manner. So I'll shut up and get on to the real news which I've saved for last. Though maybe you know it already, in which case I shall be extremely full of chagrin. It is that Joanna has got herself engaged! Engaged, yet. Can you imagine anything more middle-class than that? It was in the paper! And she's got a *ring*, a damn great expensive thing that practically blinds you when you look at it. And they're going to have a *wedding* – when she's got her doctorate – a proper wedding, not like you and me: in at the door of the register office, sign the paper and out again – but a wedding with church bells and bridesmaids and silver horseshoes, the sort of wedding we'll have to buy hats for. My father's tickled pink. He says, the next thing she'll be joining the Labour Party, those liveried footmen of the bourgeoisie. *She* says it won't kill her to sacrifice her principles for one day of nonsense in order to satisfy the parents. Neville's parent, it seems, is losing her marbles. You've met Neville? Neville the gynaecologist. I said, 'Great, we'll be able to get our wombs scraped on the cheap when the time comes.' It fell like a stone. He's one of those men who make you feel about twelve years old and retarded to boot. I think, though, that he and Joanna are very well suited, they will devote themselves to life's important issues while the rest of us just continue to be flippant and trivial and egotistic. Oh I'm so glad you acted un-sensibly too and followed your inclinations. It comforts me to know that I'm not the only one. Joanna makes me feel so dreadfully inferior. After all, anybody can produce kids. You don't get awards and certificates for that.

I must finish now and take over from Bridget who has to go and start preparing for one of my mother's unspeakable dinner-parties. My mother is a selfish cow. Please write soon. You're a lousy correspondent, you know. Almost as bad as Joanna. If you knew how much a letter brightens my life you wouldn't be so remiss.

Regards to Desmond and lots of love,
Beatrice.

She folded the letter, put it into an envelope and hunted for a stamp. There were no stamps. She'd forgotten. David would be annoyed. She debated with herself whether to dress the children in their outdoor clothes, strap Toby into his pushchair and haul them all the way up the hill to the post office or whether to put up with David's annoyance. Sloth won the day. As it usually did. She'd tell him that one of the kids had got hold of the stamps. Of course that meant he'd tell her she ought to have more control over them. That meant they'd have an hour or two of the heavy father, the breadwinner who slaved all day long only to return to a houseful of ungrateful dependants. But it was raining outside and Felix had a cold and she couldn't be bothered to change out of her paint-spattered jeans.

'You haven't any stamps, I suppose?'

Bridget puffed and panted from the effort of lacing up her shoes. 'I don't write letters often enough to carry stamps. When I do, I use one of your father's. Why, what's the panic?'

'He said he was going to write off for that lawn-mower and the do-it-yourself book tonight. He particularly asked me to get stamps.'

'Tell him the world won't come to an end. He can't post them before tomorrow anyway.'

'You know that. I know that. But you know what he can be like if he's in a bad mood. The least little thing and he goes off the deep end.'

Bridget pushed hairgrips into the sides of her hair. Her hair, as ever, was arranged for convenience rather than style. The priest's housekeeper gave her a trim once a month. The priest's house-keeper also did home perms but Bridget hadn't the time. 'He wouldn't go off the deep end with me. Sometimes I think you women ask for everything you get. You give in to them too much. They get pampered by their mothers and then they expect it from their wives. They never have the chance to grow up.' This from Bridget, chief of the pamperers. 'Your father's just the same: "Where's my shirt? Why aren't my shoes cleaned? I can't find this, that and the other." I say to him sometimes, "I can't think how ever you managed during the war with no women around to fetch and carry for you." '

'What makes you think there were no women?'

'That'll do with that kind of talk. He's your father. Give him some respect. By the way, young Einstein has screwed the bathroom tap off and I can't get it back on. That'll please his lordship.'

Young Einstein was Felix, a child never content until he had reduced everything to its component parts. Sometimes Beatrice wished she'd produced an ordinary average child with an ordinary average IQ and no burning curiosity about mechanical objects.

'I thought I heard water pouring down the drain.'

'That's what you heard. Until it's fixed nobody can have a bath.'

'Christ, that's marvellous. He'll love that.'

'It won't kill him. You'd think he was an old man with the cares of the world on his shoulders, the way he carries on sometimes.'

He did look older than his years. He came into the house slowly, almost unwillingly, it seemed to her. He was over-conscious of his responsibilities, he found it difficult to rationalize the ambiguity of his work position: there had been times when he'd almost handed in his notice and looked for a job where there would be no possibility of whispers of 'the boss's son-in-law, the heir-apparent' sounding in his ears – almost, but not quite. He was afraid of change. And besides, he knew that Robert Martin had no intention of promoting him beyond his capabilities. He was steady and he was efficient, but his father-in-law was shrewd enough to realize that he lacked initiative, that he ran from the making of decisions, that he was no future captain of industry.

Beatrice heard the thud as his briefcase hit the floor, the sound of his automatic coughing as he inhaled his third cigarette of the day – he was trying to give up, a course of action which was very welcome from the financial point of view but disastrous from the point of view of the effect upon his nerves.

If it hadn't been for me getting pregnant so often, Beatrice sometimes thought, he wouldn't have those lines on his face, he wouldn't find it so difficult to relax and laugh. It would be the same as it was at the beginning, when we used to bung Sam into the back of the car in his carry-cot and drive aimlessly for miles, when he used to buy apples purely for the pleasure of watching me eat them, the beginning when we used to go to bed at half past seven just to be close, when we'd wake up in the mornings wanting each other. Those times were in the past. Now the sound of her crunching got on his nerves, and their sex life, subject so often to curtailments and accommodations on account of her pregnancies, had never recaptured its momentum. Brief and cursory it was, when it happened, with both of them on edge, waiting for the first hint of a cry from one or other of the bedrooms.

She poured him a drink. She wished she could get rid of the feeling that they had retreated into the set attitudes of adversaries. She said, 'I forgot your stamps and Felix has buggered up the bathroom tap.' She had discovered from experience that it was best to present him with the bad news straightaway rather than lull him into a false sense of security and then spring it on him.

He closed his eyes, finished his drink and then went out of the room. She heard the slam of the door of the kitchen cupboard where they kept the tools. She heard him say, presumably to Matthew who must have returned prematurely and unknown to her by the back door, 'I thought you were supposed to be next door until seven o'clock?'

She heard Matthew say, 'They told me to come home,' and, reluctantly, she went to find out what had happened. Matthew had been invited to Nicholas Glover's birthday party. No doubt he had fallen prey to a spasm of wreckage. He would tell her, he wasn't a liar, made no moves in the matter of his own defence. Pamela Glover would tell her too, at length, over and over again.

'I broke his plane. It was a birthday present. He cried and she sent me home.'

He regarded her steadily. He had Amy's rather protuberant eyes and her long sweep of forehead.

'Was it an accident?'

He didn't answer. He scratched at a scab on his knee. David, sorting through a box of spanners, said, 'Roll on next term. See what they can do with you at this free-for-all place. The price they charge, they should turn you into the Archbishop of Canterbury. Are you sure that Felix did the tap? It sounds more like one of his tricks.'

Father and son regarded one another with mutual antipathy. Beatrice came to Matthew's defence, as she so often did, trying to fan some sort of affection into life between them. Matthew simply turned his attention to the biscuit tin and David found a suitable spanner and made for the bathroom.

He managed to mend the tap but by that time she'd shoved them all to bed unwashed. As Bridget said, there were worse things than clean dirt. But she knew that her standards were falling and despite Bridget's assurances it bothered her. It bothered her to see the expression of distaste on David's face when he found a ring round the bath, or Toby with his lunch still adhering to his front at tea-time. She still hadn't the faintest idea how anyone coped without help.

'We might go down to visit Madeleine,' she said after dinner. 'Take the kids. Or leave them at my parents' with Bridget. It wouldn't kill my mother to put up with them for a day. My father likes them anyway.'

'Your father likes them when they're all cleaned up and fast asleep.'

'Could we, then?'

'As long as you make sure that Desmond is out of the way. I'm not bursting with enthusiasm for another meeting with him.'

You're not bursting with enthusiasm for much, are you? she thought. 'Joanna wrote and said they're on a kind of back to nature thing. Next thing you know, she said, Madeleine will have taken up weaving and Desmond will be thatching the roof.'

'I very much doubt that. Desmond struck me as being more of a talker than a doer.' He opened a desk drawer where they kept the receipted bills. Her heart sank. He had a horrid little book in which he kept count of their incomings and outgoings. He held it out towards her. 'We're in the red again, aren't we?' he said. 'That rug.' He poked at it with his toe. 'We could have existed without it. It wasn't vital to our lives.'

'The carpet looked so shabby. All stained from when Felix had that accident . . .'

'But we could just, conceivably, have managed without it? Look, Beatrice, it's as simple as this . . .'

'I know, I know. Annual income twenty pounds, annual expenditure nineteen pounds nineteen and sixpence . . .'

'Well, then. Add up what I earn and add up what you spend and you can tell whether the two tally. A child could do it. Why can't you?'

'I don't know. Maybe I had a bad experience with an abacus.' The black columns of figures wavered and swam before her eyes. Tears splashed on to her jeans. It was the damn Pill; it made her over-emotional, touchy.

'Oh, for Christ's sake,' he said, slammed the drawer. 'We can't even talk these days without you dissolving into tears. What the hell's the matter with you?'

She wiped her eyes on Toby's bib which happened to be lying at hand. 'I told you, it's that Pill. It's messing up all my hormones.'

'And before that it was pre-menstrual tension, and before that it was pregnancy. Just when can we expect your hormones to settle down into a state of calm?'

'Not while you're always on at me.'

'I'm not always on at you.'

186

'Yes, you are. You're always finding fault. I'm on tenterhooks every time you come through that door for whatever I may have done wrong. I feel afraid of you. I never used to feel like that.'

He lit a cigarette, overstepping his quota. He said, 'You're paranoid.'

'I am not paranoid. You're always picking on me and picking on the kids and everything's always wrong. You never want to make love to me any more. And when you do you make it seem as though you're doing me a big favour.'

'I'm bloody tired, that's why. I'm grafting my guts out all day to keep four kids and two wives and a house that never seems to be finished with. I spend my weekends gardening and mending and trailing the children through the damn park and wiping their snotty noses and putting plasters on their grazed knees and being woken up by their damn yelling. Large families are for rich people.'

She looked at him amazed. 'They're your kids. I didn't fertilize myself. What do you think I do all day? What kind of a thrilling daytime life do you suppose I have?'

'You have Bridget to help you . . .'

'Oh, I wondered how soon that would come up.'

'And in view of that fact I think you could make more of an attempt to tidy yourself up a bit.'

'What?'

'Well, look at yourself.'

She did. At her paint-caked jeans and her stained jersey and her decrepit sandals, at her hair that needed washing and no longer made any pretensions to style. He could have a point there. She said, 'If somebody makes it plain that he finds you undesirable it tends to make you cease to care.'

'If somebody looks as if she's just finished the spring cleaning every day of the week it's a bit difficult to work up much desire.'

'I didn't think you were like that.'

'Like what?'

'One of those awful men who want women to look like something off the Christmas tree.'

'I remember how you used to look.'

'Before I had three, no, four kids to look after. Before you went off me.'

He put out a hand awkwardly towards her. 'I haven't gone off you.'

187

She held on to it, turned it palm upwards. There were callouses under each of his fingers. She said, 'I think I need more affection than you want to give me. I know you were never in love with me. But we had fun, once, didn't we?'

There was an embarrassment between them that had never existed previously. He pulled her close to him, forcing a response. 'It's just a phase,' he said. 'We'll get over it. I do love you. Of course I do. Do you think I'd stay in this madhouse if I didn't?' It was a joke, a feeble one, but a joke all the same. She helped his response along. They might be fooling themselves. But sometimes you needed to fool yourself to get by.

Dear Beatrice,

I really am sorry that I haven't written sooner. I know just what you mean about letters – receiving them, that is, not writing them. The only excuse that I can offer is that I've been ill. Nothing much, but I'm afraid letter-writing went by the board.

I'm glad to hear that you're all well and that the children are thriving. Yes, of course, three is an ideal number. Though, knowing you, I'm quite prepared to say that four is an ideal number, or even five. I think I can safely leave the task of going forth and multiplying to you.

At the risk of filling you with chagrin, I have to tell you that I had heard Joanna's news. They came for a brief visit at Easter – on the way to see his mother. Joanna says she's a very weird specimen. I bet Joanna soon knocks her into shape, whatever she is. Neville seemed all right to me. Perhaps he's just sensitive to references to his profession. I don't think he'll alter Joanna, just perhaps supply stability and a check to her impetuousness. But you're quite right, for all her impetuousness, she's managed to do very well. She was telling me she's done a paper on Wittgenstein which is to be published in some very learned journal. And to think she might have followed Fred to Katmandu and back again and ended up packing sweets on a production line, or whatever it is he's doing now. I expect we'd have done just that.

Life is pretty quiet here. We're still working on the cottage. The more we do, the more there is to do. Isn't that Somebody's Law? Desmond put in vegetables in the spring but the carrots got root-fly and the cauliflowers got some awful sort of mouldy grey fungus and the birds ate the peas. We watched a gardening programme on somebody's television and it all looked so easy and Desmond was sitting there bursting blood vessels and saying that the chap obviously had an army of helpers and the might of ICI behind him to achieve those results. Perhaps it really is a matter of green fingers, after all. At the moment he's trying to locate the source of the damp that's spreading in all directions – an awful job which involves chipping off all the plaster.

Just when we'd painted too. Desmond thinks it's jinxed, the cottage, I mean. He gets very dispirited sometimes. He thinks effort should be rewarded in exact ratio. Life's not like that, is it?

Of course we'd love to see you. But I can't make any definite arrangement just yet because we aren't sure about our plans. Desmond's a bit disillusioned with this school. It isn't what it seemed. I think he's a bit disillusioned with country life generally. I think he made the mistake of expecting too much. Anyway, he's written off for a job in Chester. So if he gets it obviously we'll be moving. I'll let you know.

Desmond sends his love. And so do I. To David and Bridget and all the young Rosses too.

Madeleine.

She laid the letter on the bedside table – she'd ask the district nurse to put it in the post; if you gave Desmond a letter he carried it around in his pocket for weeks – and she adjusted the coverlet around her waist. She was recovering from a miscarriage, a nasty five-months miscarriage. They'd wanted to keep her in hospital for longer, but all she could think of, throughout the pain and the descent into the anaesthetic, was Desmond eating cold food out of tins and blaming himself, so she'd persuaded them to discharge her to the care of a loving husband and a brisk district nurse.

From below came the sound of a chisel and lumps of plaster falling on to bare floorboards. She took her iron tablet. It was imperative that she should return as quickly as possible to good health so that she could help him in what seemed to be an endless battle against a malignant force that seemed determined that they should labour in vain. No sooner had they dealt with the woodworm than wet rot showed its ugly face, no sooner had he re-slated the roof than the guttering fell off. They'd redecorated when the wiring went and that meant digging channels in the walls from every switch. They'd redecorated again and then the damp patches appeared, and a local builder called in for his free opinion (though he didn't know it) had said mournfully, 'That's fundamental, that is. No amount of damp-proof paper or paint will hide that. That's a job that lies behind the plaster.' So now Desmond chipped away with a chisel, chipped away at his hands quite often, got dust in his eyes and down his throat and cursed the day that had brought him to this spot. All she could do was to offer him her help and support, to be there when he brought in a clump of deformed carrots or a crawling cabbage, or when they looked up and heard the steady drip of water above the ceiling and he raced upstairs with a bowl and then came down again and put his head in his hands and said, 'Fuck it.'

It might not have been so bad if he'd been content with his job. But he wasn't. He didn't fit in with that bunch of provincial reactionaries who were opposed, on principle, to all forms of experimentation. He couldn't think of expending his energies on classrooms full of clods who were destined for the plough or the rugby field. Their collective bovine gaze made the back of his neck crawl. He might have got a lousy degree, but by God he deserved better than that. She comforted him, she massaged his aching shoulders, drew him towards the bed where everything, for a brief time, was made right. They'd had bad luck, that was all. Perhaps the place was jinxed. Their lovely valley was rotten at the heart. And the valley people with their lilting voices and their neighbourliness were nosy peasants with whom it was impossible to carry on a stimulating conversation. It had been a trick of the eye: just the sun setting in a certain way that gilded the landscape. Yes, she said, yes, and pressed his face to hers and said, 'Things will improve. You've worked so hard. You will be rewarded. I know it.'

'Do you want anything?'

He stood in the doorway. His hair and his shoulders were white and his eyes were red with plaster dust.

She shook her head. 'Have you found it yet?'

'No.'

'Leave it, then.'

'I thought I might go for a drink. If you're all right.'

'I'm fine. I'm getting up tomorrow.'

'Like hell you are. You still look like death. I'll ask Mrs Whatsit to come in again. If you can stand her.'

She felt like death: weak and washed out and as though she'd never get up again. Mrs Lewis was very good: putting casseroles in the oven and attending to the personal things that she didn't like to ask Desmond to do. She got on quite well with Mrs Lewis. It was Desmond who couldn't stand people.

He ran a hand through his hair. 'Well then,' he said, 'if you're sure?'

'Of course I'm sure. We might hear about Chester tomorrow.'

'Yeah.'

Oh Desmond, don't give up hope. It will be better, really it will.

I hate it when you look so – hostile to everything around you, as though inanimate objects were capable of malign intent. In Chester, it will be different.

He went downstairs. He ought not to leave her. He'd been in the pub the night she started with the miscarriage. They'd sent for him and when he got back there were newspapers on the bed soaking up the blood. They'd looked at him reproachfully, made him feel guilty. He'd thought she was dying and they'd made him feel guilty. He picked up the chisel and made a fresh assault on the wall. He'd do a bit more and then he'd make her a cup of cocoa. The edge of the chisel slid across his thumbnail and into his knuckle. He flung it across the room. 'Fuck it,' he said, put on his coat, wrapped a handkerchief around his hand and went out.

Joanna put two sheets of paper, separated by a carbon, into the typewriter. 'Dear,' she typed and left a blank space. 'A little impersonal, isn't it?' Neville said.

'I intend to write exactly the same thing to both of them – except for the last paragraph, I'm short on time, my handwriting was never famous for its legibility – I think it's very sensible. When I'm an old retired person I'll write screeds in copperplate on scented paper. Until then, they must make do.'

'You could just write one, enclose a stamped addressed envelope and ask Beatrice to send it on to Madeleine, or vice-versa.'

She stuck out her tongue at him. 'Shouldn't you be off to play about with your speculums – specula?'

'I've got a couple of hours off. In return for doing a hundred and seventy hours last week.'

'There aren't a hundred and seventy hours in a week.'

'It felt like that.'

'In that case, you wouldn't like to be an angel and sort those notes for me? You're so wonderfully efficient. Do you think you'll end up like your mum, having the heebie-jeebies every time somebody puts something back in the wrong place?'

'It's possible.' He picked up a sheaf of loose papers. 'What's it worth?'

'Stick around. You never know your luck. You like doing it, anyway. You like making order out of chaos. And then I can get on with these wretched letters.'

She typed:

Apologize for long delay in putting pen to paper. Have been up to my eyes for the last month or so. It's only when deadlines approach that I can really start working. And deadlines are approaching fast. You think: ah, wonderful, original research, and two weeks afterwards you're wishing to God that you had the old despised disciplinary guidelines: 'Write an essay of not more than 2000 words on – ' you know? However, I've broken the back of it, I think. You say I'm always boring you with details of my enthusiasms, so I won't bore you. Suffice it to say that the work I've been doing inclines me more and more to decide to go into education at some level or other.

You'll have noticed change of address. Couldn't stand bazoukis any longer. Not to mention Lebanese psychopath in the Cypriot's old room. So I won't. Neville found me this place. Very posh. Rent reasonable. Owned by a philanthropic Labour MP. Grates a bit. Still, beggars can't be choosers.

We are getting married on August 3. St Mary's. *You must come.* If it's only to laugh at me. If you don't come I shan't get married. I need some moral support. After that, Neville's mother is cashing her chips – no, that isn't the right expression, is it? – flogging a few shares and sending us to Jamaica for three weeks. I don't particularly want to go and Neville couldn't care less, but we daren't thwart her in case she decides to be mad in a more inconvenient sort of way.

She then removed the two sheets of paper from the typewriter, put one back and typed:

How's Welsh Wales? Is Desmond behaving himself? You know, Madeleine, if you ever move back to civilization, there may be a chance for you to take up where you left off. Some places might agree to your doing a shorter course. The money would be the problem though, wouldn't it? You'll just have to wait until Desmond moves up the Scale. The only alternative I can think of is that external degree you can do from here, but I believe it's a swine and it takes ages, and it's back to the money again. Anyway, whatever happens, don't let your mind go to sludge. You must be bored stiff there with nothing to do. I see you're not being daft, at least, and spawning hundreds of kids. That *would* tie you up for a good few years to come.

See you on August 3,
Ciao,
Joanna.

On the other sheet she typed:

I am very pleased to hear that you've finally curbed your awesome

192

fertility. You have three very nice kids – as kids go. Now give someone else a chance.

Apropos Matthew, I think this school you talk about may be the best idea. If it isn't too late. A. S. Neill had a lot of success with disturbed kids much older than Matthew. I take it he's had psychoanalysis of some kind? Unfortunately, with the best will in the world, the analyst is always fighting an ongoing bad home situation. Can't you persuade Amy to get herself sorted out? A progression of fellows through his mother's life can't do much for his ego.

So your ma's taking up with queers? Ageing film stars do that, don't they? I think it's to avoid the pain of rejection. When you've been used to men desiring you all your life I expect it's difficult to adjust to the fact that your allure is fading. Much nicer to have a non-masculine man worshipping at your feet. Give them both my love. Tell your father I deplore his lifestyle, but I still think that he's lovely.

Love to you and your brats, and David too, of course,

Joanna.

PS. My paper got some good reactions in the right quarters. I'm really chuffed.

PPS. I'll bring some books back for you. And you must read them. It'll stop your mind going dead over those endless nappies. See you soon.

J.

Part Two

Part Two

I

Joanna almost missed the exit from the motorway, managed it at the latest possible moment, a concerto of horns blaring in her wake.

Her absorption had almost caused her a journey up to Penrith and back again: judging by the map there wasn't another slip road for miles. Mind you, the map was ancient. Neville kept the current AA guides, the torches that had functioning batteries, the spare can of petrol, the jack, the change for telephone boxes, the anti-freeze and the vacuum flask: Neville drove five hundred yards equipped as if for a trip around the world. Joanna's car contained only a half-empty packet of fruit gums, a copy of *Social Trends 1975* and a glove compartment full of used paper handkerchiefs.

She could have sworn that she'd know the way blindfold, that the configuration of these minor roads was imprinted indelibly on her memory. She was amazed to find that without the map, ancient as it was, she'd have been lost. Certain landmarks had changed, or disappeared – the gas container that used to loom as a beacon over the town, its level constantly changing, had gone and so had the water tower, and there was an estate of council houses where once prep school boys in yellow and black blazers had foregathered for sports day. But other topographical features, by nature unalterable, appeared to have altered: this road was longer, that hill was steeper, more thickly wooded, the river ran with a rush not a feeble trickle. It took us an hour to reach it on our bikes, our picnic lunches in our saddlebags. We rode behind Madeleine who'd borrowed Beatrice's second bicycle. Every ten minutes or so we'd yell, 'Mad, you've got a puncture!' She fell for it every time. In the afternoon we'd ride back into town, mooch around, rubbing different shades of Woolworth's lipsticks on to the backs of our hands, trying on every hat in C & A until they threw us out, sitting in the Tudor Café for hours over three cups of coffee, making patterns in the brown sugar, waiting to be noticed.

The Tudor Café had been re-stuccoed, fitted with mullioned windows and re-christened the Golden Something-or-Other. She went in and ordered a lemon tea and a sandwich. She felt that she needed a neutral interval to collect her thoughts before walking into the thick of it.

She'd known that it was coming, of course, that it was on the cards. Neville, over a terrible line from the airport, had advised her to keep well clear, said that other people must mop up their own messes, that those who sought to intervene very often got the worst end of the stick. She'd agreed with him wholeheartedly. That was her policy: to agree with him and then proceed to do what she'd first thought of.

A phone rang in the private quarters at the back of the café. It rang on the same fretful note as it had done in Joanna's home the previous morning. Sometimes you knew, before you lifted the receiver, that news of a disturbing nature was about to make the electronic journey and issue from the earpiece. She'd been asleep, dreaming of a cinema which became a railway station and all the trains were running in the wrong direction. Bangor was her intended destination. 'There are no trains to Bangor,' a dark, doll-like girl in a pink frilled skirt told her, 'ever.' The organist disappeared into his pit and the ruched curtains swished open, but the stage was empty. A bell rang and rang, signalling the *mise-en-scène*, summoning the players to their appointed places.

She'd tied her dressing-gown cord and shuffled her feet into her slippers and remembered that it was Beatrice who always used to have the train dreams.

It was Beatrice at the other end of the phone. For a moment she had allowed herself to imagine that it might be someone else, the someone else who had said, 'I shan't ring you; there just wouldn't be any point. We're not interested in remaining friends, are we?'

'Yes,' Joanna said, rubbing condensation from the window and discovering rain and the likelihood of more rain and the fact that three weeks of incessant rain had caused an outcrop of moss to form on the outside wall.

'It's me and I'm in a call-box. Will you ring me back?'

'Why are you in a call-box?'

'Because our phone's on the blink. Wednesday it was the washing machine and Thursday the drains were blocked and the iron died in a shower of sparks. Today it's the phone. Do you think these things run in cycles?'

'You'd better give me the number before we get cut off.'

'It's cheap on Sunday,' Beatrice said when they were re-connected. 'It's seven-thirty,' Joanna said, having just caught sight of a clock. 'In that case it's very cheap. I'm sorry. I couldn't sleep. Joanna, will you come? You said you'd come.'

'It's happened then?'

'Yes, it's happened. You'll say, "I can't just drop everything and drive across England to hold your hand." You'll say, "I told you so," and "You had it coming," and "Why don't you pull yourself together and grow up?" You'll say, "I have my own life and I really couldn't care less. Other people's squalid dramas don't interest me in the least." But you did say that you'd come.' Beatrice's voice sounded very faint and far away. 'There's nobody else,' Beatrice said, 'nobody else at all.'

'What about – ?'

'You know perfectly well. She just wants me to die. Well, maybe she'll get her wish. Maybe I don't want to carry on any more.'

She's been reading again, Joanna thought. When I meet her she'll be wearing black and she'll say, 'I am in mourning for my life.' When I meet her. Because of course I shall go. I could never keep my nose out. Not even after all these years of Neville telling me what a thankless and pointless activity the poking in of one's nose invariably turns out to be. Besides, if ever I needed the divertissement of Beatrice and her woes, that time is now.

'You won't do anything stupid?'

'Such as? I haven't got enough pills. My doctor doesn't like to prescribe them. He's one of your psychosomatic merchants: an ingrowing toenail is merely an outward manifestation of neurosis. Talking of doctors, where's your horrible husband? Don't bring him.'

'He's in Saudi Arabia. He left two days ago.'

'Dilating and curetting the wombs of the wives of oil sheiks?'

'Blowing through their tubes, probably. They need to be fertile.'

'Christ, he must be stinkingly rich by now.'

'Stinkingly.'

'I should have been the wife of an oil sheik,' Beatrice had said. 'It's just about all that I'm good for.'

In the days when it was the Tudor Café they'd baked their own cakes and made salads out of stuff that grew in a greenhouse at the back. Elderly ladies in dotted Swiss muslin aprons had poured your tea, so genteel they'd been that you were afraid of tipping them in case it might offend. In the days when it had been the Tudor Café a cup of tea and a sandwich cost one and three. Joanna wiped her mouth with her handkerchief while a young girl with maroon hair and fingernails and an expression of weary disdain cleared away the remains of thirty-five pence worth of stale curled bread, limp lettuce, dry lemon, and hot water that had been briefly impregnated with a single tea bag.

'Can you still get up to Maddock's Hill by the short cut, the back road?' Joanna enquired of her. The girl stared. I don't care about the fact that they're barely literate, Joanna thought; I don't care if they're insolent, discourteous and wear safety-pins through their noses; if only they'd answer when spoken to. They look at you as though they were being addressed in medieval Latin, as though you didn't share a common language. Perhaps they are all deaf – perforated eardrums – a legacy of years of discothèques. Perhaps that immutable stare is actually lip-reading.

'They haven't closed it down, bulldozed it away, built a new town across it?' she said. The girl shook her head.

Beatrice no longer lived by the golf links. When Oliver arrived they'd moved to an old draughty rambling house that had once been a vicarage where, for nine months of the year, everyone had to wear woollen vests and go to bed with their socks on. There had been no alternative; newly-built, easy-to-maintain dwellings were not constructed to house large families, at least not those dwellings in the price-range that they could afford. Oliver had come about when Toby ate Beatrice's birth-control pills and in the panic of hospital and aftercare she'd forgotten to get them replaced.

Joanna drove past her parents' house, her old home. There was no longer a brass plate on the gate-post. Group practices flourished now all over the town in plate glass and pink brick health centres, and her parents had retired to the Scottish village of her father's birth. Her mother was a marriage guidance counsellor and her father fished a bit and drank milk and ate digestive biscuits for his ulcer.

The Martins' place was a home for delinquent children – the bars on the windows had served a purpose after all. The terracing and the patios and the smooth lawns had been laid waste to make way for a netball court and a workshop. The huge elms which had provided Emmett with fuel for so many bonfires had been chopped ruthlessly and trellis-work fencing erected in their place.

These changes caused Joanna no sentimental pangs. The Martins' place had been far too large for four people, and there was no doubt about the improved efficiency of health centres: they could have you cross-referenced and diagnosed and hospitalized in the time it used to take her father to answer the phone and back the old Standard 8 out of the garage. Nevertheless. Even the estate beside the golf links had mellowed, had achieved a sense of permanence, some full-grown trees and some residents advancing into middle age.

She changed down for the hill's last twisting gradient and hastily wound up the car window; the wind at this altitude assumed gale force; no doubt the temperature dropped a couple of degrees as well. Most of the houses on the solitary road that crested the ridge of the hill had been gutted, reconstituted internally with underfloor electric central heating, double-glazing, waste-disposal units and fitted kitchens, and advertised for sale as high-class flats for superior people. Beatrice had said, when this reconstruction was taking place, that she intended to make friends with all the superior people and then she could go in there for a warm.

Beatrice's was the last house. The limits of Beatrice's garden were enclosed by galvanized iron fencing to protect unwary children from the sheer drop that lay on the other side. Joanna left the car at the front because progress up the drive was impeded by two brimming dustbins. The dustmen wouldn't walk a step further than the gate, Beatrice said. Every week David or the boys had to heave the wretched things round to the front.

It wasn't a sight to cheer the soul of the weary traveller. Perhaps in the summer, in full sunshine, with all the weeds blooming and ladybirds crawling in and out of the couch grass and the brambles thick with fruit and the swing creaking to and fro from the bough of the gnarled and sterile pear tree, perhaps then you would think houses ought not to be square and new and pink with neat gardens; this is how houses ought to be, gabled and covered in creeper and slightly dilapidated and open to the elements. But it was Monday, March 21 in the year of grace 1977 and the sky was leaden and the ground was dank and you looked at the place and you saw flaking paintwork and defective pointing and guttering that leaked in a green slimy stream down the wall. You walked up the path beside a neglected garden littered with débris: punctured footballs and old yoghurt packets and milk-bottle tops, two rusting bicycles and a sandpit, a small tent, its canvas sodden, its guy ropes sagging, a pair of pram wheels and one child-sized boxing glove, you tripped over the broken tiles of the porch step and you put your finger on a bell which, you suspected, wouldn't produce any reverberation inside the house.

It didn't. She banged on the stained glass panel with her gloved fist. After a few moments it was opened by a boy of about ten years old who had a look on his face which children adopt when they are instructed to say, 'Not today, thank you,' or 'Will you come back next week?'

'Is your mother in?'

It must be Oliver. Oliver was the one who looked like Felix. And Felix was the one who looked like his grandfather.

'She's in the back garden.' He wore unmatching tennis shoes and a baseball hat pulled down over his forehead. He sneezed and wiped his nose on the sort of handkerchief that Joanna preferred not to look at.

'Can I come through? I'm Joanna. Don't you remember me?'

'No,' said Oliver, but held the door open for her to enter. She stepped into the great high-ceilinged hall that was full of undusted and undustable surfaces. There was a coat rack covered with duffel coats and anoraks and parkas and there were different sized wellington boots everywhere.

Beatrice was clad in anorak and wellington boots. She backed out of the hen house cradling two warm eggs. She said, 'Hello, Joanna, how's your ideology?' as she always did, much in the same way as someone else might say, 'How's your dreadful cold?' She held up the eggs. 'Two,' she said. 'We used to get a dozen a day. Still, what can you expect when nobody bothers about them but me and I haven't the time? It's a wonder they're alive, let alone laying.' Oliver sneezed again. 'I thought I told you to stay indoors? He gets bronchitis,' she explained. 'We all get bronchitis. The healthiest person in the world would get bronchitis if he had to sleep in these bedrooms. Get *in*.'

Oliver ignored her. He rattled a stick against the fencing and said, 'Are you the one who sent me the catcher's mitt from America?'

'Yes, that's right. Did you play with it much?'

'No, not much.'

She decided that what she disliked most about children was their honesty. 'Why did you come back?' he said.

202

'From America? I was on an exchange visit. I could only stay a year.'

One year. One academic year. Most extra-marital affairs had to be conducted in the shadow of the doorstep, so to speak; it wasn't often that sheer coincidence could be so arranged that it yielded an undreamt-of opportunity. They were fledgling lovers when the opportunity had arisen. She remembered him, buttoning his shirt at the window of that borrowed flat on a sun-gilded Oxford afternoon and saying, 'There's a chance that I may be going to the States,' and the awed look on both their faces when she raised her head from the pillow and said, 'There's a chance that I may be going too.'

Without that opportunity, it might have lasted three months – his commitments would probably have prevented him from committing himself anew, and she could never have settled for the twice-a-week-in-a-borrowed-flat-and-if-you-don't-scratch-my-back-I-won't-scratch-yours routine; it wasn't in her nature. America had a lot to answer for, not least the pain in her heart.

It began to rain, great spattering drops that rattled like machine-gun fire on the corrugated iron hen house roof. Beatrice turned Oliver around and pushed him towards the door. 'Come on in. I'll make something to eat. And then we'll bring your case in. You are staying? It isn't just a visit for China tea and cakes on doyleys?'

'*You* won't have any doyleys. I know you.' Joanna shivered, pulled her collar of Arctic fox around her ears. Beatrice reached out a hand and stroked it. 'Nice. Very nice. You look like the lady of the manor on a visit to the workhouse. To each,' Beatrice said, 'according to his needs.' She hung her anorak behind the kitchen door, touched the strip of rabbit fur that was sewn to its hood, said, 'Mine came from the Famous Army Stores. It's Sam's, actually, his cast-off.'

So was the rest of her wardrobe by the look of it. She wore a maroon rugby jersey and a pair of jeans fashionably frayed at the bottom that betrayed their masculine origins by the width around the waist. She filled the kettle and watched as Joanna divested herself of her coat. 'God, aren't you slim! And elegant. And all the rest of it. You remind me of my mother. Clear the junk off that chair and sit down. My mother used to bring a cushion from the car to put on the chairs in case she soiled her two-hundred-guinea frocks. Oliver! Are your hands clean? Hang this coat in the hall. No, don't. Take it upstairs and put it on my bed. Very carefully.'

Oliver snatched at it nonchalantly. Joanna removed a roller-skate and a toy car and a copy of *Shoot* from a chair and sat down. 'How is your mother?'

'Still living in sin in Lytham St Anne's.'

Joanna raised an eyebrow. Beatrice decided that being able to raise one eyebrow must be an innate talent, like singing in tune; she'd practised for years without any success. 'Is Archie steering a new sexual course, then?' Joanna said.

'Don't know. Doubt it. All right, she's living in sinless companionship. It's even worse. Bung some coal on the fire, will you? No, on second thoughts, you'd better not. It smokes like hell and you'll get filthy. I'll do it.'

Joanna drank her coffee and ate her cheese sandwich and looked around her. Sometimes these big old kitchens could be so arranged that they resembled pictures in magazines advertising pressure cookers or food mixers. This one didn't. A thin coating of emulsion paint could not conceal the uneven surface of the walls. The ceiling sagged in one or two places. The plumbing was ancient. A hissing, gurgling gas heater provided hot water – periodically it sent forth from its recesses an alarming roar of blue flames. Not one piece of furniture matched another piece of furniture. Dripping flannelette sheets were draped over a clothes-rack which was suspended from pulleys on frayed ropes. Every so often, when the wind swirled in a certain direction, the room was filled with clouds of smoke.

Beatrice followed her gaze. 'Not quite the same as the other place, is it?' she said. 'Not in the same class at all.'

'I don't know how you even keep it clean. Without help.'

Beatrice emptied the dregs of her coffee into the sink. It was horrible coffee, the supermarket's own brand, seven pence off. 'Oh, didn't you know, I have a Nubian slave comes in four mornings a week. To do the rough.'

'You miss Bridget.'

Beatrice picked up a tea-towel, stared at it as though she couldn't for the life of her understand its function, its purpose, its place in the scheme of things, laid it down again. 'My eyes for the blind,' Beatrice said, and gave a jerky little laugh. 'She had glaucoma. Don't let's talk about it.'

'It would be better if you did talk about it. It, and the other. Or else why have I come?'

'For the pleasure of my company?'

'I cancelled a trip to Brussels.'

'Sacrifices, sacrifices. And Neville said, "Oh, don't get involved with *her*. She's a walking disaster area." I know.'

'I don't give a damn about Brussels, or Neville's opinion either. I came because I thought I might be able to help, to offer some practical suggestions. How can I if you won't talk about it?'

'Later, later. After they're all fed and watered and in bed. I'll talk then. Let's get you unpacked now and I can admire all your swanky clothes and you can tell me *your* news.'

Beatrice hauled the case up the stairs, opened doors – one door revealed Oliver sticking replicas of regimental badges on to a piece of card, sneezing still and occasionally emitting a raw hoarse cough like a bark. He said, 'I thought I'd got the Royal Engineers. I didn't swop it, did I?'

'I don't know. Perhaps you've dropped it.'

He eased himself off the tumbled bed, groped underneath it. His long fair hair fell forwards over his face. Joanna looked at Beatrice. 'It's uncanny,' she said, 'the likeness.'

'Wait till you see Felix. Sometimes, in profile . . . It gives me a shock.'

'It isn't here. I remember, I put them all in that tin. I remember it quite clearly. You've shifted it, I suppose. You shift everything.'

She closed the door upon his complaints. 'They used to give them away with petrol,' she said. 'Regimental badges and glasses and jars of spices. It's a good job they've stopped doing it, because we wouldn't be getting any more, would we?'

'How do you manage for transport?'

'The kids have got bikes. I borrow one and cycle down the hill and wait for the bus. Occasionally I get a lift from one of our very superior neighbours. You're in here.' She opened a door. 'Bedrooms,' Beatrice said, 'we have aplenty. Was there any specific reason for vicarages being huge?'

'Men of the cloth always seemed to have large families.'

'The Reverend Thing didn't. His wife was barren.' She put the suitcase on the bed and blushed. Joanna said evenly, 'There is no need to bite your tongue on my account. I got over that kind of embarrassment years ago.' She had. After all the polite counterings of impolite questions to do with the starting of families and leaving it too late and wasn't it a little selfish, she'd changed her tactic, answered straight out, 'I don't want to and what's more if I did want to, it seems that I couldn't.' 'A barren woman,' her mother-in-law had called her; it had a fine biblical ring to it.

She clicked open the clasps of her case. 'It's a jolly good job really. I'd have made a lousy mother and Neville would have made an even lousier father. Babies wouldn't have fitted into his world of order and symmetry.'

'No, I suppose not.' Beatrice stowed away a bundle of assorted male clothing in the wardrobe. 'Gets more like his mother every day, does he?'

'Yes. He doesn't think so, but he does. She's in a home now, by the way, mother-in-law. She finally went completely loco, lost the papers on which she used to note down her *ordres du jour*.'

'I remember you telling me,' Beatrice said. 'Get up. Brush teeth. Read one chapter of *Anthony Adverse*. Call vet apropos neutering of cat.'

'Yes, well, when she lost them she just didn't know what action to perform next. We went to see her at Christmas but she didn't recognize us. Just sat there stroking her lap and gibbering. God, I hope when it's time for me to go, I can go cleanly, alive one minute and dead the next.'

'Like my father?'

'Well, no, not quite like your father.'

'Look, let me show you how this fire works. If it isn't lit in a certain way you're liable to lose your eyebrows.'

Joanna knelt while Beatrice struck a match – like so, adjusted the gas tap – *voilà*, reached towards the fire at an acute angle. They both thought of the manner of Beatrice's father's death and how amusing it would have seemed had it happened to a total stranger and they'd read about it in the newspapers.

'It was a fitting death,' Beatrice said, as the gas fire spluttered. She tossed the spent match into a big patterned jug on the mantel-piece. 'He died as he lived.'

In mid-thrust. In a German hotel bedroom. In the company of a girl who hadn't the sense to extricate herself and return to her own room before raising the alarm, a girl who'd run out into the corridor screaming hysterically. The press had got on to it, of course. Despite an attempt at discretion by colleagues and manage-ment. 'Industrialist,' the press had called him, 'Industrialist dies suddenly of heart attack.' 'His companion,' the German press called the girl. The English press called her his secretary. They couldn't stop her jabbering mouth. Fräulein Bech. Twenty-two years old she was and unused to men reaching the final climax of their lives when sunk in her luxurious flesh. And oh what sniggers there had been, and newspaper editors trying to compose obituaries, straight-faced, and telegrams of condolence from the CBI, and men in the factories saying what a way to go and how did they manage to screw down the coffin lid, and the doors of the big white house on Millionaires' Row double-locked and inside it Beatrice crying for all the lost years and Bridget faint with embarrassment and Helena going completely bananas.

'Is there enough room in there for your things?' Beatrice said, opening a cupboard door. 'I keep telling Felix to move his chemistry stuff but for all the good it does I might as well talk to the wall.'

There were shelves covered with test tubes and retorts and pipettes and little squares of gauze and bunsen burners and jars filled with brightly-coloured substances. 'Is he still keen?' When she'd last met him, Felix had spent most of his time performing experiments that resulted in bright blue crystalline substances or anhydrous white powder, had bored them rigid with blow by blow accounts of efflorescence and effervescence.

'Never touches them. He's writing a book now.'

'Really?'

'It's porn,' Beatrice said. 'I found the key to his diary and read it.'

'Wasn't that a bit unethical?'

'Probably. It was awfully derivative, actually – young virgins clad in wisps of white lace, lots of heaving and thrusting, that sort of stuff. What I imagine to be a précis of the entire oeuvre of the local skinflick palace. Do you think I've raised a potential pervert?'

'I think it's highly unlikely. I suppose he's just at the age for smut and snigger. Of course I've not seen him for what – nearly two years?'

Beatrice gave the bedcover a final tweak. 'You'll see him in just about – twenty minutes. You'll see all of them. All of them that are left.'

2

They came with a rush and a roar, a cacophony of bicycle bells, blasts of cold air and a thunder of feet. The sound of feet was the most vivid impression, heavy feet upon creaking floorboards, huge heavy out-of-control adolescent feet. Coats were flung in the general direction of the hallstand. Voices, at full volume, vied for supremacy: one baritone, two shrill and treble, and one cracking painfully on every high note.

They entered the kitchen, they stared at Joanna. Beatrice reminded them of her identity. They stared a moment longer, nodded their heads abruptly, and then began to talk again, all at once. 'You never put my shorts in.' 'They weren't going to give me any dinner.' 'Can I have a biscuit?' 'I hope you've ironed my neckerchief. It's Cubs tonight.' 'I came top in Biology.' 'Mum, they've still got that Telecaster in Draper's. If I saved up the deposit, couldn't I get it on the HP?' 'You can't even play the guitar.' 'I can learn, can't I?' 'Can I have another biscuit?' 'Well, *have* you ironed my neckerchief?'

Beatrice chopped carrots. 'I thought the whole idea was that you ironed your own neckerchief.'

'He hasn't got a proficiency badge for ironing.'

'What did you get one for – bedwetting?'

'Nose-picking. Belching. Flatulence.'

'You're not going tonight anyway. Not with that cold.'

'A-ah, but it's the *competition*. I'll lose *marks*.'

'Dib dib dib and dob dob dob.'

'It's not that any more, you know it isn't . . .'

'Akela wears a truss. I would like to thank you for your support . . . I wear it at all times.'

'Can I have another biscuit?'

'Here! Take the tin. When those are finished there aren't any more until Tuesday. Now go away and get washed and do your homework. Leave it alone, Oliver. Sam, did you find that shirt? Feet *off*, Toby. And do it properly. And don't keep flushing the loo, wait until you've all been. You know what happened yesterday.'

'I'll mend it.'

'Oh yes. Remember what happened when you mended the light?'

'Only because the rotten plaster's rotten.'

'Push off! And bring down your dirty shirts when you come. Oliver! Use your handkerchief!'

Voices and feet receded. Joanna closed the door. Every so often there was a thud or a crash above their heads and a few flakes of plaster floated down from the ceiling.

'Well, they seem cheerful enough. Hasn't it affected them at all?'

Beatrice opened the oven and stirred a rice pudding. She said, 'They don't know yet. They think he's just on a trip.'

'Oh Beatrice!'

'Oh Beatrice nothing. What am I supposed to say? Anyway, I told you, leave it till afterwards.'

Over dinner Joanna had her first chance to look at them. For a few brief blessed moments, a very few moments when they were comparatively still and their mouths were silenced with food. All of them, except for Oliver, towered above Beatrice. All of them seemed to treat her as Beatrice had once treated Bridget, as charwoman, cook, some-time confidante, recipient of grumbles, ironer of shirts, finder of ties, provider of money and food and clean socks, wiper of noses, butt of jokes, archetypal grown-up person incapable of understanding the finer nuances of life. And, towards them, Beatrice behaved with a kind of bewildered uncertainty, reiterating a perpetual and compulsive monologue: wipe your nose, don't bite your nails, where are you going, change your trousers, don't speak with your mouth full – as though this in some way reassured her, gave a structure to the relationship.

She'd always carried a mental image of them en masse, a multitude. It was a way of ridiculing Beatrice's fecundity: to imagine them as a tribe, rather than four individuals. But here, around the dinner table, she was forced to appreciate that they existed singly and separately: Sam, thickset, with his father's grave gaze and a quick grin that had nothing to do with his father; angel-faced Felix, self-contained and fastidious and given to sudden bursts of temper; Toby, Beatrice's child, dark, a mutinous stare and a smile full of sweetness, and Oliver, the last of the mistakes, for ever placing himself in precarious positions, laying himself open to

209

teasing and then crying when subsequently teased. How curious it must feel: to produce issue, *persons*, who were like you and not like you; to be responsible for somebody else's existence; what a disconcerting thought.

They accorded her the small amount of attention that courtesy demanded. She was just some ancient friend of their mother's who had visited them from time to time and sent them presents on their birthdays: unappreciated presents mostly: educational toys from Hamley's when they preferred garishly coloured plastic objects made in Hong Kong with built-in obsolescence. She was much posher and swankier-looking than their mother. Her fingernails were long and polished and her face was covered in stuff and she smelled of something rather more exotic than Palmolive soap and Domestos. Her husband was that thin dark balding chap who'd nearly had a heart attack when Toby was sick over his trousers.

'This meat's tough.'

It was. Joanna chewed until her jaws ached, eventually pleaded a small appetite, decided to put herself IC cuisine for the rest of her stay.

'And the carrots aren't done. When are you going to learn to cook? It's worse pigswill than we get at school.'

'Oh *not* rice pudding. I *hate* rice pudding.'

'Since when?'

'Since always. Re*volt*ing.'

'Worse than Dead Man's Leg? Or Blood and Bandages?'

'Fly's Cemetery today. Oh God.'

'We know. It's all over your blazer.'

'Blame Mason. He chucked it at me.'

'Spotted Dick.'

'Spotted Dick!' Spotted Dick sent them off into mounting waves of hysteria. All except Sam who said, 'Mum, can't I eat in my room? It's absolutely disgusting down here, like joining in at a trough.'

'You can all stop showing off. Or leave the table and do without. Joanna is unused to feeding with savages.'

Felix put his elbow on the table, leaned his chin on his hand and contemplated her. 'Are you still at Oxford?' She nodded. 'Is it OK?'

'I think so.'

Beatrice lit a cigarette, smiled a little one-sided smile, said, 'Joanna is involved in the perpetuation of an élite. Or that's how she'd have described it fifteen years ago. Have you clinched the Chair yet, Joanna?'

'What are you on about?' Felix said.

'Nothing. Nothing at all.'

'I might go there,' he said. 'Oxford.'

'Oh I say, that's awfully good of you.' Sam cut himself a chunk of cheese. 'They'll be awfully pleased about that.' He cut himself another chunk. Beatrice said, 'Sam, that cheese has to last till the weekend. You can't still be hungry.'

'Nag, nag, nag nag nag.'

'What are you planning on, Felix? Chemistry still?'

'Good grief, no. What's that thing you teach?'

'Philosophy.'

'I might do that.'

Sam spluttered into his coffee cup. 'He doesn't even know what it is. Cretin. Felix Ross, reading Pornography. Your starter for ten . . .'

Felix blushed, made mountains in the sugar bowl. 'What's that place Grandfather was at?'

'Magdalene. And it was Cambridge, you cretin.'

'I might go there.'

Beatrice tapped her cigarette against the edge of the ashtray. 'I don't think you should follow in his footsteps. He got sent down.'

'Did he really?' Joanna swivelled in her chair. 'I never knew that. Whatever for?'

Beatrice pursed her lips, shrugged her shoulders, blew on her coffee. Sam said, 'Having it off, probably. Randy old so-and-so.'

'That will *do*, Sam. If I hear any more of that I shall clip you round the ear.'

'You couldn't reach,' Samuel said, very quietly. Felix sniggered. Oliver said, 'Having what off?'

Joanna poured more coffee. 'How about the rest of you? What about you, Sam?'

'Mechanical engineering. If I pass the rotten exams.'

Toby came out of his trance. 'I'd like to be an astronomer.'

'You haven't got the eyebrows for it.'

'He has a telescope in the shed at the bottom of the garden,' Beatrice said. '*When* he can be bothered.'

Oliver said, 'Having what off?'

'Shut up, Oliver, and *blow your nose*.'

211

'Shut up Oliver, shut up Oliver, that's all I ever hear.' He sank under the table until only his eyes and his fringe were visible. 'I don't suppose anybody's interested in what I'm going to be?'

'We are all agog.'

'Absolutely agog.'

'Dying to know as well.'

'Well, go on, what do you want to be?'

He hauled himself back into his seat. 'I just changed my mind,' he said.

Toby finished off the cheese. 'We don't have to clear up, do we? Only I'm going round to Grayson's. He's setting up his fish tank tonight.'

'And I'm going to the Photographical Society.'

'And I've got masses and masses of stinking Geography.'

'And I'm going to the Cubs.'

'*You're* going to bed. I'm going to rub your chest with Vick and then you're going to bed.'

'You are rotten.'

'I dare say.'

'Can I have the portable telly, then?'

'Oh Mum, don't let him have it. Remember what he did last time. We couldn't watch the match.'

'You can have it provided that you promise not to fiddle with it. Be quiet, Felix. And the rest of you – come back here and *listen*: put your scarves on because it's cold and mind the traffic and *don't* take that short cut over the fields and I want you back no later than nine-thirty.'

'It doesn't finish until ten,' Sam said. 'Good God, Mum, I'm not a kid. When *you* were my age I was almost born.'

'You're getting your dates a bit mixed, aren't you?'

'No, that was you. You got your dates a bit mixed.'

'I shan't tell you again . . .'

She raised the ashtray. He ducked out of the door. He said, 'I may be a little boy, but I can *count*.'

Toby and Samuel left, scarf-less, their coats flying wide open. Felix went unwillingly to his bedroom. Beatrice and Joanna cleared the table and washed six sets of dishes plus odds and sods left over from breakfast and lunch. By the time they'd finished, and Oliver's chest had been rubbed and the portable television had been adjusted until there was more picture than snow, and Felix had been told to turn off that racket and get on with your homework and they'd made another cup of coffee to sustain themselves after their labours, Toby and Samuel were back and it was supper-time and mugs of Ovaltine and plates of sandwiches and another load of dirty dishes.

'Sometimes I could be quite happy with them just changing their socks and brushing their teeth and keeping out of my way,' Beatrice said. She drew the curtains, threw half a bucket of coal on the dying fire and sank back into the sofa. 'Sometimes I long for the day when they're old enough to leave home. Or rather, I used to do. Now I need them, don't I?' In the firelight, in her jeans and ridiculous rugby jersey, she looked eighteen years old again. 'There's a bottle of plonk and some glasses in that cupboard. I'm sorry, I should be waiting on you, shouldn't I? I'm shattered. Some mornings I can scarcely find the energy to push back the bed-clothes. I just want to bury my head and stay there till I die.'

'You were awake early enough yesterday morning.'

'And some nights I can't get to sleep at all.'.

Apart from the occasional muffled thump, the house was quiet. 'Listen to them,' Beatrice said. 'Children of the night. What music they make!' They drew their legs underneath them and sipped their drinks. It wasn't plonk. It was Blue Nun. For which Joanna was profoundly thankful. You got to the age when plonk would no longer do. After a long pause, during which Beatrice did a lot of unconscious sighing, Joanna said, 'When did he finally depart?'

'Last Tuesday.'

'To the bosom of . . . ?'

'Yes, Greta, whatever the hell her name is. The red-haired cow.'

'She's not called Greta?'

'No. She's called Gillian. It's just that, looking at her, you'd expect her to have one of those ghastly working-class film star names: Greta or Rita or Marlene.'

'You're all right?'

'Oh yeah. I'm hysterical with joy.'

'You're too calm.'

'I don't know the appropriate reactions. It's a bit late for weeping and wailing, isn't it? And I can't say it came as a bolt from the blue.'

'And what about – that man?' Joanna said, making a big pro-duction number out of wiping the base of her glass and setting it down on the carpet.

'Didn't want to know. Did not want to know. I could hear him

213

trembling in his shoes when I phoned him. Said he was probably being posted to the Midlands. Scared stiff of being *named*. I don't know why I rang him. I can't stand the sight of him. I couldn't stand the sight of him sometimes when it was happening, let alone after it was over.'

'Well then – why?'

Beatrice tore the Cellophane from a fresh packet of cigarettes. 'Why did you desert your husband for a year and go off to America with another fellow?'

'What?'

'You heard me.'

Beatrice blushed when she was embarrassed. Joanna went pale.

'Well, you did, didn't you? And Neville got to know about it and now he punishes you by staying married to you and not married to you, buggering off for six months of the year and then making you kiss his feet every time he returns, showering you with furs and jewels and sodding Lotus Elites and then reminding you of the way you used to think. It's a far subtler form of cruelty. My husband's just buggered off, period.'

Joanna bit the inside skin of her cheek. 'You're quite wrong. We have a workable relationship. It may seem unusual to outsiders but it works for us. We do care for each other. And, besides, I didn't just pick up with the first man who cast an eye in my direction.'

'I was never very discriminating, was I? Anyone would do. Oh, stop going on about him, as if *he* was important. All this started happening five years ago and you know it. Long before he came on the scene. Or the others.'

'What others?'

'What others!' Beatrice refilled her glass to the brim. 'Have some more of this and stop giving me that shocked-to-the-depths-of-your-soul bit. Others. Others who looked at me rather than looking through me. Others I fancied, momentarily.'

'You needed them?'

'I needed something. After my father died and Bridget died, after Bridget died in the middle of doing my washing,' Beatrice said slowly, 'and then that awful business, I think I went a little bit mad. I was on tranquillizers for six months. It was open my eyes, greet the dawn and reach for a Valium. And David not communicating with me, not knowing that it was then we could have started again, properly, with our eyes open. I was in hell, a kind of do-I-exist-or-is-somebody-dreaming-me state. They made me feel real. They were therapeutic, that's all. They should have been prescribed on the National Health, instead of the Valium.'

'And David knew about these others?'

'Perhaps. I don't know. Yes, I suppose he did. As long as I was fairly discreet he didn't give a damn. The damage was done as far as he was concerned. For five years we've communicated via the kids. Oh, I don't mean we didn't address one another. We said, "Have you got the car keys?" and "What time will you be home?" and "Your striped shirt's in the wash," and occasionally we gritted our teeth and had sex and we lay on various beaches for three weeks of every year and went together to parent/teacher meetings and we had people to dinner and we managed not to stick knives into each other and at Christmas he filled the children's pillow-cases and he paid the bills and bought me flowers on our anniversary and a card that said "To my darling wife", and year by year I knew him less and less.'

'Perhaps he'll find out that this woman's not· what he wants. Perhaps he'll be back with his head in his hands.'

'Oh Joanna don't give me that mouthwash!' Beatrice mopped up spilled drink with her handkerchief.

'Eyewash.'

'Eyewash, then. She's exactly what he wants. She's got a home, she's got money and she hasn't got any kids. She'll devote her life · to mopping his brow and healing his hurts. She's the woman he's been searching for ever since his voice broke. So don't give me any crap about reconciliations. It's over. It's final. When all desire and affection between two people has died, you might as well accept it gracefully. You think I should go and castrate him and poison her tea?'

'I think he should be made aware of his responsibilities. He has, after all, fathered your children. Or is that a fact you simply shrug off when it becomes inconvenient?'

'Oh he'll come to see them. If it's only to make sure I haven't smothered them in their beds. He thinks I'm unbalanced. And incapable of coping. He remembers all the times Bridget looked after them during the day and he got up at night to give them drinks of water while I sat on my backside reading *Crime and Punishment*.'

'You ought to tell them.'

'I know. I'm too much of a coward.'

'Or he should have told them.'

'He's a coward too. I know just what will happen: Sam will want to know every last detail, will want it all logical and straight-forward – everything proceeds according to certain laws in Sam's estimation; Felix will go white round the mouth and say, "So what?"; Toby will yawn, and Oliver will cry because whenever people's faces assume a certain sort of expression Oliver cries automatically. There'll be traumas, will there? It's inevitable?'

'Nothing's inevitable. It depends to a great extent on the state of the relationship before the split. Presumably they've been aware of a somewhat strained atmosphere for the last few years?'

'I don't know. They've always been so wrapped up in their own concerns. Perhaps they thought that all parents behave towards each other as we did: just sort of moving parallel through the days rather than actually touching.'

'Did you think, when you were a child, that all parents behaved the way yours did?'

'Heavens, no. I knew that other people just didn't function at the same pitch.'

'And would you have been shattered if they'd parted?'

Beatrice considered. 'No, I don't think I would, but then I had Bridget. And David and I certainly didn't spend fifty per cent of our time together screaming at one another and the other fifty per cent in bed. I'll let him explain,' Beatrice decided, draining her glass. 'When he comes to see them. He'll do it less vitriolically than I should. And I dare say that's for the best. They've never been all that close to him, anyway. It was always "Your father's tired. Don't bother him. I'll do it, whatever it is." He considered that putting a roof over their heads and food in their mouths and clothes on their backs was the sum total of fatherhood.' She placed the cool bowl of the glass against her forehead. 'Maybe that's unfair. No it bloody isn't. It's bloody true.'

Joanna yawned. Beatrice said, 'I'm sorry, you must be tired. All that driving. Do you want to go to bed?'

'I'm all right. Will you divorce him?'

She shrugged. 'I don't want to marry anyone else. Let him sweat.'

'You might be better off financially.'

'Oh, he's giving me the same amount of money. He told me that. Very noble. I think he expected me to touch the ground with my forehead. And as I won't have to keep him out of it, I suppose

I'll be better off. Such as it is. He had to take a big drop, you know. He was lucky to get another job. Six years ago redundant sales executives who'd ridden on their father-in-law's shoulders for a considerable number of years were an extremely dodgy proposition. They probably still are. We manage. Just.'

'Why don't you get in touch with your mother?'

'And have her gloating? I'd rather starve in the gutter. Besides, the rate that she's going there won't be much left.'

'I thought he'd have left you something. Separately.'

Beatrice smoothed the creases in her forehead. 'He was playing Monopoly,' she said, 'towards the end. With the bank in the leading rôle. We didn't know. David didn't know. A retinue of accountants came to explain the situation. All his life he'd gambled and won. For the first time he didn't have the chance to see it through. He'd hit a bad patch: strikes, rising costs, *I* don't know. He was in hock. He knew, the state things were in at the time, that if he left anything directly to me, he'd be depriving her. And he couldn't do that, not even after death. Besides, a lot of stuff was in her name anyway. For death duties, etcetera. The Yanks bought her out, closed two factories and made a clean sweep. With David, as you know, the first one out of the door. Perhaps the Yanks don't care for nepotism.'

They sat for a little while longer, yawning, forcing their eyelids open, worrying around the edges of the situation, not yet sufficiently at ease with one another to go directly to the heart of the matter. There were events, five-year-old events, that couldn't be hauled forth by the scruff of the neck but had to be gently, tactfully, disinterred, brought out into the light and inspected. But it was too soon. Beatrice gathered up the bottle and the glasses and the brimming ashtray. 'You'll stay? You won't dash off at the earliest opportunity?'

'I'll stay if you want me to, until after Easter. Though I'm not sure that I'm necessary. You seem very calm. Of course, if, as you say, you no longer love him, if it's simply a matter of hurt pride and disorientation – '

Beatrice turned round abruptly. 'Who said anything about not loving him? Just because I said there was no desire or affection between us doesn't mean to say I didn't love him. I think I'd only just started to do that.'

3

'I shall have to go to see her,' Joanna said. 'Well, there's no "have to" about it. I shall go to see her.' She cradled an armful of plates. 'Where do these go?'

'In that cupboard.'

'After all, I've never had any quarrel with her.'

'Of course not.' Beatrice began to sort socks out of the dirty washing. 'Of course not. She is beyond reproach. Always has been. You take this lot to the launderette. You'll see her there. The one in Sadler Street, opposite Marks and Sparks. Now, I must remember to segregate Toby's. He's got athlete's foot.'

'What do you mean, I'll see her if I go to the launderette?'

Beatrice shook soap powder into the sink and put eight pairs of underpants to soak. 'She works there. What a pity that we fell out. No doubt she could get me cut-rate prices on this lot.'

'She works in a launderette!'

'Yes, that's right.'

'But why?'

'Maybe they don't need a new governor at the Bank of England. Maybe she just missed being elected a Fellow of All Souls.' Beatrice rubbed vigorously at the Y-fronts. 'It may have escaped your notice, Joanna dear, but there are round about one and a half million unemployed persons in this country. Besides, I suppose it's convenient for her; it's just around the corner from where they live and perhaps it fits in with school hours.'

'But surely there must have been something better than that.'

'She is unqualified and inexperienced. Like me.'

'You have *some* qualifications.'

'The odd GCE in Latin and Greek,' Beatrice said, 'somehow seems to have no relevance to the scheme of regarding oneself as a marketable commodity. And I don't suppose an alcoholic husband is much of an asset in that direction.'

'You don't ever see him?'

With a soapy hand Beatrice pushed her hair behind her ear. 'No, never. Even in a town this size you can succeed in avoiding some-body if you really set your mind to it.'

Joanna folded the sheets. 'There wouldn't be any message?'

'There wouldn't be any message.'

Joanna parked the car, posted a letter to her husband, bought meat, eggs, fruit, vegetables, cheese, bacon, two bottles of Nuits St Georges and, on impulse, four boys' sweat shirts from a very expensive teenage boutique. She then cashed a cheque at Lloyd's Bank and walked round to Sadler Street opposite Marks and Spencer's.

And there another girl with maroon hair – it couldn't be the Tudor Café girl; perhaps it was her sister? – sat filing her green fingernails beside a stack of clothes baskets. A youth in denims with a St Christopher medal arranged throttle-fashion around his neck shuffled stamped-out fag ends into a pattern on the floor. Joanna smiled. The girl stared. The youth looked away. 'Is Mrs Russell here?'

The girl inclined her head without taking her eyes off Joanna's face and yelled, 'Mad! There's a woman here wants you,' into the recesses of the establishment.

Madeleine came through from the back. She said, 'Hello, Joanna,' as coolly and casually as though they'd parted from each other ten minutes previously, as though there hadn't been a gap of three years, punctuated only by the odd letter, so unforthcoming that it amounted to nothing more than a waste of paper and effort.

It was Joanna who lost her composure. 'I've brought my washing,' she said fatuously, holding out her polythene bag.

Madeleine lifted the lid of the nearest washing machine, began to pull the sheets out of the bag. 'You mean you've brought *her* washing. You'll need five pence for the detergent machine. Unless you've brought your own.'

She continued to stuff sheets into the interior of the washer. She wore a green overall and her feet were bandaged and there was a yellow bruise on her forearm. There were signs of settling-into-middle-age in her gestures, in the way she bent to retrieve a pillow-case, the way that she straightened slowly, one hand to the small of her back. Joanna thought of those long-ago women in her father's surgery with their kids and their gynaecological troubles, members of an amorphous age-grouping that manifested itself physically at a mean average of fifty years old. Working-class women aged quickly, she had thought then; it was patterned in their genes. Though her father had said no, had said it was due to worry, poverty and worry.

Well, probably Madeleine had had her fair share of those. Down the years.

'Look,' Joanna said. 'Could you spare a few minutes while those are washing? There's a Kardomah next door but one, isn't there?' There was no possibility of a conversation with the glassy-eyed girl and the youth hanging on to their every word.

Madeleine looked up at the clock. 'Would you mind, Dawn? You won't forget to check the dry-cleaner?'

Dawn filed her thumbnail to a fearsome point, looked up and stared. 'I just don't understand them,' Beatrice had said, 'the Dawns, the Tracys and the Sharons. They are alien beings. I never got on particularly well with the Carols, the Barbaras and the Susans, but at least we were of the same era, we had once held certain erroneous beliefs in common: ladies always wearing gloves and children being seen and not heard and men wanting to marry virgins.'

They carried their coffee cups to a vacant table. We could all get by on much less food and drink, Joanna reflected, if we didn't use them as props. We don't seem to be able to open our mouths to one another unless we've a cup or a glass or a loaded fork in our hands.

'You're staying with her?' Madeleine said. 'Dispensing comfort and moral support? Mopping up the tears?'

'You've heard?'

'That sort of news comes on jungle drums. The rest of the town probably knew about it before they knew it themselves. She probably said, "Ask Madeleine if she's satisfied now."'

She had covered her green overall with a coat, a cheap shabby coat. Wisps of soft hair escaped from her woollen hat. Appearance-wise, like Beatrice, she had given up. The difference being that Beatrice could veer towards the eccentric: rugby jerseys and boys' anoraks and wellington boots and still, somehow, manage to look striking, whereas Madeleine, who had always needed good clothes and good hairdressers before her attractiveness was apparent, now assembled her wardrobe from market stalls and the counters of the cheaper chain stores.

'Surely it's time that all that business was dead and buried?'

'She has every right to feel aggrieved. She was always used to getting what she wanted from life. She thought there was no limit to what she could take. With absolute impunity. She never realized that eventually you have to pay for what you've had.'

'You sound like the voice of the scriptures.'

'I believe in justice.'

Joanna stirred and stirred her sugarless coffee. 'Children believe in justice, adults can usually encompass the concept of mercy.'

'I expect she still hates me. As I hated her.'

'Oh, I doubt it. I don't think Beatrice is much of a hater. Let's not pursue it. Let's talk about you. Let's talk about finding you something other than that ridiculous job. You're thirty-three, Madeleine, you can't spend the rest of your life sweeping the floors of launderettes.'

Madeleine ignored her, said, 'You look as though you're doing very well for yourself. I somehow never could visualize you teaching. I didn't think that you'd have the patience. How clever you are, Joanna. How clever you have always been. Even if your intelligence quotient was blush-making.'

'I find myself teaching less and less and administrating more and more. What do you mean, clever?'

'You always knew what mattered and what didn't and which people were dangerous and just when to say goodbye and just when to work and when to be idle. You always knew how to take the long view. You'll get your professorship and Neville will make a fortune and be knighted. It'll be half-a-crown to talk to you soon.'

Joanna made an attempt to stand outside herself and see herself as Madeleine saw her. Rich. Successful. Fulfilled. A woman with a high professional standing who had published at least one definitive work, who counted among her friends some of the best minds in Europe and North America, whose husband was the darling of fabulously wealthy menopausal matrons because of his air of discreet concern as well as his clinical and surgical skills, who divided her time between an architect-designed house on the outskirts of Oxford, a Welsh cottage and her husband's London flat, who drove an expensive car and holidayed in places that package tourists had never heard of.

The dice had always fallen for her. 'Lucky cow, aren't you?' he'd said – that man who'd been her lover and could never be her friend. 'The sort who falls down the sewer and comes up odourless, aren't you?'

So it had always been. Until now.

'How are things with you? How's Natasha?'

Natasha, eight years old, pale, pretty and asthmatic, the only survivor of a series of miscarriages.

'She still has attacks. But not quite so badly. Not like they used to be.' Two o'clock in the morning and they'd had to break off their quarrelling because there was a three-year-old child trying to crawl up the wall towards the window, towards the air, going blue in the face, the furious workings of her lungs visible beneath her nightdress. A pretty, pale, sickly child who'd learned that an attack of asthma could be relied upon to stop the quarrelling. For a while. Until the novelty wore off.

'And Desmond? Working yet?'

'No, not at the moment. I have to go,' Madeleine said. 'Perhaps you could come round this evening?'

'Would I be welcome?'

'He probably won't be in.' She put her foot to the floor and winced with pain. Joanna looked at the bandages and the bruise and looked at her queryingly. She said, 'I tripped and trod in some glass.'

'Weren't you wearing any shoes?'

'No. I was on my way to bed.'

'Did you go to the doctor? Slivers of glass can be nasty.'

'They're not so bad. Just sore. I'll expect you this evening, then?'

Oh well, into every life a little rain must fall.

She collected Natasha from school. Natasha was too old to need collecting from school but there was a busy main road that had to be crossed on the homeward journey. Natasha would walk quickly, apart from her, mortified, while the other kids, unaccompanied, fooled about and dashed between the traffic without looking either to the left or to the right.

She said, 'Will he be in?'

'No. He's gone for an interview.'

And it was as if the grey skies of March had parted to disclose the radiance of summer. The tightness in her chest dissolved, the threat of that first ominous wheeze was no more. Separately, she could feel affection, even love, for them; together, she hated them.

Madeleine unlocked the door, picked up the two buff-coloured envelopes from the mat and checked the five rooms of the flat. On the mantelpiece in the living-room he had left her a note. It said not to expect him before ten: he was taking the opportunity to visit an old acquaintance of his who worked at the Polytechnic in the town where his interview was being held. Once, years ago, there had been another note left propped behind a clock and the words of that note – 'I hate you, you bitch' – written with such force that the pen had driven through the paper, had bored into her brain with the intensity of a great truth, finally acknowledged.

Fragments of glass, trapped in the carpet fibres, glinted outside the bathroom. A dustpan and brush wouldn't be effective; she would have to use the vacuum cleaner attachment and suck them up. As well as finding some way of removing the jagged edges in the empty panel of the bathroom door. It was thin fragile glass that had yielded readily to his elbow. She didn't know what impulse it was that had prompted her to flee from him, to run into the bathroom and lock the door behind her. Usually she submitted. He hit her silently and she submitted to it silently. That way his rage worked itself out quicker and the child slept. Her attempt at escape had only enraged him further. She had locked herself against him psychologically; that she should attempt to do it literally was beyond endurance. His elbow had come through the glass and his hand had turned the lock and he'd hauled her, from where she stood in the corner between the lavatory and the bath, across a sea of jagged glass. And throughout the agony she had wondered dully if the noise had wakened the child and whether there were any important arteries or whatever in your feet that could cause you to bleed to death.

Sometimes she read leaflets distributed by Alcoholics Anonymous and the Samaritans and once she'd even got as far as pushing her twopence into the slot of the telephone before sanity intervened. Alcoholics were persons who could not function without drink. Desmond could go for several months without touching it, weeks and weeks of sobriety before going on a bender. Desmond was not an alcoholic. The violence was not due to the drink; the drink merely allowed expression of the violence. And as for the Samaritans: the idea of attempting to articulate her problems to some disembodied voice on the end of a telephone was too daunting. She couldn't even articulate them to herself. Her family doctor

(Beatrice's family doctor too; they had often, all unaware, escaped meeting one another in the waiting-room by the merest fraction of time) was the most obvious source of help. He would say, 'Perhaps you enjoy being beaten? Some women do, you know.' Or he'd make her an appointment with a marriage guidance counsellor. Or send her to a refuge for battered wives. Sometimes she'd sit, mute, while he examined Natasha, opening her mouth and closing it again. He said that children who suffered from attacks of asthma were often under severe emotional strain. He said it with a question mark at the end of the sentence. But always she sang dumb. He couldn't help her any more than the AA or the Samaritans could help. He couldn't roll back thirteen years of time and remake the world so that it suited Desmond's psyche. He couldn't cancel out all the snubs and rejections that a person with Desmond's temperament was bound to attract, all the hard work brought to nought, all the rotten ill-luck. He couldn't bring back the Desmond she'd once known, she *thought* she'd once known.

The flat above the bookmaker's. Joanna rang the bell, hoping to heaven that he would be absent. She hadn't met him for seven years and if she didn't meet him for another seven it wouldn't be a moment too soon.

Natasha received the book that Joanna brought for her quietly and politely, proceeded to unwrap it and read it. 'You always bought books,' Madeleine said, 'as birthday presents. So that you could read them beforehand. It was obvious. You were a messy child. You've altered.'

'I expect we've all altered.'

'Beatrice's father always used to say that you'd end up voting for the Labour Party.'

Then Beatrice's father, dying thrillingly, ecstatically, you were wrong. 'I don't vote for anybody. The people I agree with ideologically, I deplore individually, and usually vice-versa.'

'You're outside it all then? You've abdicated your responsibility?'

'I try to transmit the views I hold. I try to educate and re-educate.'

'You once said that nothing was ever achieved by appealing to reason.'

'I once thought that the world lay at my feet just waiting for the word. I lost the belief in my messianic abilities along with a good many other misconceptions.' She smoothed her skirt. 'What about you? Are you performing some kind of penance? Can't you just go to church once a year and do that?'

'There aren't any other jobs.'

'*No* other jobs? I know it's practically reached the state where you need two A-levels to work behind Woolies' counter, but I can't believe that a trip to the Occupational or Vocational Guidance or whatever it's called might not produce something a little more suited to your talents and capabilities.' Joanna accepted a second slice of cake. Something that obviously hadn't changed was her appetite. 'Usually, when someone takes a job that is unrelated to either of those categories,' she said, 'it's because they're researching, or they need to do something mechanical and boring while they devote their minds to higher things, or because their self-esteem has taken a hammering. Or else it's because they're seeking some kind of absolution. And you're not writing a novel about launderettes, are you? Or unravelling the secrets of the universe?'

'I thought you'd given up instant psychoanalysis. Why am I seeking absolution?'

'To return to a state of grace, of course. Isn't that what it's all about, your religion? You're doing a sort of physical equivalent of a few decades of the Rosary. Like nuns flagellating themselves. I take it you've lapsed totally?'

She nodded. *Ego te absolvo a peccatis tuis,* she remembered. It wasn't even that any more; it was in the vernacular now. She remembered the confessional and the priest's little dry cough, her First Communion veil and her white kid shoes and all those horrible rough boys that she knew from school transformed, their thin pure voices raised in the *Gloria*, the bland nothing taste of the wafer on her tongue and the belief that she had something that all those Protestants at school, singing 'Eternal Father, Strong to Save' with such gusto and practising their religion on a Sunday, could never have. She remembered the Paschal candles and the Sanctus bell and the very last time that she'd felt safe.

'I should have thought you'd be glad. You were always so anxious to rid me of cant. Or to rid me of one sort and replace it with another.'

'Was I? Did I? I thought I wanted you to be free.'

'What's freedom?' Madeleine said. Although that concept which had once seemed merely a mystifying abstraction was now becoming

225

more familiar; freedom was possibly being able to do without someone who hit you and hated you, someone who'd dragged you half across England in his search for a place where his talents might be appreciated and then blamed you for his failures because you were the only one who gave a damn about what became of him. To be free would be to be without a need of him, without the love or the hate or whatever it was that she felt for him; to be eternally indifferent.

They spoke guardedly. About Desmond's interview. (To say that he had a slim chance of success would have been an over-statement; he had been too long out of teaching and there were certain to have been a hundred and thirty-three applicants for the position. Oh, for those golden days when everybody was having babies and nobody gave a hoot about your sense of vocation and Desmond could blithely turn down offers all over London! Still, he had an interview.) They talked of the quaint power structures in Joanna's college and her sojourn in America, of Neville's Arabian appointment and the technique he had perfected for the unblocking of blocked tubes, of the changes that had taken place in the town since Joanna had last visited it, of Amy Bellamy's second marriage and subsequent divorce, of her third marriage. The presence of the child acted as a deterrent against speaking of what Joanna really wanted to speak about and what Madeleine, despite herself, really wanted to know: the state of affairs in that house up on the hill. And then, when it was finally time for Natasha to close her book, drink her hot milk and go to bed, in came Desmond – two hours earlier than anticipated.

She could tell now, instantly, whether he was or whether he wasn't – something about the eyes, the fixity of his gaze – even before he moved towards her and she saw his exaggerated gestures and smelled the drink on him. He wasn't. There was an automatic release of tension: her hands relaxed their grasp on the arms of the chair, the lines around her mouth disappeared, her breath was exhaled in a deep sigh. He wasn't. Sometimes it went on for days, and so did the subsequent oblivion. But tonight he wasn't. And tonight she could sleep peacefully beside the warmth and security of his sleeping body.

He and Joanna contemplated one another for a few moments without speaking. My God, how grand she's become, he thought: one of those women who strike the fear of God into everybody around them, one of those women who get up to speak and everybody falls silent. Why ever did she desert politics? She'd have been a wild success. She always had presence but when I knew her she hadn't learned to ally it to appearance and manner. She used to wear whatever her hand first landed upon in the morning and her approach was about as subtle as a battering ram. She's come a long way with Neville, Neville and his civilizing influence. Then, she would have burned at the stake for what she thought she believed in and everyone regarded her as a joke; now, when no one would ever dream of regarding her as a joke, she's opted out.

His once firmly-muscled taut physique was becoming a memory. There was a fold of flesh at the back of his neck and the hint of a paunch. There was loose skin under his eyes and lines on his forehead and a lot of grey in his hair which had receded dramatically from his brow. You kept a picture in your mind and, on re-encountering someone after a number of years, it was that picture you used as a key to recognition; the changes, the depressing changes became obvious only gradually: he turned his head and you saw a slackness of the jawline, he moved towards you and you saw that those straight shoulders now incorporated the suggestion of a stoop. He had been a young man: firm-fleshed, athletic, with a profusion of black curls and now he was a grey-haired man with bags under his eyes and a furrowed brow; a grown-up person. We are all grown-up persons, she realized: Madeleine, her hips spreading beneath her green overall; Neville, carrying the responsibility of life or no life in his hands; Beatrice with her childbirth scars and her children; and me. We are approaching middle age, half way along the journey. She had a picture of each of them as being at the extremes of an axis or, perhaps, occupying different positions on the vast boardgame of their accumulated experience: Beatrice stuck in a corner, queen of the crèche, Madeleine trying and failing to negotiate an insurmountable obstacle, and Joanna herself, racing round the track, lapping them both, side-stepping the obstacles, avoiding the trap of Beatrice's corner, not even daring to look.

And then Madeleine rose to take Natasha to bed and he sat down and offered her a cigarette – which she declined – and said, 'Given up all your bad habits?' and the moment was broken and he was only Desmond again whom she disliked, Desmond the wrecker, Desmond who, seemingly, couldn't move in one or other direction through life without leaving chaos and ruination in his wake.

'You're staying with her?'

His face was quite impassive. You mentioned the name of a former lover to a woman and a little shadow flickered across her face: of regret, or affection, or amusement; men didn't seem to be affected by retrospective emotion in the same way.

'Yes. You know all about it, I expect?'

The implication being: you ought to know all about it but, so often, those who initiate have no knowledge of the consequences of their actions.

'Him slinging his hook? Oh yes. It's no loss, I should have thought.'

'He speaks very highly of you too.'

'I once threatened to break his head. I'd do it again if he came within shouting distance of me.'

'I rather thought that that should have been his prerogative. If there was a head to be split open I should have thought that it would be yours.'

He looked at her silently. She was disturbed to find that he could still goad her, could still curl his lip and she was eighteen again and incoherent with indignation. Why, she didn't know; she didn't respect his intelligence or his opinion or anything else about him; it was just that air of challenge he had, a sense of flung gauntlet that she just couldn't resist picking up.

He leaned forward, ground out his cigarette in the ashtray. He said, very quietly, 'How is she taking it?'

'Unnaturally. I think she'll carry on, continuing to cope, for just so long, and then the balloon will go up.'

'There'll be someone else for her. Someone better.'

'Someone better than you?'

Madeleine stood in the doorway. Madeleine had heard. She encircled the wrist of her left hand with the fingers of her right. It was a gesture that Joanna had noticed several times since they'd met, a gesture of restraint perhaps. She said, 'Do you want something to eat?'

'No, thanks. I ate while I was waiting to change trains. Ralph wasn't there. He's been given leave to do post-graduate research or something. Maybe that's what I should do. How would you rate my chances, eh Joanna?'

'Very slim. How was the interview?'

'A wash-out. The one in front of me had a First Class degree and the one after me had just come fresh from in-service training. Very important, in-service training. Helps you to understand all that jargon they throw at you in interviews. Of course, you wouldn't know about that, would you, Joanna? Not from the dizzy heights of your pinnacle.'

'I have to take part in interviews just like everybody else.'

'Really? I thought, for you, it was simply a matter of inclining your head in a gracious yes or no to various invitations. I thought it was only scum like me who had to bow and scrape and bite my tongue when those sneering bastards feel the need to make snide comments on what they call my chequered career: "Bit of a chequered career, isn't it, Mr Russell? Any particular reason?"'

'And was there? Any particular reason?' For the way you moved on and on, exiting acrimoniously from every job that had seemed just the thing, shifting your belongings and your wife and, later, your child from rural Wales to Chester to a commune in Dorset, to London, to Manchester, to Norfolk, and all the places in between, from schoolteaching to commerce, to industry, back to schoolteaching, to community work, to a brief spell in administration, and finally back here to the Dole? .

Madeleine shifted nervously in her chair. She didn't want him to begin it: the long explanation, of the houses that had fallen apart, the people who wanted to do him down, the cultural deserts, the intellectual tundras, the aesthetic slag-heaps, the closed minds and the malice, the uncertainty within himself, the feeling that nothing held together at the centre, that there *was* no centre, the tuberculosis that had kept him idle for the best part of a year, the novel that had gone the rounds of nineteen publishers, the proposed *Aspects of the Industrial Revolution* that never got beyond the early stages of research, the sudden wild enthusiasms that flared and died so very quickly. She didn't want him to begin it; it made him sound – paranoid.

But he merely said, 'I needed change. And now society can't accept that way of life. You have to dive for your niche and hold fast to it. No longer any little diversions on the way. You've clung all right, haven't you, Joanna? Nothing could dislodge you now. Well, tell us all about it. That's why you came, surely, to dazzle us?'

And so their discourse proceeded in a fairly amicable fashion. Madeleine made more tea and Joanna talked about herself and

Desmond only interrupted every now and then to say, 'The people's flag is deepest red,' or 'Man is born good; capitalism corrupts him.' And they talked of Natasha and how Natasha was really going to fulfil her potential: she was going to be a painter or a writer or a musician, something outside the system; no second-class seat on the academic gravy train for her, no supercilious bastards pulling rank or class on her; creativity was the only thing that could see you sane through this stinking world; he hadn't had it, but she had. And he produced some drawings she'd done for Joanna to see. They were talented, they were accurate and they were horribly neat.

Joanna made polite noises and wondered what it was about parenthood that destroyed one's critical faculties. She had noted it time and time again: people who could distinguish wheat from chaff almost blindfold suddenly developing these blind spots when it came to the creative or intellectual abilities of their children. Nevertheless, she said, 'Yes, very good,' and 'Remarkable,' and was a little touched to see that Desmond too was incapable of true objectivity; it made him seem more natural. She'd always thought of him as being completely devoid of all natural human feeling.

4

An altogether unproductive visit, of course. She searched for her toothbrush in amongst six other toothbrushes, most of them quite hard and dry. If they could get away with neglecting it, they neglected it. And, as Beatrice said, she simply didn't have the mental energy, let alone the physical stamina, to follow them around enquiring into the nature and extent of their ablutionary omissions.

Joanna ran the water, wiped off rings round the bath and got into it. She soaked for a long time, regulating the water temperature with her big toe, ruminating on that unproductive visit because otherwise other pictures, unbidden, would pervade her consciousness: her lover's bathroom with its six toothbrushes; the flurry of bath-time; she imagined him towelling down his youngest children, gently – he was one of those heavily-built, almost brutal-looking men who surprise you with the tenderness of their touch. Six toothbrushes, six egg cups, and a wife called Sylvia married young, crowned with orange blossom in the second half of her first pregnancy; she'd held her stomach in valiantly for five long months until he'd taken his Finals and then he'd done the right thing, in accordance with the strict working-class morality that was his heritage, that he'd accepted. Sylvia the hairdresser-as-was, collecting recipes from women's magazines by day, serving him relays of coffee in the room where he sank himself in his work, his other life, opening her legs for him in bed at night. She couldn't imagine Sylvia's face, she thought of Fallopian tubes instead.

The water rose above her heart. It hurt. Neville treated erosions of the womb. Could you have an erosion of the heart? She moaned briefly into Beatrice's sponge. 'We can have a year,' he'd said. 'I won't leave her. It wouldn't be fair.' Simple, clear-cut. Winter in Boston. Oh God! She'd never dreamed that it could hurt so badly. One academic year. And an afternoon in a borrowed flat, to say goodbye. Brown eyes, he had, limpid, steady, that refused to be compromised. And a fine, razor-sharp intellect. 'What on earth do you have in common?' You and Sylvia Fallopian Tubes? The kids.

Her skin began to pinken and pucker. Such complacency! To imagine that she'd be immune. 'Perhaps you'll be able to identify it for us – that bit reserved for that sort of thing – isolate it,' Robert Martin had said, 'and save us all a tremendous amount of bother-ation.'

She'd had it all under such perfect control: her job, her marriage, her entire lifestyle. Babies just hadn't happened – but then she'd never wanted babies. Nor had Neville; they'd wanted fulfilment in their careers and the freedom to enjoy the fruits that those careers afforded. With Neville's assistance, her future had been mapped out; he liked order, rhythm, harmony. He liked to be able to say, 'Next week, we will do such and such a thing,' in the certain knowledge that it would come to pass. He was intelligent and ambitious, he was organized and reliable – if he said he'd meet you at half past two, he'd meet you at half past two if he had to crawl there on his hands and knees. And he had an unerring instinct for the particular course of action that would yield the greatest satisfaction. She'd never really appreciated just how much he'd smoothed the path for her, ironed out the irritations, groomed her to be what he thought she was capable of becoming. It wasn't until she met that man – her lover – that she'd realized that with no uncertainty, there can be no excitement.

For he was dangerous. That much she recognized at the same moment as she recognized the prickling of her skin and the thud of her heart as he reached out his hand towards her, dangerous because he seemed to have walked out of a past that she'd abandoned: a past when every day could amaze you by presenting some unusual opportunity, some unsuspected facet of social experience. He'd smiled at her as he'd turned towards her on the not-very-clean sheets in that borrowed bedroom and his smile had said: 'This you couldn't plan for, incorporate smoothly into your scheme of things, however much you tried. Nice middle-class lady having a fling with a bit of rough – you'll moan underneath me in just the same way as any street-corner tart; all your fancy manners and your suitable friends and your napkin rings won't make the slightest difference to that. I'm one of those real people that you used to talk about in those days when you were just dying to escape from suburbia and the nice boys that were lined up for you. Neville's as safe as houses; he'd no more let you down than walk naked along the high street. But when was the last time that he encouraged you to recognize the world beyond your own private concerns, when was the last time that he put his finger on your pulse and made it race, when was the last time that the two of you laughed together like a couple of kids?'

She'd wanted to argue with that smile, to say, 'No, you have it all wrong. I'm just a ten-years-faithful married woman wondering what she might have been missing all these years. It happens all the time. Your appeal for me has nothing at all to do with the fact that I have reached a point, a pause, in my life when order and predictability seem to be narrowing its horizons, when I wake up in the morning and look around at my beautiful bedroom and remember my bedsitter in Islington and all the passionate, illogical fervour that characterized those years, before I was forced into a rational reappraisal of every belief I held dear. You believe still that the dream can be made real, that self-interest is not man's fundamental motive; you move uncorrupted through your life as aflame at injustice as ever you were. You will never compromise, and if reason interposes itself between you and your vision, then you'll just kick reason into orbit. You remind me of Fred. I admired

Fred. For his intensity. I admire Neville too. For his self-discipline. It seemed then that I had to choose between the two of them. I hadn't met you then. I didn't know that in you the two could coexist.'

She'd wanted to argue with his smile, but she was forced to admit that it told the truth, that the logic that she valued so highly collapsed beneath the impact of an emotional need that she'd tried to deny. She loved him: not just in her head as she loved Neville, but between her legs and in her heart. And he belonged – in the real sense of the word – to other people.

The water was cold. She roused herself. Stop it, stop it, she thought. Think of Beatrice, deserted, think of Madeleine diminished, think of all the anguish, the waste and disorder of lives ruled by the emotions. Pull yourself together.

She dressed and went down into the kitchen. Beatrice was mixing scones and reading a magazine that had been donated by an inquisitive next-door neighbour; a pretext for gaining entrance and discovering the marital state of play. She had left no wiser than before she came; she remembered, with chagrin, that she hadn't even read the magazine herself.

'She said there was a recipe in it. All I can find are articles about sado-masochism and are you sure you're satisfying your man.' Beatrice turned a page with a greasy forefinger. 'I suppose the short answer to that is no. Perhaps if I'd read this years ago . . .'

'You should have read one entitled "Are you satisfying someone else's man?" Beatrice?' Joanna perched herself on the edge of the table, gathered a handful of raisins and ate them slowly. 'Can I ask you one question without you being mortally offended?'

'It depends what it is.'

Joanna eyed her. 'Did you ever get the impression that – that Desmond might have a tendency towards violence?'

Beatrice presented her back, made a meal out of opening the oven and lighting the gas.

'Well?'

'You can ask me a question. I didn't guarantee that I'd answer it.'

Joanna ploughed grimly onwards. 'When I saw Madeleine yesterday she had an enormous bruise on her arm and her feet were covered in bandages. When I asked her about it, she said that she'd slipped and trodden in some glass.'

'Yes? Well?'

233

'If you slipped and fell it wouldn't be your feet that would get cut, would it? And if you were walking, you'd only tread once, you wouldn't tread twice.'

'Is there a point to this conversation?'

'Yes, there is. When he came through the door, she went – kind of rigid and you could see little muscles jumping up and down in her cheek and nerves beating in her neck and her heart thumping under her dress.'

Beatrice banged the oven door. 'My, aren't we observant?' she said. 'Did her mouth go dry as well and her knees start to tremble?'

'I just wondered if he'd – exhibited any signs of – those sort of tendencies when – you knew him.'

'Bit of the old S-M?' She drew out points from the pool of spilled milk on the kitchen table. 'Did we rush outside and grab a chain and padlock off somebody's bicycle? Did we burn each other with cigarettes and equip ourselves with black boots and riding crops and hang upside down from chandeliers? We haven't got a chandelier, and your prurient curiosity is nauseating.'

'Did he ever hit you or show any inclination that he might want to hit you?'

'No,' Beatrice said, 'he never did.' She fastened and unfastened a button on her shirt, kept her face turned away.

'I'm not being nosy,' Joanna said, 'simply for the sake of being nosy. It's just that I thought a bit of background information might be useful – if there was any background information.'

'Before you jump in there with both feet?'

The phone rang. Beatrice went to answer it, saying en route, 'It'll be the engineers. They've already rung twice to check whether it's working. I keep thinking it's heavy breathers.'

Joanna moved round the kitchen gathering up dirty crockery and toast crusts and half-empty packets of breakfast cereal, wiping away tea stains and marmalade stains and elderly stains from meals of long ago. In Bridget's day, all the spoons were in the spoon drawer and there were no cobwebs hanging, streamer-fashion, from the ceiling. Bridget had worked herself to a complete standstill.

Beatrice reappeared in the doorway. She gnawed nervously at her thumbnail.

'That was a very long conversation – just to ascertain that the phone was working.'

'It was him. My dearly beloved husband. Wanting to know if he can come round this evening.' She sat down on a kitchen chair and began again the irritating process of un-buttoning and re-buttoning her shirt.

'And you agreed?'

'I could hardly do otherwise. He's still got a doorkey and we haven't changed the locks. He says he wants to talk to the kids. Oh Joanna, he's not going to try to entice them away, is he? Leave me with nothing. Is that his idea?'

'I don't know. I don't know him. You should know. You've been with him for fifteen years. You should know the way his mind works, the tricks he might be likely to pull.'

'I don't know him any better than I know the man who delivers the milk, the man in the tobacconist's where I buy my cigarettes.'

Joanna rinsed out a battery of milk bottles. 'There isn't a court in the land,' she said, 'that would countenance him having custody of them. Not in view of the fact that he's deserted you and is, presumably, engaged in an adulterous relationship.' Her words had a ring of assurance that she didn't privately believe. Courts made all sorts of weird decisions and people, prompted by guilt-engendered rancour, were quite likely to act in all manner of malicious ways. 'If this is definite and irrevocable, this parting, then perhaps it would be as well if you got yourself to a solicitor at the earliest possible opportunity.'

'Yes,' she said, half-heartedly. And Joanna knew that Beatrice was no more capable of positive, decisive action than she had been years ago when she'd spent her time agonizing over inevitable examination failure rather than actually doing something to banish that inevitability, when she'd endure being bitten by ants because moving to an ant-free part of the garden was too much bother. If Beatrice and a solicitor were to be brought within shouting distance of one another then someone else must do the arranging.

In the afternoon Joanna made apple tarts, a fruit cake and two dozen currant buns. She worked rapidly and neatly, peeling and slicing and kneading and mixing and cutting off edges of pastry with precise economical movements. Beatrice sat and watched her, smoking, occasionally chewing a piece of one of her hard scones. She watched the way that the cake rose to a perfect uncracked symmetry, the way that the buns, light and golden, tumbled from the baking tin, the fragrant bubbling that arose from the glazed surface of the tarts. She said what a rotten housewife she was, a rotten cook, a rotten mother, a rotten everything. 'A lousy wife,' she said, 'a lousy mistress and a lousy mother. I never really expected to be very good at being a wife or a mistress, but I did think that I might be passing sufficient at motherhood. I did resolve to try. To give them my love and my interest and my affection. All that's happened is that I fuss too much – or I neglect them: they go to school with holes in their socks and string in their shoes and once Toby was the only boy in the school choir wearing a grey shirt instead of a white one. Once, years ago, I came to stay with you for a few days – do you remember? – and Oliver – or was it Toby? – whoever was the little one then, thought he was coming too and he packed up all his little jumpers and shorts and stuff inside this old attaché case and I didn't have the guts to disillusion him; I just left him sleeping the next morning and went. And once I trapped Felix's fingers in the car door and told him to stop fussing and then I found out that one was broken. And now,' Beatrice said, wiping away a few indulgent tears, 'they have moved completely away from me. They hardly touch me in passing, rushing off to their own affairs, their own friends. Even Oliver. They have lives separate. And soon they'll grow up and go away and visit me once a year and draw lots as to who'll be lumbered with me when I'm old and past it.'

A button came off in her hand. 'At some point,' she said, staring at it disconsolately, 'it all got out of control.'

Joanna cleared away the magazine, Oliver's scarf and a broken pocket calculator from one corner of the table and laid her tarts to cool. She said, 'I think you've done a very good job. They're brave and exuberant and independent. Would you prefer timid clinging children without an ounce of self-confidence, children afraid to bawl and shout and quarrel because they're fearful of the outcome? Madeleine's child's like that, in a permanent state of held breath, afraid to make any spontaneous movement in case it causes a row. You can tell just by looking at her. And why this sudden bout of self-denigration? If he's coming, wouldn't it be better to start bolstering your self-esteem? Why don't you go and get changed and do your hair? Let him have a good look at what he's abandoning.'

Beatrice made no move. 'It was him, sorry, *he*, who said most of those things anyway, about me being lazy and disorganized and clueless.'

'Well, naturally. You'd hardly expect him to leave you with a paean of praise ringing in your ears. There's a kind of formula for this sort of situation, involving the gathering up of every genuine complaint that ever arose during the relationship and then garnishing them with pure fantasy, you know: "on three occasions you didn't sew on my shirt buttons" becomes "you are the laziest slut who ever drew breath", or "you once eyed a woman at a party" turns into "your illicit sexual exploits leave Casanova standing" – if you'll pardon the expression. Oh come on, Beatrice, move yourself, for God's sake. You *do* possess some clothes of your own? Well, go and put them on. There's hen muck all over your jeans.'

'If ever I used to make an effort for him, he used to say, "Whose benefit is this for? I take it you're embarking upon another sordid little relationship – although relationship's too grand a word for what you do, isn't it? Back-seat screwing, that's about your mark, isn't it?" Oh,' Beatrice said, 'all those years of being beyond reproach and dispensing divine forgiveness, and then he does the selfsame thing and thinks he's perfectly justified. Oh, the bastard,' Beatrice said, 'I wish he'd get knocked down by a car on his way here and I'd stand and laugh as the life-blood seeped out of him. I'd dance on his grave and rejoice at his passing and poison the minds of his children against his memory.'

She was holding a saucer in her hand. She threw it at the wall. It slid to the ground and rocked gently, unbroken. Joanna said, 'That's the first normal reaction we've had out of you.' But she realized that the rage was assumed, just as the tears had had to be conjured by the resurrection of sentimental memories. Beatrice was in a wilderness, a padded cell of a wilderness where no emotion had yet penetrated. Maybe this numbed apathy, this refusal to acknowledge the true impact of the situation was normal, but Joanna had visions of it increasing steadily, encompassing all areas of her life until nothing was left but a token adherence to routine, a thin thread of contact with reality.

The evening meal passed in the usual clamour of imparted news, quarrel and complaint. Though rather less complaint than usual. 'This is terrif,' they said, bolting huge mouthfuls and reaching for more. 'Don't tell me you cooked this?' 'Joanna cooked it.' 'I thought you were a teacher of philosophy.' 'Does that mean I shouldn't be able to cook?' 'No, suppose not. Mum's nothing and her cooking's feeble, to say the least.' 'To say the very least.'

Beatrice put a forkful of food into her mouth and chewed at it for the duration of the meal. She had changed into a jumper and skirt but her face, winter-pale, was devoid of artifice and her hair was lustreless and ragged at the ends. As much as to say: 'Here I am, looking like hundreds of other women who have four kids and a home to look after. No more and no less. I am not a young girl, nor a fashion-plate. I am what I have become after fifteen years with you and it is your bounden duty to accept me as I have become, chapped hands and laddered stockings and stretch marks and all.'

'I'll make myself scarce, shall I?'

'Oh no, don't go. Please.'

'You can hardly expect him to be delighted to find me here. And I can't add anything fruitful to the discussion. I'll go to the flicks or somewhere.'

'There won't be a discussion. Please don't go. I might pick up a knife and kill him.'

She had never liked him. She had always found him humourless and slightly patronizing. But she had to admit, when she saw him, that he had turned into one of those middle-aged men whom women tend to find attractive, men who look as though they are waiting to be rescued from the demands of a life they chose by mistake but have spent loyal years attempting to come to terms with. He was handsomer too. Until she saw him, she'd wondered what on earth the Gretas or even the Gillians found so irresistible about him. Now she realized that he had become the type that elicits the lurking nurse in a lot of women. The Florence Nightingale syndrome. She'd seen instances of it before: women who thought they wanted to take weary men and cherish them back into a love of life. They really didn't want to do anything of the sort; if ever those men did recapture their *joie de vivre*, they immediately lost their attractiveness.

He didn't take off his coat. He said, 'Oh hello, Joanna, where's my wife?' And immediately she remembered why she didn't like him, him and the other men who said 'my wife' as they said 'my car' or 'my right shoe'.

'She's in the kitchen. Your children are all in *there*. She told them that you wanted to talk to them when you came in. Perhaps

238

I ought to tell you that they don't know that you've left.'

He paused with his hand on the doorknob. 'I didn't expect that she'd spare me that happy task. Would you mind asking her if she'd join us?'

Joanna moved towards the kitchen. He said, 'Rang you up straightaway, did she? So that you could rush over and commiserate with her?'

'Don't you think that she needs someone to commiserate with her?'

'Oh I know I'm the villain of the piece. Always have been. Made her pregnant, made her marry me, kept her chained to the house with kids, took the best part of her life and then threw her on the scrap heap when I fancied a change. Isn't that the general gist? Of course, her little peccadilloes had to be overlooked; she wasn't responsible. A law unto herself, my wife. I expect that's about the strength of it, the tale of woe?'

'It's no concern of mine. I'll fetch her for you.'

Beatrice was cleaning the cooker. Joanna said, 'He's here. Isn't it a most inappropriate time to do that?'

Beatrice scrubbed away with wire wool and Vim. 'Cookers have to be cleaned. The world doesn't stand still.'

'And marital separations have to be discussed. He's waiting for you to join him.'

'Then he'll wait. He can do his own dirty work. As I'm doing mine.'

She scrubbed it, she rinsed it and she wiped it dry. You'd have thought that an inspector on behalf of the society of oven hygiene was due to call at any moment. She had a grey streak down her cheek and her skirt was spattered with soapy water. Joanna stood with folded arms and watched this essay in intractable obstinacy. Desmond and Beatrice, Joanna thought, must have found a lot of common ground; they both gave you the impression that they derived pleasure from sheer contrariness.

'There!'

But she lingered still. She didn't want to see him, that cruel-faced stranger who was spelling out her fate to her children, calumniating her, enlightening them as to the precise nature of her worthless character.

'All the more reason that you should get in there and put your side of the story.'

'What side? I haven't got a side. There isn't one. Oh, I'm going. Just hide the bread knives.'

Joanna washed up everything that she could find to wash up, mopped the floor, made a few beds that were unmade from the morning. Passing the door of the lounge, she heard his voice: steady, reasonable, Sam's voice, occasionally raised in interjection; once, Toby's voice, but never Beatrice's voice. It was when she was coming downstairs with *The Lord of the Rings* that she'd borrowed from Felix's bedroom that the door banged and Beatrice came tearing up the stairs and almost sent her flying.

She was incoherent for a while, lying in the middle of the big bed, screwing up handfuls of candlewick coverlet. Then she sat up and switched on the light and said that she hadn't heard so many platitudes mouthed by one person all at once since morning prayers at school assembly. 'Your mother and I,' he'd said! 'Your mother and I think it best if we live apart.' And, 'This in no way affects our mutual feelings for all of you.' And arrangements he'd made, visiting dates. And he was sorry, they were both sorry, but they both thought that continuing to live together could only have a bad effect on all concerned. He would see that they didn't suffer materially any more than he could help. This was his phone number by which they could contact him any time, day or night. Like a taxi service. And Sam had said, 'But . . .' and, 'What . . .' and, 'Explain . . .' And Felix had shrugged his shoulders and curled his lip. And Toby had yawned. And Oliver's bottom lip had begun to tremble. And not one word had he said about the harlot, the red-haired cow, his paramour. He'd said instead, 'Sometimes people outgrow each other. It's not a question of blame. It's just life.' It was at that point that she'd banged out of the room.

Suddenly she sprang from the bed, dived for the wardrobe and began tearing ties off the rail, shirts from their hangers and dreadful old moth-eaten jerseys from its recesses. A heap of clothing arose on the floor. Cufflinks were added, a pair of slippers with holes in them, half-empty bottles of aftershave, Christmas-present packets of handkerchiefs still in their wrappings, a defunct electric razor and a pile of collar-stiffeners from the days when collars came complete with stiffeners. She hauled down a suitcase from the top of the wardrobe and proceeded to stuff this motley collection into it, snapped down the fasteners and carried it on to the landing.

Hiding the bread knives had not been the only necessary precaution. Joanna placed her hands over her ears as the suitcase was tipped over the banister rail and launched into space. The crash seemed a long time in coming but when it did it brought them all out into the hall. Five faces contemplated the spillage – it had, of course, burst open on impact, and five upturned faces awaited pronouncement. Or action. Would she throw herself after it?

She would never have a better vantage point in her life. She wasted it. She merely turned on her heel and went back into the bedroom. And her husband left his belongings where they had fallen and let himself out of the front door. And Joanna came down and led the kids into the kitchen and said, feeling very foolish indeed, 'Look, cakes and pies and buns,' as though what they most wanted in the world were cakes and pies and buns.

Fresh commotion broke out in the hall. Beatrice and David were struggling for possession of the phone. Beatrice won. She cradled it to her chest. Short of attacking her, there was no way that he could prise it from her grasp. His arms fell to his sides. 'You petty, malicious bitch,' he said.

'It's my phone.'

'It's paid for out of my earnings.'

'And don't we know it? Haven't we always known it? Your earnings! Every crust we ever put into our mouths, every rag we ever put on our backs – your earnings paid for them. Why didn't you have the babies and then I could have gone out to work and supported you?'

'I just want to make a phone call.'

'You can go to hell and take your stuff with you.' She kicked at the clothing that lay dispersed on the floor. A cufflink rolled and rebounded from the skirting-board. 'I suppose you told that streetwalker you're living with that you came to her with just what you stood up in. The grand gesture! I suppose you told her you couldn't afford any other clothes, not with your great ravening family to keep. The cow! Does she know your procreative propensities, by the way, the cow? Does she know that that's all you're good for? Maybe that's what attracts her. Tell her not to confuse procreativity with performance. You may be proficient at the former but the latter always left a great deal to be desired.'

A faint spasm of disgust crossed his features.

'Tell her that in that department you're by no means Alpha +. More like D – . No big deal, no great earth-mover. Of course, she'll know that for herself, won't she? The cow. Perhaps she's so overcome with the wonder of it all that she's prepared to overlook your shortcomings. Literally.' Beatrice hauled the phone lead out of its socket. 'There! Make your phone call now.'

He made another unsuccessful grab for the instrument. Beatrice taunted him with the unattached end. Joanna stepped between them. 'Whatever is this all about? Lower your voices. Don't you *care* what your children think of you?' The voice of the adult. The schoolmistress. Neutral.

'The car won't start,' he said. 'I wanted to phone a taxi.'

'Bloody walk! It's what I have to do!'

Joanna picked up her car keys from the hall table. 'I'll take you,' she said.

'Oh thanks, thanks very much. There's loyalty for you.' Beatrice sank down on the bottom step of the stairs, the phone in her lap. 'My God! Whose side are you on?'

'I thought you said there weren't any sides.'

She felt that he'd rather have walked. Five miles. In the rain. He didn't know what tone to adopt, what demeanour to present. There were sides all right, and he knew which one she was bound to be on.

She should have concentrated on her driving, chatted inconsequentially about the weather, occupied the neutral zone. But that was not in her nature. She voiced, instead, all the fatuous comments that onlookers are wont to voice in such situations: 'Are you sure you're doing the right thing? Beatrice doesn't mean what she says. Couldn't you have another try? You'll destroy her. She'll never get over it.'

'She'll get over it. She'll have somebody else before you can turn round.'

He spoke without rancour. His expression, in pale moonlit profile, combined a sort of deadly resignation with fleeting regret. There seemed to be no possibility of appeal. Nevertheless, she tried. 'You can't know her very well if you think that.'

'Maybe I don't know her very well. I don't care any more.'

'But you did care. Once?'

'Yes, I cared once. When I was being cuckolded. She said she'd fallen in love with him and it was because she'd never had the opportunity for any falling in love, never got it out of her system. And so I forgave her.'

'That was big of you.'

242

He gave her a sharp glance. He said, 'I was supposed to agree to her adultery? Accept it as right and proper?'

'Maybe she didn't realize that she was married to God.'

'Don't try to be funny. I wasn't blameless. And I'm willing to take the blame – for certain things: for marrying her, for not having myself doctored – I never wanted all those kids, and for not having the guts to go when I first realized that it was over between us.'

'Doesn't it take guts to stay?'

He picked nervously at a thread on his trouser leg. 'No,' he said, 'it was easy to stay, to accept and accept and accept and close my eyes to all the rottenness. Like her, I'm used to letting things happen. I could have carried on that way: paying the bills and watching the kids grow up and looking in the other direction whenever she came into the house all illuminated after some plausible bastard had told her she was a great lay. That was easy. And all my life I've taken the easy way, the line of least resistance.'

'Left here?'

He nodded. 'It's not just a spur-of-the-moment decision, some passing infatuation,' he said. 'You know as well as I do when it started happening. She told me it was a madness, that it was all over, that sometimes it was necessary to look outside before you could appreciate what you had at home. So I forgave her – oh, I'm sorry, you don't like that word, do you? I tried to understand her motivation, to put into our life together whatever it was that was missing, not knowing, in my complacency, that he needed only to crook his little finger and back she'd go to him. Like iron filings to a magnet. As she did. After that, when I got to know, something just clicked off. After that second time I stopped caring one way or the other. It was as if something shut off in my head. Or my heart. It wouldn't have worried me if I never saw her again.'

She hadn't expected any such insights. He was discussing a relationship that had been laid to rest, from his point of view, years ago.

'Here,' he said, 'number twenty-seven.' And she braked outside a neat detached house of red brick with a poplar tree in the garden and lanterns outside the door and a welcoming glow of light behind the curtains in the front windows. 'Thanks,' he said. 'Tell her I'll ring the garage about shifting the car in the morning,' and opened his door. She saw that Beatrice was right: that in his mind she had been annulled, made part of an old forgotten life. Still she

243

tried, detaining him by the sleeve, the engine running. 'She said that was the time that you could have started off at a different level, with your eyes opened to one another, both realizing what it was that you wanted.'

He swung sideways out of the car. A shadow moved behind the curtained window. His face, greenish in the sodium light of the street lamp, was not hostile towards her. He looked like a man who had just relinquished a long-time burden. 'I'm sorry,' he said. 'But she always wanted more of me than there was.'

5

Sam mended the chain on Oliver's bicycle. He worked silently and gravely and methodically, brushing the hair out of his eyes, wiping his oily hands on a rag, answering Oliver's repeated queries with monosyllables and occasionally moving him firmly but gently out of the way. He seemed taller and heavier-set than he had done the week before, the last week of his childhood.

They watched him through the window. 'His new responsibility sits heavy,' Beatrice said and refilled her glass. The morning had passed in a frenzy of activity: ceiling-brushing and paint-washing and dusting and vacuuming; the afternoon was to be given over to the emptying of a bottle of wine. It was as though she was experimenting with different approaches to banishing the realization of her situation from her mind. Tomorrow she might dig the garden, or she might take the kids to the pictures. Apart from her basic routine, there were no longer any regularities left.

'He won't talk to me,' she said. 'He might talk to you. Mind you, what is there to talk about?'

Joanna put on her coat and went outside into the desolate rain-sodden stretches of the back garden. He acknowledged her with a nod. He put his hands on his hips and surveyed his territory: the balding lawns, the decrepit outbuildings, the vegetable plot that had long since been given over to ever-spreading bramble and convolvulus. 'What a dump,' he said. 'You know, it wouldn't be too difficult to knock it into shape. Dismantle those sheds and mend that fencing and tidy up that wilderness at the bottom.'

They walked together, discussing improvements that could be made. The hens scratched in their earth enclosure, turned their backs and exhibited ragged tail feathers. They weren't laying. No one knew why.

He kicked at a piece of rotten wood that lay on the grass. He said, 'I'll have to get the others to help me. They're such lazy swine, that's the trouble. You know, they start off full of enthusiasm and then rapidly lose interest. Toby stands scratching himself and Felix just vanishes and Oliver's too young to realize . . .'

'You don't have to become their father,' she said quietly, hesitantly, afraid that she might be putting her foot into forbidden territory.

'The one they've got isn't exactly a resounding success,' he said, without looking at her.

'Is that what you really think? Or is it simply reaction to what's happened?'

'It isn't what I think, it's what I know. I dare say as a person he's OK. But as a father he's always been pretty futile. He's never been very – interested in us. I don't mean we've been neglected or anything. It's just that you could always tell he was forcing himself to play football or take us camping or whatever it was. That he'd rather've been doing something else. They had to get married, didn't they?' he said, turning to face her, demanding her answer.

She equivocated. 'What makes you think that?'

'I've seen their marriage thing. And my birth certificate. They had to get married because I was on the way.'

'Does it bother you?'

'It doesn't bother *me*,' he said scornfully. 'But perhaps they wouldn't have got married at all except for that.'

'They didn't *have* to get married. They chose to do so. They thought they'd be happy together. And I think they were. For a considerable time.'

'So what changed things?'

'*They* changed, I suppose. People do. Life's a dynamic process – we alter from day to day, in our needs and our aspirations. Husbands and wives don't always go in the same direction. Some people manage to adjust to the changes. Others don't.'

He dribbled an old bald tennis ball around the edge of the grass. He said, 'People who have children shouldn't be allowed to do that sort of changing.' In his face she saw all the fierce, undiluted morality of the young: black is black and white is white and there are no indeterminate shades of grey. It reminded her, with a pang, of her own girlhood: the way she'd felt that any right-minded person must be bound to agree with her point of view.

'Try not to judge them,' she said. 'Try not to align yourself totally with one of them or the other. Oh, I know, it's easy to say. But their relationship with one another doesn't affect their relationship with all of you. Not fundamentally.'

Oh shut your mouth, Joanna, she thought. You're just making noise. And she thought nostalgically of her parents' generation and its seeming certainties, when some things were right and others were wrong and the concept of blame existed and could be used quite righteously.

He tried to make the tennis ball bounce, without success. 'You'll stay?' he said. And for that moment his face was thin and tense and childish again and his lip trembled like Oliver's.

'Yes, I'll stay. For as long as I can.'

Felix said, 'I'd rather not discuss it if you don't mind,' in direct response to her cowardly and indirect hedging. She'd knocked on his bedroom door but he hadn't heard her because of the ear-blasting volume to which his record-player was tuned. He was lying on his bed, his head in the crook of his elbow. She went up close to him, mouthed, 'Do you mind if I turn it down a bit?' The very walls were vibrating. He made a non-committal gesture and rolled on to his back.

'I quite enjoy the music,' she said. 'It's the loudness that gets me down.'

'The loudness is the main part of it.'

She sat down, flicked through a book about the Apollo landings. 'I can't rid myself of the suspicion,' she said, 'that it wasn't all an enormous hoax – you know: cardboard cut-outs in the television studio and back projection. It comes, I suppose, of nurturing the habit of scepticism. I expect you'd be able to disabuse me straight-away.'

He stared at cracks in the ceiling. 'I doubt it,' he said.

'Oh? I thought you were interested in this kind of thing?'

'Was.'

It was like trying to make progress through a swamp. 'You've turned from science to music?'

'Yeah.'

'Do you play anything?'

'Used to play the piano a bit. I was hoping to get a guitar. I don't suppose there's much chance of that now.'

'Why not?'

He gave her a look that would have withered a plant in full bloom. She remembered how, in the presence of his grandfather, she'd always felt gauche and uncharacteristically unsure. Felix had the same effect upon her.

'Things won't change as radically as you suppose,' she said. 'He's not taken off to the ends of the earth.'

He turned on her the full contempt of his glacial blue eye. It felt as though the temperature had dropped ten degrees. 'No,' he said. 'He's taken off with a red-haired woman. And I'd rather not discuss it if you don't mind.'

'And that's the way the land lies,' she reported back to Beatrice. 'I'll have a glass of that, if it's only to prevent you from guzzling the lot.'

'Inebriation,' Beatrice mused, 'it's a peculiar process, isn't it? Sometimes I can drink till it comes out of my ears without any effect and other times, two lagers and I'm anybody's. What does it depend on, do you suppose?'

'I don't know. One's metabolism? The phases of the moon? God, it's foul! What is it?'

'In the supermarket it was called Red Wine,' Beatrice said. 'There was also White Wine. And Rosé Wine.'

'I should think it would remove rust from chromium plating.'

'It's what I shall have to get used to. Our standard of living, never exactly luxurious, is bound to drop. Whatever his gracious assurances.'

'Don't take everything away from them, Beatrice. Not all at once. Sam seems to have a fairly philosophical attitude. But Felix isn't showing anything except total hostility. I don't know about the other two.'

'They haven't yet acquired the power of reflective thought. Every so often it dawns on them and they look perplexed – Toby came bounding in the other day, saying, "Will Dad pick me up from Grayson's on Saturday? He's going to mate his guppies." And then he remembered and blushed like fury. But by and large they're too quickly distracted, too concerned with the here and the now and immediate gratification, to lose a lot of sleep. Oliver cried a bit, and then I said that he could have a track suit in Manchester United colours and he perked up instantly. Of course, every child psychologist from here to eternity would doubtless tell me I'm quite wrong and they're simply repressing away like mad and when they're sixteen or so they'll probably go out and hit some old woman over the head. Or take to arson.'

'Like Matthew.'

'I keep thinking of Matthew, as a kind of talisman against my worst dreads. Here, did you see this?' She pulled out a snapshot from a sheaf of bills on the mantelpiece. Joanna saw a tall tanned youth, smiling, his arm around a tall tanned girl, against a background of Jamaican vegetation. She tried to link that relaxed and confident figure with the child who'd rocked himself to and fro and lit fires in garden sheds.

'They're getting married next year. Her father owns the plantations. A shrewd boy, obviously. Shrewder than his father. Let's hope his expectations aren't dashed in the way that his father's were.'

'Oh Beatrice, he didn't marry you in hopes of an inheritance. He was always yelling at you for accepting money from them. You told me so.'

'The thought must have been at the back of his mind. As my father said. Good old Dad, you thwarted him at the last.' She raised her glass. She was a bit tiddly.

'What about Amy?'

'Last I heard, she was in Switzerland, having just negotiated a hefty alimony settlement from the Italian count or whatever he was. How come that Amy, without looks, intelligence or personality, managed to hook herself such a variety of catches?'

'She really tried. She's rich herself. Money smells money.'

'You're probably right. I don't envy her in the least. She's like my mother. They have nothing. She's worse off than my mother. At least my mother has Archie.'

And speaking of angels or devils . . . Joanna sat up straight in her chair, peering through the window. It was years since she'd seen Helena Martin and naturally time had taken its toll – but the person who was walking up the garden path, skirting the brimming dustbins, was undoubtedly Beatrice's mother.

'What are you gawping at, Joanna? Do you want the last of

this rut-got, got-rut – I am a bit plastered, aren't I?' She articulated each word carefully. 'Do you want the last of this gut-rot? Or can I finish it? I wonder that Amy hasn't taken to the booze. With all her money. I wonder why anybody who has the money doesn't take to the booze. Madder music and stronger wine. Come, fill the cup, and in the fire of spring the winter garment of repentance fling: The Bird of Time has but a little way to fly – and Lo! the bird is on the wing.' She put the empty bottle down on the hearth, unnecessarily precise. 'Do you remember, Joanna, Miss Thing asked us who translated the Rubaiyat of Omar Khayyam and you put your hand up and said Ella Fitzgerald? Joanna? Whatever is it that's so interesting out there?'

'Your mother is coming up the path,' said Joanna. And Beatrice choked on the dregs of the wine, said, 'God Almighty,' and became instantly sober.

She was ringing the bell. Or thought she was ringing the bell. Soon she would realize that it didn't work and she would tap at the glass panel in the door. Joanna and Beatrice looked at one another. 'I conjured her into being,' Beatrice said. 'If I hadn't spoken her name she wouldn't have appeared.' Joanna said, 'Hadn't somebody better let her in?'

'Perhaps she'll go away. Perhaps if we just sit quiet.'

'Don't be ridiculous, Beatrice.' She rose from her seat.

Beatrice clasped her arms around her body as though for protection. 'Tell her I'm not here. Tell her I don't exist any more. Is she alone? Or has she brought her pet prancing queen with her?'

'Can't see anybody else.'

The tapping became more staccato, more insistent. 'Tell her,' Beatrice said, 'that I'm just a figment of her imagination.'

'Well at last!'

Helena at sixty: not what she was. Obviously. The soft caress of mink as she passed Joanna in the hall, a waft of expensive scent and hair lacquer, a lizard-skin handbag flung down on the table, a rattle of gold bracelets and a flash of precious stones on a pale manicured hand. But. Age-freckles on the back of that hand, crêpey skin at the base of her throat, large tinted glasses concealing a maze of wrinkles under her eyes, the tint of her hair not quite approximating to its original hue, a deep line incising her forehead. 'She's marvellous for her age,' they said, no doubt, in Lytham St Anne's. And Joanna understood how terrible it must be, the process of losing your looks, when your face really had been your fortune, when you used to spend hours looking at yourself in a mirror because your beauty demanded admiration.

'Joanna.'

Mutual reappraisal. When last seen, Joanna had been wearing thonged sandals and a garment that resembled a patchwork quilt, had talked of soup kitchens and vagrants and the social order. A very clever girl, a research student, who marched to Aldermaston and sat in and sold copies of subversive literature on street corners and said she'd as soon wear a ring through her nose as one on her finger.

She wore one now. And a dress that hadn't come off a second-hand stall and shoes that had more in common with Bond Street than a Chinese paddy-field.

'The telephone wasn't working.'

'No. There was an accident.' Beatrice had not only torn the lead from the socket, she'd torn the socket from the wall.

'How is she?' She removed several anoraks from the hallstand and hung up her coat. Her figure was good still, at any rate to the outward view and aided and abetted by corsetry, long sleeves and a high neckline. 'There's no need to look discountenanced,' she said. 'I'm quite *au courant*. I have a few friends left around here, even though my own daughter doesn't think fit to communicate with me. Where are all those children?' She looked around her suspiciously, as though expecting them to materialize out of the walls.

'Sam's doing the garden, Felix is listening to music, Toby's out helping to mate somebody's guppies and Oliver's playing in a school football match.'

She seemed relieved. She said, 'Perhaps one of them would carry my case in later.'

'You intend to stay?' Beatrice stood in the doorway, chipping paint from the jamb with her thumbnail. 'Hello, Mother. Have you come to tell me you warned me?'

'I've come to offer you what help I can.'

'I'm being inundated, aren't I? There I was, thinking that no one gave a damn and here you all are, like vultures around carrion.'

'You invited *me*,' Joanna said, wounded. She hadn't seen this side of Beatrice since their schooldays: the tongue of silk that could turn into a viper's tongue so rapidly and so unexpectedly that the easily-discomfited tended to keep their distance.

'I didn't invite her.'

She turned her back on them, went to the drinks cupboard and opened another bottle of Red Wine. 'One of your informants got the news travelling, did he? Runners with cleft sticks? Where's your page-boy? Didn't you bring him with you?' She poured three glasses. 'A toast,' she said, 'to the oft-disputed fact that our mothers always know best,' and took a big mouthful.

Helena, who had seen the label, left hers untasted, settled herself in an armchair, her legs crossed to their best advantage. She looked quite formidable: the mistress of a women's college, the governor of a house of correction, the power behind anybody's throne. 'Just exactly what are the arrangements?' she said.

'There's only one. Quite simple and straightforward. He's slung his hook. Is that a reference to shepherds, or what? Who else has a hook? Clergymen? Shepherds don't have hooks though, do they? They have crooks. Maybe it's nautical, something like splicing the mainbrace or keel-hauling.'

'I mean what are the arrangements apropos maintenance and a roof over your head, amongst other things.'

'There aren't any.'

'My dear *child*.'

'I am not your dear child,' Beatrice said. 'I *was* your most un-welcome child. I am now a grown-up woman. So for Christ's sake don't start using that tone to me. Save it for your tame poofters. How is Archie, by the way? As lovely as ever?'

'We are business partners.'

'And who could doubt it? Unless they were deaf and blind. I think it's a lovely arrangement. He's gorgeous. Well, he's not as gorgeous as he used to be. In fact he's going to seed a bit in the region of the hairline and the paunch, and his matinée idol profile isn't what it was. Nevertheless he'd still put us in the shade. Isn't that right, Mother? Doesn't anyone want any more of this lovely liquid? You're wine snobs, that's what you are. If it said Château Something-or-other you'd be gulping it down.'

Helena smoothed her skirt over her lap. She produced a little unamused smile which said, I am determined to hold myself in check however much you try to incite me to lose my temper. 'He's left you,' she said, 'it's quite definite?'

'A big hand for the lady on my right. You can't put much over on her. Not only is she, was she, a pretty face, she's as sharp as a razor too.'

'Is your idiocy due to drink? Or don't you even have that excuse?'

Beatrice poured another glass. *'In vino veritas*, Mother, *in vino veritas*. I often wonder what the vintners buy one half so precious as the goods they sell. They are not long, the days of – Still the vine her ancient ruby yields. That's all I know. Apart from Out of the strong came forth sweetness.'

'Don't quote the Scriptures at us.'

'It's off the golden syrup tin. I'm the one that didn't get the education. Remember? Due to my natural idiocy.'

'Due to your natural perversity.'

'I shall go and get the meal ready,' Joanna said. She was not usually squeamish, but those two were squaring up as for the world title, and they were not evenly matched.

And she, Joanna, was unused to playing a rôle as impartial as that of referee. The chatter of the boys would cover up any hidden hostilities – even, perhaps, certain overt hostilities, she thought with relief. But the boys were disinclined to chatter. They answered her enquiries politely but succinctly and concentrated on their food. Joanna kept starting conversations condemned to die in their infancy from lack of nourishment; Beatrice kept on refilling her glass, occasionally quoted at length and irrelevantly; Helena observed the level in Beatrice's glass and shot her glances that palpitated with meaning. 'Perhaps,' she said, 'afterwards, we can have a sensible discussion.'

The rate at which the level in the bottle of wine was diminishing made that seem an unlikely possibility. For 'sensible discussion' substitute 'vituperative screaming match', Joanna thought; she tried to enlist the support of the boys, tried to detain them with subterfuge. To no avail. With healthy regard for their own skins and selfish disregard for her predicament, they severally excused themselves.

She gathered the dishes together and carried them into the kitchen. As she left, she heard Helena say, 'We must get you to a solicitor.' As she washed up she had no difficulty in imagining the general tenor of any conversation that might proceed from that remark. And when she rejoined them, Beatrice had reached that point where she was due to say, 'You never gave two hoots about my welfare. Why start now?'

She made for the bookcase. She said, 'I'll get something to read and take it upstairs.'

'Don't go,' Beatrice said. 'I might murder her.' The drink was affecting her motor nerves rather than her cognitive mechanisms; she had not yet reached the stage where she lost sight of the end of her sentences, but coordinating the bottle, the glass and the angle of inclination was beginning to pose problems.

'Stay,' Helena said. 'You might be able to drum some sense into her head.' She turned towards her daughter. 'Or do you really relish the prospect of being penniless and roofless and having your children taken into care?'

'What rubbish are you talking?'

'You may think that you can predict his actions, but you have to predict for two now, not just one. And I don't suppose *she's* particularly well-disposed towards you. Where on earth did he meet her, anyway?'

'At the Cactus Society.'

'Dear God,' said Helena, as though the idea of such a meeting touched unplumbed depths of banality. 'What were *you* doing, letting him go to such places alone?'

'I said a Cactus Society not a Blue Film Society. It was his *hobby*, for God's sake. I didn't think that we had to be attached at the navel throughout our entire married life.'

'You didn't think much at all, did you?'

'Well, as far as I knew, *I* wasn't married to an accomplished lecher.'

She let that pass. Gracefully. She said, 'The point I am trying to make is that unless you stir yourself to safeguard your rights, you may very well find yourself in a precarious position.'

'Afraid I'll come begging to you?'

'She's quite right, Beatrice,' Joanna said, feeling like the holder of the casting vote who may be sacrificing principle to expediency.

'She's always right. When will she realize that I have a mind of my own and a right to some dignity?'

Helena studied her nails. 'From what I've heard, you gave up all pretensions to dignity some time ago.'

Oh no, Joanna thought, that wasn't wise. There was a look coming into Beatrice's eyes which reminded her of the look a confused bull has when it finally focuses on the matador.

'Of course I'm not sitting in judgement,' Helena said. 'God knows you probably had reason enough. I warned you, didn't I, about allowing that dreadful routine boredom to become a constituent of your life? I told you that some men need change and excitement as they need food and drink.' Forward she went, piling Pelion upon Ossa; Beatrice tightened her grip upon the stem of her glass. 'Post-mortems don't do any good,' said Helena, 'nevertheless, I can't help feeling that a good deal of this has been self-engineered. There were signs, surely, that you could have interpreted? Even with such an unemotional and inscrutable man as that. He always made me feel a hundred and three.' And then – oh, inevitable and fatal phrase – 'Of course you should never have married him.'

The glass flew from Beatrice's hand and tinkled into hundreds of pieces on the hearth. A fraction to the right, and it would have hit Helena full in the face.

And while they contemplated the aftermath of this gesture and Helena automatically raised a hand to her cheek, the dam burst and released into the quiet air was a flood of hate and rage and pain and humiliation – incoherent, most of it, mingled with tears and mucus, but they caught the odd salient phrase: *complete* failure, aren't I? Never gave you anything to boast about . . . not at school, or in my marriage. All I could do was have kids . . . anyone can have kids . . . can't even keep my husband . . . such as he is . . . all you could do was to criticize and turn your face away. You made me the way I am. I *loathe* you. You and him, leaving me. I got married to *escape* from you, to have something of my own, something *decent*. You were hateful. You went to Lausanne and Palermo. And you left me. And I made you a Mother's Day card at school and you left it unopened. Don't mess me, you said, don't touch me, your hands are dirty. And you left me . . . only Bridget cared and I worked her to death, I killed her and she left me . . . and I killed *him*, the person he was, and he left me. And Desmond, he left me too . . . and she . . . I begged her and pleaded with her and she had a face like a cat . . . she said I'll destroy you, because she thought I'd enticed him . . . perhaps I did . . . I just want to make myself different from how you made me.'

She was completely devoid of reticence or restraint. She recounted episodes they'd rather have not heard. She said that she hadn't even the guts to do away with herself. And then, quite suddenly, while her chest was still heaving with sobs and tears were splashing over her collar, her eyes closed and she fell back against the sofa.

'It's good,' Helena said, though her face was stiff with disapproval. 'Better than suppressing it. Just re-directed hostility, that's all. He isn't here for her to attack,' she said, 'so she attacks me instead.' She sounded as confident as Joanna herself used to sound in the days when she quoted facile generalizations from works on psychiatry as though they were messages brought down from Mount Sinai.

6

Madeleine made out her shopping list. Essentials, she knew, were food and clothing and heating: there was a gas bill and an electricity bill and a telephone bill that gazed back at her with silent reproach every time she dusted the mantelpiece. But essentials were, to a certain extent, relative: it was essential that Natasha should have a pair of ribbed tights and a long party frock and jeans embroidered with butterflies; every other girl in her class had a pair of ribbed tights, etc., etc. She crossed butter off the list. They could make do with margarine. Margarine was better for you. And to hell with the bills. Perhaps, before they got to the stage of sending around the forces of disconnection, he'd have a job.

'Scouring powder' she crossed off – absolute cleanliness was an expensive process. She wrote her list on a piece of cardboard torn from the cornflake packet. But any resemblance between her mother all those years ago, and herself, she would have considered to be purely coincidental.

'Beatrice,' Joanna said softly, into her ear, 'Beatrice, aren't you getting up?'

Beatrice moved her head on the pillow. Her throat was sore, her stomach was churning and her head ached. She could have coped with all that. Part of the ritual of having a hangover was that you didn't pamper it; you just soldiered on grimly wishing you were dead until it decided to take its leave of you. A mere hangover was not the reason for her disinclination to move.

'Can you get their breakfasts, see them off to school?'

'Yes, of course. You stay where you are. A rest will do you good. I'll bring you a cup of tea.'

The tea lay untouched on the bedside table. She buried her head under the bedclothes until the extent of her world was a safe and undemanding cocoon of warmth. The muffled sounds of feet and bicycle bells and milk deliveries and cars starting up barely penetrated. She understood why hermits became hermits and monks became monks – Fred had become a monk, Joanna said, a member of a very strict order. It was perhaps significant, Joanna said, that having experienced more facets of society than most people, Fred had opted for a place and a life that was apart from society.

Bed was better. Monks had to adapt themselves to a rigorous routine, even hermits, presumably, had had to sweep out the cave occasionally and bestir themselves to trap a few locusts and gather a drop of wild honey. Bed was the place where everything lost its significance: night and day, summer and winter, seed time and harvest. As a child she'd luxuriated in it; they'd had to prise her out of it: Bridget, swishing open the curtains, saying, 'It's eleven o'clock. You're wasting your life away.'

Oh Bridget, she thought, why did you have to die and leave me? And her pillow was wet with tears, not the tempestuous tears of the night before, but slow calm tears that welled and flowed effortlessly. She remembered how she had tried to prepare herself for the eventuality, tried to anticipate the extent of her desolation and, by means of such anticipation, to shape it to manageable proportions. But the day that Bridget collapsed in the middle of the kitchen floor, her arms full of washing, she found that her attempts at controlling her reactions by the simple expedient of forecasting them had been useless.

And no one could help. Not David, not the kids, not her mother. The only person who knew how it felt to lose someone upon whom you relied and about whom you felt guilty was Madeleine. Madeleine and Desmond and their child had moved back to the town, into a poxy flat above a bookmaker's shop. To Madeleine then she went for comfort. Madeleine listened while Beatrice talked, and told her that, impossible though it seemed, the feeling would pass. She would either become more independent, said

Madeleine, or she would transfer her dependence to someone else as she, Madeleine, had done.

But Madeleine, who had taken a clerical job, was very often out, and Beatrice would arrive at the flat to find only Desmond – who was recovering from tuberculosis – and his daughter.

Things were not good between himself and Madeleine, that much she knew. In the same way that a child unhappy at school but forced to obey will make its parents' lives a hell, so Desmond, unsatisfied, unfulfilled and unaware of what exactly it was that might constitute satisfaction and fulfilment, used Madeleine as whipping boy. Once she arrived at the flat and heard him in full spate: 'I wish I'd never married you, I wish I'd never met you.' Well, there was nothing unusual in that. She'd said it herself, more than once, over the years. What was unusual was Madeleine's apparent disinclination to stand up for herself. It was as though she felt that such punishment was only right and proper for someone who ought not to have aspired so high as to expect love to be returned in the same degree.

His life was in a shambles, he told Beatrice. It lacked direction. It lacked purpose. Whatever he attempted seemed to be doomed to failure. Anyone else would have dismissed these remarks as mere exercises in self-pity. Not Beatrice. Beatrice considered the failures to be persons such as herself and David, those who clung to what they had because they had neither the energy nor the courage to try for anything other, those who didn't dare to dare. Desmond at least *tried*, refused to fool himself into thinking that what he'd got was what he wanted.

They talked of books. He'd got through a lot of literature during the past inactive year. She began to quote a poem of Dorothy Parker's; he finished it for her. He showed her his novel, newly-returned for the sixth time, a privilege which had not been accorded to anyone else, not even Madeleine. She took it home with her but she never read it, afraid that if it was dreadful, he would be automatically diminished. It was inconceivable that she could be in love with anyone who betrayed ineptitude in his chosen sphere: the violin teacher of old had been an extremely good violin teacher, and so it had been with the ski-instructor and the tennis professional. Being in love had to incorporate a large measure of admiration; Desmond did not fit into the world of employment because he was a novelist manqué. Actually reading the book might have disabused her of that notion.

For by now she was in love with him. It had taken her some time to recognize and identify the emotion, so long had it lain dormant. At first she couldn't imagine why she so looked forward to those visits. In the mornings she would wake, open her eyes and be out of bed in a trice, resisting the lure of whatever it was that tried to drag her back into unconsciousness. She didn't remember that years ago she'd woken just as easily and jumped out of bed with similar alacrity when it was the day of her violin lesson or she'd arranged for some tennis coaching.

When the realization dawned – she had been chopping cabbage, she remembered, and it came between an upward and a downward stroke – her immediate reaction was one of joy, the emotion you'd feel upon meeting a very old and dear friend after an interval of years. The feeling existed and Desmond was its object. Nothing could alter it or banish it; it would remain until its course was run, despite the remonstrances of reason. She was only surprised that she had been free of it for so long, amazed that she had managed to live through all those days of her life without its help and support.

Somebody's socks went down the side of the machine, between the drum and the casing, and they had to send for the engineer. Dawn was always pleased when a breakdown occurred; she fancied the engineer. He showed no sign of returning her interest, but he'd got the message all right, Dawn said, as she applied frosted gold shadow to her eyelids and pink blusher to her cheeks in the room at the back of the premises where there was a gas ring for making tea and a tin of soft ginger biscuits and a heap of torn magazines. She applied herself to this task as Michelangelo probably applied himself to the ceiling of the Sistine Chapel: a millimetre too much colour here, a line slightly out of true there, and the whole business was begun again from scratch. Sometimes she offered Madeleine the choice from her vast selection of beauty aids. 'I bet you could look OK,' she said, 'if you did yourself up. Give your old fellow a surprise. He might get up off his backside then and you wouldn't have to come out slaving in this dump. Catch me working in a hole like this when I'm married. I bet Trevor's on a good wage, don't you think?' Trevor was the engineer.

'Perhaps he's married already.'

'Never.'

'How can you tell?'

That seemed to fall into the category of silly questions, warranting only a deep sigh and a sideways glance of unmixed condescension.

Well, how did you tell these things? What was it about the non-verbal code that some could decipher it instantly while for others it remained impenetrable? Dawn went off to dazzle Trevor and Madeleine sat and drank another cup of stewed tea.

Pupil dilation – Joanna's old favourite, relative distances between persons, certain gestures, expressions, configurations of limb composure: she'd missed them all. She'd thought that that would be the last thing on Beatrice's mind, Beatrice who'd been almost inconsolable with grief. And if Desmond could help, then she'd been perfectly willing for him to offer that service; it would, she'd thought, give him a feeling of usefulness which had been sadly lacking in his life for the last year or so. She'd known, of course, that he found Beatrice attractive. He'd told her so. She knew also that he no longer loved her, Madeleine, with the same intensity as he had done; she supposed that was inevitable. That he needed her as much – and more – than ever he had done, she didn't doubt for a moment. Once he had kept her sane, he had been the bulk against which she leant while everything disintegrated around her; their positions were reversed: she was the anchorage now, the safe harbour to which he returned after his unsuccessful forays into the public world. She understood, she comforted and she forgave. She knew how it must be to consider yourself special and yet have no outstanding ability or capacity for serious application. She knew how galling it must be to have to defer to minds that seemed inferior to your own and how he was incapable of doing so, to want to excel at something without possessing the necessary ambition or patience, to hate and despise yourself without being able to alter any facet of your character or personality.

They had a lot in common, Beatrice and Desmond. They both viewed life as a deterministic process. The choices were made by some external authority and however hard you tried, if that authority did not look favourably upon you, then you were beating your head against a brick wall. 'There is something,' Beatrice said, 'outside myself that prevents me from getting things done.' 'The cretins they promote!' Desmond said. 'Jobs for the boys. My face doesn't fit. If they think I'm going to lick someone's boots to remain in favour, they've another think coming. It's not what you know,' Desmond said, 'it's how you hold your knife and the stripe in your tie, or your talent for sycophancy, or your family tree, or your penchant for blinding everyone with science. It's the con-merchants who get to the top of the heap,' Desmond said. 'The imbeciles who occupy top jobs! The stuff that gets published!' Desmond said.

And all that time she was sitting at her desk in the Department of Health and Social Security, processing claims for sick benefit or disability pension, watching the sky changing colour and the cineraria on the windowsill bursting into bloom, never once did she suspect. Such was her complacency that she actively encouraged their association; liaisons between unsuccessful tubercular novelists and mothers of four occurred only in the pages of society magazines or the gutter press.

'I say, dear!' A woman in a floral headscarf poked it and her head around the door. 'Have you got the change of fifty pence?'

Dawn and the engineer were nowhere to be seen. No doubt they had repaired to the Kardomah to drink coffee and get better acquainted. Dawn, like Beatrice, wasted no time when it came to hunting down the object of her desires.

In that no-man's-land, that neutral territory between sleep and wakefulness, Beatrice sensed that Joanna had departed with her tray. A portion of poached fish there had been, and a dish of jelly – invalid food. With the combined talents of her mother and Joanna in the kitchen it couldn't fail to be appetizing, but actually eating it demanded that she sit up in bed and stretch out her arm, so there it lay, the lure of semi-consciousness being more enticing than any morsel of *haute cuisine*.

Muddled images, out of sequence, passed behind her eyelids: the steamed-up windows of his car – he'd still had a car then; Madeleine paid for its upkeep and running costs; that very first time he'd turned his face towards hers and the knowledge that they must make love was present in their eyes. Where? Anywhere, it didn't matter, it mattered only that they should be together. The Film Society on a Thursday evening: she paid her subscription and she read the programme, Antonioni, Pabst, Pasolini, she became word-perfect on the little printed résumés – she never saw any of them; the way he kissed her like a man dying of thirst, and all the differences, so many, many differences that she – love partner to only one other man – had never suspected; that walk to the bus stop, her heels clicking on the deserted pavement, a quick glance and a crossing over to the other side of the road, the other bus stop, and travelling out to where the car was parked in a lane that led to a disused railway siding; the heart-stopping moments when she thought she saw a face she knew, at the bus stop, on the bus, but it was always merely an approximation to a face that she knew; the glow of his cigarette and the angle of his dark jaw, the plastic and chromium pubs where they swallowed down their drinks and departed because their mutual desire was too urgent to suffer delay, the moon silvering the outline of his face, the trite love phrases they couldn't help but utter, the exquisite, intoxicating sweetness of his mouth on hers and once, a black cat with neon eyes, frozen in the headlights.

And those afternoons in the flat when Natasha, exhausted after an attack, finally slept, and he led her into what she had always imagined would be the prohibited spaces of the matrimonial bedroom. Not so. They were without shame, had lost any pretensions they might have had about preserving the niceties, the delicate distinctions and ambiguities of their position. On Madeleine's blue-striped, drip-dry, non-iron sheets they explored the potentialities and the limits of sensation. It seemed inconceivable that they should accede to some social rule that preached restraint. They echoed the sentiments of generations of adulterers who have found themselves to be in total sexual accord: 'It seems so right. And how can anything which seems so right be wrong?' They said also, 'We are hurting no one else.' They said, 'It must surely be once in a lifetime that one experiences such fantastic biochemical complementarity.' At least, *she* said that. He said, 'Come again?' and when she explained, he agreed because he had forgotten that he'd experienced it before, with Madeleine, with Polly.

They fitted together like two pieces of jigsaw. In every way. Once she mentioned having been impressed by a particular painting. An obscure painting it was, by an obscure Dutch artist. Wordlessly, he'd opened a drawer and produced a photograph of the selfsame painting, torn from an ancient copy of *Studio*; he'd had it since his schooldays. They were not awed by this amazing coincidence since they did not regard it as being a coincidence. In some other place, some other time, some other dimension, they'd known and loved one another. Or they'd been the same person. Their mutual exploration was simply a re-discovery. She was the face that had always existed in his subconscious and he was the original of those others, those pale imitations, the violin teacher and company, by means of whom she had been groping towards the source, before nature intervened and curtailed her quest.

Madeleine's curtains fluttered in the breeze and the room they were in was a place set apart from the world, the confines of the only real existence; beyond it, everything was mere shadow-play. They never thought beyond the moment, because the moment was all and it would last for an eternity. Their hands moved constantly, touching, defining, committing to memory the scroll of an earlobe, the jut of an ankle bone, the smooth sweep of a shoulder-blade; they wanted to absorb one another in some way beyond the commonplace words they exchanged, the essentially limited physical activities in which they indulged. By means of passion they willed themselves through some personal black hole into a different dimension where a more satisfactory means of communication existed, where the laws of relativity that bound their relationship to the other parts of their lives ceased to have significance.

It was nothing to do with 'I love you' or 'I like you'; it was simply, 'Without you I would cease to be, as I would cease to be if deprived of food or drink.' Neither hope nor expectation had a place in their affair; their spouses, their children, they were situated in that other world that existed beyond the window, the one that reclaimed them after they had put on their clothes and combed their hair.

She was happy, she was energetic, she was patient and understanding and companionable with the children. And when David made love to her, well, that was enjoyable in its way – as far as the mechanics went. The fact that she had discovered a centre, a core, in her life enabled her to function so much better in all the other areas. Which was why, when they were found out – and perhaps they had invited discovery; it seemed too marvellous to be kept secret – and the tears and the reproofs and the threats were raining down upon her head, she couldn't really understand what all the fuss was about.

Madeleine collected Natasha from the house of her schoolfriend and together they went into town to buy the jeans, the tights and the long dress. In Marks and Spencer's she saw women pushing trolleys laden with expensive and hygienically-wrapped foodstuffs: perfect, unblemished apples they had, plump pink ducklings, packets of lasagne and cartons of double cream. She tried not to look at them. She went to the butcher's and bought half a pound of mince and some spare ribs. Her life, like her mother's, was ruled by choices: food *or* heat *or* clothes. Of course, there was nothing preventing her from *attempting* to get what Joanna called a proper job, nothing except lack of confidence and the fear of what might happen if she were to leave Natasha in the care of her father and he should chance to get drunk. He never *had* done, but that didn't make her feel any more confident. Besides, she was nervous and she looked awful and there was no money for decent clothes or hairdressers, and who on earth would want to employ anybody like that?

She caught a glimpse of Desmond going into the Job Centre and for a second or two she couldn't quite place him: dark, jowly, corduroy jacket, pausing to extinguish a cigarette stub under his heel – her husband, a man who had misused and abused her, who had never allowed her a wife's proper security, who had assaulted her and squandered their livelihood on drink, who had betrayed her in her own bed. Joanna would say, 'You must enjoy it or you wouldn't stay.' Oh, to have Joanna's clear-cut vision of life: either you do or you don't. Joanna probably had an operational definition of love and if she found any discrepancy between theory and practice then the emotion experienced could not be called love. 'Once,' Joanna had said, four years ago, 'once – well, nobody's perfect, but *twice* . . .'

It was over, he'd told her. It had been an obsession and it was over. Beatrice might be desolated, but neither of them had ever assumed that it could amount to anything more than it was; a husband, a wife, five kids between them and lack of money made any such assumptions impossible. It was just something they'd had to get out of their systems. He'd begged her forgiveness. She couldn't take it in, that there was no part of him with which Beatrice was not familiar, that Beatrice had made coffee in *her* percolator, and then got into *her* bed and afterwards washed in *her* bathroom. It was over, he said, he had a job now, things would be different. 'I get into a temper and say things I don't mean. The fault lies in me. But it's you I need.' She looked at him wonderingly, remembered

263

how she'd been wearing Beatrice's clothes on their very first date together. The image of Beatrice had been with him before ever he met her. His confession was total. He was sure of her forgiveness, her not forgiving him would have shaken the very foundations of his existence. 'You don't hate me, do you?' he said, confident of an answer in the negative. He stretched out his hand towards her and she covered it with her own. Try as she might, she could find no vestige of blame attaching to him. He had simply taken what was offered, what he'd probably desired from the very beginning: that first evening when he'd seen her in the velvet suit and the silk blouse; borrowed plumes. Beatrice was the villain.

The wind rattled tendrils of creeper against the window pane. A quantity of soot fell down the chimney and hit the hearth with a faint hissing sound. The electric clock on the bedside table whirred and then ticked away at a furious rate. Beatrice turned her pillow over to its cool side. Pillows, she thought: you sighed into them and wept into them and sank back on to them in ecstasy. Bridget used to starch the pillow-cases. Perhaps Bridget had invented work for herself: starching pillow-cases, ironing the toes and the heels of stockings, cutting the crusts off toast. None of those things got done any more and no one seemed to be any the worse for such neglect.

If one was a naturally dependent person, Madeleine had said, then one simply transferred that dependence on to someone else. Before, Bridget had been her rock and refuge; afterwards, after all was discovered and she'd cried and promised and promised and he'd walked round with a look on his face as though someone had hit him in the solar plexus, afterwards she'd attempted the trans- ference. But David was not Bridget, content to sublimate his personality for the sake of the health of Beatrice's psyche. He could not be her husband, her mother, her father and God all rolled into one. He was quite prepared to overlook her solitary lapse from marital fidelity, but he could not alter himself, for her or anybody else.

For a year she had moved mechanically: cleaning, cooking, knitting, mending and washing. Everything seemed slightly out of focus. But sometimes she thought that she'd come to terms with her loss: some afternoons when they rushed in from school brandishing their gold stars and their Alpha pluses and their hand-made Christmas cards; some evenings when she went from bedroom to bedroom noting the different expressions and postures they assumed in their sleep and yet how alike they looked. It is over, she'd think then. I am free. And yet, the very next day, an autumnal twilight thick with nostalgia or a bright, wet, windy April morning that seemed to promise unlimited possibilities, that old hand would squeeze at her heart and she'd find the idea that he was alive, living, breathing and functioning, not five miles away from her, quite insupportable.

The wind howled, rattled the creeper, more soot fell down the chimney and Joanna said, 'You must eat something, if it's only a boiled egg.'

'If it'll make you happy.'

'An egg, then. And is there anything in particular that the kids need: football gear or ironed neckerchiefs, etcetera? Never mind, I'll ask them when they come in.'

She heard them whispering outside her door. She laid down her egg spoon and her tea cup and pulled the clothes up to her chin. She heard the door open and one of them – Felix – say, 'She's asleep. Ssh.' And then there was a clatter of feet and individual doors slamming. They'd have awakened a catatonic from his trance. She felt no twinges of guilt at this neglect of them. She desired only that they should stay away from her and leave her to her private world of kaleidoscopic visions.

She saw his face again. The way it was the day they'd encountered one another by sheer chance – though neither of them believed in the concept of sheer chance – and how she realized instantly that all those assurances she'd given herself about being cured were nonsense. An addict is never cured of his addiction; one drink, one cigarette, and all the months or years of abstinence are as nothing.

They could have smiled and passed by but of course they didn't, they resumed exactly where they'd left off. David was away from home two nights of every week. This time the Literary and Debating Society provided her with an alibi. She'd attend for the first half an hour or so and then excuse herself and make the old familiar journey to the railway siding. 'This house,' Desmond said, 'supports the motion that Desmond and Beatrice are meant for each other. All in favour, say aye. Motion carried.' Natasha had started at nursery school and he had every Wednesday afternoon free from his teaching duties at the technical college. The only difference was that Madeleine had exchanged her blue-striped sheets for lilac ones.

Her Tuesday afternoons and evenings were fraught. She tried to anticipate everything that could possibly go wrong. Once Oliver woke on a Wednesday morning with a rash and complained of a sore throat. 'Stop feeling sorry for yourself,' she'd said, and packed him off to school. When she got back at half past three in the afternoon, she'd found him crying his eyes out in the hen house; they'd sent him home after lunch and he'd lost his key.

That pulled her up short. For a day or two. And then it was forgotten. German measles was, after all, a very mild illness, and all the other catastrophes that had come into her mind at the same time – road accidents, overturned paraffin heaters, gas explosions, the front door being opened to homicidal maniacs – could be averted by the simple expedient of engaging a babysitter for one evening a week; and why, if calamity were due to strike, should it choose to strike on a Wednesday afternoon?

In the car, in his bed, they talked desultorily and with lack of conviction about the future. He would leave Madeleine and she would leave David and they would go off somewhere together and live happily ever after. This particular vision depended upon their disregarding the existence of their children. Perhaps she could leave hers. She didn't know. Whenever she tried to think about it a kind of psychological safety curtain came down. What she was certain about was that he wouldn't leave his. She had seen his face whenever Natasha had a particularly bad attack of asthma, the way he guided her across the roads and aired her clothes in front of the fire, testing the temperature against his cheek.

But naturally calamity did strike, and naturally timed its striking for a Wednesday afternoon. Not a paraffin heater bursting into flame, or acute appendicitis and ambulances at the school gates and policemen putting out messages for absent next-of-kin, but in the form of a crucifying period pain which incapacitated Madeleine to such an extent that her immediate superior in the Department of Health and Social Security insisted that she take the rest of the afternoon off.

It grew dark in Beatrice's bedroom. Outside, birds twittered frantically in the dusk. Beatrice curled herself up very small, clasped her arms around her knees. If there was one memory from that entire period that would remain with her until the grave, it was the look on Madeleine's face when she'd opened the bedroom door upon them. It could not have been described as shocked or disorientated or horrorstruck; it was, purely and simply, quite merciless.

7

'And how long does Madam intend to remain incommunicado?'

Helena sank on to the sofa, lit one of her very occasional cigarettes – it was not the fear of lung cancer that had caused her to reduce her once high intake; it was the discovery that smoking accelerates the ageing process of the skin.

She had cooked an excellent meal for all of them. Now she had set the boys to washing up. 'Washing up's against her religion,' Sam said, through a symphony of grumbling and groaning – she had worked with the careless abandon and concomitant messiness of one who knows that someone else will clear up afterwards.

'She's not actually ill, is she?'

'I don't think so,' Joanna said. 'I think she's just tired.'

Helena mused, gazing down the length of her silver-banded cigarette. 'I shall ring the doctor in the morning,' she said eventually.

'Oh, I don't think that would be a very good idea.'

'You don't?'

There was an inflection in her tone, a note of genuine query. At last, Joanna thought, I am considered worthy of holding a sensible opinion. Once, and not so long ago, she would have simply regarded me with that 'oh-Joanna-is-so-amusing-we-must-bear-with-her' look that she reserved for me ever since my childhood.

'I think she might consider it to be an unwarrantable interference.'

'She can't stay up there indefinitely, shutting herself off from reality. She needs to see a solicitor, to get her affairs put in order, to think about her future.'

'Perhaps she's had a bit too much reality of late. Perhaps she needs a period of complete switch-off, a hibernation.'

Helena thought it over, poured them both a glass of the sherry that she'd brought with her. 'Why is it,' she said, 'that you have turned out to be so sensible and capable, whereas my daughter behaves like an adolescent? Is it because you had the chance to pass through that phase of silliness and she didn't?'

'Phase of silliness?' .

'Yes, yes.' Helena made an explanatory gesture with one hand. 'In your case it was up the workers and setting the world to rights and rejecting the values you'd grown up with. In other cases, it would be falling in love with unsuitable people, or religion, or drugs, or whatever it was then. You had the opportunity for self-discovery. She was married at eighteen. I tried to persuade her to have an abortion. If anyone else had been doing the persuading,' Helena said, 'she would have agreed to it. I realize now,' Helena said, 'that she resented me, regarded me as a rival, therefore any suggestion that I made would be rejected out of hand.'

Oh God, Joanna thought, working-class women take up bingo in their declining years; with ladies in Helena's socio-economic grouping, if it's not bridge and good works, then obviously it's Freud. And that's something that some fortunate few of us managed to work our way through at an earlier stage of our development.

'I knew from the very beginning that it was unlikely to be successful. He couldn't give her what she needed. Wretched man. She thought she was reforming a rake. She was far too young to realize that all that was simply a gloss on his essential dullness. Hardly the ideal partner for one who was so badly afflicted with boredom. Naturally, as soon as she stopped having those babies and found herself with time on her hands, she looked around for someone with a little more verve.'

Joanna played around with the idea of 'verve' and Desmond, tried to relate them, gave up, defeated.

'And of course when that dreadful po-faced man found out, he behaved like some Victorian paterfamilias, oozing moral indignation, making her feel like a fallen woman. And when you feel like a fallen woman you behave like one. Which, of course, explains all these silly affairs she's been having with these dreary men. If she'd only applied a little of that intelligence she's supposed to possess, then there wouldn't have been any question of him leaving her.'

She paused, awaiting Joanna's response.

'Of course,' Joanna said.

'I beg your pardon?' Her calm, composed expression said, I am willing to acknowledge you as an equal intellect, I am willing to enter with you into a process of negotiation and redefinition, just so long as we regard certain facts as being self-evident.

'I'm sorry. It's just that my comment would appear to be unnecessary. You have it all worked out: what she did and why she did it and the inevitable outcome. I can't deal in your sort of certainties. I just don't think that x necessarily results in y. I don't know what you mean by "dreary men" or "regarding oneself as a fallen woman". And I don't understand why you should think her affairs any sillier than, say, your affairs.'

She had overstepped the mark by a mile. Helena's eyes were hidden by her glasses, but the shape of her mouth betokened the extent of her outrage. Joanna sipped her sherry, continued imperturbably, relishing the realization, newly-dawned, that Helena no longer commanded a special sort of respect, a feeling of awe, just because she was Helena. She was simply a woman, an adult, and if she wanted to engage in a serious conversation with another adult concerning the reasons for her daughter's withdrawal, then she must accept the fact that neither age, rank nor status protected her from the utterance of certain home truths.

'You see,' Joanna said, 'Beatrice, having had the opportunity for close observation of an explosive relationship, and the way that it can affect any dependent children of that relationship, was drawn towards the opposite extreme: marriage to a man who would be her friend rather than her lover. When she made that choice she was unaware of her own instincts and the likelihood that, sooner or later, they would surface and she would crave excitement just as you and her father did.'

Getting it off your chest was a most appropriate phrase. She felt as though she could float up to the ceiling.

Helena regained her control; it had been a momentary lapse. She said, 'It's always the parents who are to blame. We can't do right for doing wrong.'

'Well, I'm afraid, if you insist on pursuing psychoanalytic theory, that's the route it invariably takes: the royal road to parental mismanagement.'

'How long do I have to take the blame? She's a woman now, with children of her own.'

'Then accord her the courtesy of treating her like one. Either give her equal footing, or else *be* a mother – you know? – bosom to cry upon, clean handkerchief and kiss it better. Stop behaving like the queen faced with a recalcitrant peasant. And why *blame*, for heaven's sake? Everyone's so anxious to grab a share: "It was my fault", "*I* made her do it", "She's the way she is because of me". That kind of guilt's an indulgence and an insult to common sense. People do what they do. Life may be eternal impingement, but we're not simply marionettes dancing for ever to someone else's string.'

Helena got up and walked to the window, affected an absorbed interest in something that lay outside it, although all that she could see was her own reflection. Her back to Joanna, she said, 'What impeccable order all of your relationships must be in.'

'We've finished.'

Sam came in, followed by Oliver. Helena turned from the window. 'You've done all the pans?'

'Yes. All the pans and the oven dishes *and* cleaned all the muck off the stove. Why d'you think it took us so long?'

He squared up to her. He was quite as tall as she and no longer as afraid of the implications that lay behind her cool stare as once he had been. Whenever his grandmother came to stay, his mother tended to behave as though she was at her children's level, a child herself: naughty, mutinous and stubborn. He was old enough to realize that parents ought not to have that effect upon their offspring.

'It won't do you any harm to help in the house. She lets you get away with murder.'

Helena looked him straight in his bold eye. He might be a well-grown youth with a degree of maturity not often met with in boys of his age but, to her, he was just the young Beatrice all over again: defiant to the last, presenting a face that asked to be slapped.

'When's she getting up?'

Her withdrawal had followed rapidly upon Helena's coming. Consequently he felt quite justified in transferring to Helena a measure of the aggression that had been directed towards his father.

'Who's *she*?'

'The cat's mother,' Oliver said. He wiped liquorice from his mouth and on to his trousers, sneezed and sniffed. Helena avoided direct contact with Oliver at all times; he seemed to be in a permanent state of stickiness and viral infection. Her presence didn't bother him in the slightest. She could stay, she could go; he didn't care.

'Well? When is she?'

'Oh, quite soon, probably. She's just having a rest. If there's anything you need, then I'm sure that your grandmother and I can see to it between us.'

It was a most unsatisfactory answer but he could tell that it was all that he was going to get. He sat down, flicked through the pages of Helena's *Vogue*. Helena said, 'Isn't there some homework or something that you should be doing?'

'If you want us to leave, why not just say so?' He got up from his seat so energetically that dust rose from the sofa cushions. 'Come on, twerp. Can't you tell when you're not wanted?'

Oliver went without demur. For him, to be in the presence of adults meant only: 'Stop sniffing, wipe your nose, wash your hands, no, you can't, why, because I say so.'

Helena lit another cigarette. To the devil with wrinkles! If she'd admitted to having nerves, then those children would have got on them: Sam, so insistent on knowing the whys and the wherefores, Toby, impervious to exhortation, and Felix and Oliver, living reminders, provokers of memories that hurt. 'Unnecessarily harsh,' she said, 'isn't that what you're going to say? I'm sorry, I just don't like children. I never have done.'

Joanna looked sideways at her – not without admiration – this formidable elderly woman who had picked herself up from the depths of the worst humiliation and made for herself a new way of life, a cosy, undemanding way of life. Helena could teach them all a lesson or two in the art of survival.

' "An unnatural woman," my daughter once called me. I suppose it's true. At least I don't pretend any maternal instincts that I don't possess. I'm honest with myself. I don't retreat into inaction as an alternative to facing up to myself. She's getting up tomorrow,' Helena said, suddenly vehement, 'if I have to drag her out of there.'

Joanna refrained from comment. She merely regarded the mother: strong, forceful, positive, and considered the daughter: lying upstairs, escaping into a private universe from which the need for decision had been banished, and wondered if it was at all possible that somebody had muddled two babies and the real

Beatrice was somewhere else entirely, organizing her life with the efficiency and single-mindedness of her natural mother.

No degree of force was necessary. They persuaded her downstairs where she sat, still wearing her dressing-gown, in an armchair in front of the television set. She ate a poached egg, dipping fingers of toast into the yolk as she watched the screen, avidly. *Grandstand*, she watched, globs of egg dripping from the toast on to her lap. She watched as though she'd put her life savings on a horse running in the 1.30 at Kempton Park, as though she'd suddenly developed a fervent interest in the skull-crushing and collar-bone-fracturing fouls perpetrated by rugby league footballers. When they spoke to her she answered politely but absently. She gave the impression of immovability, as though she would sit on, her hand half way to her mouth, while one programme followed another across that convex rectangle: cartoons, talent contests, all-in wrestling, Westerns, broadcasts about quantum mechanics put out for the benefit of students of the Open University.

The boys, in their best clothes, fidgeted about the room, whistling, combing their hair, quarrelling, over-watering the cactus plants on the window-sill, humming tunelessly, flinging themselves together or severally on to the sofa. They were awaiting their father's arrival. He was taking them to a football match and then for a meal. The incidence of football matches on Saturday afternoons solved quite a few problems.

Beatrice lit a cigarette and used her dirty plate as an ashtray. Helena, with a look on her face that gave you the impression she'd just trodden in something unpleasant, removed the plate and replaced it with a proper ashtray. Beatrice appeared not to notice. Hull Kingston Rovers had just scored a try.

'I'll give her until Monday,' Helena said, placing the plate on the draining-board in the kitchen, 'to come out of her trance, and then I'm calling in the doctor.'

'You don't call in doctors these days,' Joanna said. 'Not unless you're dying. You make an appointment for two weeks next Thursday.'

'When you pay them,' Helena said, 'they come when you call. Meanwhile, I have a word or two to exchange with Mr Ross. Another thing I find most peculiar about Beatrice is her apparent lack of interest in this dreadful woman. All I can get out of her is that she has red hair and is called Greta.'

'She's called Gillian, actually. And I have a feeling that the supposed colour of her hair owes a lot to Beatrice's strange and peculiar conviction that redheads are inveterate husband-stealers.'

'I shall require a little more information from *that* gentleman,' Helena said, 'than her name and her colouring. When he brings them back this evening I shall expect rather more of an explanation than *that*.'

She'd been to the hairdresser that morning, her face had been created with care, her scent was subtle yet pervasive, the chains around her neck made a clinking noise, like armour.

'You don't mind if I go out for a while?'

Beatrice might remain seated before the television set or she might take a knife and stab him through the heart. Helena might provoke some fresh drama. David might take the kids and their passports and escape with them to foreign parts and never be seen again. At that moment, Joanna couldn't have cared less. She just wanted to go out of the house and get into her car and drive to where there weren't any people.

'Not in the least. What there is to be said will be said more effectively without an audience.'

They passed each other in their cars at the bottom of the hill. Either he didn't see her or he pretended not to see her. I wouldn't be you, she thought, for a gold clock as big as a banjo, as Bridget used to say. Coming all unaware to face an avenging mother-in-law. She'll make mincemeat of you. She'll make you squirm and shuffle your feet. Not because she's a mother defending her cub, but simply because she's always resented you, ever since the beginning when you were quite a handsome young man and you had the temerity to fancy Beatrice while Helena herself was still eminently fancyable.

She drove out to what used to be the countryside before it had been blighted with a rash of bungalows and an egg-packing plant and a pumping station. They'd held their picnics on what was now the forecourt of a garage. Beatrice always had lovely sandwiches with the crusts cut off, wrapped in a damp linen napkin, and a brand new bicycle with a dynamo and three-speed gears and drop-handlebars that Emmett serviced whenever he'd run out of leaves with which to make bonfires. Beatrice would sacrifice her sandwiches to the insatiable demands of Joanna's appetite and lie on her

273

back eating a Mars bar, acquiring spots and foretelling their futures. Those futures as predicted by Beatrice bore little relation to the presents they had become.

She switched off the engine, tilted the driving mirror until she could see her reflection. It didn't look in any way different. A little paler, perhaps.

Her features dissolved before her eyes. It was his face that she saw. His brown eyes, his moustache, his upper lip pulled back over his teeth at the moment of release. 'Hadn't we better take some precautions?' he'd said. 'I tend to hit the target with an almost monotonous frequency.' Four already and another one on the way. Sylvia liked having babies so he gave her them. Perhaps she was no great shakes when it came to discussing Theories of Occasionalism or the Ghost in the Machine, but she was possessed of a hormonal regularity par excellence. 'In my case,' she'd said, 'there is no target to hit.'

An examination, years ago, conducted by one of Neville's colleagues: 'You don't seem to be ovulating. We can treat you . . .' No. No thanks. I don't like babies. I don't intend to have any. Ever. Neville's not bothered either. He doesn't like kids. He's stopped just about as many as the ones he's made possible.

She remembered his face in that borrowed bedroom, smiling. 'I might make you pregnant,' he'd said. Oh, the overweaning male pride of it – I can impregnate any woman who'll open her legs for me. She'd laughed at him, dismissively.

Of course, when you believe yourself to be barren you don't bother to check your dates. It comes around and you deal with it. That morning she'd woken up and looked at the date on her watch and said to herself, 'I must remember to buy some Tampax.' Then she'd looked again, and started to do a few calculations.

'Shock can do it, you know. Or a cold. Once I went for three months. All kinds of things can do it. Nerves. Or an emotional upset.'

'Or going to bed with someone. How soon can you have that frogs and rabbits thing?'

She shook her head to clear it. Three weeks overdue. A slight touch of nausea as she'd got out of bed that morning. What a turn-up for the book: in the club and a choice to be made between two responsibilities. Watch it grow? See if it turns out to be tall and slim or dark and heavily built with eyes like treacle?

Pull yourself together. It may not even *be*. One way to find out. Your friendly local chemist. Fast, confidential service. Wait until the shop is empty and then hand over your sample and your two pound notes, wait with beating heart for the verdict.

She drove into town, purchased a small bottle of aspirin, flushed its contents down the lavatory in the nearest public convenience, did what was necessary and made for the appropriate chemist's shop. She found that she was blushing. Too ridiculous. The whole business; just too ridiculous.

And her timing was rotten. They didn't test for pregnancies on a Saturday afternoon, the girl said. She'd have to wait until Tuesday. She could ring for the result. Tuesday? 'It's Easter,' the girl said, gave her a funny look.

Of course it was. Out there in the real world, the world where people weren't being deserted, beaten up, trying to decide which of two men might have fathered an embryo whose existence hung in the balance between now and Tuesday afternoon.

And sufficient unto the day. Don't panic. Put it out of your mind. Think of other things, other people's problems.

Driving back through the thronged centre of the town, she caught sight of a figure that resembled Madeleine. It was Madeleine. She was carrying a bag full of shopping on one arm. The other arm was supported in a sling.

Joanna braked rapidly and wound down her window. She accepted scurrilous observations about her character and parentage, and threats to her person quite calmly while she attempted to attract Madeleine's attention.

'The high street welcomes careful drivers,' Madeleine said, entering the car sideways and with difficulty.

'Home?' said Joanna, waiting humbly and patiently to rejoin the line of traffic.

'Where else?'

A new note, a note not heard before in Madeleine's voice. Joanna turned her head sharply, but not sharply enough, it seemed. The voice might have betrayed something, but the face was quite composed. And she talked ceaselessly, not allowing Joanna a word in edgeways, until they'd reached the flat. She talked about the price of food, about Beatrice and Beatrice's zombie-like condition, about the new job Desmond was starting after Easter – supply teaching at the comprehensive. She talked about anything and

275

everything except her arm swathed in its precise white hospital bandaging.

'Well, thank you very much. I expect I'll see you again before you leave.'

Joanna leaned across and opened the door for her. 'Aren't you going to invite me in? I need a refuge for a while. Just until the skirmishes chez Ross are over. I'd go to the flicks but it seems to be a straight choice between soft porn and King Kong and, besides, this town always used to be famous for its cinema-frequenting gropers.'

'I think as a breed they're extinct now. The only patrons of the cinema are old-age pensioners who get in half-price. Not groping material by any stretch of the imagination.'

'Can I come in or can't I? If you're entertaining a lover or starting your spring cleaning just say so, and I'll continue my aimless driving for another couple of hours. Or I'll sit in Beatrice's hen house.'

As Oliver once did when he had the German measles and Beatrice and my husband were otherwise engaged, Madeleine thought. Or so David told me. She hesitated, half-in, half-out of the car. It would be easy to put Joanna off, to manufacture some excuse. Joanna watched her steadily. Joanna could be properly regarded as her only friend. Friends were hard to make, harder still to keep, when you moved from place to place, when you had to keep your private life extremely private. And, somehow, she realized that she had reached the point where she needed a friend.

Though still some obscure shame prevented her from voicing any direct statement. She moved about the kitchen unpacking her shopping and putting it away while Joanna leaned against the door and said, 'You've been in the wars again, I see.'

She tipped a packet of tea into the caddy, put the kettle on to boil. 'I tripped and fell down the stairs,' she said.

'Very accident-prone lately, aren't you?'

'They say it goes in cycles.'

'Mm. Beatrice says that. The difference being that Beatrice's accident-proneness involves irons and drains and washing machines, whereas yours is all in the sphere of broken glass and arms and bruises.'

Madeleine took two cups and saucers from the cupboard. Her good hand trembled slightly. Joanna watched its trembling, said, 'You know what your sort of accident-proneness reminds me of?

276

Those babies that are carried along to Casualty so often for cuts and abrasions that eventually someone gets suspicious and contacts the social services.'

'Beatrice used to be the one with the fertile imagination – weaving exotic tales out of mundane events. You always wanted facts and conclusions.'

'That's what I'm doing, drawing a conclusion from the facts. Simple logic, that's all. No imagination involved.'

'Then you're working from a false premiss.'

'And you're a lousy liar. Good liars, as well as needing perfect memories, have to be able to coordinate their vocal and facial expressions. Your face is OK – it's like looking into a mirror, but your voice gives you away.'

'Don't play about with me – your clever verbal games – I'm just not up to it this afternoon.'

'They wouldn't be necessary if you'd speak the truth. He hits you, doesn't he? He uses physical violence towards you. Why are you afraid to admit it? Because I'll feel sorry for you?'

She slammed the teapot down on the stove. A misty vision of Joanna swam into her eye corner: expensive coat, well-cut hair, discreetly made-up face, kid gloves, gold watch, valuable rings. 'What the hell business is it of yours?' she shouted, as she'd wanted to shout at Helena Martin years ago when she'd stood in their hall, in the middle of that gleaming expanse of parquet, waiting for Beatrice, wearing her too-long gymslip and her sensible shoes. 'What gives you the right to patronize me, to talk down to me as though I were a mental defective? What gives you the right to make any comment, unfavourable or otherwise, about my life? It's *my* life and I don't see any reason why it should conform to your standards.'

Joanna knotted the belt of her coat. She said, 'Nothing gives me any right, except the responsibility every human being ought to have for the safety of another member of the species. Once you accused me of having concern for humanity and not giving a damn about individuals. I took your criticism to heart; I tried to remedy the omission.' She picked up her handbag from the kitchen cabinet. 'I'll go,' she said, 'if that's what you really want me to do.'

They felt themselves to be crystallized within the moment, like flies in amber. Joanna waited. And Madeleine fought the ultimate battle with her reserve and her shame and won it and said, 'Yes, he hits me. And it's getting worse. What started off as a slap across the face has developed into full-scale assault. And I'm frightened.'

And, once those four simple explanatory sentences had been uttered, the rest was easy: the drinking, the nature of the violence, his apparent subsequent amnesia. She stared past Joanna as she recounted her story; she didn't want any expression of horror or sympathy to divert her from her course until she'd reached its conclusion.

Then she took a deep breath and poured milk into the cups. Neither of them wanted tea; it was just an occupation for her hands. Perhaps, after all, she could have told it to the Samaritans. But the Samaritans were, primarily, listeners. They would not say, as Joanna said, so surely and definitely, 'He's ill. He needs treatment. And you need to be away from him. You realize that?'

'I don't know that I could manage without him.'

'Would you be willing to try?'

It was a direct question that required a direct answer. She tipped the spout of the teapot towards the cup and poured. So intense was her absorption that she kept on pouring and scalded her hand. The pain recalled the pain of her arm, the pain of the broken glass, his grasp on her elbow, his hand across her cheek, the sheer unmixed viciousness in his face as he hurt her. She ran cold water from the tap on to the tender flesh. 'Yes,' she said.

8

He came in while they were packing two suitcases: a small one for Madeleine, a larger one for Natasha who, as luck would have it, was at the house of a schoolfriend. The plan was essentially short-term: a hotel for the pair of them. Financed by Joanna. Ethical considerations were laid aside for the present; Joanna had money and Madeleine had none. Joanna moved rapidly and ruthlessly. Clothes were needed and toothbrushes and a few toys and books for Natasha. And that was all. She discovered Madeleine dithering, a pair of flowered curtains in her hand. 'You won't need flowered curtains. Not yet awhile, anyway. If you're going to do it, you must *do* it.'

'If it were done when 'tis done, then 'twere well it were done quickly,' Madeleine said. Only Madeleine could have rendered that quotation accurately. She had made a decision, she had said the word, but the impression she gave was of an unresisting element being borne along by a greater force.

Joanna grabbed a tin of talcum powder and a comb from the dressing-table, threw them on top of an assortment of clothes and snapped shut the clasps of the case. And Desmond walked into the bedroom. 'Have you come to stay?' he said, quite politely, nonchalantly. 'I wouldn't advise it. There's only the sofa and it's not sprung for peaceful slumber.'

He folded his arms across his chest. He was wearing his good suit, he'd had a close shave and a haircut. Anyone passing him in the street would probably not have picked him out as a wife-beater. She swung the suitcase off the bed and on to the floor. She said, 'I'm not staying. She's leaving.'

'She is?' He stayed where he was, blocking her exit. 'On whose say-so?'

'On her own say-so.'

Other people's husbands: she had tried, unsuccessfully, to elicit a response from David; a response was the last thing she wanted from Desmond.

'And just exactly why is she leaving?'

'Because she's grown weary of acting the part of your punch-bag. Excuse me, please.'

He appeared to be sober. And Madeleine had said that he was violent only when drunk. Nevertheless, she couldn't suppress a very obvious flinching motion as she attempted to pass him.

He moved suddenly and abruptly. He looked rather surprised. As though he was unused to people regarding him as a threatening presence. He said, 'Just put me in the picture, will you? Madeleine is leaving me? At your instigation?'

Once past him and with the outside door in view she felt more confident. 'Your wife is leaving you because she can't take any more of your abuse. You understand? I can't put it more plainly than that. I'm sure you understand. Whatever your faults, being slow on the uptake was never one of them.'

'What the hell are you talking about – abuse? Christ Almighty, I should have known it. Every time you come near us there's trouble.'

She had never seen such a skilful portrayal of perplexity. He gave the impression that she'd walked into the middle of a scene of domestic bliss and sowed dissension simply for the sake of a perverted satisfaction.

'I seem to remember,' he said, 'that I had to tell you to piss off once before. Well, I'm telling you again now. Go and conduct your crusade somewhere else and leave us in peace.'

'Peace?' The bathroom door, still minus its glass panel, was conveniently at hand. She gestured towards it. 'Does your idea of peace encompass smashing glass and then forcing her to walk across it? You're the one, Desmond, who leaves destruction in your wake. Everything you touch, you ruin. You're responsible for a broken marriage, you were partly responsible for a death. If you continue the road you're travelling you may well be responsible for another.'

'That was an accident. I'd had too much to drink. I put my elbow through it.'

'It was not an accident. It was a deliberate act. They were all of them deliberate acts.'

He looked at the space in the door as though attempting to remember the exact circumstances of how it had come about. He said, 'What do you mean – death? Whose death?'

'A girl called Polly. She drowned herself. You haven't forgotten, surely? You were mad about her once. You were going to marry her. Until your feeling for her ceased, as suddenly as if you'd turned off a tap. She went home and she put herself in a river.'

Madeleine came out of the kitchen, carrying Natasha's pills and her inhaler. She stopped dead in her tracks at the name. They formed the points of an equilateral triangle, the three of them. He turned his head from Joanna to Madeleine. He said, 'Is that true?' She nodded.

'Why didn't you tell me?'

'Because I suppose I wanted to protect you from the knowledge.'

'She thought you weren't responsible. She didn't realize that it is in your nature to fall madly in love and out again and to hell with the consequences. She didn't realize that you'd vent your frustrations on whoever was misguided enough to return your affection. Poor Desmond. The world doesn't appreciate you. So Madeleine must suffer for it.'

He passed a hand across his eyes as though attempting to brush

280

away some cloudiness that impeded the clarity of his vision. He looked pathetic and despicable. She couldn't imagine why she'd ever felt afraid. 'These accusations,' he said, 'abuse, suffering. You mean that because of me Madeleine has to take a ridiculous, menial job? It wasn't my idea. She only does it for a kind of martyrdom, to make me feel small, smaller than I feel already.'

'I mean that you hit her and you hurt her. You see her arm, Desmond?'

'Of course I see it.' But he made no attempt to look.

'There's something special about it, isn't there? It's in a sling. Do you know why that is?'

'Have you gone quite mad?' he said. He focused on Joanna's face so that Madeleine and anything to do with Madeleine was outside his range of vision. 'It's in a sling because it's broken. Will you go, you bitch, and leave us alone?'

'In my own good time. Why is it broken?'

'Because she fell down the stairs.' He articulated each word slowly and carefully as though communicating with an imbecile.

'No, not because she fell down the stairs. Because you pushed her. I'll refresh your memory.'

Madeleine said, 'No, Joanna, no.'

Joanna said, 'Yes, Madeleine, yes. If, as you say, one half of him doesn't know what the other half's doing, then it would be as well if someone introduced the two of them to each other. You came home on Thursday night, Desmond – well, Friday morning, actually. You were drunk. You pulled her out of bed, dragged her along the landing and when she resisted you pushed her down the stairs and locked the door behind her. When she came to and realized that her arm was hanging in a most peculiar fashion from her shoulder and it hurt like hell, she tried to get back into the flat. But you wouldn't open the door. So she was forced to go to the phone-box on the corner – in her nightdress and bare feet, mark you – and ring for an ambulance. They collected her from the bottom step of the stairs, they took her to hospital where her arm was X-rayed, set and bandaged. And eventually, towards morning, they brought her back. She was afraid that the door would still be locked against her but the ambulancemen banged very vigorously and you opened up. You seemed astonished. They asked Madeleine if she was sure that she was going to be all right and she said yes. They looked at one another and at the pair of you. They

281

were drawing certain conclusions. But, like the police, they aren't empowered to interfere in domestic disputes. So they got back into their ambulance and they drove away. And Madeleine came back to await your next bout of brutality. There. Does any of that register, conform to your conscious memory?'

He had closed his eyes while she was speaking as though he was experiencing some sort of sensory confusion, as though if he closed his eyes, he wouldn't be able to hear her and she wouldn't be able to see him. She said, 'The charitable view, Desmond, is that you're sick, that you're not responsible for your actions. I'd advise you to get yourself to a doctor and explain them to him as I've just explained them to you. In the meantime I'm taking your wife to a place of safety. When she's settled, she'll let you know where to contact her. But until you've either curbed your drinking and your viciousness, or got yourself some effective treatment, she has to stay away from you. For the sake of her own health, mental and physical.'

'And my daughter?' He made queer little grasping gestures with his hands as though he needed to hold on to something and there was nothing there.

'For purely practical reasons, your daughter must go with her mother.'

She took Madeleine's coat from its hook and draped it across her shoulders. Madeleine seemed frozen into position. She lifted the two suitcases. She said, 'I've never thought much of you, Desmond, but I can recognize the fact that you need help.'

He took the suitcases from her grasp and threw them, one, two, at the door. They didn't burst open; they were obviously more soundly constructed than Beatrice's suitcases. He turned towards Madeleine. 'Haven't you a voice?' he said. 'Is this bitch to be your mouthpiece? You stand there – a wronged woman. Christ, you've been doing it ever since that night I happened to be in the pub when you started to miscarry. Never a word – just those fucking soulful, wronged eyes staring at me – in my dreams. You never did anything deserving of blame, did you? Eternally beyond reproach, pure, forgiving. Christ, perhaps I do hate you. Clinging to me like a fucking leech all these years, accepting, accepting, forgiving, forgiving. You're too good to live, you know that? Why don't you go out and get drunk, get laid, rob a bank? For Christ's sake, *anything*. Saints should be in heaven, not down here married to me.

Why don't you go and put yourself in a river too? Why don't you? Because it's against that religion of yours that you've never entirely freed yourself from? Surely God will forgive your indecent haste to get to him. Because, by Christ, you're too wonderful for any human being to put up with.'

Madeleine's tongue moved around the inside of her lips. She said, 'I gave you my love.'

'You smothered me in it!' He grasped his head between his hands. His jaw trembled. Joanna shifted the suitcases, opened the door, ushered Madeleine forth. His teeth were clenched. It was difficult to understand what he was saying. Except for the last sentence, delivered at full volume, following them down the stairs: 'You go, and you never come back. You think you can do without me. You never could and you never will.'

They tried the Crown. The Crown was full up. The receptionist said, 'It's the Conference, you see.' They tried the Majestic. The Majestic was full up too. 'We've got them three to a room,' the receptionist said. The foyer of the Grand bristled with placards and seethed with men wearing lapel badges. The same was true of the Imperial and the Metropole. In the White Boar Joanna wove a course through a tangle of elbows and half pints of beer and gin and tonics towards the reception desk. 'I've got to be joking, haven't I?' she said to the girl behind it. The girl said, 'I'm afraid so. They're all over the place.'

They were indeed. They had spread like a fast-growing fungus throughout the town. From the grandest hotel to the sleaziest boarding-house, every space that could be fitted with a divan and two wire coat-hangers and called a bedroom was occupied. Joanna sat in the car, tapping her fingernails on the steering-wheel. There was nowhere else left to try. They were resident in every hotel within a radius of fifty miles. Natasha, in the back seat, read *William's Happy Days*, Madeleine shivered, though it was a mild evening, said, 'Having made the grand gesture, now we turn round and go back?'

'For God's sake, this is ridiculous. A plague on all conferences and their delegates. Haven't you any extant aged relatives who'd be willing to put you up for the night?'

Christ, what am I doing, she thought. Why don't I just drive home and see to myself?

'I might have, but I don't know of them.' She'd always been a shiverer, trembling uncontrollably at bus stops on frosty nights when everyone else was glowing, exhilarated. Desmond said she had the coldest feet in Christendom.

'The Social Services,' Joanna said, 'don't they have an emergency number and some sort of provision of temporary accommodation for these sort of cases?'

'The Samaritans, the Salvation Army Men's Palace, Aggie Weston's. Don't call me a case.' She might have known that it would end in farce.

Natasha yawned, longed for sleep, which would obliterate the questions she dared not ask. Joanna switched on the engine and said, 'There is, of course, one place.'

'The police station? They'd tell me to go home like a good girl and we'll sort it out in the morning.' If only she could get *warm*.

'I meant Beatrice's.'

'Why not? She can fall on my neck with tears of joy.'

'I'm serious. *She's* got a spare bedroom.'

'You *are* out of your mind. I'd rather sleep under the viaduct. I'd be in as much danger from Beatrice as I am from – ' She turned round quickly; Natasha's eyes were closed but she wasn't asleep. 'From other quarters.'

'The state she's in, I doubt whether she'd notice your presence.' Joanna backed into a side road. 'It's worth a try, anyway.'

Madeleine put a detaining hand on her arm. 'Joanna, will you get it through your skull: Beatrice's home is the last place that I am entitled to enter or desire to enter. I hate her guts and she hates mine.'

'I don't think she does. And are you sure that you do, still? I know perfectly well that it's the last place you'd choose. But it's Hobson's Choice, isn't it?'

'Let's just go back, forget it ever happened. Please.'

'You know what he'll do to you?'

'No. I've never left him before.'

They listened to the child's rhythmic breathing. She had fallen asleep on top of her books; she would have cramp when she awoke. Madeleine tore at the edge of her handkerchief with her teeth. She felt profoundly tired. If some decision wasn't taken soon, like Natasha, she would sleep where she sat. She heard Joanna's voice, distantly, saying, 'You know what he'll do. He'll get drunk and you'll have another broken arm. Or a broken head. Maybe not tonight. Or tomorrow. But it'll happen. If you go back now you'll never leave him. Not until he injures you badly. Or kills you.'

Madeleine yawned and shivered alternately throughout the journey. You reached a pitch when your grasp of events was not what it ought to be, when you couldn't comprehend your own feelings. She loved Desmond and she hated Beatrice. Beatrice hated her. Wasn't that the order of relationships? Or had she got it mixed somewhere? Was the equation not so clear-cut as that?

'I'll do a recce,' Joanna said. 'I expect she'll be exactly where I left her.'

She was. Watching *Match of the Day*, surrounded by her sons. Helena was absent, Joanna noted with relief. Perhaps she had pursued David to his love-nest and was, even now, making his paramour wish that she'd never been born.

'Have you eaten?' she enquired of them. Though the question was pretty redundant, considering the plates, the crumbs and the apple cores that littered the room. 'Where's your grandmother?'

'This is the match we *saw*,' Oliver said. 'We *saw* this match this afternoon.' An expression of anguish crossed his features as he was treated to an action replay of the wrong team scoring a goal. 'Grandmama,' Sam said, 'has swanned off to visit some posh friend of hers. I think we're beginning to get on her nerves.'

The footballers trooped down the tunnel. 'It's over then, is it? Are you going to bed now?' Joanna's hand moved towards the control knob. They protested vociferously: 'Of course it's not over.' 'There's the round-up yet.' 'And Goal of the Month.' 'We've entered for Goal of the Month.' 'If we'd won, we'd know by now, you jerk.' 'Oh yeah.'

'Well, please could you watch the rest of it upstairs? I want a word with your mother.'

They raised every sort of objection imaginable, but eventually they went, calling out, 'Good night, Mum,' as they jostled one another for precedence in the doorway. 'Good night,' she said, without turning round. She didn't say, 'Don't forget to brush your teeth and put your socks to wash,' which was part of the routine of her normal nightly farewell. Joanna turned off the television. Only then did she look up and say, 'Why ever did you do that? It's probably the Midnight Movie on next.'

'I don't care if it's probably the four-minute warning and last one to the fall-out shelter's a sissy on next. You've been watching that since noon. You'll go blind and you'll get piles. How did the visit go?'

'From my point of view? Never saw him. He simply collected and dumped. *She* saw him. She came into the room flushed with triumph. But I didn't want to know. So she strode off in a huff to visit one of her old flames. Imagine having old flames you can actually visit! Mine would have apoplectic fits if I turned up on their doorsteps.'

At least she was talking. Which was more than she'd done for the past few days. Though she still gazed at the screen as if hoping that it would form a picture as if by magic and despite Joanna's dictatorial hand.

'Beatrice, there's a favour I want to ask of you.'

Outside, in the car, Madeleine awoke jerkily from a doze. She could wake Natasha and together they could open the doors, step out into the night and make for – where? Home? She had a picture of the door locked and the window barred against her, as in the scene from *Peter Pan*. Her mother had taken her to see *Peter Pan* at the Hippodrome when she was seven. A treat. She remembered the smell of plush and oranges and the thrilling impact of the words: 'To die will be an awfully big adventure.' She slept.

Beatrice wiped her mouth on her sleeve. 'For all I care,' she said, 'you can open my house to the public at five bob a throw. Come one, come all.'

'You're sure?'

She shrugged. 'I suppose she's entitled to her share of gloating as much as anyone else. More so. Though I would have thought that this would be the last place she'd choose.'

'It is. There are no other options. She thinks that you hate her.'

Beatrice began to peel another orange. Five days of semi-starvation had restored her appetite wonderfully. 'As well as being no good at anything else,' she said, 'I'm no good at that either – sustained hating. They can sleep in the attic on those camp beds. I expect there are some sheets around somewhere. And now can I switch on the television again?'

Joanna opened the car door and they emerged, asleep on their feet. She led them into the house and up the stairs, made up the beds, undressed Natasha, put on her pyjamas and took her to the bathroom. Sam was in residence, searching his reflection for spots and wondering whether the amount of down on his upper lip warranted his very first shave. He eyed the child and eyed Joanna queryingly. He said, 'We used to keep mice in the shed. Every time you went to look, there were a few more of them. It's getting to be like that in this house. *They* ended up eating one another. Who on earth is she?'

'She's the daughter of a mutual friend of your mother's and mine. Madeleine. You probably wouldn't remember.'

'Yes, I do. I remember her husband. He taught us to whistle through blades of grass.'

That sounded like Desmond, and one of his major accomplishments.

'What's she doing here, anyway?'

'It's a long and complicated story which will be better saved till morning.'

Not that you'll be told then, she thought. Why is it that we shield our children so from the unpleasant facts of life? Like Mrs Brennan, who thought that if sex was never mentioned, Madeleine would never find out about it.

She helped Natasha into bed. She said to Madeleine, 'Is there anything you need?' But Madeleine was already asleep.

It wasn't the Midnight Movie. It was some moronic variety programme and even Beatrice, with her indiscriminate ardour for the moving picture, was showing signs of disenchantment. She turned her head when Joanna entered the room. Joanna said, 'They're both out like lights. I take it you weren't sorry to miss the formal re-introductions?'

'You take it correctly. I can do without that martyred expression at this time of night.'

'How do you know about a martyred expression? Have you seen her recently?'

'No. It's how I always think of her, as having a martyred expression.'

'That's what he said.' Joanna yawned, supposed that his was a name that ought not to be mentioned, but she had grown weary of treading delicately through a kind of personal index prohibitorum.

Beatrice combed her hair behind her ears with her fingers. 'Will he turn out into the night, do you suppose, seeking her?'

'Don't know. He won't come here, that's for sure. Or will he?'

287

She sat up straight in her chair. 'Oh God! I never thought! He knows that David's gone. Oh God! You don't think – ?'

'Will we bolt all the doors and bar the windows, push heavy furniture against them, sit up all night listening to our own heartbeats?' She seemed neither excited at the idea, nor alarmed. She began to smile. 'Poor Joanna. Whatever did you do that you should be lumbered with the troubles of such a pair of dumkopfs? Why don't you just get into your car and drive back to where all your acquaintances lead gentle, ordered lives?'

'I nearly did. This afternoon.'

'But something stopped you. You found your nature would assert itself after all. You could never be a non-participant, however you tried. You've missed having a cause, all these years, haven't you? Admit it.'

'How on earth could I turn you two into a cause?'

'Our rehabilitation, of course. That's a cause. Not as romantic or as immediately gripping as rousing the proletariat or even returning meths drinkers to wholesomeness. But it looks like the best you've got.'

'I'll just settle for bed. It's been a long, long day. And *you* can damn well get up in the morning and wash all those disgusting dishes. If you're having a breakdown, then have it over the sink.'

Beatrice threw orange peel towards the fireplace, missed her target. 'You shouldn't talk to me that way,' she said.

'I've tried kid gloves. That simply drove you to your bed.'

'And you can't go up yet.'

'Why not?'

'Because here comes my lady mother. And she'll want to tell you all about the assault that she mounted upon her son-in-law and she'll want to know all about our midnight visitors. And I'm damned if I'm going to explain.'

288

9

Madeleine and Natasha slept, turning inwards towards each other for warmth in the cold attic. Beatrice and Helena slept, relishing their muted Nembutal-induced dreams. The boys slept in their various individual postures: Toby and Felix curled embryonically, Sam on his back, his arms outspread, Oliver on his face, the covers over his head as protection against the bogeys that might just possibly exist, despite his daylight insouciance. The house was thick with sleep and Joanna, resentful, turned and turned again, pummelled her pillow and interpreted every nocturnal noise as evidence of Desmond's attempted forcible entry. Not that she was afraid. Not with Helena in the house. Helena would tame dragons and disarm axe-murderers with a single one of her glances.

At five o'clock, after two solid hours of sheep-counting, she went downstairs, lit the kitchen fire and waited for the dawn to announce itself at the window.

The kitchen was littered with adolescents' effects: motor-cycle magazines, rugby shirts, the internal workings of various pieces of machinery. Present or absent, the evidence of their existence was inescapable. She tried to imagine her own house disordered, invaded by an alien presence. Fifteen years ago she'd asked Beatrice how it developed, that maternal instinct, how it developed and overcame what surely must be a natural resentment at playing host to some unknown parasite. 'Your hormones see to all that,' Beatrice had said. 'Sylvia is a good mother,' he'd said. Calm, she supposed, all lap and mammary glands.

The thought made her retch a little. She ate a Garibaldi biscuit and did subtraction sums down the side of yesterday's newspaper. If it *was*, then it was more *likely* to be Neville's. But children came to look like the people they grew up with, just as husbands and wives grew to resemble one another. Didn't they?

Farcical. At the back of the form room they'd read out desperate letters from women's magazines, giggling, scornful: how *could* people get themselves into such ridiculous predicaments?

All her life she had acted in her own best interests; there had never been any confusion, they had always been apparent. All her life she had relied upon sweet reason for guidance, had used the fortunate falling of the dice to her own advantage. What, in these circumstances, did reason dictate? Obvious. She was fond of Neville. She respected him. And the other one? 'I will never leave her,' he'd said, all through that Massachusetts autumn, that dead winter, the early days of green spring. 'I shouldn't have married her but I will never leave her,' he'd said, blowing smoke rings up to the ceiling in that borrowed flat. 'There's been too much between us.' Blood-knowledge, cold-water flats where she addressed envelopes while he struggled through his doctorate, confinements and quarrels, that long tradition of shared class customs, his children, emerging, one after the other, stamped with the imprint of his features. 'Most women like being pregnant,' he'd said. 'Family life has a fair bit going for it.'

She couldn't, wouldn't, tell him. They were bound for Scotland and a new job, all six and a half of them: Sylvia and Paul and Simon, Jenny and Tessa and the one that hadn't yet made its début, all the goldfish and the rabbits and the guinea pigs crammed into his old estate car, with him at the wheel: the patriarch, the protector. Throughout the long journey he would see to it that they were kept amused. She saw him, delivering his jokes in that wry, offhand way he had, pulling into lay-bys for the little ones to be sick, leading his entourage into some motorway café and leaving with a pocket full of sugar lumps – in his dockside youth he'd robbed telephone boxes of their change and pinched apples from barrows; old habits died hard.

She saw him singing as they progressed along the road, singing silly songs with his head thrown back, orchestrating the kids in the occasional vulgar chorus, biting into one of Sylvia's home-made sandwiches. He'd make it fun, an adventure for them, as he made everything fun. She thought of journeys undertaken with Neville when she'd know exactly where they were going and precisely when they'd reach their destination. She remembered her lover and the way that he'd change direction in mid-stream, the way he stood on his head in the middle of her study when he thought she was getting too intense and humourless about something, the way they'd made love on the floor. It was his spontaneous gaiety – and his street-toughness that had attracted her. Neville squired her to drinks parties in Belgravia drawing-rooms, bought tickets for the opera, brought her home to an elegant bedroom where he made love to her with a professional expertise; *he* turned up unexpectedly and said, 'Get your coat on,' and took her to the sort of pub that she hadn't frequented for years where they drank with miners and factory hands and listened to raucous women singing at microphones and afterwards they did it in the back of his car all among the toffee papers and the dismembered Action Men and the children's drawings and he had none of Neville's skill or delicacy – just an intuitive knowledge of women that resulted from a childhood of innumerable sisters and aunts and a history of satisfying a large sexual appetite that dated from the time he was thirteen and had his first girl behind a bricked-up air-raid shelter.

And it was as though she was eighteen again, without responsibilities, social position or a string of letters after her name, as though he had waved a wand that brought it all back: drinking too much and laughing in the dark, changing your mind at the very last minute, opening unfamiliar doors, and sharing a last cuddle as the dawn rose over the brickworks. 'Life's not just doing what's expected of you,' he'd said.

He had loved her, in his way. She had no doubt about that. They had found in each other a rare complementarity of thought and feeling. But there were others who needed his love more than she did. Dependants, in the true sense of the word. His fidelity might have been suspect, but his loyalty had never been in doubt.

Reason dictated one course of action only. There were certain advantages in being married to a gynaecologist. She knew the ropes, the people you contacted, the signatures necessary for that simple, efficient procedure that could be fitted in between lunch and dinner. Vacuum-extraction. Neville had endorsed it enthusiastically. So simple, so efficient. Difficult to believe that it was in any way connected with the nullification of an existence.

Helena came downstairs saying, 'I don't suppose there's the faintest chance that everyone might act in a civilized fashion today?'

She looked younger, more attractive, this morning. Her joust with her son-in-law had brought a sparkle to her eye, a bloom to her cheek. It wasn't often, these days, that she got the chance of a good fight. Not that David could be described as a serious contender: he was, fundamentally, a blusterer and, ultimately, a sulker, but he had put up a sufficiently spirited display to afford her a little of that exhilaration she remembered from the old times.

I could ask her, Joanna thought, I could lose hold of my sanity and I could say, 'Dear Mrs Martin, I'm in an awful spot. Perhaps you were once in a similar awful spot at some time in your life. You admit that you don't like children so therefore you must have been tremendously relieved that you had the means to condemn them not to be. *Were* you relieved, after it was over? Or are you still haunted, in your private moments, by the sacrifices you made for what you considered to be the life you wanted? Dear Mrs Martin, you see perhaps I didn't escape the phase of silliness after all – perhaps I'm simply experiencing it a decade or two after everyone else. I met this man, you see, and we had the chance of a year together and I thought it wouldn't make any difference to anything, that I could return to how it was before without a pang. I was wrong. Do you understand? That even if I can't have him, I might want to keep something of him?'

She kept hold of her sanity and she listened while Helena recounted the course of the battle and Beatrice washed up. Beatrice had dressed and come downstairs quite voluntarily. Curiosity had impelled her. She had combed her hair and done her face and chosen female clothes that matched each other out of her wardrobe; she wasn't going to have that frozen-faced bitch witnessing the extent of her discomposure.

Joanna scrambled eggs. Beatrice wiped plates. Helena unsealed her own private packet of decaffeinated coffee. 'You are, as the saying goes,' she said, 'well rid. After last night, I realize that there's no limit to the depths to which he'll sink in the attempt to justify his conduct. I heard things that no self-respecting husband would divulge about his wife.'

'Fascinating,' Beatrice said, wringing out the dishcloth. 'Fascinating. That's the effect you have upon people, Mama; you bring out the worst in them. Why don't you make yourself useful and take up some breakfast to our guests? Act as an intermediary. No, perhaps not. She was always in awe of you. Well, of course, we all were, *are*. Except for Joanna.'

Joanna smiled above the scrambled eggs. Beatrice sniping at Helena was infinitely preferable to Beatrice mute in a dirty dressing-gown.

The boys came down as a merciless carillon of church bells announced Matins. They hunched their shoulders, swung their arms, distorted their features into a variety of slavering leers and staggered about the kitchen yelling, 'The bells! The bells!' and 'Sanctuary!' They did that every Sunday morning; for them the joke never palled. Helena seized Toby by the back of his collar, brought him to an abrupt standstill and placed a carefully-laid tray into his hands. There were scrambled eggs and there was toast and coffee and there were two crumpled napkins that she'd unearthed from a drawer. 'You've forgotten the single rose,' Beatrice said. Toby said, 'What am I supposed to do with this? Don't tell me.'

'You're supposed to carry it upstairs. Come along,' said Helena, helping him on his way with little prods in the small of his back.

'Who's up there?'

'Who've we got in the attic?'

'An acquaintance of mine and her daughter.'

'Which acquaintance?'

'Ask no questions,' Beatrice said, drinking from Helena's coffee cup, 'and you'll be told no lies.' That was pure Bridget, who hadn't been aware that children's questions must always be answered, patiently and accurately.

'Madeleine Russell,' said Joanna, as she scrambled away madly in an attempt to keep pace with their plate-clearing fervour. 'She was probably before your time.'

'No, she wasn't,' Felix said. 'I remember her. I remember her husband. He showed us how you make a whistle out of a blade of grass.'

'And Michelangelo was remembered for his proficiency on the Jew's harp,' Beatrice said. 'And everyone talks about how T. S. Eliot could entertain a roomful of people with a glass of water and a folded handkerchief.'

They looked at her and looked at one another and pointed their fingers at their temples. 'She's having one of her flights of fancy,' Felix said. Sam said, 'One of her famous non-sequitur sessions. It's just affectation.' Oliver said, 'I thought Michelangelo was a painter or something stupid like that.'

She leaned over and ruffled his hair and kissed his pale forehead with its two childish indentations in the flesh above the eyebrows. 'I love you,' she said. He blushed and ducked away from her and crammed his mouth full of toast. 'They're all lovely, aren't they?' She appealed to Joanna. Joanna nodded. Sam said, 'Oh God,' and Felix said, 'Oh, bloody hell, don't start *that*.'

'Can I *eat* now?' Toby said, having accomplished his mission. Helena said, 'Do you *allow* them to use that sort of language? They sound like street urchins. I know what I should do with them if they were mine.' Beatrice said, 'Would you like to adopt them? They'd bring joy and comfort to the time of your few sad last grey hairs.' But it was Beatrice who had the grey hairs. One, anyway. She'd pulled it from its follicle that very morning.

'Are they coming down?' Joanna said.

'I told them to take their time. I thought perhaps the boys could organize something to include the little girl. A picnic, perhaps? It's a lovely day. They could take their bicycles, go over to Shooter's Wood. Or the estate. It will be full of bluebells now, I should think.'

'Bluebells,' murmured Felix. 'Oh God.'

Sam said, 'This is our *home*, you know. We do *live* here.'

Beatrice said, 'It's an *excellent* idea,' and jumped up and began to haul loaves of sliced bread from the bin. 'Come on, Toby, you can butter and I'll spread.'

'Why me?' Toby said. 'Why's it always me?'

'Because you're efficient and thorough and biddable – when you choose to be. When it comes to sandwich-making, you're my very favourite son.' She hugged him to her. He struggled within her grasp. 'Oh don't start that stuff,' he said, and began to butter, fending off her advances with his elbow.

'You mean we've got to drag some *kid* along on a *picnic*?' Felix enquired of her. 'Are you *serious*?'

'Some *kid*?' Oliver said. 'Oh *lord*!'

'Look, Mum,' Sam said. 'I'm not a *child*. I'm a bit past *picnics*.'

'If he's not a child, then neither am I. He's only fifteen months older than me.'

'And *he's* only eleven months older than *me*.'

'And if he's not a child – '

She banged a spoon against the sink until they were silent. She said, 'You are all going to do me a favour, a *kindness*. You are going to take an eight-year-old girl on a picnic. You are going to treat her decently and make sure that she enjoys herself, because she's had a pretty rough time recently. Understand? Comprenez? Roger and out.'

'*She's* had a rough time? What about us?'

'It's going to rain, and if it rains I'll get another cold and you'll be sorry then.'

294

'We don't even *know* her.'

'And how do you know she'll want to come?'

She didn't want to go. That was obvious. She stood with her eyes fixed on the floor while they surveyed her. They were huge, strange and frightening. All strangers were huge and frightening. The smallest of them, a blond, shaggy-haired boy who wore a tee shirt with a picture of Snoopy as the Red Baron on the front, said, 'How can she come if she hasn't got a bike?'

'She can ride yours. And you can ride the old one.'

'No, I can't,' he said triumphantly. 'It's got a puncture. *And* the saddle's off.'

The intensity of their half-circle was immediately dissipated. Their faces lightened as they began to turn away, to relish the prospect of a long Sunday with nothing to do. Natasha brought her feet into perfect alignment and chewed the skin on the inside of her lip. 'I'll get off to Grayson's then, can I?' Toby said. Oliver juggled an imaginary football from toe to toe. Beatrice said, 'Couldn't one of you ride her on your crossbar?'

'It's *illegal*.'

'You might have done that sort of thing in *your* day . . .'

'In the dark ages.'

'I'll take you,' Helena said. 'We can all just about fit into the car. So stop making excuses and go and equip yourselves with whatever it is that you want to bring with you while I change into something more suitable.' Not that she *possessed* anything suitable for forays into muddy bluebell woods. Beatrice stood with her mouth agape, said, eventually, 'Do you want the loan of an anorak and wellies?'

'I don't think that will be necessary.'

'Isn't it all rather above and beyond the call of duty?'

'Isn't that what grandmothers are supposed to be for?'

'Whatever has come over her? What will she *do* all day? It *is* going to rain, you know.'

'She can drive them around. And she's taken *The Interpretation of Dreams* with her. That'll while away the time.'

'But she can't bear them. She thinks human beings should be shut away from civilized society until they're at least eighteen. What's her motive? Has she some plan?'

'Perhaps she just meant what she said: "That's what grand-mothers are for." '

'And what do we do about the unseen presence?' Beatrice

jerked her chin towards the ceiling. 'The lodger,' she said. She remembered that film: the pacing feet and the glass ceiling; it had been shown on one of the evenings when she did actually attend the Film Society. 'If she does intend to come down I expect she'll want you to act as escort. What's your plan of campaign, anyway?'

'Tomorrow morning,' Joanna said, 'after the circus has left town, I'll book her into a hotel and we can look around for some accommodation for her. She'd also be wise to consult a solicitor, I suppose. Like you. You could go together. You might get cut rates. Like block bookings and coach parties.'

'Highly comical,' Beatrice said. 'And she's agreed to all this, has she?'

'Hardly. We haven't even had time to discuss it. It just seems to be the logical procedure.'

'And then, having brought about all these changes, you'll hand over the reins to her and swan off back to Oxford? And you think he'll accept it all quite calmly?'

'I don't know what he'll do. You're more of an authority on him than I am.'

Beatrice winced. 'You'd better get her down. There's no point in postponing the evil moment.' She picked up what seemed to be a rather dirty communal comb from the side of the sink and drew it through her hair. Joanna hovered in the doorway. 'You won't . . . You'll . . .'

'I'll be the soul of tact and understanding. I just hope that we can depend on similar behaviour from *her.*'

If nothing else, Joanna thought as she climbed the stairs, Madeleine's personal crisis has drawn Beatrice out of her bed and persuaded her to drag a comb through her hair. Sweet are the uses of adversity. She opened the attic door. Madeleine was standing beside the neatly-made bed. She said, 'I suppose I've *got* to come down, say, thank you, Beatrice, for your kind hospitality, for taking us in as victims of the storm?'

'Yes, I think you do have to come downstairs. Come carrying a white flag, if you like. Or should it be Beatrice with the white flag? I've lost track of who's supposed to be the injured party, who exactly it is who has right on her side.'

'She didn't have to say yes to him.'

'Perhaps she couldn't help falling for him any more than you could. Perhaps you didn't have to tell David after she'd sworn to

296

you that it was finished between them. Perhaps when God wakes up we'll all cease to exist. *Come* on.'

Beatrice had made coffee, and got out the best china in preference to the usual assortment of mugs that said: Toby or Capricorn or Property of HM Prison Dartmoor. But she left the pouring to Joanna, afraid that the nonchalance of her manner might be belied by the trembling of her hand. She said, 'Madeleine,' and Madeleine said, 'Beatrice,' and Joanna, pouring, felt as though she should drop a handkerchief between them and say, 'Let battle commence.'

They sat at right angles to each other, silently, each recognizing that safe small talk was beyond their capabilities. Joanna stared at the clock which, she had noticed, was either slow or fast. David had been meaning to regulate it since about 1974. Madeleine and Beatrice timed their covert glances so that they didn't coincide. The composite pictures they finally built up were arrived at by a kind of mental painting-by-numbers process: a glimpse of profile, a patch of skirt, a nervous hand fluttering within the field of vision. She's not young any more, Beatrice thought; she looks like somebody's mother. Madeleine thought, she doesn't look much older than she did when she used to say *'Merde alors'* in the French class and spend most of her time shading in the capital letters all the way through a textbook. She cleared her throat and said, 'Thank you for taking us in. It's very kind.'

The phone rang. Joanna went into the hall, closing the door behind her.

'Neville, probably,' Beatrice said. 'They'll discuss us, at three quid a minute or whatever it costs. They'll weigh up all the pros and cons. He'll tell her to get herself back to civilization and leave us to our own devices. She'll say, "I'm sure that everything can be sorted out. If we discuss it rationally. It's a bore for me, I must admit, but I can't leave until I've pointed them in the right direction; they're so clueless – " ' She put down her coffee cup. She said, 'Joanna has it all sewn up, hasn't she?'

'Joanna was born knowing the ropes.'

'Not like you and me.' They looked directly at one another.

'Joanna could always sniff people out. She knows instinctively, at ten paces across a crowded room, whether or not she ought to get involved.'

'Perhaps we all have that instinct but some of us don't heed it.'

'Neville's safe. Why didn't we settle for safety?'

'I didn't have much option.'

'What an excuse! You'd never have gone after him in the first place if you hadn't smelled danger.'

'I thought that he was some kind of ladykiller who had never known True Love. He wasn't. Why didn't you stick to one of those nice, decent young men that Joanna was always finding for you?'

'They bored me rigid.'

Beatrice refilled the cups. Her hand was calm. She said, 'Do you ever look back along your life and it seems as though that person who went through those experiences was somebody different – a different you? As though your life was a series of discrete phases with a different you participating in each of them? I feel that if I could only go back and stand beside the me of that time and try to understand how I felt, how I saw things, I might begin to know what I'm all about. I have a picture of, say, me at sixteen, sitting in the El – whatever it was called – you know, the obligatory meeting place for the town's gilded youth – smoking a Gauloise and listening to Roy Orbison singing *Only the Lonely* and watching the scarlet MGs draw up outside. I see that picture, clear and vivid, but I can't remember being that person.'

Madeleine nodded. She understood. Who was that girl who had painted black round her eyes and sat in darkened rooms kissing total strangers while somebody loaded the record-player with Pete Seeger and the Everly Brothers, Miles Davis and Charlie Parker, Beyond The Fringe and Buddy Holly and The Crickets? What was it that that girl had expected from life? What had impelled her steps along those various dark roads into those various rooms where someone draped a coloured scarf over the light bulb and someone said Carlos was coming with the hash and someone's period was three weeks late and someone read Kerouac in the corner with the aid of a flashlight and all the art students dyed their hair bright yellow and painted cans of soup? What on earth had led her to imagine that there was anything worthwhile to be gained by seeking companionship among the uninhibited, the outlandish, the downright dangerous? It had been different for Joanna, Joanna going down the road with vicious old ladies shouting 'Beatnik' after her. She could consort with drunks and hopheads, derelicts and drop-outs, without being altered in any way; she could share their joints and drink their booze and listen to their pathetic self-

298

justifications with the appearance of avid interest, but all her imitations of their way of life were external phenomena; at the centre she was untouchable.

She came back into the room. Beatrice said, 'Joanna has permanence and continuity.' Joanna said, 'Thanks very much, you make me sound like the Albert Memorial.'

'And how's Himself? Have they provided him with a harem of concubines as one of the perks? Has he fallen for a pair of eyes darkened with kohl and brilliant above a yashmak? Isn't it frightfully unethical to bugger off to the Middle East when this country is teeming with prolapses and National Health waiting lists five miles long?'

'He's fine,' Joanna said, and ignored the rest. 'We don't have to cook lunch, do we, groan, groan? as Oliver would say. Can't I get us something from the takeaway?'

'On Easter Sunday?'

'They're Chinese. Unless Sunday means something in the Year of the Snake or whatever it is, I don't see that they have any justification for closing. If they are closed, if they're Hong Kong Christians or something, I'll go to the delicatessen. That's Jewish.'

Beatrice stacked the coffee cups on a tray. 'Why aren't I the sort,' she said, 'to have found myself a Neville? You know, those nice genial smiling sort of men that you see on the six-fifteen – the sort of men *other* women are always married to – they have creases round their eyes and they help you with your case and strike up pleasant impersonal unflirtatious conversations with you? They have a boy at university and a girl at training college and they mend plugs for elderly female relatives and if they saw you standing at a bus stop they'd give you a lift – you know the sort? But I'm probably deluding myself. Those selfsame men probably go home and snarl and grunt and thump their wives. Oh, sorry,' she said. 'I wasn't aiming to be offensive. I just forgot. How is your arm, anyway?'

'Mending, I suppose.'

'You'd rather not discuss it. I'd rather not discuss it. The subjects I'd rather not discuss at this present moment would fill a book. My mother thinks I'm repressing, and Joanna thinks I'm doing my ostrich number and the kids deserve a better explanation than they've had. But I just don't see the point of chewing over and over an unpalatable morsel that'll only have to be spat out in the end.' She balanced the tray on her hip while she opened the door. She said, 'Joanna thinks that your little contretemps has rescued my sanity. Something along the lines of there's always someone worse off than oneself, and natural human curiosity mingled with superstitious delight – you know, thank God she's getting it instead of me.'

'How *is* it, Beatrice?'

She'd hated and hated. For years. But, after all, it was only Beatrice and no emotion could be as unmingled as that.

'It's like balancing on the high wire,' Beatrice said. 'And this is the first time that I've worked without a safety net.'

10

'What a very rich lady you must be, Joanna.'

Beatrice extracted a large prawn from its bed of rice, leaned her head back, brought it to her mouth and neatly and viciously bisected it with her teeth. 'It's terribly expensive, that Chinese caff. In your heyday you would have gone in there and enquired about their profit margins. You'd have tried to persuade them to stick posters of Mao in their window next to the Frying Tonight sign.' She arose from her cross-legged position on the hearth rug to refill their glasses, waved away Madeleine's demur, her shielding hand.

The rain slid silently down the window. 'Whatever can they be doing?' she said. 'You'd think she'd bring them back, wouldn't you?'

Joanna said, 'She's probably immersed in her book, probably gained some important new insight into the roots of her personality.'

'While the kids run round in the peeing rain?'

'Oh no,' Madeleine said. 'She wouldn't let them do that? Natasha's chest – '

'Don't *worry*. She has *sense*, my mother. More sense than all of us put together. Anyway, I don't care.' Beatrice stretched luxuriously. 'This is lovely. Girls in the dorm. I *suppose*. That's an episode of which I have no experience. *She* wanted to pack me off to a boarding-school but he put his foot down. Is this what it used to be like in college: wet Sundays and music and wine and self-analysis and the whole world out there just waiting for you to make your mark? I was deprived of all that. I suppose I resent it still. Straight from wooden desk to connubial couch. Why, in the name of God, didn't someone try to dissuade me from my course, talk sense to me, stand over me with a rhino whip until I passed those sodding exams?'

'Oh Beatrice! Everybody did. We tried to persuade you to work. Your parents wanted to haul you off to Harley Street. No doubt they'd have provided you with a dozen full-time tutors if they'd thought you had any serious intention of applying yourself.'

'I was too young to know any better,' Beatrice said wistfully.

'Take those exams again, now,' Joanna said. 'You're going to have to think of something to do with your life, aren't you? A few bits of paper might help.'

'Now? If I couldn't do it then, what chance would I have now? One's brain cells start dying off at the age of sixteen or so, don't they?'

'I have quite a few mature students among my bunch this year. Seventy-year-old persons have been known to gain Open University degrees. New careers that blossom at forty are commonplace.'

'If you ask me,' Beatrice said, 'it's downhill from here on. Children growing and growing away, one cup of coffee in a café lasting an hour, conversations with oneself, small idiosyncrasies becoming major obsessions, policemen getting younger and younger, six library books a week, intercepting a glance of masculine approval and finding out that it's not for you but the eighteen-year-old girl sitting next to you – '

'And there's the rub.'

'What do you mean?'

'You know what I mean. You can't conceive of life unless you're proceeding in lock-step with a partner. There are other ways of going about it.'

'Such as?'

'An absorbing interest. A career. Good works. A philosophy. A programme of self-education.'

'Balls.'

'I'm just pointing out that alternatives do exist to continually burdening one other person with your emotions.'

Fine words. Physician, heal thyself. She felt abnormally hungry. Wasn't that a symptom too? There must be some way of asking Beatrice or Madeleine without arousing any suspicion.

'Hark at her,' Beatrice said.

'And aren't we being a trifle hypocritical, lecturing others on rational behaviour? Anybody'd think you'd always followed your head. That's not true, is it? Or is it OK for you to refuse to divulge your frailties? You can smack your lips over our squalid affairs, but yours are on some private higher plane altogether.'

Madeleine looked up, startled. Joanna eased off her right shoe with the toe of her left foot and vice-versa, balanced her wine glass between her knees. 'Nothing earth-shattering,' she said. 'I fell in love.'

'And?'

'And nothing. It could not be, as they probably say in True Romances.'

'Why not?'

She tapped out the rhythm of a tune on her glass. She said, 'Too many people stood to be hurt. It wasn't the end of the world. It never is.'

'So you just turned your back and said goodbye for ever and made up your mind that life was going to be your work and Neville?'

'Something like that.'

'But at least you have your work. You're defined and classified. You mean something in people's estimation. What have we got?'

'Five kids,' Joanna said, 'between you. And you have to define yourself; you can't leave that to other people.'

Madeleine sighed deeply. 'Why can't I be like you?'

'Why on earth should you wish to be like me? Be like yourself.'

'But you have become what I always imagined myself becoming. When I was seventeen I wanted to be Beatrice's mother: Chanel suits and hair like silk, heads turning, eyes lowered deferentially, possessed of a bright hard unshakable self-confidence. Now I want to be you.'

'They *are* rather alike, aren't they?' Beatrice said, looking from Joanna towards the opposite wall upon which – presumably – she projected the image of her mother. 'That same no-nonsense attitude, that same cool smile and steely calm, that implicit assumption of superiority.'

Joanna raised her eyebrows.

'Well you are superior. Both of you. You're diligent and thorough and unsusceptible to side-tracking. You don't vacillate. You don't fool yourselves. You are essentially *en face* in your approach. Whereas *we* sidle up on our experiences crab-wise, thinking that if we declare our interests we shall be doomed to disappointment.'

'You would never be afraid of standing up for your principles,' Madeleine said. 'If someone jumped the queue ahead of you you'd tell them politely but firmly to get back into place whereas I would step back humbly to make way for them and *she'd* burst blood vessels with interior silent rage. You don't have the faintest hidden suspicion that everybody else is somehow morally superior to yourself, you're sure of right and wrong.'

'Can I have it in writing?' Joanna said. She found it incredible – and a little frightening – that they should have misread her so, that they hadn't an inkling of just how far she was from achieving the state of grace that they'd described.

At four o'clock they ate crumpets. Butter oozed through the holes and on to the carpet. It didn't matter much: children and dogs and carelessness had bequeathed ineradicable stains already. The clock struck. Ten minutes later the church clock struck. 'We usually take the mean average,' Beatrice said. 'It's all relative anyway. The moment existed, exists, always will exist.' That much she had learned, in Madeleine's bedroom, crumpling her immaculate sheets. 'Just as I refuse to be decimalized and metricated and convinced that half past three is really fifteen-thirty hours, so I refuse to accept someone else's arbitrary divisioning of my life. As far as I'm concerned, March 1977 lasted for thirty-three years and morning is when I choose to get up.'

'Terribly confusing for the rest of us. How do we coincide? Co-in-cide,' Joanna said. 'Now if I had another "i". Are there any more "i"s?'

They were on to their third game of Scrabble. Some of the pieces were missing and the blanks had been defaced and nobody wanted to be responsible for keeping the score. However, Madeleine always won, whoever kept the score. Joanna began dramatically, disposing of 'x's and 'q's wholesale, but then tended to sink to the level of 'it' and 'do'; Beatrice invented words and definitions of those words and, as there was no convenient dictionary, often got away with them, but her style was too impulsive, her ability to recognize multiple relationships almost non-existent; Madeleine it was who progressed steadily, assembling modest little words on high-scoring squares, making use of others' groundwork. 'I bet you do crossword puzzles too,' Beatrice said, 'and belong to Mensa. Quod,' Beatrice said, 'that's admissible, isn't it? As in *quod erat* something or other.'

'It's Latin.'

'Well you had "shebeen" and I'm sure that's Gaelic. Or Erse. If you can have Gaelic, or Erse, then I'm having Latin. Why is it that crumpets look so delicious and yet taste like boiled face cloths? Christ, that rain! I think we ought to be building an ark.' It created a solid white wall between the window pane and the garden. They heard the muffled sounds of it bouncing off the hen house roof and dripping and trickling from the broken place in the gutter. 'Perhaps Mama and the kids have been washed away.'

'You don't think there's been an accident?' Madeleine said, pausing in her accounting.

'We'd have heard. You always get to hear about accidents. I used to be like you: every time I let one of them out of my sight, I'd imagine him being run over by a ten-ton lorry or lured away by some slavering pederast and his poor little body lying unidentified in the morgue. And, in fact, the only real accident that we ever had occurred at home in the bathroom under my very nose.'

'My mother,' Madeleine said, 'used to put pieces of paper inscribed with my name and address into all my pockets whenever I went out.'

'Your mother used to meet you from children's parties to escort you two hundred yards along the road. Your mother, I seem to recall, wouldn't allow you to ride a bicycle in case you fell off and injured yourself. All things considered, it's a wonder that you aren't an inmate of a locked ward.'

Madeleine, after long deliberation, made 'axe' and 'fealty'. 'And Joanna expects me to walk out towards the world, bold and unafraid,' she said, 'can't understand why I have no confidence. Yes, please, I will have some more of that wine, if you don't mind.'

'Joanna simply wants to make you realize that most of your terrors are groundless,' Joanna said. She put an 'a' above the 't' in Madeleine's 'fealty' and scored two. 'All other people *aren't*

cleverer, brighter or more capable than you; they just have a more
realistic – or a more workable – conception of their own value.
Beatrice, what's a flunt?'
'A flunt,' said Beatrice, 'is an ancient device, dating from primitive
times.'
'Go on!'
'Fragments of flunts,' Beatrice said, 'have been discovered during
the course of archaeological digs and are believed to have come into
existence during the palaeolithic age. The Cenozoic era, actually.'
'And what was supposed to be the function of this particular
artefact, this flunt? Did it bear any resemblance to a *flint*?'
'Yes,' Beatrice said, 'there were certain similarities. It shared
many common characteristics; it just wasn't so sharp, that's all: a
blunt flint. Shall we pack it in? Her genius-level score is giving me a
pain.'
'We've nearly finished now. We might as well press on to the
end. You can't continue to pack everything in just because you're
not winning, you know, Beatrice.' 'Let's play another game,'
Beatrice had said, in her ruched party frock and black patent
shoes, eyeing Dr McCloud beseechingly, while the cleverer
members of the party moved unerringly towards the slipper, the
thimble, the treasure trove.
'Oh, all right. This, then.' She spelled out D-I-L-P. They queried
it. 'Another ancient device?' Joanna said. 'And what era does this
date from?'
'The Cretinaceous. No, that's not right. I mean the Cretaceous.
The Cretinaceous is what we're in now, isn't it?'
'Stop arsing about. Look. You've got an "o" and a "v" and an
"e". If you can find a spare "m" or a "d" or an "r", you're laughing.'
'So I have.' She found an 'l'. 'There, will that suit you? Or does
it count as obscene?'
Madeleine, apparently blind to the implications, added an 'r'.
Joanna had to pass. She juggled her remaining letters and thought,
how curious it must be to sit beside a woman who's slept with
your husband. I'm sure that I couldn't do it. Not with any measure
of equanimity. I should be horribly, degradingly, jealous and full
to the brim with chagrin. Perhaps, after all, they have a more
mature outlook on life than I do.
I once pleaded with her, Beatrice thought, after her husband –
my lover – and I had called it quits. I abased myself. I offered to

undertake whatever penance of sackcloth and ashes she cared to dish out, just so long as she kept the knowledge from David. I had hurt her, I knew, but mostly it was in her pride and, when all's said and done, that's only a flesh wound and as with other minor injuries, the more it hurts, the quicker it heals. But she was implacable. She sat, her hands folded in her lap. She was Nemesis. I had sinned, I must suffer. QED. *Quod erat* – something or other.

Madeleine read what she'd made: 'lover'. It was difficult to remember, that time: Desmond slamming out of the house and Beatrice crying, with her hair in her eyes and a ball of crumpled paper tissues in her fist. 'Please, oh, please,' she'd said. 'I'm a whore and a bitch and all stuff like that. I know. But if you tell him you'll finish us. And I need him.' Or words to that effect. It had been hard to decipher amid the sniffs and the hair and the tears.

She had thought then that what Beatrice had done was the worst sort of betrayal that one person could inflict on another. It was as though her life had been divided into two eras: Before Beatrice and After Beatrice; the first part an idyll, the second beset with drinking and violence. She was glad that she had told David; she knew that he was a man who would use his wounded pride as an excuse to end a relationship he had begun to find far too demanding.

She shuffled her letters and got rid of them at one fell swoop. She made 'lone' and 'fire'. Beatrice's marriage was over. She ought to have felt triumphant. But she didn't. She sat next to her deadliest enemy and played Scrabble. She had had to admit to herself, at last and reluctantly, that Beatrice had been catalyst rather than cause, that there never had been any idyll except at the very beginning and that his excessive drinking hadn't begun as a result of the Beatrice episode: he'd been half-seas over the very first night she'd encountered him; the only difference being that in those days he hadn't yet accumulated a weight of frustration and resentment to be expressed by means of that drinking.

Joanna passed again. Beatrice disposed of her remaining letters by attaching them to a spare 'm' and forming 'man'. 'Joanna,' she said, hesitantly. 'What was he like?'

'Nosy.'

'No. Just thought that you might want to talk about it. I can't imagine the sort of man you'd fall full tilt in love with. What was he like?'

Like a gangster. How they'd laughed over his passport photograph. The Godfather, she'd called him, said that his academic appointment was probably just a cover for his real mission, watched at the airport for a welcoming committee, all swarthy jowls and gold teeth. But there was only the thin harassed Dean of the Faculty and his thin harassed wife who had difficulty in interpreting her lover's accent. His appearance, his lovingly-nurtured accent, they kept him tied to his roots, to the world that Sylvia was at home in. She thought of the way that he abandoned the sherry parties, the gatherings that might have advanced his career, in favour of football matches and grim public houses and darts teams and men who echoed his speech patterns and his mannerisms; how he scorned the artificial world of the intelligentsia, went dog-racing in a combat jacket and a flat cap, said, 'Bollocks' when she told him that he couldn't belong to those places any more. She thought of the way that he made love: without any of the ritual, the aesthetic niceties that she'd been used to. She thought of the way that he never told her lies, not even to be kind.

'Well?' Beatrice said.

And the opportunity was there: to spill everything, to say, 'Beatrice, Madeleine, if you had your time over again, would you choose not to have children? What is it like? What should I do? Yes, me, Joanna, the sensible one: should I make the sensible decision, or should I accept what both of you would recognize as the working out of my destiny?'

They were her friends. They'd had experience that she lacked. And they were sufficiently distanced from her to consider the dilemma objectively, just as she'd attempted to consider theirs. But the words stuck in her throat. It took courage to climb down from a pedestal, even if that pedestal wasn't of your own making. 'It's past history,' she said.

II

He'd expected her back by nightfall. Where could she go? The hotels were all full up. He'd encountered some of the more vigorous of the conference delegates in search of after-hours entertainment: signing themselves into back-street clubs and paying over the odds for their drinks in the hope of discovering talent, tipping assorted night porters to turn their heads away when they ushered whatever talent they'd found up to their rooms. He'd encountered them and observed them wonderingly as though they were members of a different species. He envied them in a way: that a quick poke at unfamiliar flesh could constitute pleasure, could bolster their egos, render them pleased and proud and give them something to dine out on until the next conference came around. He remembered all those girls before his marriage – and some afterwards – who'd shared his bed, recollected with disbelief how his life had been ruled by something as insignificant as the sexual itch. Women – they were all the same, at bottom: the prim ones who clamped their legs together and the easy ones who couldn't wait, the ones who loved you for your mind and the ones who couldn't tack together two coherent sentences. He'd married the best of them, but even she was no different, essentially, even she couldn't help herself from wanting, wanting, taking, taking, trying to squeeze herself into those personal places inside him where no one was allowed.

He heard a clock strike two as he let himself into the flat. They were back, he knew it. He had to check each room half a dozen times before he could accept that they weren't. Sometimes, when they were there, he hadn't been aware of them; their absence created more of a space of nothing than their presence would fill.

There was no possibility of sleeping. He took off his coat, lit the gas and settled himself into an armchair. He hadn't had enough to drink, not enough to blur the edges. The amount of alcohol in his veins only served to make him see his surroundings with a lurid clarity, and to make him shiver. He turned up the fire. Madeleine was always cold. Like sleeping beside a corpse. She'd be cold tonight. Wherever she was. Wherever that bitch Joanna had taken her. That bitch Joanna: she'd probably swept into the Grand or the Majestic and demanded that they tipped the conference organizer out of his suite in favour of her charges. Or perhaps she'd driven them back to Oxford with her. He looked up the number in the book beside the phone and dialled it. He heard a telephone ringing in an empty house. There was a difference between someone not answering a telephone and no one being there to answer it; somehow you could always tell. Where else? The abandoned Beatrice? No. Never. The last place she'd go. He'd once been mad for Beatrice, her honey skin, her perfect face, her dreamy be-clouded eyes. He'd looked at her and it was as though he was looking at himself. The only one who hadn't built up walls around him, the only one who didn't base her behaviour on some damn set of principles or other. Nothing between them – except recognition and the shared understanding that nothing made sense and what seemed real might be fantastic, and vice-versa. He wished that he could have loved Beatrice, but it would have been like loving himself, and how could you love yourself?

He put his coat back on but still he couldn't get warm. Perhaps he had the 'flu. She'd come back when she knew that he had the 'flu. Wherever she'd gone. Wherever that bitch Joanna had taken her. That bitch Joanna, symbolic throughout his life, it seemed: the blind goddess, the angel with the flaming sword barring his entrance to Eden, Joanna and her ilk: the collective voice that said you must, you ought, just look at you! Seeing nothing, understanding nothing, except how you manipulated the world to your own advantage, braying about right and wrong and good and evil, forcing their perception of reality on all around them, judging you by their own artificial constructs of morality, placing you, classifying you, measuring you against some criterion they'd invented, they administered, they maintained. Joanna, who was all the headmasters, all the employers, all the interviewers, all the publishers who'd rejected his book, all the bossmen he'd ever encountered; Joanna, who wore the implacable mask of some ultimate authority who, unseeing, saw everything you did, and judged it.

He went into the bedroom to see what she'd taken. He pulled the eiderdown off the bed and draped it over his shoulders. He had a fever, there was no doubt about it; his head tolled dully every time he moved. She would come back and nurse him as she had nursed him through the tuberculosis. She hadn't taken much. Skirts and frocks and jackets still hung in the wardrobe. They were cheap, shoddy-looking. He fingered their various textures. He remembered vividly the velvet suit and the silk blouse, and a white frock there'd been, dazzling in the dusk. Beatrice's all, it transpired. She'd come to him in disguise. This was her real self, this tatty, mass-produced frock with its trailing threads and its unfinished seams, this skimpy skirt, thrown together in some foreign sweat-shop. But he needed her, unsatisfactory as she was. He needed her because there was no one else.

At the back of the wardrobe was his manuscript, curled at the edges, dog-eared from all those unappreciative thumbings, turning yellow. He carried it into the living-room, crouched in front of the fire, adjusted the eiderdown around himself, and read it. Some of it. It was pathetic. Kafka he'd read, and Scott Fitzgerald and Lawrence. His eyes scanned the sentences. He sweated. It wasn't the fever; it was mortification. Words, just words – piled against each other, saying nothing, going nowhere. He threw it across the room and it burst apart, releasing its constituent pages. A whirlwind of black and white. Nothing more than defaced paper. The only thing he'd had in common with Scott Fitzgerald and Kafka and Lawrence was his tuberculosis.

Beatrice hadn't said. Beatrice hadn't said, 'This is a waste of paper and ink.' Perhaps she thought she was being kind. That wasn't kindness: to think one thing and say another; it was simply an insult to his dignity. He'd never believed those publishers and their rejection slips, he'd merely assumed that getting a book published demanded some qualification he didn't possess – like not being able to become a member of Lloyd's unless you had assets of however many thousands of pounds it was; he'd have believed Beatrice.

He was burning up and freezing all at the same time. But he made no move to get himself to bed. He stared into the orange radiants of the gas fire and forced himself to confront this new knowledge. He felt totally bereft. The very last layer of self-deception had been torn away. He had no gift, he had no vocation, and there was nothing that life could offer him that would satisfy him. Except for his daughter. To see her grown and successful, to protect her from life until she'd learned to use the weapons that you needed to fight it with. He'd have to settle, for a job that wearied his soul and a routine that would stifle and deaden his intellect. He'd have to learn, at last, to accept, to knuckle under, to curb his tongue and bend his knee, to send his body through the motions of everyday life, to mimic conformity until it became as natural as breathing.

And he'd have to learn to do it without the periodical anaesthetic of drink. Her bruises had puzzled him at first, but lately all sorts of dimly-reflected images had begun to invade his sober mornings: the way she stood there, or lay there, frail, defenceless, somehow inviting attack.

Men who hit their wives were brute-beasts. He'd read the horror stories: burns with lighted cigarettes, broken jaws, fractured skulls, inert bodies defiled, children huddled wide-eyed and screaming in corners. Men like that ought to be locked up, he'd thought. He raised his hand and touched his burning forehead. His temperature must be well above the hundred mark. The psychological johnnies would call it psychosomatic, just as they said that those brutish men were deeply disturbed and therefore not responsible. The picture of her bandaged arm came into his mind. He couldn't have wanted to push her downstairs; she was necessary to him. However much he resented her, she was necessary to him. All he'd wanted to do, surely, was to push her out of the way, or to provoke a reaction, a flash of hatred across those impassive features. That saint-like fortitude would drive anybody to violence. He remembered the years of packing up and moving on, the lack of security, the lack of money, the lack of friends. And never a word of reproof had she uttered; she'd just taken down the curtains, wrapped the plates in newspapers, spread the butter less thickly, darned and mended until there was more darn and mend than original, done sums on pieces of cardboard, adapted herself to new houses and new faces and new accents. It wasn't normal. A normal person would have protested, would have said, 'What about *me*?' And yet, in acceding to him, she took from him, drained him of whatever dignity, whatever integrity he'd once possessed. Perhaps the wives of those brute-beasts were the same. Perhaps their saint-like acceptance incited you to find out just how much they would accept.

He stumbled into bed, fully-clothed. He was very ill. He might die. It was a thought that had attracted him often in the past: never

311

to wake again. But not this morning. Not alone, with nobody to give a damn. He wouldn't drink again – if that was what happened when he drank. He needed her marginally more than he needed oblivion. 'Let her come back,' he said, to the black devil, the monstrous imbecile who controlled things. But of course she would come back. It was only a gesture. She would be no more capable of envisaging a life without him than he could contemplate his existence without her.

He'd spent the morning walking around the town, clutching at walls or holding on to gate-posts whenever he felt his legs going from under him. The Sunday morning bells jangled through his head, a procession of small black children wearing white straw hats moved demurely along the pavement towards the entrance of the . Pentecostal Church, parted politely, like the Red Sea, to let him through. It was bloody cold and only the hardiest of the old men sat around the War Memorial, at a safe distance from an ancient female lunatic who had marked out the limits of her territory with newspaper parcels. He knew them all: the dispossessed, the disturbed and the unemployable. Fellow-frequenters of the same haunts: the library reading rooms, the cheap cafés, the post office queues, he had observed their shamblings, their mutterings and spittings, their eyes which stared out dull and impassive or shifted continually, on the look-out for the authority-figure who invariably said no. He had mingled with them, but he was not of them – he had a job waiting, didn't he, and countless scraps of paper testifying to his intellectual superiority, didn't he? He had read Kafka and listened to Brahms and walked through the Uffizi prepared to be astonished. He had written a novel and fathered a child, bought and sold houses, traversed the length and breadth of England, constructed the sort of image that inspired relatively sane persons to offer him employment.

The madwoman cursed him as he passed her by. He recognized in her face that all-embracing hostility that he felt within himself. All his bits of paper, all his jobs, all his experience: it wasn't enough. There was something he didn't have, something lacking, but he couldn't, for the life of him, put a name to it.

A mean wind curled in the alleyways and blasted him around every corner. His temperature had gone down but his head was light and his legs weren't functioning properly. He couldn't remember what it was that had prompted him outside into the deserted Sunday streets, except perhaps the hope that she might be there, sitting mournful but tranquil on a municipal bench or a doorstep, like a damn Hindu, letting fate take its course.

He bought a paper and a bottle of Haig and made for home. A car passed him while he dithered at a Pelican crossing – he needed to wait until the road was quite clear in case his legs should crumple unexpectedly. It was a dark green car, gleamingly clean, driven by an elderly woman who signalled him impatiently to cross and then, recognizing his hopeless indecisiveness, accelerated to avoid him. In the back seat of the car, squashed between many other children, was a child who bore a faint resemblance to his daughter. He almost gesticulated after the car, but the effort of raising an arm was too much for him. Besides, it had probably been a hallucinatory effect: he wasn't seeing anything clearly. The tall edifice of the Royal Insurance building loomed to the sky and the Town Hall clock said first a quarter to three and then five past one. There was a hollow feeling inside him which he didn't think to associate with not having eaten for almost twenty-four hours. He would go home and huddle beside the fire and drink the whisky – for his 'flu, or whatever it was – and wait. Though she might be back already.

She wasn't. Not even ensconced within the broom cupboard, nor hidden in the wardrobe, nor under the bed. Apparently he had underestimated the flamboyance of her gesture. But of course she was moving in the wake of Joanna's resolve. And Joanna, like all others of her kind, picked up the cause of other people and put it down again, rapidly, as soon as it began to interfere with her own concerns. The novelty would wear off; from being a cause, Madeleine's status would decline to being that of a nuisance. 'It's up to you now,' Joanna would say, returning to her own world. And Madeleine, because she was unequipped to rely upon her own initiative, would return to hers.

He ate a few hard pieces of cheese that he found in the fridge, opened the whisky and almost fell into the armchair beside the fire. The shivering had begun again. He shouldn't have gone out. She would be sorry when she returned, returned to find him with a raging fever, pulmonary complications and the faint ominous shadow of the lesion in his lung.

The whisky warmed him. Old friend. No caprice. Just there,

313

golden, aromatic and eternally reliable. He would ration it. By the hands of the clock. But the hands of the clock had paralysis. He turned his attention to the paper. The usual number of Irish people had been killed or maimed. Mrs Gandhi was out for a duck. The price of spring vegetables was likely to be high because of the continual rain. (He'd thought he'd read drought at first, but that was last year and another reason for the price of vegetables being high.) A terribly amusing lady wrote a terribly amusing letter about the skimping and cheese-paring that was necessary for managing on fourteen thousand a year. The memoirs of a peer of the realm and an ageing Fitzrovian queer jostled each other for space. The best-seller list had its usual quota of television spin-offs, how-it-ought-to-have-been autobiographies, and manuals of instruction on how to survive with a goat and a hedgeful of nettles when the bad times came.

He flung the paper to join his dismembered manuscript at the far side of the room. Sunday culture: a choice between unfrocked vicars and gang bangs on the one hand and the thin neighing tones of the intelligentsia on the other. The bad times could not be long in coming; the life of the culture was always the first thing to expire.

It wasn't yet four o'clock. Why didn't she come? For the first time it entered his head that she might not come. The cruel, heartless bitch. Well, he'd show her. First thing tomorrow he'd be down to the solicitor, have a posse of private detectives on her trail and a battery of injunctions, custody orders, divorce papers and veiled threats raining down on her head. He'd sue the bitch Joanna for enticement.

He was burning again; the room was a furnace. He threw off his jacket, called to her from within himself: come back, please come back. He felt tears dropping on to his cheeks. She loved him, she had always loved him; it had been, it was, it must always remain. She couldn't give up on him, not at this late stage. After he'd had a good cry and a few more whiskies and a sleep he felt a bit better. He rose to his feet and contemplated his face in the mirror above the fireplace. His face wouldn't keep still. It reminded him of how drink used to affect him in the early days: it didn't merely blur then, it made him take one too many steps on a staircase, persuaded him that whatever he wanted was within his grasp, rendered his face in the mirror amorphous, alien. One feature was obvious though:

he badly needed a shave. He walked slowly towards the bathroom, testing each footstep before he executed it. He put his hand on the glass panel of the door but there was no glass in there and his hand went straight through and he was thrown off balance. He tried to remember back to the old drunken days. There was a particular way of angling your head so that the room stopped revolving and the laws of perspective reasserted themselves. He seemed to have lost the knack.

He saw his razor lying on the shelf. It was an old-fashioned open razor – not an affectation; it was simply the only instrument that made any effective inroad upon his beard. He saw two razors until he shook his head and cleared it. He hung on to the hand basin for support while he lathered his face. Only the weight of his feet anchored him to the floor. Water hung in a column of suspension from the mouth of the tap, eventually released individual rainbow droplets that chased one another around the plughole. The blade glittered so that he hardly dared look at it. He applied it gingerly to the left side of that monstrous bloated reflection; he supported his right hand with his left. His jaw felt gross and dead. He calculated unfamiliar distances and drew the blade upwards and downwards. A series of little red mouths gaped at him, oozed. He continued grimly. Once his knees buckled. He slid to the floor, cracking his chin on the basin. The razor embedded itself in the fibres of his pullover. Christ, he thought, hauling himself upright, I could have cut my throat, and felt tenderly and with blunt fingertips for the whereabouts of his jugular. It did not declare itself; there was a muscle or a tendon or some damn thing down the side and the gristly rings of his larynx in the front, and that was all. His jugular would have to take care of itself, wherever it might be situated.

He rinsed the soap from his face and tried feebly to staunch the bleeding. By the time he was clean-shaven and collapsed in the angle between the bath and the basin where a few fragments of glass glittered still, like mica in a pavement, it had begun to clot.

'Sleep it better,' his mother used to say, drawing the blind. There'd be firelight on the walls and rags to spit into and a poultice for his chest that made him yelp whenever it was applied. From delirium he'd pass into sleep and in the morning he'd wake to find that it had burned itself out of him.

315

Sleep was evidently no longer the automatic cure. If he'd been asleep. In the bathroom it was almost dark. It took him twenty minutes to ease his cramped limbs into action. Tears of weakness flowed down his face and he remembered his mother for whom he'd exhibited scant regard and he said, 'Madeleine' over and over again under his breath as he drew himself into an upright position. Once, as a young man, he'd been self-sufficient, moving unencumbered from one rented room to the next, knowing many people superficially, needing no special relationship with any of them. Until Polly came along. And Madeleine. And Beatrice. He turned on the tap, splashed water on his face, thought of Polly and her drowned features. All his nerves cringed. He was not the sort of person other people killed themselves for. He simply didn't make that much of an impact. And nobody was responsible for anybody else. He'd coped alone once; he'd cope again. His reflection with its pattern of healing cuts in the puffy flesh gave the lie to such heroic ideas.

He looked at the clock and saw that his collapse had at least earned him a respite of three hours from time. Nine o'clock. It would soon be tomorrow. Tomorrow she would come back. It was logical to stay away for the weekend, to allow him time to learn his lesson. 'I am sorry for what I have done,' he said. He said it out loud and that seemed to lend weight to the sincerity of the feeling. He drank what remained of the whisky and re-covered himself and got out his cigarettes. There weren't many left. He would have to ration them. Tomorrow his fever would have abated. He would wake and find that the floor stayed where it was when he stepped on to it, that the walls no longer receded or came forward to meet him every time he shifted his eyes. At ten-thirty he fell asleep. The cigarette that he had been smoking fell from his fingers down the side of the chair. A sudden shift of his weight might have extinguished it, but he slept like a statue, head thrown back, breathing stertorously through his mouth. In sleep all the lines seemed to have been erased from his face; he was the young man who had thrown Pedro's sherry trifle through the window and believed that eternity was at his disposal, the young man who had found the only person in the world who didn't make him wonder if he belonged to the same race as the rest of them. He slept and dreamed pleasant, floating, flower-bedecked dreams. And the cigarette smouldered on.

12

Oliver had a Church Parade. In the cold kitchen Beatrice cursed and grumbled, made him toast and combed his hair. Nobody else was abroad. He arranged his green tags under the turned-down tops of his socks and folded his neckerchief carefully around his jersey. She raked the ashes in the grate, arranged lumps of coal upon twists of newspaper. She said, 'When I was your age, it would have needed an explosion to get me out of bed at this time in the morning.'

'You don't get anywhere by being lazy,' he said primly. 'This toast is burned. As usual.'

'Where, exactly, do you want to get?'

'I want to be an officer in the army.'

'Might one enquire why?'

'You go all over the world and people have to do what you say.' He grabbed his cap from the chair. 'I'm *late*,' he said. 'And I'm supposed to be carrying the standard. Everybody else's mother wakes them up in time.'

'My youngest son,' she said to Joanna who came down yawning hugely, 'the littlest of my lambs who once went into purdah for a week when we had to have the hamster put down, has just announced to me that he wishes to become a licensed killer.'

'Why did you have to have the hamster put down?'

'It had hamster disease.'

'What's hamster disease?' said Joanna, fumbling blindly in the interior of the bread bin.

'Oh *Joanna*. I mean to say, how could anybody born of my flesh want to join the army?'

'Do you think that your mother would object to me pinching a couple of her Ryvitas and her Acacia blossom honey secreted by hand-reared bees and specially imported from the Balkans?' She salivated at the thought of it: honey, honey! It was all that she could do to restrain herself from creeping downstairs in the middle of the night to raid the larder. 'The result is positive,' the girl had said at the other end of the telephone. She'd said it twice, in a mechanical voice. Joanna had thought for a moment that she might be listening to a recorded message.

Beatrice blew on the reluctant flames. 'Bridget used to throw sugar on it,' she said. 'Imagine! A time when you could throw sugar into the fire rather than shake it from the tablecloth back into the bowl. The army!' Beatrice said. 'Once, you'd have sought him out and explained to him the error of his ways. You used to say that armies and wars and stuff were capitalism's way of dissipating the threat of workers' collectivism. You used to sit down at Ban the Bomb meetings and get carted off to clink. What exactly did happen to that crystal vision?'

Joanna licked threads of honey from her fingers. 'I discovered that a mass of people is composed of individual persons who simply refused to fit into my pre-established categories. I used to think that events followed logically one after the other. I used to think that the entire random universe could be tamed and controlled. When I began to open my mind and listen and learn I found all my certainties to be weak at their foundations.'

Beatrice rattled the kindling with the poker. 'And we all thought that it was Neville,' she said, 'seducing you with posh possessions.'

'No. Not Neville. Just time and change. An interaction between what you might be and what happens to you. The unlikeliest things can happen.'

It was as though that telephone verdict had made any further heart-searching redundant, as though that verdict was the end of the whole affair rather than its beginning. An uncharacteristic lethargy possessed her; she thought of these last few days at Beatrice's house as being a respite from the need to make a decision. Of late, her behaviour generally had been most uncharacteristic, and to be at the mercy of one's hormones was a disconcerting thought.

'You're not having much success with that fire, are you?'

'When you *want* them to blaze up,' Beatrice said, 'they never do.' After a pause, she said, 'Have you ever been to an inquest?'

'No.'

'They're open to the public, aren't they? I can't remember.'

'I think so.'

'Christ! A mammoth washing of dirty linen?'

Joanna put down her Ryvita, suddenly satiated. 'Absolutely not,' she said. 'No reason.'

A little flame spurted suddenly and blazed. Beatrice crowed delightedly and fanned its vigour with the *Observer*. She said, 'She had just left him, walked out on him. Wouldn't that sort of information be regarded as highly relevant?'

'The only item of undisputed relevance is the empty whisky bottle and the only fact that can be fully validated is that poly-whatever-it-is that they use to stuff cushions with is highly inflammable and gives off toxic fumes. She stayed the night with a friend. He had a few too many and dropped his fag-end. It happens all the time: smokers in bed run the risk nightly; you're safer walking down the fast lane of the motorway.'

Beatrice started in on the Ryvita where Joanna had left off; it was a conditioned reflex, generated by years of scraping out the pans after everyone else had been fed. She said, 'Will you take the breakfast up or shall I?'

'Have you seen her shed one tear?'

'No.'

'Neither have I. She's reacting most abnormally. It's as though she's in limbo. Like you. A good weep might do the pair of you a power of good.'

Beatrice took two shop eggs and placed them in a pan. The hens' diet was deficient, or some trauma had inhibited their normal physiological functioning, or they were doing it for spite – or not doing it, actually. She said, 'I don't intend to waste my energy grieving over that sad apology for a husband and father whom I had the misfortune to meet at a precarious stage of my emotional development. I intend to regard what has gone before as a sort of computer error.'

'You can't just *negate* past experience.'

'Oh can't I!' The egg shells split and disgorged frilled lumps of clotted albumen. Beatrice's eggs always cracked in the boiling. 'I can and I shall,' she said.

'Well, bully for you. D'you think that *she* can?'

She had been aware that something was about to happen a split second before it occurred. She had been sitting half way along the coach in an aisle seat and as they swung into the bend a hand had squeezed at her gut and suddenly her throat was dry and her adrenalin was pumping like fury. The whole of her past life hadn't flashed before her eyes, but then she hadn't *had* much of a past life.

An age had elapsed between initial lurch and final impact. And before the screams there had been a susurrus of rapidly-intaken breath. She had identified the fat knee of Dorothy King and the sharp articulated elbow of Miss Mee and the wide, wide eye of Jane Porter. She'd thought that she'd suffocate, trapped among navy blue serge and wool and poplin, but they had cushioned her against the ultimate shock. Saviours, they had been, with their plump thighs, their school-dinner silhouettes, their ample flesh thrusting in Maidenform bras. But she remembered thinking even then, as they lifted her and placed her gently on the red blanket and all she could see from that angle was a single blood-filled shoe, 'Saved for what?'

She'd dreamed about the crash every night since he died. Sometimes he was an occupant of the coach and his face would loom at her beseechingly just before the life was crushed out of him. She tried to help him, she struggled and she fought, but his face slipped further and further away and her name echoed only faintly in her ears. Once she woke herself up crying, 'It's not my fault. I couldn't help you.' Mrs Martin said that one trauma was bound to recall an earlier trauma. She couldn't believe that there wasn't some deeper significance.

She slid out of bed without waking Natasha, washed and dressed herself in her new black dress and her new black coat. Voices issued from the kitchen: Joanna's resonant, Beatrice's hoarse from too many years of cigarette smoking – she was beginning to sound like an elderly blues singer.

She embarrassed them. She embarrassed everybody, with her calm demeanour and her inability to display emotion. They didn't understand that she'd done her grieving in advance, down all the years of hoping and hoping less.

It was a cold morning. The congregation wore their winter coats and handkerchiefs were much in evidence among the choir. She couldn't take communion. She tied a scarf around her head and slid into a back pew and, as the service progressed, recognized faces around her familiar from long ago when Sunday morning provided an oasis of certainty among the continual fears and insecurities of childhood, when she had still been able to believe that it represented something: the *Gloria*, the raising of the host and those final words, sonorous, solemn, and invested with complete certitude: *Ite, missa est.*

'Your pagan rites.' She heard his voice in her ear as it had sounded sometimes at Christmas or Easter when, wistful for that lost familiarity, she had inclined her head and listened for the bells. 'It draws you back,' he'd said, 'despite yourself, back to your comfortable state of peasant ignorance, back to the time when a few words intoned in a particular way could wash your soul clean. Words! That's all they are. And your soul doesn't exist except in your imagination.'

'Are you performing some kind of penance?' Joanna had said. The phrase had remained with her, going round and round in her head, disturbing her with its implications. She remembered another phrase of Joanna's, a quotation from Lenin, something about two sorts of people in the world: the who and the whom – those who do and those to whom it is done. Desmond had been unhappy, or disturbed, or psychopathic, or unsocialized – the label you applied depended upon your school of thought; any rational being would have brought him into contact with agencies that could have helped him. Any rational being would not have taken the blame. Perhaps, for all those years, she had deliberately assumed the rôle of victim, accepting punishment as her due. She had neglected her mother and resented her mother's self-sacrifice. She had abandoned her faith – according to its tenets, her marriage was null, her child born out of wedlock. She had survived while better people had died all around her.

She looked up at Christ crucified in stained glass. Perhaps she had deliberately chosen a hard path, somehow invited his assaults. The mysteries of the psyche were like the peace of God, according to Mrs Martin.

Thirteen years. Long enough, surely, for the purposes of expiation. The service passed her by; it meant nothing. But there was comfort in the atmosphere, in the once-familiar ritual. Returning after a long journey to a place that felt like home. He had undermined her certainties, corrupted her capacity for belief, but the framework persisted, the externals – they remained, despite her abandonment of them.

She turned, in the porch, at the sound of her name. She remembered him vaguely – the man who had uttered it – a colleague of Desmond's from the technical college. 'A fellow fish-eater,' Desmond had called him.

'I was sorry to hear about . . .'

He managed it badly, stuttering, looking away. What an embarrassment we are, she thought, the bereaved. She helped him a little by remaining calm, nodding her head gravely in the right places. He said that afterwards, when it was all over . . . well, *afterwards*, there was a social club attached to the church . . . not that she'd *feel* like it . . . but, well, it had helped him, in the same circumstances three years ago, helped him to overcome the loneliness, the feeling that nobody else cared, well . . . she mustn't ever think that she was entirely alone . . . well, if there's anything I can do to help, well, goodbye.

Embarrassed, but he had seemed kind. Perhaps there were ordinary uncomplicated kind people who tried to abide by certain rules of conduct with whom one could have relationships; she'd never allowed herself to attempt to find out. Perhaps it wasn't all loving and hating, after all. Perhaps there could be affection and understanding and acceptance. Perhaps she wasn't so much a murderer as a prisoner set free.

Sam had them all digging in the garden. 'I'm going to dish out a few spades and forks,' he'd said. 'And if they come moaning to you, *don't* pamper them and tell them that if they don't want to do it they don't have to, because they jolly well *do* have to.'

'Yes, master,' Beatrice had said. Now she searched the medicine cabinet for salve: Felix's blisters were a sight to behold.

An old unfinished packet of Ovulen fell out. She flushed them down the lavatory. She wouldn't be needing them again, not in the foreseeable future. On impulse, she also flushed away her ancient Valium and all but three of Madeleine's sleeping pills. Madeleine was behaving most oddly; best to be on the safe side.

'Will you live?'

Felix uncurled his fingers and winced as she anointed the stigmata of his toil. There was a fragility about Felix, a thin-skinned unsuitedness to physical exertion. Touch him and he'd bruise. She dabbed at his blisters and thought of the contents of his diary: all that heaving and panting, all those strenuous contortions and tremendous ejaculations with nameless, faceless, female figures. The ugly thrusting words blotted out everything except immediate sensation. Was he so afraid of feeling? The others shrugged off her attempted embraces: 'Get *off*; don't be so sloppy; oh *Mum*' – until they had earache, or their best friends deserted them, or they weren't picked for the team – except for Felix. Felix denied his need, to her and to himself. Hunched, waggling his anointed hands in the air, he surveyed the tamed garden: the lawn mowed bald, the soil raked to a weed-free tilth. 'What's it all in aid of anyway?' he said. The grass would grow again, the weeds would proliferate.

'Sam thought that we could plant vegetables.'

'Oh. Is that what it's all about? Him acting like Hitler. Vegetables. Are we *that* hard-up?'

'No, we're not that hard-up. And no, that's not what it's all about. It's just Sam's way of coping.'

'Can't he cope without turning himself into Simon Legree?'

'Can *you* cope?'

He didn't answer her. His hands began to clench, until the pain reminded him. She sat down on the edge of his bed. She said, 'I'm sorry, Felix.'

He presented his back to her: thin neck, shoulders beginning to broaden. 'Sorry for what?' he said, his voice travelling from baritone to treble. As if it wasn't enough that he inhabited that unsignposted no-man's-land between childhood and maturity; his unsuccessfully disguised vulnerability made her heart ache. 'Sorry that parents should inflict such things on their children,' she said, and waited, hoped, for a response. She couldn't remember the last time that she'd had a conversation with him. With any of them. The days were filled with words, but they formed a monody, a Gregorian chant of instruction, reminder, warning and exhortation; counterpoint was rarely heard.

'It isn't you who should be sorry,' he said. 'Is it?'

Torn between wanting an answer and not wanting it. She remembered the twilight world of childhood: never being given the facts in full, always having to piece together a conclusion from insufficient evidence; yet afraid of knowing lest the knowledge should be too much to bear.

'I'm not a saint,' she said. 'And neither is your father.'

'But *you* haven't taken up with somebody else.'

Or have you? Is there some as yet unknown figure waiting in the wings? Are we to be subjected to *that*?

'No, I haven't. Nor am I likely to.'

Felix needed a new pair of shoes. And his trousers were worn shiny at the seat. And she was practically certain that he'd missed a dental appointment. The idea of romance, of that early-morning tingling – heart fever – seemed very remote. Perhaps Joanna was right. It became less important.

'Will you be getting a divorce – all that stuff?' he said. He still hadn't turned to face her.

'Eventually, yes, I suppose so.'

'And he'll marry her?'

'Presumably.'

She tried to picture Gillian in her mind's eye. All she could get was red hair. And it wasn't red, after all. It was pale blonde. She tried to force herself to be interested but Gillian insisted, somehow, upon remaining an off-stage character, the type who steps behind the footlights during the very last minute of the last scene of the last act of a play. Gillian's rôle was nothing more than that of fortuity.

'I saw her once, you know, at that annual exhibition thing, standing behind her *Carnegiea Gigantea*.'

'Her what?'

'A big cactus – phallic symbol type.'

He turned from the window. Their eyes met. 'I must say, I don't think much of his taste,' Felix said.

'Why not? What's the matter with her?'

'Oh nothing – nothing at all – except that she had a face like an Identikit picture assembled by a cretin.'

'She hadn't?' said Beatrice delightedly.

'She had. Like that advert for painful piles.'

It was delightful, this conspiracy of scorn – they could have continued it indefinitely, but it was self-indulgent and she ought not to encourage him.

'I ought not to encourage you,' she said. 'Anyway, it's wicked to mock the afflicted.'

'Sam thinks he ought to be shot.'

'You don't?'

He shrugged. 'Everybody's got their own life, haven't they? I can't see that it'll make an awful lot of difference to us. We'll see almost as much of him as we ever did. Anyway, we shan't be here for very much longer.'

Already, the shadow of the future was imminent. Oh, callous youth. 'You talk as though you'll be leaving me for ever,' she said.

'We have to grow up. It stands to reason. What will you do?'

324

Joanna and Helena talked of plans and schemes and insurances, of charting a course towards the future, maintaining an accurate compass setting. Solicitors, they spoke of, training, a job, fixing a landmark on the horizon and advancing upon it, doggedly. It was the sort of prospect that had always filled her with gloom. She'd wanted her options to be left open, to be available for whatever was in store for her; she'd wanted life to surprise her. Perhaps it was necessary to create your own surprises.

'If I aimed towards any sort of a job,' she said (the word 'career' seemed unduly pompous), 'who'd look after you lot? You'd be neglected.'

'Neglect,' he said, 'is a different thing from ceasing to fuss. You'd just have less time for fussing.'

She looked out of his bedroom window, looking for evidences of trauma. Oliver was kicking a football against the fencing. Every so often he performed a bit of fancy footwork, nonchalantly, looking covertly about him to see whether it had been appreciated. It hadn't. Toby stood guard over two jars of frog spawn that were balanced precariously on the edge of the rainwater tank. 'You're not getting rid of *these*,' he'd said. Toby had lately taken to stepping out of the path of beetles and tenderly lifting stranded spiders from the sides of the bath and conveying them into the garden. 'Peace and love,' Toby said, except when roused, when he was liable to hit people.

Sam was teaching Natasha to ride Oliver's bicycle. He had lowered the saddle but her feet barely reached the pedals. She rolled perilously from side to side. Sam held on to the back of the saddle and a handful of frock. 'Don't let go,' she kept calling as she made the desperate journey to the hen house and back. 'I won't let go,' Sam said. '*Pedal*, you nerk, don't just let them spin round.' She crashed to a halt as the front tyre hit the fence. 'I don't think I'll ever be able to do it,' she said, twisting in the saddle to look up into his face. 'You will,' he said. ' 'Course you will.'

She went downstairs and took from a drawer the prospectus she'd obtained from the local college of further education. Not that she had any serious intention . . . Just going in there to collect it had demanded an enormous effort of will. Still, it might be one way of filling those idle hours hitherto devoted to fussing.

13

'Death By Misadventure.' The coroner's court proclaimed it. There was a small paragraph in the local paper, and a daily paper that was doing a survey concerning hazards in the home used Desmond as a statistic. He'd have taken umbrage; it was a daily paper of decidedly right-wing inclination.

Joanna lay in bed, reading them both. Madeleine had gone to the hairdresser's. Sounds from the next room indicated that Helena was packing her belongings. Real life was calling her, sending its reverberations all the way from Lytham St Anne's via phone calls from Archie saying that he just couldn't cope any longer.

Today was departure day. She too must pack her suitcase and turn her car towards the south and try to make up her mind. There was a man in Riyadh, a just man, fair-minded, who had never broken a promise he'd made, who lived by his head, a man who'd be quite prepared to discuss the situation rationally, dispassionately, as though the person concerned were someone other than his own wife. And there was another man in Lanarkshire who'd intoxicated her blood and said that the word loving could encompass any number of feelings, that there was always sufficient of *something* in any long-standing relationship to make it a going concern. Neither of them, it seemed to her, were involved centrally with the making of the decision. It was her decision.

She attempted to line up the alternatives in her head: she could do nothing, say nothing, let nature take its course. No drastic alteration in her lifestyle would be necessary. She could bear it and wean it, employ a nanny to look after it and return to work. Neville would adjust, no doubt, might even discover unsuspected paternal talents. Many women, faced with the same problem, had done that very thing, managed to live with that same uncertainty, built on a foundation of deceit in order to maintain the stability of their marriages.

Or she could tell him. He wouldn't strike her or throw her out of the house or pack his bags and leave. But cruelty could assume subtler forms than that, and she'd already experienced small evidences of his capacity for cruelty. He'd never known for certain about her lover, but he wasn't a stupid man, he'd suspected. And saw to it that she was punished, forced her into a recognition of the damage that she was capable of, the mess into which her emotions might lead her. He'd gone abroad, he'd left her to sort it out for herself, refused to acknowledge her weakness as a normal human characteristic. Perhaps a swift blow would have been kinder.

Or she could book herself into a clinic first thing tomorrow morning and get rid of it. That microscopic parasite. Pregnancy: it had been just words on paper; she'd only ever thought of it theoretically: meiosis – gametes – zygote – cell division – embryo – foetus incapable of sustaining an independent existence much before the seventh month; she hadn't understood that when it happened to you, you didn't just recognize and appreciate it in terms of those impersonal biological categories, you were forced to realize that here was a situation where your glands took precedence over your cognitive processes.

She took a mouthful of tea, swallowed twice, rapidly, and hurtled out of bed. She elbowed aside an astonished Felix, locked herself in the bathroom and was sick. I haven't had this sort of sickness for years, she thought, as it subsided, not since I grew out of my migraine attacks. There was a pain behind her eyebrows and her left eye wasn't focusing. Lilies and stained glass, she remembered, horsehair and cannabis resin – her own private touchstone that warned of situations and substances that must be avoided. She walked slowly back to her bedroom. Which way could the dice be expected to fall? She felt curiously fatalistic.

'There's a woman coming up the path,' Felix said.

'What sort of a woman?'

'*I* don't know. Youngish. Quite glam.'

'Oh God, not the Jehovah's Witnesses again. Go and get rid of her, Felix.'

'Do your own dirty work.'

'Hell's teeth! As if I haven't enough on my plate this morning.' Beatrice went to the window. 'What do you mean – a woman? It's Madeleine.'

'Is it?' He joined her. 'She looks different.'

'She always did. When she made the effort.'

327

'She doesn't look so old and decrepit –'

'Felix!'

'By the way, Joanna was being awfully sick as I came downstairs. It must be your cooking. I told you you'd poison someone sooner or later.'

'Go and bring down your Grandma's cases.' Sometimes, Beatrice thought, nothing happens. Months and months of nothing happening and then, all of a sudden, the whole world revolves rapidly and everything you've taken for granted is turned on its head: Madeleine blueing her insurance money on clothes and hairdressers, my mother offering to have the boys for a holiday, taking them to Blackpool – Blackpool yet! I didn't realize that she even knew that it existed; Joanna, eating and not eating, feeling faint, rushing for the bathroom for all the world as though she was in the club.

'I think I may be getting a migraine,' Joanna said. She had on about two pounds of make-up but her pallor was still apparent.

'You'd better go back to bed.'

'I have to leave today.'

'You can't drive in that condition.'

'I only said "think",' Joanna said irritably. 'Don't fuss.'

They went outside to speed Helena on her journey. The sun had come out. The house seemed less dilapidated in its benevolent glow, even the front garden looked less woebegone. The boys carried out her luggage and then lined themselves up for the receiving of gratuities with the single-mindedness and the lack of subtlety of a cohort of foreign waiters. She distributed largesse. 'You'll come over in July?' she said, pulling on her driving gloves. 'It's a good thing that you're all boys – for the sleeping arrangements.' They nodded graciously. Toby said, 'Will you take us to that aquarium place you told us about?' Their day out with her had obliged them to revise their opinion. She was bossy all right, dictatorial, but not entirely immune to their blandishments – Felix particularly, for some reason, was adept at getting round her. And she didn't keep on and on at them, like Beatrice. They could understand, in a way, why she didn't get on with Beatrice. Chalk and cheese.

Beatrice looked at her mother, thought of that house in Lytham St Anne's, the muted ticking of clocks in elegant rooms, the chess set with its ivory chessmen ever disposed, the long autumn evenings solaced with companionship. Helena had made a new life for herself out of the ruins; she'd compromised, she'd adapted. She returned Beatrice's gaze. 'You'll do as I advised you?' she said. 'You'll let me know . . .?' She didn't say, she couldn't say, I'm sorry that I wasn't able to give you the love and attention that you needed. She clasped Beatrice's arm above the elbow. I was selfish and greedy and I loved him so. You were pretty, you were going to be beautiful and I had rivals enough. I thought that love for you would have meant less love for me, as though it were a kind of constant sum.

'Yes, I'll let you know.' Beatrice detached her arm gently but firmly, kissed her mother on the cheek, did not say, Now is not the time for an uprush of maternal solicitude, Now is too late; said instead, 'Don't worry, I'll survive. I'm a survivor. Remember?'

'They told me to tell you that lunch is almost ready. I can nearly ride Oliver's bike now.'

Natasha stood in the doorway of the attic bedroom. Her hair ribbons had come undone and she seemed to be rather dirty and she'd discarded the anorak into which Madeleine had so carefully zipped her that morning. None of the *boys* wore anoraks; they wore tee shirts and jeans and stayed out in the rain and *they* didn't catch pneumonia.

'Can I have a bike when we go home?'

Madeleine put down her lipstick. It was a new lipstick, purchased in Boots that morning. It was so long since she'd bought one that she'd had to ask the assistant's advice.

'Can I?' Natasha said.

She'd tried to explain that Daddy was dead, that there was no longer a home to go to. And Natasha's lip had wobbled in just the same way as Oliver's lip had wobbled in similar circumstances. But eight-year-old memories are short and the fact of death is difficult to internalize at any time of life. How long would it be before relief at the prospect of no more quarrelling gave way to the realization that she was half way to being an orphan? 'We'll see,' Madeleine said. She heard Toby's voice at the bottom of the stairs. 'I'm coming!' Natasha bellowed in reply. 'Toby's going to show me his guinea pigs.' There was the diminishing sound of wellingtons squeaking on lino and a crash as she jumped the last three steps of the stairs.

The old-fashioned cheval glass in the bedroom had to be propped at a certain angle with *The Complete Home Doctor* before it would tender you your reflection. That morning she'd looked into it and it was her mother that she saw: a widow woman with untidy hair, a face creased with anxiety and lines where there ought not to have been lines. She'd closed her eyes while history repeated itself in her head: poverty, loneliness, life lived vicariously and obsessively through her daughter; she saw herself purchasing her clothes from jumble sales, sitting with the light off, making do with a slice of bread and butter for her lunch so that Natasha should have her chances; she realized that such self-sacrifice satisfied something perverse in one's nature: if all parents sacrificed themselves for their children eternally, who benefited? No, she had thought, no!

She applied the lipstick and smoothed the new hairstyle. Black suited her, made her look wistful, fragile; the hairdresser, as she came out, had looked at her not as a hairdresser looks at a client but as a man looks at an attractive woman. *That* was something she hadn't experienced for a good few years. She went down for Joanna's farewell lunch.

'Must you leave?'

Felix passed his plate along the table and belched dramatically. 'It's not fair – introducing us to decent grub and then deserting us. It'll be back to the usual crud tomorrow, I suppose. Pastry like shrapnel and peas like bullets.'

'Lumpy custard.'

'Her speciality – chickens on Sunday and chicken soup on Monday.'

'Heavens, yes, the inevitable potage.'

Beatrice shook her head. 'No. Tomorrow you're making your own.'

'Why?'

'I have to go out.'

'Where? You can't be going out *all day*.'

'I'm going out in the morning and again in the afternoon.'

'Where to?'

'To see a man about a dog.'

'Twice?'

'Get on with your meal.'

She'd made two phone calls, one to a solicitor – picked at random from the book, and another to the admissions office at the local college. The effort of making those phone calls had drained her. But it was a small triumph. She felt as an agoraphobic must feel having made it as far as the gate.

'How's the headache?'

Joanna was rearranging the food on her plate rather than eating it. 'I don't think it can decide whether to come or whether to go.'

'You haven't had migraine for years, have you? I wonder what triggered it off? It's foul, isn't it?' Beatrice said. 'I remember I had it once or twice when I was carrying Oliver. Your father told me that it was something to do with the change of hormonal balance.'

There was a curious little lull in the conversation. Beatrice seemed to be trying to understand the implications of her own words. Then Sam pushed his chair back from the table, and, as if they had been waiting for the signal, the others followed suit. 'We're going to the Odeon,' Sam said. 'It's that Monty Python thing on. Yes we will take care crossing the road and no we won't talk to any perverts. 'Bye.'

Madeleine called Natasha back, tidied her hair, straightened her collar. Natasha fidgeted from foot to foot, anxious to be off. She had found a place with them, a rôle. They treated her with the same kindly condescension they'd have treated a new pet.

'But you were going to plant vegetables,' Beatrice said to Sam.

'Oh, it'll wait. There's stacks of time for that.'

She was glad. That childhood had reclaimed him, for however short a time. Duty must be subordinated to pleasure. Vegetables versus Monty Python – no contest.

'Say goodbye to Joanna before you go.'

'Goodbye, Joanna,' they chorused. 'The trouble with children,' Neville had once said, 'is that they are incapable of intelligent conversation until the age of twelve or thirteen. The strain of attempting to communicate until that time would be intolerable.'

But of course it was a different kind of communication, she understood that now. Her headache hovered. Oh, make up your mind, she thought, and then I can make up mine.

Madeleine was doing a lot of throat-clearing, working herself up to some sort of statement. The words came, eventually. She said, 'When would you like us to move out?' She didn't look directly at Beatrice. There was still a good deal of reserve between them; perhaps there always would be. The sharing of Desmond had

331

brought them both closer together and further apart.

'Where will you go?'

The insurance money wouldn't last long and there was no pension; Desmond hadn't remained in anyone's employ long enough to qualify for pension rights. Madeleine was poor. Beatrice had never known poor; she only thought she had.

'I suppose I can get a room somewhere. Until I find a job.'

It was inconceivable: rooms and Social Security and your shoes letting in the wet and not being able to meet the insatiable demands of the electricity meter – they were conditions that appertained to other people, denizens of the world out there, a kind of abomination of half-concealed desolation, a world with which it ought not to be necessary for Madeleine to have truck. 'You'd better stay here,' Beatrice said, aware that she had adopted the same surly tone as Felix did when he was being magnanimous and embarrassed about it.

'I can't be obliged to you.'

'Why the hell not?'

'Were you ever patronized, Beatrice, made to feel that you ought to be grateful, expected to accept other people's pity and advice and cast-offs with exclamations of delight?'

Poor Madeleine Brennan. In her long macintosh. Trudging through the puddles as the long sleek black car slid slowly past. Poor Madeleine Brennan, aspiring, tugged downwards, encouraged to rise, rebuked for her aspiration: contradictory forces on every side. Beatrice did understand, a little: the deforming pressures. 'That was then,' she said. 'Now you have no choice. You have someone else to be responsible for.'

'Are there never any choices?'

'Lots, I expect. But I've only ever recognized them retrospectively.'

'What if you were to be reconciled?'

'No reconciliations.'

'But you said that you loved him.' Joanna spoke up. Love had always been a very important word in Beatrice's vocabulary.

Madeleine stared into her coffee cup as she had stared into it years ago at the Martins' dinner-party, seeking for omens, explanations, answers. Beatrice had loved David. And she herself had loved Desmond. You had a longing, a desire to matter to somebody, to ease your aloneness – and you took the material available and you imagined that, in some magical way or other, it would be shaped exactly to your requirements. In the mortuary, the cemetery, the coroner's court and the various eau-de-nil offices through which Helena and Joanna had steered her, while officials brought his life to an end, officially, with certificates and rubber stamps, she'd realized that it was a presumption to suppose that you could predict or control or take the responsibility for the actions of anyone but yourself. She'd thought, at first, if I hadn't left him, then he wouldn't have died, but she knew now that that wasn't necessarily true; it might have happened, whether or not.

Love: it was a word to be used in the past tense. And – in the future – one must try to separate it from its alter ego: delusion. If there *was* any kind of future that might contain the possibility: she felt scarred to the soul. But her scars might heal.

'He doesn't love me,' Beatrice said. 'He never did. None of them did. I deluded myself. You can't rely upon it, anyway – love.'

'What can you rely upon?' Joanna felt her head gingerly. She had begun to see properly again.

'Work, perhaps. I'm taking your advice. I'm going to try to get myself some training, some qualifications. I'm not thick, I never was thick. Just misdirected.'

She sounded defiant. As though someone had said, 'You! You don't stand a chance.'

'Well – look pleased,' she said. 'You were always so keen for us to take your advice, to act rationally and not be influenced by signs and symbols or the beating of our hearts or the phases of the moon. You always said that we were our own worst enemies, that there are answers to everything if you search long enough.'

Joanna looked from Beatrice to Madeleine and back again. Madeleine looked quite pretty. Helena, in confidence, had wondered if Madeleine wasn't a little callous – or perhaps it was just delayed shock. To Joanna, she looked like someone who was about to make a conscious, independent choice for the first time in her life.

'Don't rely on my advice,' she said. 'I'm not qualified to dispense it. I doubt very much whether many people are.'

She'd always thought of them as being permanently fixed in the images they'd created for themselves: Beatrice, the bearer of children, who could only define herself through sex and fecundity, who looked upon life as an Apache dance; Madeleine, the penitent, who saw it as a kind of endless school report; and herself, the one

333

who'd always made her own decisions – the correct ones, who'd scorned the idea that sometimes the decisions could be made for you. Perhaps a certain redefinition was in order. Perhaps their lives weren't steps taken, one after the other, along some self-selected, self-defined and therefore predetermined course, but rather resembled one of those circular games that children play where, periodically, everyone moves around one place to occupy someone else's previous position.

She glanced at her wristwatch. The pain was going, the nausea had gone. 'It doesn't seem as though I'm going to have an attack after all,' she said. 'I must leave now.'

Beatrice smiled. 'Back to the rarified atmosphere of the groves of academe where life is ordered and subject to control and the books are full of explanations.'

'Back to make a decision.' She'd know, by the time she turned her key in her lock, what she was going to do; she thought, perhaps, that she knew already.

'Some deep philosophical dilemma that is beyond the understanding of our meagre intellects?' Beatrice said. 'Still, it's better than working.' She fished inside the dresser drawer. 'Here,' she said, 'take this with you. I found it the other day when I was looking for a safety-pin to keep Toby's zip up. It'll remind you of the time when we were considered to be quite special.'

It was a snapshot. Circa Bridget's Box Brownie. Elm trees in the background and Emmett's wheelbarrow. A patch of check shirt in the corner indicated that Emmett hadn't quite managed to get out of the way in time.

They studied it. 'Bridget wasn't exactly Cartier-Bresson, was she?' Beatrice said. 'Do you remember, taken soon after we felt that we could decently leave off those black armbands they gave us? Sunday morning. Madeleine came back with Bridget after church and Bridget wanted to finish the roll so she could send Cousin Molly the holiday snaps. You in your accordion-pleated skirt. You'd saved up for months to buy that – you reckoned that it was the height of chic.'

'So I didn't have your advantages. That was when we were being especially loved and cherished by all around us, wasn't it?'

'Was it? I was aware only of muted hostility: Why those three?'

Madeleine took the photograph. The blouse she'd made in Domestic Science. Beatrice's dark fall of exquisitely-barbered hair.

334

Joanna, taller, behind them, a hand on each of their shoulders. The same face then as now: jaw angled upwards, eyes direct, unblinking at the camera, seeing through it towards the future. She and Beatrice, startled, as though caught unawares: mouths slightly open, eyes dazzled, expectant but unwary. Could anyone seeing it have foretold anything at all about them, from the tilt of a jaw, the curve of a smile, the blink of a startled eyelid? She handed it back to Joanna. 'Why us three?' she said, 'do you suppose? Sheer chance? A random event? Or *is* it significant?'

'Oh, there's bound to be a reason,' Beatrice said, 'isn't there, Joanna?'

But Joanna only replied that it was too soon to tell.